Pride Publishing books by S. J. Coles

Single Books
Blood Winter
Straight to the Heart
Dark Summer
The Devil You Know

Once Upon a Holiday
Your Christmas
Our Valentine's
My Summer
His Halloween

Blood and Bonds
Touch in the Night

Collections
My Bloody Valentine: Blood Red Roses
Sun, Sea and Small-Town Secrets
Enemy Territory: My Iron Knight

I0636300

Blood and Bonds

TOUCH IN THE NIGHT

S. J. COLES

Touch in the Night
ISBN # 978-1-80250-579-5
©Copyright S.J. Coles 2023
Cover Art by Kelly Martin ©Copyright November 2023
Interior text design by Claire Siemaszkiewicz
Pride Publishing

TOUCH IN THE NIGHT

Dedication

For Hannah B, Queen of the Night

Chapter One

"Can you see all right, Olly?"

"Yeah."

Jesse looked up. His nephew's face was solemn under his blue bobble-hat. Jesse patted his knee and shifted the boy's weight on his shoulders.

"You know there's nothing to be scared of, right?"

Oliver didn't answer right away. "Dad says the baron is dangerous."

"He said that to you?"

"Not to me. To Mum."

"And what did your mum say?"

"I dunno...I snuck away before I heard. They're arguing a lot again."

Jesse edged to the side as a woman brought her phone up to photograph the illuminated front of St. Helen's church. The snow-flecked air was rich with the smells from the mulled wine cart and bratwurst stall but stiff with a sense of unease. Jesse scanned the crowd, noting the unusual lack of children.

"He's not dangerous, Olly," he said. "He's just a man."

"He's not a man, though, Uncle Jesse," Oliver whispered urgently. "He's a vampire."

Jesse suppressed a smile. "There's no such thing, mate. Just wait. You'll see he's just a guy, like me…like your dad."

"Dad says they *kill* people." Oliver's grip tightened on Jesse's head.

Jesse muttered under his breath. "There are bad ones and good ones, Olly…just like people."

Lights flooded the stage before his nephew could answer. A woman Jesse recognized from TV stepped up to the microphone, raising her hand in response to the muted applause.

"Good evening, ladies and gentlemen. Thank you for braving the cold to be here tonight. We have a truly unique Christmas light display for you this year. Leaflets with a walk-around guide can be picked up at the tourist info center, or you can download the York Christmas Festival app." She smiled wider, darting her focus behind her. She took a deep breath. "Without further ado, I would like to welcome our special guest, someone who has funded this year's illuminations and who has kindly agreed to switch them on. Please welcome, Baron Emory Von Magnusson."

More hushed applause and whispered comments punctured the frozen air as a tall figure stepped onstage. Oliver tensed. Jesse stared.

He'd seen pictures of Von Magnusson, of course. It seemed to Jesse that you could hardly look at your phone these days without seeing something about 'The Undying Baron' and his recent move back to his ancestral lands. He was a handsome, broad-shouldered figure with styled black hair and dark blue eyes, the color of a nighttime ocean. Hot? There was no question about that. Jesse didn't mind admitting to himself that the haemophile was the stuff of fantasies—chiseled jaw, flawless skin, a body he'd be happy to take a flying run at. But still just a flesh-and-blood guy, not the inhuman demon the hate groups touted him as.

In person, however, he literally took Jesse's breath away. He was the tallest man Jesse had ever seen. He towered over the woman, who was easily five-eleven in her stiletto heels. His shoulders were so wide that the black wool overcoat, dotted with snow, had to be custom-made. Under the coat, he wore a tasteful suit in Oxford blue, a crisp, white shirt and a blood-red tie. Jesse blinked, wondering if that had been deliberate. But then the haemophile's eyes met Jesse's, and all intelligent thought fled.

There was an electric moment when Jesse was convinced the haemophile was reading every inappropriate thought that rolled through his mind, then he lifted his cobalt gaze and Jesse was able to breathe again.

"A very warm welcome to all of you," the haemophile said, his voice deep and rich as coffee liqueur. "I am honored to be here. York is a city very dear to me, and any chance to make it shine brighter warms my heart."

More staid clapping. Every gaze was fixed on the speaker, but the expressions on the faces around Jesse were uncertain. Magnusson never blinked, and his smile never wavered. The glimpse of his over-long canines Jesse had got as he spoke had sent a needle of uncertain excitement over the back of his neck. He shook himself and patted Oliver's shin.

"See? Just a bloke…like I said."

Oliver's gaze was locked on the haemophile, but his grip on Jesse's head had loosened, and he sat a little easier across his shoulders.

"He's big," Oliver murmured.

"You're not wrong there, mate," Jesse said, drawing a deep breath, hoping it would cool the sudden heat in his veins.

"This year's Christmas display is something a little different," Magnusson went on. "I wanted to try to recreate the York I was born in. – the one I knew as home, to show the world the timeless nature of our city's beauty. So, if you'll allow me…"

The smiling woman stepped aside, gesturing toward the large switch on a table next to the mic. Magnusson wrapped one large, gloved hand around the lever. He pulled it back with a click.

The streetlights dimmed at the same time as countless points of white light sprang into life around the square. Hundreds of simulated candles flickered along every eve and window ledge, their flames appearing to sway in the chill breeze. The building fronts were dotted with points of cooler white, creating the illusion of an unclouded night sky crowded with stars. A full moon wreathed in wisps of silver cloud was projected on the front of the church. The uneasy murmuring silenced as the crowd turned to take in the display.

"It's moving," Oliver whispered, his voice hushed with awe as the projected clouds appeared to drift away, leaving the moon shining and full on the front of the building.

Magnusson was gazing up with a smile on his full, tilting lips.

"Ladies and gentlemen. I give you a winter night in eighteenth-century York—cold but warm with welcome, dark but lit by love." He gestured around the square "The stars and moon are true to their current positions in the sky above us and will move as they do. As you walk throughout the city, you will find constellations, planets and galaxies. The candles will burn down before dawn but tomorrow"—he smiled wider—"it all begins again. A very Merry Christmas to you all—and a Happy New Year."

The clapping that broke out as he raised his hand was far more enthusiastic. The square filled with chatter. Phones were lifted to photograph the lights. Magnusson shook the hand of the woman on the stage and withdrew into the shadows.

"Come on, Uncle Jesse. I want to go see over there…"

Oliver was trying to scramble down Jesse's body. He lowered his nephew to the floor but was unable to resist glancing back, trying to see if the haemophile was still there, in the dark, watching.

But Oliver tugged on his hand again, and he allowed himself to be dragged down Stonegate to follow the trail of flickering candles. Oliver squeaked in delight and pointed to where the sparkling band of the milky way shimmered over the closed-up shop fronts. He hustled them down Minster Gates toward the towering hulk of the Minster itself, asking ceaseless questions about the constellations that Jesse was only able to answer with the aid of Google and a Wi-Fi hotspot.

When they had completed a circuit of the moonlit, star-speckled Minster, weaving between the swelling crowds with increased difficulty, Jesse drew Oliver aside.

"It's getting late, mate. Better get you home."

"But I want to see if the moon's moved!"

"It'll be back tomorrow night," Jesse said, tucking his chin into his threadbare scarf and wincing again at another missed call notification from his brother. "Come on, pal. Time to go."

The crowds thinned as they walked toward the river. Oliver started to shiver, and Jesse picked up his pace, thinking to get Oliver back in the warmth as quickly as possible, even though he wasn't keen to face the sort of welcome he guessed would be waiting for him at his brother's house.

"What's that?" Oliver stopped in his tracks and looked back up the deserted street.

"What was *what*?"

"Didn't you hear that?"

Jesse heard it—a muffled cry, almost too quiet to hear.

Oliver pointed back the way they'd come. "I think it's coming from over there."

Jesse backtracked to the mouth of an alley. He could hear the traffic from the main road and the hoot of a boat on the river, but inside the alley was silent and dark.

Jesse knelt by Oliver. "I want you to stay here, okay, mate?"

"But what is it, Uncle Jesse?" Oliver whispered, his face crumpled with concern.

"I don't know, but you're going to stay here, yeah? Hold on to this railing, and don't let go. I'll be right back."

Oliver nodded, pursing his lips, and Jesse squeezed his hand and crept into the alley.

"Hello?" he called. "Hey, is anyone there?"

Silence. Jesse took another step and spotted a pale shape in the shadows. A little girl sat against the wall with her knees drawn up and her face buried in her arms.

"Hey," Jesse said, his heart going into his throat as he knelt next to her. "Hey there. Are you okay?"

She squeaked and curled into a tighter ball.

"Hey, love, it's okay," he said. "I'm not gonna hurt you. What are you doing here on your own, huh?"

The girl shook and clutched her arms tighter about herself. Jesse bit his lip and pulled out his phone to call the police then swore when he saw his battery had died.

"Hey, Olly," he called. "Come here a sec, mate." Oliver crept into view, his eyes intent as he spotted the girl. "Looks like this little lady's lost. She's scared. Can you tell her it's okay?"

"Hey," Oliver said uncertainly, approaching the girl. The girl finally raised her head. Even in the dimness, Jesse could see her face was tear-stained and puffy. "Hey," Oliver said, kneeling next to her, putting his mittened hand on her arm. "Hey, what's up? You lost?"

The girl nodded, screwing her face up like kids did when they were trying desperately not to cry.

"It's okay," Oliver said with a smile. "We can help. Can't we, Uncle Jesse?"

"Course we can," Jesse said. "We'll get you home, love. You'll see. Can you tell us your name?"

She sniffed. "Dimity."

Oliver giggled. "That's a funny name."

The girl scowled. "No, it isn't."

"Yes, it is," Oliver said, smiling wider.

"No, it *isn't*," Dimity insisted.

"Okay, okay," Jesse said as Oliver's smirk threatened to break into another giggle. "Dimity? Can you tell me where you folks are?"

"I'm…I'm looking for my dad," she quavered. "I've looked everywhere… He was supposed to be here."

"It's all right, honey," Jesse said. "We'll find him. But let's get you inside somewhere warm first, okay?"

Dimity stared warily at Jesse.

"It's okay," Oliver said. "Uncle Jesse's nice, really. He only looks scary."

"*Oi*," Jesse said with what he hoped was a reassuring smile, and Oliver laughed, startling a chuckle from the girl. "He's right though, love. They're only piercings. I'm soft as soft inside, promise. Up you get. I know a place around the corner that does the *best* milkshakes."

Her face brightened, and Oliver exclaimed excitedly. They helped Dimity to her feet, and Jesse instructed his nephew to take the little girl's hand and not let go. Oliver obeyed, and Jesse took his nephew's other hand. They left the alley, the little boy chattering about the moon and star lights, the Minster, the candles.

"I wanted to see it," the girl sniffed again as they turned onto another side street. "My dad was supposed to be there."

"We'll get you back to him, love. Don't worry," Jesse said. He ushered them into the warm, steamy space of Ditzy Daisy's Ice Parlor with relief. His hands pulsed as they warmed. The children's faces lit up as they took in the counter, laden with sponges, brownies, trifles, cupcakes and cookies.

He steered them into a booth near the door just as a smiling middle-aged woman in a bright blue apron appeared from behind the counter with a notebook.

"And very nice to see you again, Jesse," she beamed as she took in the children. "On babysitting duty again, I see?"

"Hey, Daisy," Jesse said, keeping an eye on the children as they began scanning the laminated menu of colorful ice creams. "Can I borrow your phone?"

She gave him a mocking look. "Out of credit again?"

"It's sort of an emergency."

Daisy's face clouded. "An emergency?"

Jesse nodded to the girl and lowered his voice. "Found the little lass in an alley. Got separated from her dad at the switch-on, I think. My phone's dead, and I need to call the police."

"Oh Lord," Daisy whispered, handing over her phone. "Sure thing, Jess. The poor little mite. You get on with that, and I'll sort them out with some sugar."

"Thanks, Daze," Jesse said with a heartfelt smile and stepped to one side to make the call.

"Police, please," he answered the emergency switchboard operator. "Hey," he said when a woman answered after a number of beeps, "I'm at the cafe on Huntington Road, York. I've found a lost little girl, Dimity. She's looking for her dad."

"Did you say Dimity Hawthorn, sir?"

Jesse blinked. "Don't know her surname, but I think she was at the Christmas light switch-on—"

"We have a call in for her, sir. Did you say she's safe?"

"Yes, she's safe. She's a little shaken up, but she's with my nephew now and seems better."

"Your name, sir?"

Jesse watched Daisy start loading ice cream into the milkshake mixers, keeping one eye on the children. "Jesse Truelove."

"And the cafe?"

"Ditzy Daisy's."

"We're on our way. Please keep the child in the cafe."

"Yeah, of course. So you're gonna tell her dad?"

"Officers are on the way," the woman repeated. "Please do not move from your current location."

She hung up. Jesse stared at the phone for a moment with unease sneaking through his insides. He returned to the booth just as Daisy set two glasses overflowing with whipped cream, chocolate shavings and sprinkles in front of the wide-eyed children.

"There you go, me dears," she said, tucking a glittery straw into each glass. "That should keep body and soul together until we get you home."

"*Amazing*," Oliver enthused. "This is the *biggest* one I've *ever* had." He slurped noisily. Dimity watched him with a shy smile. "Go on. It's caramel choco fudge, my favorite."

The little girl sipped from her own glass. She smiled shyly through a cream mustache.

"Good, huh?" Jesse smiled, and the girl nodded. "And I've got some good news," Jesse said. "Your dad's on his way."

She beamed. "He is? Really?"

"He'll be here any minute," he said. "So you better start work on that."

She grinned wider, showing a gap near the front where a new adult tooth was just starting and went at the whipped cream with the long spoon Daisy had laid on the table.

"Thanks, Daze," Jesse said, handing the phone back. "You're a lifesaver."

"Don't worry about it. Poor little thing must have been terrified. And you can forget about that, too," she added, as Jesse started rummaging in his pockets for money. "It's on the house."

Jesse smiled sheepishly. "A double lifesaver."

"Not a problem, hon. Want a coffee before the coppers get here?"

"That'd be great."

Jesse perched at the counter with his coffee, grateful for the bitter heat warming him through from the inside. Daisy flipped the sign to *Closed*, just as blue flashing lights filled the cafe and three police cars crowded the curb outside. Jesse straightened as a black car muscled between them and out climbed a tall, thin woman, immaculately turned out in a peach belted overcoat and black patent heels, her silver-streaked hair gathered into an artful arrangement at the nape of her neck. She screamed money, and her tall, rigid posture screamed control, but the look on her face was unmistakable. She was scared.

She strode into the cafe with three police officers and what looked like two members of private security at her heels, her eyes darting everywhere until they landed on Dimity. The worry in her face stiffened into hard lines of anger.

"Dimity Hawthorn, there you are. Do you have any idea how worried we've been?"

The girl cowered into her seat. Oliver glanced between the girl and the gathering in the doorway with wide eyes. Daisy watched with a wary expression from behind the counter.

Jesse frowned and stepped forward. "Uh, hang on…"

The woman's gimlet-sharp gaze transferred from the girl to Jesse. He saw her take in his undercut, nose ring, tattoos and leather jacket and watched a familiar look of disdain fill her amber eyes. "And you are?"

"Jesse Truelove. I called the police."

"Oh," the woman said, looking down at his ripped jeans and worn-out trainers. "Well, we thank you for keeping Dimity safe, but she's coming with us now. Dimity? Come along at once."

"Just hang on one second," Jesse said, stepping between them. "She said she wants her *dad*."

"Mr. Truelove," the woman said, her thin, dark brows drawing together in a sharp frown. "Please, step aside."

"Where's her dad, lady?"

Dimity was clutching her glass tight, a small frown of defiance creasing her forehead. "I want Daddy, Aunt Helena."

Helena's face flushed. She glared at Jesse. "I regret to say my niece has no father, Mr. Truelove. And she ran away from her minders today when they took her to the Minster for the carols."

"I wanted to go to the *lights*," Dimity said, her face screwing up. "Daddy was supposed to be there."

"She seems pretty sure," Jesse began, but the woman nodded to her security men, who hustled forward and manhandled Jesse out of the way. Dimity burst into tears, and a diminutive, somber-clothed woman came forward to take her hand and drag her from the booth.

"At least let the lass finish her milkshake," Daisy put in.

"Dimity does not eat such things," Helena said as the little girl was steered toward the exit. The police stepped aside to hold the door open.

"Hey, wait." Jesse moved to follow them, but Helena stepped into his path.

"Again, we thank you for your assistance," she said, producing a leather wallet from her oversized handbag and extracting out two fifty-pound notes. "We can take it from here."

"I don't want your money, lady—just to know the lass is okay."

"She's fine," the woman insisted, holding out the notes. "She is back with her family now, where she belongs. Take it. I insist."

Jesse took the money with numb fingers, and the woman swept out of the cafe without a backward glance. She exchanged some brief words with the police officers before they doffed their caps, climbed into the police cars and drove away. One of the security staff held open the back door to the big black car to allow Helena to climb inside. Jesse caught a glimpse of Dimity sitting in the back with her stony-faced minder before the door was closed and they drove off.

"Poor wee thing," Daisy said, shaking her head. "Guess the rest of that milkshake's yours, lad," she added to Oliver.

"No, we'd better go," Jesse said. "Olly? You done?"

Oliver nodded, his face strangely solemn as he watched the black car disappear from view. "Do you think she's okay, Uncle Jesse?"

"Yeah," Jesse lied. "Yeah, I'm sure she's fine. Here," he said to Daisy, laying the money on the counter. "You take this."

"Oh no, honestly." Daisy waved it away. "Jesse, that's yours."

"I don't want it," he said, shoving it toward her. "Put it toward your Christmas staff booze-up or something."

Daisy smiled an uneasy smile and took the money. "Okay, I'll do that. Thanks, Jesse."

"See you around," he said, taking Oliver's hand and leading him outside. He heard Daisy lock the door behind him and stood looking in the direction the car had gone for a long moment until a yawn from his nephew reminded him how time was getting on. He steered them back toward the river then over the road bridge and back toward Heworth.

Chapter Two

Jesse stood in the overheated, over-decorated living room, glowering at the designer rug rather than meet his brother's eyes.

"I just cannot believe you took him, Jess."

"I take him every year."

"Not *this* year. I specifically said I don't want him anywhere near that *thing*."

Jesse fought a sigh. "That's *why* I took him, Ant. The poor sod thinks there's a *vampire* living up the road."

"There *is*."

Jesse gave him a look. "Perhaps you should try getting your info from somewhere that's not Facebook."

"And the dark web's so much better?"

"Ant..."

"I was *there*, Jess. I was there in London when that guy got slaughtered."

"Yeah, I know. You never stop bloody going on about it." Anton's face darkened and Jesse pursed his lips. "Look... You and Sareena don't go around teaching Olly it's okay to judge people by their race or anything, do you? So, you shouldn't—"

"The key word there is *people*, Jess. Those *things* are not people."

"It was just one rogue haemophile, Ant."

His brother's handsome face was tight with anger. His green eyes, a shade darker than Jesse's own, blazed. "It only takes one."

"You're being daft."

"They are *dangerous*. And I don't want my son anywhere near them. Understand?"

Jesse was grateful to be shown the door. He made for the gate, but someone calling his name made him turn.

Sareena crunched down the snowy drive toward him. Her breath hung around her in clouds, and her warm, kind face held an unfamiliar strain of worry.

"Try not to think too badly of your brother, Jess," his sister-in-law said. "He's just trying to protect Oliver, that's all."

"Olly was scared out of his wits until I showed him this guy's just a guy," Jesse said, lowering his voice. "His own dad telling him there's monsters living up the road? Jesus Christ."

Sareena winced. "You have to understand how much Blood Winter shook him. His conference was in the same building where that man got killed."

"I *know*. And that would shake anyone up. But this is about Olly. And I don't think he needs to be scared of some dude who's just trying to live his life."

"I know, and I agree with you," Sareena said, laying a hand on his arm. "But it's not your fight."

Anger, instantly doused by sadness, flared in his chest, and he looked away.

"I'm working on it, I promise," Sareena said, squeezing his arm. "Just…give Ant a break, okay? He's been finding everything tough since your dad passed."

Jesse closed his eyes, a dull ache in his gut. "Yeah. Yeah, I know."

Sareena's smile was gentle, but her brown eyes were concerned. "You're okay, right? You don't need any money or —"

"I'm fine."

"You don't usually miss calling Ant back. Are you out of credit again?"

"My phone died is all."

Her gaze was knowing. "A contract phone would be more reliable, you know. There are some good deals around now. And we can help out with the payments."

"I don't need charity, Sareena." Jesse regretted the words the minute they left this mouth and lowered his gaze. "Sorry. I guess it's getting to me, too."

Sareena put her hand on his arm. "You don't need to apologize. And it's not charity, Jesse. It's for Oliver. He wants you to keep in touch, too."

"I should get some work any day now," he said softly. "The first thing I'll do is buy credit."

"And pay your heating bill?"

"Yeah. Sure."

"Promise?"

Jesse looked into her deep caramel eyes, welling with love and concern. Like always, he didn't know how to handle it.

"Get back inside. It's freezing. Tell Olly I'll see him around, yeah?"

Sareena nodded. "Of course. And come back soon. Your brother misses you, too."

Jesse clenched his mouth of his response, nodded and turned away before Sareena could say anything more.

He soon found himself at the end of Chestnut Avenue, looking left along Heworth Road toward the university district and his poky flat then right toward the river and the city center. He searched through his pockets, found a crumpled fiver and headed toward town.

The Evil Eye was crowded and steamy, the air thick with the smell of warm humans and spilled spirits. He made his way to his normal stool at the bar, weaving between the usual mix of townies and tourists, laughing and sipping elaborate cocktails. He ordered a Dark and Stormy then sat, sipping his drink and searched the crowd.

It wasn't long before a guy hanging on the edge of a group near the door caught his eye. He weighed Jesse up a moment with seeming interest building in his square-jawed face. He leaned in to shout something to his friends then made his way over, carefully steering his whiskey sour ahead of him in an exaggerated attempt not to spill.

"I've seen you here before, right?" the man said, overly loud.

"I dunno, have you?" Jesse said, trying to gauge if the guy really had big arms under his hot-pink shirt or if it was just a trick of the light.

"Pretty sure I have. And on Grindr, too, yeah?"

Jesse's blood started to thrum. "Maybe."

The man glanced back at his friends, who were all laughing raucously over something on a phone. He leaned in to talk into Jesse's ear. His breath smelled like whiskey and mint gum.

"Yeah, I remember your listing. Said you like it a bit out-there, huh?"

"Yeah," Jesse said, meeting his eye. "Think you got it in you?"

Dark heat lit the man's eyes. "Yeah. I reckon I do."

"Okay then…?"

"Tyler," the man said, grinning and showing straight, white teeth.

Jesse set his glass aside. "Okay then, Tyler. Your place or mine?"

"Yeah, I, uh…" He looked back at his friends. "Gimme five minutes?"

"Four."

Tyler hurried back to his friends, downing his drink as he went. He conversed insistently with them, and they looked over, sniggering and clapping the big guy on his back.

Jesse checked his watch then jumped when someone slammed a shot glass on the bar at his elbow.

"He's not gonna give you what you want." A girl with hair the same electric-aqua as the liquor sat beside him and downed her own measure. She made a face and coughed. "And you know it."

Jesse eyed her narrowly. "And you know what I want?" he said and drank.

"You want a man who can make you feel like a whore and a prince, all at once." She grinned, her teeth very white against her dark lipstick. "You're asking too much of human beings, Jess. No such man exists. Believe me, I've looked."

"What do *you* want, Trixy?"

"*I* want," she said, holding up her hand to order two more shots, "to discuss a business proposition."

"This isn't really a good time."

"From the state of those," Trixy said, nodding at the holes in Jesse's jeans that were clearly not part of the design, "I would say it's the exact right time."

He sighed, lifting the second shot. "What's the job?"

"Not here," she said. "Come to mine?"

"Can't you just email me?" he said, downing the shot with a grimace.

She shook her head, her bunches dancing. "I'm not putting any of this into emails. Come over and all will be made clear."

"I'm kinda in the middle of something here," Jesse said, sliding off his stool as Tyler caught his eye and nodded to the exit.

Trixy glanced at Tyler and snorted. "Fine. Go have your lackluster bar-pickup sex, *then* come over. I'll be awake all night anyway."

* * * *

They hadn't even got to Jesse's floor before Tyler was shoving him against the wall and thrusting his tongue into his mouth. There really was strength in his brawny arms, evident in the way he was grabbing roughly at Jesse's arse, but the movements were clumsy with drink and desperation. Jesse concentrated on the feel of the strong, male body, his warm, musky scent and the very promising feel of a hard, long member crushed into his crotch.

"I want you to hold me down, yeah?" he said as he fumbled through his pockets for his keys. "Make me beg."

"Fuck yeah," Tyler panted, grinding against him. "I can do that, baby. I'll make you beg."

Jesse got the door open and they shambled across the sitting area, shedding coats and shoes as they went. Tyler's breathing was heavy, his hands grasping, the kiss sloppy and demanding. Jesse grunted as he came up against the kitchen unit and yanked Tyler's salmon-pink shirt over his head. He was toned as an athlete, his skin tanned and dusted with fair hair. His biceps bunched invitingly, making Jesse's arousal spike. Jesse ran his hands up them. Tyler responded with a growl and fumbled at his belt.

As soon as he'd unfastened his fly, Tyler shoved Jesse's hands down the front of his pants. A frisson of excitement went through Jesse when he measured the thickness and weight of the hard flesh in his hands. He began stroking and tilted his head away from the clumsy kiss to let Tyler mouth wetly at his neck.

"Get your pretty arse out, yeah?"

"Hold me down," Jesse breathed, closing his eyes and clutching at Tyler's hard biceps with one hand, pumping the thick length with the other.

"Yeah, yeah, whatever," Tyler panted, unbuttoning Jesse's jeans. "Where's your room?"

"No. Right here."

"Fuck. Okay."

Tyler spun Jesse, shoved him against the counter and yanked his jeans down. He grabbed Jesse's wrist with his free hand and crushed himself against his arse, fumbling his thick cock toward his entrance.

"Jesus," Jesse growled. "Put a rubber on, you reprobate."

"Christ, really? Now?"

"Yes, *now*," Jesse snapped, yanking open a drawer and slamming a condom on the counter.

Tyler swore and reached over, pinning Jesse with his strong legs but then he heard the packet ripping and Tyler's grunts as he sheathed himself. "Lube?"

Jesse fumbled in the drawer and handed the bottle over. He listened to the slick sound of Tyler lubricating himself then two lubed fingers were thrust into him. Jesse swore and crushed his eyes shut. He breathed through the feel of invasion as Tyler fumbled at him, stretching and probing, breathing heavily in his ear.

"Fuck," he groaned. "*Now*?"

"Get it in," Jesse said, clutching the countertop. Tyler groaned then Jesse gasped as Tyler's length slammed into him. Jesse moaned, drinking in the sharp stretch, the feel of the counter digging into his belly, the strong frame pinning him in place, the fingers tightening around his wrist.

"Yeah, you want that?" Tyler muttered as he kicked Jesse's legs farther apart and bent him over the counter. "Fuck," he swore as he started to move. "Fuck, yes, yes, yes."

Tyler growled and grunted in time with his thrusts. Jesse closed his eyes and ears and fumbled for his own cock, concentrating on the sweet, deep pummeling and trying to angle himself so Tyler reached the spot inside that burst with pleasure upon contact.

"Harder," Jesse said through clenched teeth.

"Christ, yes," Tyler said, and obeyed, ramming him into the counter. "Ask for it. Tell me to fuck you, baby."

Jesse clenched his mouth shut, buried himself in the sensations, tried to ignore the awkward angle, the way Tyler grasped his wrist with bruising but not dominating force and stroked himself faster, willing the cloud of sparks building under his stomach to swell and spread.

But then Tyler was crying out, thrusting deep and holding himself in, trembling and groaning.

Jesse swore, freed his wrist and reached back to hold Tyler in him until his own orgasm finally spilled out.

He released Tyler, who staggered back, panting and swearing. Jesse straightened, rubbing the red marks where his hips had been rammed into the counter and pulled his jeans up with a sigh.

Tyler's face was ruddy and slack with release. Sweat beaded his forehead. His grin was wide as he picked up his shirt.

"That was awesome."

Jesse fastened his fly without replying.

"So, look…" Tyler said as he buckled his belt. "I kinda left my mate in the middle of his stag do. I'm the best man, you know."

"Door's that way, mate," Jesse said, nodding to the exit and began hunting through the cupboards for something to eat. There was a moment of shocked silence then the front door slammed. Jesse suppressed a familiar flare of guilt, retrieved a dry crust of bread from the cupboard, spread on the last of his margarine and took a bite before moving through to the bedroom.

The glow of the half-dozen computer screens bathed the small room in an eerie green light. He sat at the desk and plugged his phone in to charge while doing a check of his encrypted email and message accounts.

He swallowed the last of the bread as he binned the emails, most of which were trying to sell him Viagra and none of which was an offer of work and leaned back in the chair, rubbing his face.

His phone turned back on and buzzed. A message from Trixy.

You coming or what?

Jesse sighed. He was tired and sore — and not in a good way. But he was also still hungry and had spent his last fiver on that Dark and Stormy at the Evil Eye that he hadn't even finished.

On my way.

He sent the message, showered off the scent of Tyler's floral aftershave and left the flat.

* * * *

"Still walking straight I see," Trixy said as she led him along her purple-painted hall. "Another bust, then?"

"Got anything to drink?"

Trixy went to a cupboard in her tiny kitchen unit and retrieved a bottle of tequila and two glasses. "Perhaps you should try dating a nice guy...just for the sake of variety."

"Glen was nice," Jesse muttered. "Look how that turned out."

"Glen was boring. There's a difference. Hungry?" she said, throwing a packet of crisps at him.

Jesse ripped them open and began shoving them into his mouth, accepted a glass and sprawled on the cushion-strewn sofa.

"Thought as much," she said, dragging over the desk chair from her recording booth and sitting. "Just so you know, you look like shit, Jesse."

"Thanks, Trix. That's really helping."

"Something going on with you?"

Jesse downed the tequila and grimaced. "Just had a day."

Trixy smiled. "So, how would a grand turn things around?"

Jesse paused with the last handful of crisps halfway to his mouth. "A grand?"

Trixy nodded.

"For what?" he asked, not liking the glint in her eye.

Her dark-painted mouth twisted in a feral grin as she handed over a tablet. "I've got an idea...a groundbreaking idea. But I need your help."

It was an online article from *The York Press*.

The Undying Baron Moves to Town.

Progressive Pragmatism or a Real and Present Danger?

Jesse scrolled to the pictures of Magnusson, looking impeccable at a press conference. His blue-black eyes gazed out of the picture, cool and measured. He scrolled on to a picture of Oswald House, Magnusson's ultra-modern mansion, all glass and chrome. The article claimed it was built on the very spot of an Elizabethan hall that had belonged to the baron's family over three hundred years previously.

"I think you're a bit late trying to go viral with the haemophile thing," Jesse said, handing the tablet back. "Nothing's ever gonna rack up the hits of that phone footage from Blood Winter."

"That footage went wide 'cause it's the only *truthful* video of these things," Trixy said, her eyes dancing. "People aren't interested in the interviews and PR projects. They want to know what haemos are really like."

"Do they?" Jesse asked disbelievingly.

"Hell yeah. This guy moving here is a fucking gift. Candid footage of the Undying Baron, unguarded and unfiltered, would be prime content—bigger than any celebrity streaming their gym session or whatever. *And it'll serve a purpose.*"

"What purpose? Ad revenue for your YouTube channel?"

She tilted her chin. "A definitive answer to the question everyone is asking."

"What question?"

"Is he dangerous?"

"Trix…"

"Everyone's talking about it," Trixy said, indicating the article. "But no one's trying to find an answer."

"You don't think he's allowed a private life like the rest of us?"

"No one has private lives anymore," she retorted with an impatient gesture. "Everything's online— medical records, home movies, banking, everything."

"Speak for yourself."

Trixy huffed through her nose. "You can keep yourself off the grid 'cause you're a raging nerd. But if anyone needs scrutiny, it's bloody vampires."

Jesse opened his mouth to protest but then looked away, fatigue stealing the energy to argue.

"A thousand quid, Jesse. Half now, half when the job's done."

"What, exactly, *is* the job?"

She enlarged the picture of the mansion. "I need you to get me inside."

Jesse paused in the act of pouring more tequila. "Come again?"

She tapped her neon pink fingernail on the screen. "Get me into Oswald House. Day time."

"Why?"

She grinned. "I'm gonna open his coffin."

Jesse stared at her. "I'm sorry… It's been a long day. It sounded like you were gonna try and get yourself killed?"

"If he's really safe enough to be living outside a haemophile commune, then I shouldn't be in any danger, right?"

"They *all* lock themselves away in the day, commune or not. And by the way, they don't sleep in coffins."

"Either haemophiles are dangerous or they're not," she said, taking the tablet back. "I intend to prove it one way or another."

"He'll have a sleeping cell, bars, locks." Jesse gestured helplessly. "*That's* how they keep us safe. Breaking in defeats the whole point."

"We don't know that. Maybe the vulnerable-in-the-day thing is actually bullshit. Maybe it isn't. Either way, I'm gonna find out—and I'm gonna film it."

Jesse shook his head and stood. "You're nuts."

"Because I'm invested in the truth?"

"Because you're willing to risk your life for hits on TikTok or YouTube," Jesse said. "It's not worth it."

"A thousand quid, Jesse. I know you need it."

"Not that bad. Get someone else."

"There is no one else," she said. "I know you can do a B&E, Jess. You've done it before."

"That was years ago," Jesse snapped. "I was a stupid kid."

"Takes someone pretty smart to break into the art gallery the same time they've got a Matisse on display."

"I wanted to see the bloody painting," he said. "If they'd just let me buy a ticket like everyone else—"

Trixy slapped an envelope on the arm of the sofa. "Five hundred now. *Seven* more when it's done—and

I'll do your next tattoo for free. Come one, Jesse. What do you say?"

"I say you're crazy…as usual."

"Can you really look me in the eye and tell me you're not in the least bit curious?"

The image of Emory Von Magnusson rose in his mind — the broad shoulders. The deep, intense gaze, the sharp, white teeth.

Trixy was grinning at him.

He scrubbed a hand over his face and grabbed the envelope. "Fine. *Fine*. I'll get you into his bloody house. But I still want to be paid if he kills you."

Trixy stood, chuckling. "I'll put it in my will. Don't worry." She planted heavy kisses on both his cheeks. "Thanks. You won't regret it."

"Why don't I believe you?"

She lifted the tequila bottle. "Wanna drink until you do?"

Jesse sighed and shrugged. "Sure."

Chapter Three

When Jesse steered Trixy's van toward Askham Moor over a week later, the situation still didn't feel any more real. Jesse's head and devices were crammed with blueprints, codes, applications and back-up plans, and while the part of his mind that was on the job was steady and methodical as ever, the part of it that held the memory the Undying Baron was roiling with unease.

He snuck a glance at Trixy. A beanie hid her blue hair, and her face was young-looking without the black lipstick and painted-on eyebrows. She was grinning from ear to ear as she clicked through the settings on her action cam.

"You're far too excited about this."

"Too right, I'm excited," she said, slotting the camera back into his chest strap. "We're making history today."

"Or a huge mistake."

She beamed at him. "You're too good to make mistakes."

He repressed a reluctant smile. But when he turned onto a narrow lane signposted as the delivery entrance to Oswald House, all traces of his amusement fled.

"Here we go," Trixy said as they drove up to the gate. "Ready?"

Jesse took a breath, lowered the driver's window and buzzed the intercom.

"Yes?" came the crackling reply.

"Security contractors here to check the surveillance system." Jesse was pleased his voice was steady. He watched the camera over the gate move to focus on the van.

"We don't use external contractors," the voice eventually replied.

"I don't know what to tell you, mate. You're on my call sheet. Check with Kingston."

"Wait one moment, please."

Jesse tapped his phone and launched his radio intercept program. There was a nerve-wracking moment of silence in which Trixy clenched her fists but then, finally, it crackled to life.

"Mr. Kingston, sir?" the same voice from the intercom came through the app.

Jesse swallowed and tapped play on his queued recording. "What?" snapped an irritable, rasping voice.

A pause. "Uh, is that you, sir?"

Jesse fumbled for another recording. "What do you want?"

"Sorry, sir," replied the first voice. "We've got someone at the back gate. Says he's here to check the security system. I've found them on the works schedule all right but wanted to check—"

Jesses queued his last recording and sent up a prayer.

"If it's on the fucking schedule, it's on the schedule. I'm busy."

A burst of static then silence.

Trixy gnawed her lip. Jesse clutched the steering wheel. Finally, the gate clicked and began rolling open.

"Fuck yeah." Trixy grinned as they entered. "How did you even do that?"

"Downloaded audio samples of the security chief from online videos," Jesse said as he steered through the snow-covered grounds.

"He sounds charming."

"That was some of his milder stuff," Jesse said.

"Sounds like your type. Perhaps you should ask him out when this is over." Jesse gave her a look, but she was staring out of the windshield. "Whoa," she breathed. They had crested a rise and the back of Oswald House rose into view. "Fuck me. How the other half lives."

"A good lot less than half, I think," Jesse muttered as he stared at the three-story mansion. He parked in a space between other work vehicles lined beside a long outbuilding and climbed out. The sounds of horses stamping and the smell of hay and manure filtered through the open doors. The house rose up beyond, its walls broken by floor-to-ceiling windows, all obscured by heavy blinds. The roof was shining slate, covered with solar panels, steam gently rising as the snow melted from them. A wide patio area could be glimpsed down the side, punctuated with red-brick fire pits and covered garden furniture.

A woman on a quad bike braked to a halt at the edge of the lawn to their right, looking at them through the blank glass of snow goggles as Jesse retrieved his bag from the back of the van. Jesse looked away and closed the van then made straight for the large man with a very obvious bulge under his coat who stood at the service entrance.

He continued to survey them for a long time after they'd reached him.

"ID?"

Jesse produced his fake laminated card. Trixy did the same. The man examined them closely, turning them over in his hands and checking both sides. Then he took out his phone and photographed both the cards before handing them back.

"They're expecting you in the security room," he muttered, swiped a card and typed a code into the keypad. The doors clicked and he pushed them open.

Jesse moved inside, trying not to hurry, Trixy following.

It was very dim inside, lit only by a thin strip of LEDs in the ceiling.

"Dummy footage should be rolling…now," Jesse murmured, glancing up at the camera over the door and double-checking the feed on his phone. It showed the corridor they were in, completely empty. "We got about twenty minutes before they start wondering why we didn't go to the security room."

"We'd better get a move on, then," Trixy said, bringing the building's blueprints up on her tablet and leading the way.

They turned this way then that, finally stopping outside a single door at the end of the windowless corridor. It was made of steel. A keypad with a blinking red light was set in the jamb.

"Last chance to turn back," Jesse said, staring at the door with a heavy feeling whirling in his insides.

"You want the rest of your cash or what?" Trixy's words were sharp but her expression intent.

"Okay. Here goes." Jesse rolled his shoulders, got out his tools and began unscrewing the keypad from the wall. He hooked out the internal wiring and clamped on the leads from his homemade Crack Box. He held his breath and pushed the button.

There was a flash and a whirr. The light on the keypad turned green, and the door slid open. Inside, they found a steep staircase, its bottom lost in shadow. Trixy switched on her headlamp. Jesse did the same just as the door slid shut behind them with an ominous click.

"We can get out again, right?" Trixy whispered.

"In theory," Jesse said, tucking his Crack Box back into his bag. "Can we get this over with already?"

Trixy preceded him down the stairs. Her boots rang unnervingly loud in the narrow, echoing space. It got colder the farther they went, and soon their breath was misting in the light from their headlamps. Finally, they came against a barred gate. Beyond it there was nothing but an empty room with the thin outline of another door. Another keypad, more complex, was set in the wall to its side. Red lights the size of pennies dotted the corners of the room.

"Motion detectors," Jesse said in response to Trixy's questioning look. "I've disabled them. We've got about twelve minutes."

"Hurry up then."

Jesse swallowed his retort and dropped to his knees to pick the manual key-lock of the gate. It was a relatively simple mechanism compared to some he'd picked in his time, but that door on the other side was making his hands sweat inside his gloves, and he struggled to grip.

Finally, there was a click, and the gate swung open. They stepped inside. Jesse braced himself for alarms and flashing lights, but there was nothing. He followed Trixy to the door. There was no handle, no lock, just the keypad and a series of small, yellow lights in the frame.

"What are these?" Trixy whispered.

"I don't know. They weren't on the schematics."

Trixy frowned. "Well, can you open it?"

Jesse bit his lip. "Trix, look how tight this all is. Surely this is enough proof that he's secure."

"We don't have anything until we have footage of him doing his thing," Trixy said, jabbing her finger at the door. "Can you open it or not?"

"The Crack Box'll get past the keypad," Jesse answered. "But, Trix—"

"Fine, if you've not got the balls," she said, snatching the box from his hand. "Tell me what to do."

Jesse made a frustrated noise. "You gotta get the clamp leads into the activation wires, behind the panel. But—"

"Gimme the screwdriver," she said, holding out her hand.

Jesse hesitated, glanced at the yellow lights, then handed it over. Trixy stabbed the screwdriver in behind the keypad and wrenched it off the wall. Light flooded the small chamber. An alarm blared. Jesse covered his ears with a curse. Trixy dropped the Crack Box to do the same, swearing even more inventively as a grid of bars slammed down around them.

* * * *

"Quite a gadget, this," the detective sergeant said, laying Jesse's Crack Box on the table between them. She surveyed Jesse closely from behind her thick-lensed glasses, her bloodless lips pressed into a thin line. "Want to tell me a bit more about it?"

"Not without my solicitor, Mariama, no."

"That's DS Paul to you, young man," she replied, though she sounded more weary than angry.

"Sling him into a cell, boss. He won't talk. He never does. And DI Walker's waiting."

The detective sergeant glanced at her constable, a stony-faced young man sat at her side who looked both bored and disdainful.

Jesse was tired. He was hungry. The interrogation room smelled of damp, and the radiator gurgling in the corner was doing little to cut through the chill. He couldn't be sure how long he'd been there, but it must have been several hours.

DS Paul sighed and leaned her elbows on the table. "It's going to be at least tomorrow before we can get you a solicitor. Wouldn't you rather just save us all some time and tell us everything now?"

"Not especially."

DS Paul shook her head. "You've done it now, you know, Jesse. I can't help you this time."

"Have I asked you to?"

Anger tinged with sadness filled her tired eyes. She exchanged glances with the constable and stood. "The custody sergeant will find somewhere nice and comfy for you, until you're willing to speak to us. I believe your usual suite is available."

The next thing he know, Jesse was sat on a concrete bench in a whitewashed cell, shivering and cursing. He clenched his hands together and stared at the floor, mentally playing through the conversation he'd be having with his brother in between now and going to prison for another three-to-five.

"Christ, if Mum were alive to see this."

Then he thought of Oliver, his eyes round with sadness as his dad tried to explain he wouldn't be seeing Uncle Jesse for a while.

He kicked his heel into the bench and buried his head in his hands.

He didn't move again until he heard the door opening.

DS Paul stood there with her arms crossed and a heavy frown on her face. "Well, young man, it appears you really do have the luck of the devil."

"Come again?"

"You're free to go."

"I... What?"

"Charges have been dropped," she said, standing back and gesturing out of the door. "You better get outta my sight before your luck runs out."

Jesse stepped out of the cell in something like a dream, accepting his phone and belt from the grim-faced custody sergeant.

"What about Trixy?"

Paul raised an eyebrow. "She doesn't have your luck, apparently. Now get out of here."

Jesse stood in the slush outside Fulford Road Police Station with his mind whirling and his head pounding. A quick search of local news sites and the police Twitter feed revealed nothing. He shook his head and was turning for home when a tall woman in a dark suit and blank expression stepped into his path. Even without the goggles, he recognized the woman on the quad bike from Oswald House.

"If you wouldn't mind coming with us, Mr. Truelove," she said as she reached out and opened the back door of a waiting car.

Jesse blinked. "Uh, what?"

"It would very much be in your best interests to come quietly, sir."

"Who the fuck are you?"

The woman didn't flinch. "I represent the party responsible for your release. The condition of your charges being dropped was that you are to meet him in person."

Jesse stopped himself from backing away with an effort. "Him?"

"Please, sir," the woman said, gesturing to the car. "The heating's on."

Jesse stood shivering another moment more, then climbed in.

He watched out of the car window as they drove out of the city and into the dark, spreading countryside. Nervousness rasped over his skin like sandpaper. His companion was still and silent next to him, but Jesse didn't think it was an accident that her jacket was unbuttoned just enough to allow Jesse to see the holster under her arm.

After an hour, Jesse was beginning to wonder whether he should be trying to call someone when they turned onto a track with tire marks in the fresh snow.

Finally he could see something ahead—lighted windows of a large building. The car pulled up, and his companion climbed out and opened his door. Jesse clutched his phone tight and got out of the car.

They were outside a modern building with large windows and a stone terrace. The doors opened into a large, open-plan dining area. Round tables draped in crisp, white cloth filled the echoing space. There was a grand piano on a small stage in the corner. On his left was a wall of glass, the room doubled in its dark reflection.

Only one table was occupied. Baron Emory Von Magnusson sat at a table for two. There was a bottle of red wine and two glasses in front of him. His suit was the cold blue of an arctic ocean. His tie was a shade darker, a rich navy that brought to Jesse's mind an evening sky in the depths of winter. Jesse recognized the squat, bull-necked man standing at his shoulder with a grimace. He could feel the heat from the man's glare all the way across the room.

But the haemophile's eyes were scorching the very skin from his bones. It was like looking into the heart of a whirlpool, all shadows and roaring water. He sat still as a marble carving, with his long, pale fingers interlaced on the table. As Jesse got closer, he was able to see the fingernails were long, glass-like and pointed like claws. A shiver ran over his skin.

He concentrated on putting one foot in front of the other without throwing up or tripping over.

"My lord," his escort said as they reached the table. "Mr. Truelove, as requested."

"Thank you, Greenway." His voice in the closed space was like captured thunder. His eyes never left Jesse's face. He didn't seem to blink. "Right on time."

Jesse fought the heat threatening to crawl up his neck into his face and clenched his hands at his sides to stop them shaking.

"Mr. Truelove," the baron said, standing and indicating the chair opposite. "Please."

Jesse stared at the haemophile with fire chasing ice down his veins. Finally, he perched on the edge of the chair, glancing over his shoulder to where Greenway stood between him and the door.

"I'm sorry for the somewhat unceremonious manner of your arrival," the baron said. "I am trying my best to integrate into the community here, but sometimes I am still forced to transact business... discreetly."

Jesse glanced warily from the baron to the man at his back and down again. "And what *business* have we got, exactly?"

"You will address the baron as 'sir' or 'my lord', you gobshite," barked the standing man.

Magnusson raised a hand. "Kingston...please."

Kingston muttered under his breath, folded his arms and recommended glowering.

"I'm sorry for my security chief's manner, Mr. Truelove. This has been a long day for all of us. And please, call me Emory."

"Okay, *Emory*," Jesse managed, the feel of the name on his tongue unnerving him further, but he hoped it didn't show on his face. "Why am I here?"

A corner of Magnusson's mouth tilted in the start of a smile that made Jesse's own mouth dry out.

"You are a direct young man. I like that."

"A couple of hours ago I was under arrest for breaking into your house. And now you've hustled me here at gunpoint." Jesse made sure he didn't blink as he held the dark, troubling gaze. "You can see why I might be just a smidge suspicious."

"Yes. I can smell your fear. Along with...something else?" His eyes were going right through Jesse. His pulse pounded in his temples. "Either way, I can assure you you have nothing to be afraid of. Wine?" Magnusson was holding out the bottle.

Jesse swallowed. "Got any beer?"

Magnusson nodded to Greenway, who paced away. The baron poured wine into his own glass. He swirled the blood-red liquid around the crystal, bringing it to his face and inhaling deeply, closing his eyes and making a low sound of contentment. Jesse's blood surged.

"I didn't realize you lot drank...booze, I mean."

"Oh yes," Magnusson said. "All we can do is drink, after all." He opened his eyes. "Are you sure you won't try it? It's from our very first harvest."

Jesse squinted out of the window to where he could just make out lines of fencing. "This is a vineyard?"

"It is," Magnusson said, smiling wider so a glint of canine flashed white against the deep crimson of his mouth. "With a hotel, spa and restaurant, though it's not open to the public yet."

Jesse looked around the large dining room. "I haven't seen anything about this online."

"I'm waiting for the opportune moment to announce it. Ah—"

He nodded when Greenway returned followed by a server carrying a bottle of Budweiser and a frosted glass on a silver tray. Jesse ignored the glass, grabbed the bottle and downed a large mouthful. The alcohol fizzed in his stomach. He dared to raise his eyes again. Magnusson was holding his wine glass to his mouth, watching him. He drank then lowered the glass and licked the red stain from his top lip.

Jesse dropped his gaze again.

"You must be hungry after your eventful day. Would you like something to eat? The chef is in."

"Why am I here?" he repeated.

Magnusson set his glass down and nodded to Kingston.

Kingston produced the twisted remains of Jesse's Crack Box from his pocket and slammed it on the table.

"Tell us how you built this."

Jesse glowered. "You broke it."

"Tell me how it works."

"Why should I?"

Kingston flushed beetroot red, but Magnusson laid a hand on his arm. The man stepped back, his jaw working. Magnusson reached into his jacket and drew out an envelope. He pushed it across to Jesse, who eyed it like it might bite. He opened it. It was stuffed with cash — at least two thousand in twenty-pound notes.

"What's this?"

"Call it a consultation fee."

"For what?"

Magnusson leaned on his elbows and looked into Jesse's eyes. "Tell us how you got in, Jesse."

"I...uh... What?"

"Tell us how you broke into my system, you little shit," Kingston said, thumping his fist on the table. "You're just some scummy toe-rag. How the hell —?"

"All right, Mr. Kingston." Magnusson didn't raise his voice, but his tone had all the ruddiness draining from his security chief's face. "I think that's enough. Give us a moment, please."

"But, sir —"

"Now...*please.*"

Kingston clenched his fists. He opened his mouth, closed it again, swore under his breath and stormed away.

Magnusson gazed at his glass of wine until he heard the door slam. Then he looked up. "My security chief and I may not agree on the nuances of polite intercourse, but I, like him, would very much like to know how you got around his so-called top-of-the-range security system."

Jesse stared at his beer.

"Please. You're not in any trouble."

"Yeah, right."

"I dropped the charges, didn't I?"

Jesse bit the inside of his lip but didn't speak.

Magnusson was silent for several moments. When he spoke, he'd lowered his voice. "I heard you, you know. We don't register much when we're under. But I heard what you said to your friend."

"Look… It was Trixy's bloody idea," Jesse said. "I told her it was stupid, but I needed the cash and she, well —"

"You knew there were touch sensors on that door. You let her trip the alarm."

Jesse gripped the beer bottle tight.

"You let yourself get caught rather than let her open that door. Why?"

"Perhaps I didn't fancy being torn limb from limb."

"That's it?"

The haemophile was gazing at him, the blue of his eyes rolling like seawater under moonlight. He was smiling. He was so beautiful that Jesse struggled to get breath into his lungs.

"Most systems have a way in," he managed, "if you look hard enough."

"Or are desperate enough?"

Jesse winced. "Trixy's not a bad type. She just wants to do her thing."

"And I would very much like you to do *your* thing, Mr. Truelove…for me."

Jesse blinked. "What do you mean?"

"I want you to work for me." He tapped his long, curved fingernail on the envelope. "This is just the start. I want you to use your skills to make Oswald House safe as possible."

Jesse hesitated. "I'm not sure your pal Kingston would be keen on working with the likes of me."

"I'm not asking you to work with him. I'm offering you *his* job."

Jesse stared at him. "Come again?"

"You outsmarted his system. You are clearly better. I always have the best."

Jesse unstuck his tongue with more beer. The alcohol was starting to tingle in his veins, making it easier to meet the impossible eyes while making it harder to resist their effect. "Let me get this straight… I broke into your place and now you want to *hire* me?"

"To make sure no one else does what you did…*ever*."

Jesse clenched his fist in his lap. He stared at the envelope of cash. "Will you get Trixy off the hook?"

"I can't do that."

"Trixy walks," Jesse said, "or it's no deal."

Magnusson sighed. "Your loyalty is admirable. I only hope you are able to offer me the same, with time." He took a deep swallow of his wine. Jesse watched the muscles moving in his throat with electricity crackling over his skin. He met his eyes again, and this time Jesse couldn't fight the heat that rose in his cheeks, but the haemophile just nodded. "Your friend goes free, as long as you make my systems secure enough to stop her or anyone like her getting anywhere near me again."

Jesse looked at the envelope. "I may be broke, but I'm not some desperate loser who'll do anything for money…just so you know."

"Mr. Truelove." Jesse raised his eyes. "I'm not trying to buy you…just your skills. Don't you think it's time they served you rather than causing you trouble?"

Jesse frowned. "What do you know about me, exactly?"

Magnusson's eyes glinted. "Enough."

Jesse bit the inside of his mouth. He lifted the envelope, felt the weight of it. He thought about his holed jeans, his crappy flat, the out-of-date milk in his fridge — the patches and plug-ins he could get for his PCs if this really was just the beginning. But he could still feel the otherworldly presence of the haemophile on the other side of the table, like he was sitting near a bonfire. "I don't know."

A pause. Jesse didn't dare look up. Finally, the baron broke the silence. "I understand. This must be a lot to think about. So, how about this?" The haemophile produced a business card and slid it across the table. "Come by tomorrow. The front door, this time." His smile twitched. "Meet the team. But if you decide yes, I would like you to move in and start work immediately."

"Wait… Move in?"

"It's a live-in position," Magnusson said frankly. "I need my security on hand twenty-four-seven."

Jesse stared at the business card to try to hide the fact that he was suddenly very aware of how small the table was, of how close that large, powerful body was to his own.

"Come by tomorrow? To Oswald House?"

"Come to the house. Then we'll see where we can go from there." The haemophile stood, buttoning his jacket with one hand while pushing the business card closer to Jesse with the other. He leaned in close to Jesse's face, and Jesse could smell the wine on his breath and a cool, fresh scent that must have been him.

"You are a very interesting young man. I hope to get to know you better."

Jesse fought dizziness. Then, thankfully the haemophile stepped away and his vision unblurred.

"Greenway will take you home. And I'll send a car for you tomorrow."

"And Kingston?"

Magnusson chuckled softly. "Rest assured, I'll be firing him before I leave this building."

He walked away, his steps barely making a sound on the polished floor. Greenway appeared at Jesse's elbow.

"Ready?"

Jesse took a moment to stare at the envelope, business card and the half-drank beer. Then he stood, grabbed the envelope and card and downed the beer.

"As I'll ever be."

Chapter Four

When Jesse opened his eyes in the dim light of the following morning, he spent some time trying to convince himself it had all been a dream. But then he saw the envelope of cash on the chair next to his bed.

He sat up, tugged his hands through his matted hair and willed it to start making sense. When it wouldn't, he sighed and pushed the covers back, shivering in the chill, and padded to his desk. The screens were reeling news, searches and forum updates. He loaded the deep search he'd set running the night before but, so far, it had only found the mainstream articles on Magnusson and other haemophile affairs that had been circulating for weeks. There were no hits containing Jesse's name. Relief washed through him but then saw there was a hit on one of his sub-searches.

Trixy had tweeted in the early hours of the morning.

I got arrested tonight in the pursuit of truth. They want to hide in the dark, but it's time to shine a light.

It had thousands of likes, comments and shares. Debate as to her meaning spread out from the post like a stain. Even when he found no elaboration from Trixy and no mention of Oswald House or Magnusson, concern still fogged his insides.

His phone buzzed. He winced and hunted through his discarding clothing until he found it. There were five missed calls — three from Trixy, two from his brother.

Jess, WTF? Ring me FFS.

Trixy's text was followed by a series of emojis he couldn't untangle. He rubbed his aching head and made for the bathroom.

He closed his eyes and let the hot water run over his head. He took himself in hand to take care of his morning wood then stilled when he realized he was imagining the large, strong hands of the Undying Baron. He quivered like a bowstring, crushing his eyes shut and willing the image to leave his mind — but his brain wouldn't obey.

Jesse was pinned to the table in the vineyard restaurant, his back arched, his shoulders straining under the powerful haemophile's hold. Magnusson's teeth were scraping down his neck and chest. His breath was hot against Jesse's skin. His free hand gripped Jesse's thigh so tight that his sharp fingernails pricked his flesh. His voice was hot and heavy, and his powerful body restrained him as effectively as if he were chained.

Jesse moaned, beating himself harder. But then the Magnusson in his mind reared up, his blue eyes blazing, red mouth gaping, face a twisted, inhuman mask. He crushed Jesse's bones until they snapped, then plunged his teeth into his neck.

Jesse staggered against the wall. He breathed until the sick feeling passed. He turned the water off with a curse and climbed out with shaking legs, his arousal draining out of him faster than the water down the plughole.

He stared at himself in the mirror. The water dripped from the ends of his black hair. His green eyes were shadowed...haunted. He swallowed, rubbing his wrist, summoning the memories of Tyler, of Sid, of Jonny and all the others to wash out the images of the baron. Lastly, he thought of Glen, first tender and smiling, then grimacing when he found out what Jesse really needed from him. He sighed and grabbed a towel.

It was getting on for midday by the time he left his flat. The cold sun was high in the gray winter sky. The pavements were slick with frozen slush. He walked as fast as he dared, heading to the bank to deposit enough of the cash to buy credit for his phone. Then he went to the nearest pub, ordered a coffee and a bacon roll and rang Trixy.

"Fucking hell, Jess," Trixy said, voice high and squeaky. "About time. Where the fuck have you been?"

"Home," Jesse said, sipping the coffee, grateful for the warmth and the normal, earthy taste. "It was a bit full-on yesterday, you know? I kinda passed out."

A pause. "Did you know I'd trip that alarm?"

"What?"

"I saw your face when it went off, Jesse. You were relieved."

"Trix—"

"Don't bullshit me. I get enough bullshit from everyone else in my life."

Jesse sighed. "You were gonna get hurt…or worse."

"That was the *point*—to find out just how dangerous he is."

"It's not fair."

"*'Fair'*?"

Jesse ground his teeth. "He's set up that system to keep people safe, Trix. Doesn't he get points for that?"

"So you're his biggest fan now, huh?"

"Look… As far as I'm concerned, we got out of this by the skin of our teeth. Let's just draw a line under it, huh?"

"And that's another thing," she went on, her voice raising. "We should have been charged for breaking in at the very least."

Jesse squeezed ketchup on the roll with a frown. "You sound like you wanted to be charged."

"Then I could have at least done a post about the suppression of freedom of speech. But no, I got chucked out on my arse in the middle of the night, no explanation. There's some top-level conspiracy going on here."

"More likely Magnusson dropped the charges."

"Why?"

"I don't know, do I?"

"Jess, I can tell when you're lying."

"Look… I just rang to check you were okay. You clearly are, so—"

"Don't hang up! I've got something else you can do for me."

"You serious?"

"This time it won't go wrong, I swear. You just hack into his security cameras, download the footage—"

"Jesus, Trix, will you let this go? You're gonna get yourself in real trouble."

"Not if you get it right this time."

Jesse swallowed his mouthful. "Leave it, will you?"

"Two grand."

"The answer is no."

"Come on, Jess. I know you need the money."

"Bye, Trixy."

He hung up, shaking his head. He finished the coffee, wiped his mouth on the back of his hand, took a breath and rang his brother.

"Hey."

"Hey," Jesse replied, pushing crumbs around his plate with a finger. Anton didn't say anything. Jesse fought a sigh. "You rang?"

"Yeah, I..." Anton paused. Jesse waited, fighting impatience. "Tell me straight, Jess. Tell me you're not sliding again."

"What are you on about?"

"That Influencer friend of yours," Anton said. "She tweeted something about getting arrested last night. It's been deleted now, but Sareena and I both saw it."

Jesse took a moment to ensure his voice was steady. "And that involves me, how?"

"Because when she's in trouble, you're never far behind."

"Jesus, thanks for the show of faith, big brother."

"Were you involved or not?"

"Involved in what?"

"Anything." Anton's voice hardened. "Sareena talked me into letting you take Olly again this weekend. But I swear to God, Jess, if you got busted again..."

"I didn't fucking get busted," Jesse snapped then blushed and lowered his voice when the two elderly women at the next table sent him disapproving looks. "Would I be answering my mobile if I had?"

"Okay," Anton said after a pause. "So what were you doing yesterday?"

"What?"

"I know you weren't home, 'cause I called around."

"You spying on me now?"

"It's a simple question, Jess. Why can't you answer?"

"How is it your business?"

"If you want time alone with Olly, then you need to prove to me you've got your shit together."

Jesse clenched his fist and closed his eyes, fighting the curses threatening to spill out of his mouth, fighting the fire burning under his skin, the hot flash of fury that threatened to close his throat.

"I'm waiting."

"You sound just like Dad when you talk to me like this."

"Good."

Jesse slammed the phone on the table. Guilt choked him but he refused to acknowledge it. The women scowled at him again, as did the barman. Jesse left.

He walked aimlessly with his hands shoved deep in his pockets, waiting for his emotions to cool. It was only as he was turning into his street that he saw the big black car parked outside his building and he realized how late it was.

He swore and hurried over.

Greenway stood by the car, one eyebrow lifted over a pair of dark glasses.

"There you are, Mr. Truelove."

"Uh, sorry. I lost track of time."

"Don't apologize to me," Greenway said, opening the car door. "You answer to the baron now."

Something shivered over Jesse's skin, but he climbed into the back of the car without another word.

They entered the Oswald House grounds through the main gate. Jesse eyed the black orbs of cameras set in the gate posts with interest as they passed. The land rolled away on either side in snow-crisp undulations. The mansion lay ahead — all glass, whitewashed walls, clean lines and terraced lawns. Jesse was again very aware of his thin scarf, scuffed leather jacket and tattered jeans. He followed Greenway to the front door with his shoulders hunched.

Greenway entered a code into a keypad and swiped a card to gain entrance to the building.

"You gotta change those, for a start," Jesse said as he followed her into a vast hall. A glass staircase climbed to a gallery landing. The floor was white marble. An electric LED fire flickered on the wall, warming the air pleasantly. Spotlights illuminated black-and-white mountain photography on the walls.

"What's that?" Greenway said.

"Swipe cards," Jesse said, eyeing the camera set in the ceiling over the front door. "Too easily faked...or stolen."

"The baron said you knew your stuff," came a voice from behind them.

Jesse turned. A tall man stood in a doorway. He was smiling, his teeth straight and white in his tanned, handsome face. A mop of chestnut curls along with the tilt of his grin gave him a playful, boyish look, though the crinkles around his chocolate-brown eyes told Jesse he must be over thirty. His body was long and lean, with toned muscles visible even through his long-sleeved tee.

"Mr. Truelove," Greenway said tonelessly, "this is Baron Von Magnusson's security engineer, Mr. Addams."

"Tom," the man said, holding out a hand. "Nice to meet you."

Jesse shook it. It was warm, the handshake firm. "Jesse."

Tom's smile widened as his gaze flicked over Jesse's face and hair, and Jesse wondered if something had heated in his brown eyes. "It's a pleasure. So, what would you do instead?"

"Instead of what?" Jesse mumbled, distracted by the look in the other man's eye.

"Swipe cards."

Jesse shook his head. "Fingerprint and retina scanners are hardest to crack."

Tom nodded, approval warming his expression. "Sounds good. I look forward to hearing your other suggestions."

"I don't wanna tread on anyone's toes."

"You don't need to worry about that," Tom said with another smile. "Kingston's gone, thank God. I just want to make sure Emory's house is as safe as it can be. I hear you're the man for that."

Jesse blinked. "You really call him Emory?"

Amusement glinted in Tom's eyes. "I've known the baron for many years now."

It was then Jesse noticed the blotched snarl of scarring on the skin of the engineer's neck. Tom watched Jesse's realization dawn, but his smile never slipped.

"Thanks, Kate," he said, nodding to Greenway. "We can manage from here."

Greenway strode away though an open-plan sitting area beyond the stairs.

"I thought we could start by showing you the security room," Tom said, gesturing through the door behind him. "Walk you through the current systems... Then perhaps tour the grounds so you can see the perimeter set-up."

"I already know the set-up," Jesse said as he followed Tom through a minimalist parlor lit only by a fiber-optic Christmas tree glowing on a glass plinth in the corner and fairy lights winking around the slate mantle. "The first thing you should do is upgrade your firewall."

"Good start," Tom said, tapping a code into another locked door and opening it. "After you."

His smile made something flicker in Jesse's chest, and he looked away hurriedly.

The security room was located at the end of the corridor that also accessed kitchens, storage rooms and the staff break room. Jesse paused in the doorway of the break room, taking in an espresso machine, widescreen TV and plush couches. Several people sat around eating or drinking.

"Everything's complimentary," Tom said as they moved on. "And the fridge is always stocked. Here we are."

Jesse already knew the security system, but he wasn't prepared for the high-end hardware. Banks of servers hummed in the corner of the room. Several rack-mount PCs took up most of the floorspace, and there were a half-dozen 4k monitors mounted on the wall. A beefy man in a security guard's uniform sat at the workstation behind the door. He was drinking something that smelled suspiciously like beef stock and scowling with a set of impressive eyebrows.

"Nice, huh?" Tom said, taking a seat at a station behind the security guard. "Kingston brought in the new monitors last month. But if you think we need to upgrade the firewall, we'll need to start with the foundation systems. Oh, this is Filip," Tom said, nodding to the security man. "He heads up the patrol teams."

"You're the kid who broke in?" Filip said. A European accent sharpened the edges of his words.

"That's me."

Filip continued to glower. "Lucky you're still breathing, if you ask me."

"I didn't."

Filip tensed. "You will need to watch your back, little boy."

Jesse flashed him a grin. "Why? What do you want to do to my back?"

Filip colored but said nothing.

Jesse took the seat next to Tom as he began loading the firewall protocols.

"I'd like to build something from scratch," Jesse said as Tom worked. "It'll be like Fort Knox when I'm done. Better." He gave Tom a glance. "I got into Fort Knox once."

Tom blinked. "Really?"

"Well..." He looked away. "Just the gift shop accounts...but still."

"Sounds good," Tom said. The light from the screen warmed his gentle smile. "Does this mean you're taking the job?"

"Kid should be in prison," Filip muttered, draining his mug and slamming it down. "Not getting a job."

"Mate," Jesse said, "if you want some dick, you only have to ask."

Filip lurched out of his chair. Jesse smiled up at him. He muttered something under his breath then slammed out of the door.

Tom laughed a little nervously. "You sail close to the wind, huh?"

"If that's what you call it." Jesse slid him a sideways glance, then looked hurriedly away. "I call it my gob getting away from me. Sorry."

"Don't worry about it." Tom waved his hand. "If anyone needs plain-speaking, it's Filip. Want that tour? If he's not put you off the whole thing, that is."

"No, I, uh." Jesse fumbled for words, suddenly unable to meet his keen, brown eyes. "Let's do it."

* * * *

Tom took him past the now-empty break room and through the deserted but spotless kitchen. "It looks like it's never been used."

"It hardly has," Tom said as he opened another door. "But it needs to be as secure as the rest of it. More, even."

Jesse eyed the industrial refrigeration unit in the corner with its heavy-duty padlock warily. "Is that…uh…?"

"That's where his feed is stored, yes," Tom said as he went through the door. "The donated blood. You can ask about it if you want."

"I'm good," Jesse muttered as he followed Tom out into an airy dining room. "Just wondering why he has a kitchen at all, if the human staff have their own?"

"He's hoping to host more human guests — dinners, business meetings. He did lots of that stuff back in Austria. But here, it's still early days. There are cameras in all these public spaces," Tom continued, gesturing at the black orb in the ceiling over the thirty-seater dining table, "but not upstairs, where the staff quarters and private rooms are — or in his study, the library or the pool room."

Jesse blinked. "The pool room?"

"Oh yeah," Tom said, grinning. "We're allowed to use it, too, during the day. But boring stuff first, I think." He took Jesse through another swipe-card door, and Jesse winced to see that they were in the corridor that led to the basement.

Tom reeled off the specs of the security door, the motion sensors in the sleeping cell and the locks as they approached. Jesse told him about how his Crack Box had bested it and suggested specialist fingerprint and retina-scan technology.

Next, they went through the parlor, a sitting area and a music room with its own stage. Minimalist black-and-white photography adorned the walls. All the floors were marble. Blinds were drawn across every window, giving the place a dim, shadowy feel.

They didn't come across another living soul, and their footsteps echoed off the high ceilings. It was vast and luxurious, with no expense spared, but Jesse felt like he was walking through a museum. He wondered how anyone, even a haemophile, could truly live in somewhere so new, so...empty.

He suggested upgrading the wiring and installing some back-up wireless transmitters. Tom made notes then headed for the library.

"These are the rooms without video surveillance," Tom said, as he opened a set of double doors onto a large, dark space. "There are motion sensors active during the day, but I think Emory would like something more robust. These are his private rooms. He won't have cameras, but he really doesn't want anyone getting in here...*ever.*"

The doors shut behind them, and they were plunged into darkness. The air smelled of dry dust and old pages. Tom tapped a command into a glowing keypad and several lamps flickered to life, filling the space with warm light.

The walls were covered with shelves, all stuffed with books. They were of every conceivable color, bound in leather, wood, paper and everything in between. There were foreign titles, English titles and many without any identifying mark at all.

"Whoa," Jesse said. "That's a lot of books."

Tom chuckled. "Emory's been collecting for quite some time."

"No shit," Jesse said, wandering to a shelf entirely dedicated to horror writers. "First-edition *Dracula*. Figures." Jesse looked around again. "Huh. No windows."

"No windows."

"Well, that's one less way to break in," Jesse said, examining the blinking motion detectors in the corners. "You need better sensors and more of them—floor as well as ceiling, wired into their own network. You should set alarms on the cases, too. Guessing these ones are valuable?" he said, gesturing at a display case containing a tome laid out on velvet, ablaze with colored illuminations.

"Scarily valuable," Tom replied.

"Who has the deactivation codes?"

"Me, Greenway and Filip. And you, if you join us, obviously."

"How often are the codes changed?"

Tom put his hands in his pockets and frowned. "Kingston wasn't one for changing the codes. It meant re-programming the system each time."

"That takes minutes," Jesse said, running his hand over the back of a deep, worn leather armchair that looked like it had provided comfort to someone for decades. "Less, if you upgrade the system. I could write an algorithm to do it for you. But the codes should change every week."

"You're the boss." Jesse blinked. Tom was smiling again. He gestured to the inner doors. "Shall we?"

Jesse followed Tom into a study, again high-ceilinged and windowless. A large, cozy suite was arranged around a large marble fireplace. The fire leapt into life when Tom tapped a code into another keypad. It flooded the room with warmth. In this room, too, the furniture was old …more worn. The sofas were laden with cushions. The boat-sized desk was dotted with pen holders, strange ornaments and a carved Chinese lamp with a jade-green shade.

It was still clearly expensive stuff, but more real…homey. This felt like a sanctuary, walled away from the world. Jesse was shocked by the strength of his desire to stay, to sit in front of the fire and gaze into it, forget everything else and just listen to the warm silence. But Tom was already moving to the next door.

The smell of chlorine flooded Jesse's senses as they stepped through. This room did have windows — windows that made up three of the four walls. Tom pressed a control and the blackout blinds lifted with a gentle hum, revealing the snowbound vista of Askham Moor, stained apricot by the setting sun. Potted tropical plants wreathed the air with a heady smell. The pool at their feet was large and deep, the water crystalline blue.

"Who knew haemophiles liked to swim?" Jesse murmured as he skirted the pool, examining the motion detectors in the ceiling.

"They like lots of things," Tom said in a low voice. "They're a lot like us in some ways — and really not in others."

Jesse looked back. Tom had a distant, thoughtful look on his face.

"How long have you worked here?"

"Since Emory moved in. About a year? But I was with him in Vienna before that. We were there for about five years."

"Vienna? Nice."

"It was" — Tom's smile was a little brittle — "until it wasn't. So, are we done here?"

"Unless you want to go for a swim," Jesse ventured after a pause.

Tom's cheeks reddened, but he glanced out at the setting sun and smiled apologetically. "We're a little late tonight. How about seeing your room?"

Jesse blinked. "Does he really want me to move in?"

"That's the deal, I'm afraid."

Jesse looked around the pool room then at the tall, handsome Tom. He smiled. "Guess I could get used to it."

Tom beamed then led the way back to the public spaces of the house and up the glass stairs to the second floor.

"As I say, no surveillance up here," Tom said as they moved down a corridor with paintings on the walls and flowers on the tables, "apart from the windows. Staff quarters are all on the top floor. We have our own staircase from the break room. But thought you'd better see the whole thing."

"So what are these? Bedrooms?" Jesse said, reaching for a handle, but Tom put his hand out to stop him.

"Yes. But you don't need to see them."

"Who are they for?"

"Guests…when he has them. This way."

Jesse frowned at his tone but followed him through another locked door and up a utilitarian staircase to a floor that looked more like one in a hotel, uniform doors and spot lighting.

"This is Filip's room," Tom said as they moved along. "The rest of his personal security rotate on shift and don't live in. This is Kate's."

"Kate?"

"Greenway," Tom explained. "Though, in honesty, she doesn't really sleep much. This belongs to Alfreeda, the housekeeper. Opposite hers is mine. Then, finally," he stopped at the door right at the end. "This is yours."

"Next to yours?"

"Next to mine. But don't worry, I don't snore."

Jesse tried to decide if that look was back in his eyes, then opened the door. He hovered awkwardly on the threshold. The room was almost as big as his entire flat. There was a rich, blue carpet under his feet and the walls were painted in an eggshell color that complimented the dark carpet and the warm wood of the furnishings. A door to the side opened onto a roomy en suite. He wandered into it a little helplessly.

"It's nice."

"Glad you think so."

"I'll need network ports installed," Jesse said, waving at the desk. "And more plug sockets."

"Does that mean you're saying yes?"

Jesse paused. Tom had an expectant look on his face.

"I just…" He examined Tom's guileless expression for a moment. "What's the catch?"

"Catch?"

Jesse gave him a baleful look. "I broke into this guy's house. I helped a YouTuber try to ruin him. Now he wants to pay me to live in his mansion and play with his hardware?" Tom colored, but Jesse made sure he didn't break eye contact. "There's gotta be something I'm not getting."

"Sometimes things are as good as they look."

"You trust him then? Magnusson?"

"With my life."

Jesse was surprised at his serious tone. He resisted looking at the scar on Tom's neck with an effort. Then his thoughts returned to his cold, pokey flat with its empty fridge and damp walls.

"I guess it couldn't hurt to give it a go…"

Tom grinned. "That's great news. Emory will be so pleased." He hesitated, glancing out of the window at the gathering dusk. "We've probably got time for a walk around the perimeter before it gets properly dark? Might as well see all of what you'll be dealing with."

"Sounds good."

Tom chattered about the perimeter cameras as they descended the glass staircase, but reached the bottom, froze and fell silent.

Chapter Five

Emory Von Magnusson stood in the center of the hall, looking like a member of long-dead royalty that had stepped out of an ancient painting. Jesse thought he'd prepared himself for meeting the haemophile again. Now it seemed he'd been wrong.

He was so tall, so still and so…unreal, that the sight of him stole all rational thought away. He wore another exquisitely tailored suit, this time in such dark blue that it was almost black. His tie was gray silk. The shade of ash made his milky skin glow. There was the hint of a smile playing on the lips. His eyes were fixed on Jesse.

"My lord," Tom said with a smile. "Good to see you, sir."

"And you, Tom," Magnusson said, voice smooth and warm. "And Mr. Truelove. So glad you agreed to come."

Jesse fought the color rising in his cheeks, gave an awkward shrug and dropped his gaze to the haemophile's polished shoes. "I owe you, right?"

"If you can help strengthen my security, I will be the one that owes you."

Jesse dared another look at his face. He could make nothing of the enigmatic half-smile, but the depths of his eyes were alive with unsaid things that Jesse couldn't even guess at.

"So, Tom, what do you think?"

"You were right, sir," Tom said. "Jesse's the one we need. And he's just agreed to join the team."

"I'm delighted to hear that," Magnusson said, holding out his hand. "Welcome aboard, Mr. Truelove. I have no doubt you will be a great fit here."

"Thank you," Jesse said, awkwardly, taking the haemophile's hand. It was cool and hard. Jesse swallowed, taking in the large tendons, the glass-like fingernails and shivering at the feel of the checked strength in his grip. "I'll do my best."

"Of that, I have no doubt."

He looked at Jesse in silence for a long moment, during which Jesse wondered whether he ever blinked.

"I was just about to show Jesse the grounds," Tom put in after an obvious hesitation, glancing between them with an unreadable look on his face.

"I'll do that," Magnusson said. "If you could tell Alfreeda to make the necessary arrangements for him to move in immediately, that would be most appreciated. Providing that's agreeable, Mr. Truelove?"

"Uh, sure. I mean…yes, that'll be fine."

"Excellent." Magnusson held an arm out to the front door. "After you."

"Catch you later, yeah?" Tom said with a reassuring smile. He stepped closer, leaned in and murmured in his ear. "Don't be scared. He's safe. I promise."

Tom's words did more to set unease creeping through Jesse's flesh than anything else so far. His vision from his shower that morning returned. He almost felt his bones breaking. He ducked his head to avoid the heavy gaze of the haemophile and preceded him to the door.

"Are you sure you won't be cold?" Magnusson said, glancing at Jesse's worn jacket.

"I'll be fine," Jesse said, tucking his hands into his pockets and hoping the need to get out into the chill to calm his rushing blood wasn't obvious.

It had started to snow again. Pinhead-sized flakes whisked in the building's floodlights. Jesse drew the cold air deep into his lungs, willing it to help him focus. But the haemophile striding at his side, seemingly impervious to the cold and with footfalls making no noise beyond a slight crunch in the snow, was making it hard to concentrate.

"Nice place," Jesse ventured as they followed the path between the house and the trees toward the back of the mansion.

"Thank you," Magnusson said without looking at him. "But it is just a house. It's where it's built that's important."

"You lived here before, right? Like a hundred years ago or whatever?"

"Three hundred." Magnusson sent him another ghostly smile. "Oswald Hall burned down long ago. But Askham Moor is more home to me than anywhere else I've ever lived."

Jesse tried to decide what to ask next of all the hundred questions buzzing in his head, when they came out into the wide, terraced grounds behind the house. The snow-covered lawns and raised beds were lit by strings of white lights, giving the place the ethereal glow of a fairy glen. The boundary wall was almost lost in the gathering night. Stars pin-pricked the sky between the snow clouds. By their light, Jesse could just make out the rolling moorland beyond the walls, blanketed in smooth white, unblemished and silent as the grave.

"I regret there has to be walls at all," Magnusson said in a soft voice, gesturing at the twenty-foot barrier of stone. "But, alas, a necessity for an independent haemophile, at least for now." He looked down at Jesse. "Would you like a closer look?"

Jesse swallowed but found he couldn't look away. "Sure. There's a gate, right?"

"That's right," Magnusson said, heading down some wide steps under arches of naked rose plants. "Just beyond the trees."

"You should get rid of it," Jesse said, shivering harder as they passed into the shadows under the large trees. "Have a solid wall all around."

"I like to have access to the moor."

"And people who want to break in really like having lots of ways to do it," Jesse replied as they reached the wall. Magnusson turned and strode along it, never putting a foot wrong, despite the deepening dark.

"You'll want to stay close," he said softly. "There are no lights down here."

Jesse swallowed and moved closer, having to almost jog to keep pace. Magnusson stopped at a break in the dark stone, and Jesse put his fingers out to feel the cold hardness of steel.

"You didn't come in this way," Magnusson said.

"Being let in is easier than breaking in," he muttered, using the torch from his phone to examine the heavy bolt. "If I strengthen your firewall so people can't hack your maintenance schedules, that'll be a lot harder to do. But you could get through this with any decent pair of bolt-cutters."

"I would like to keep the gate."

Jesse put his phone away. "Then you need a better lock."

"Anything you say."

Jesse could just make out the smooth angles of Magnusson's face in the light of the moon peeking through a break in the clouds. His eyes were lost in shadow, but Jesse could feel them on his skin like laser sights.

"I sense a lot of anger in you," Magnusson said after a long, heavy silence.

Jesse blinked in the dark. "Excuse me?"

"It's in the way you move. Speak. Smell."

"I *smell* angry?"

"Among other things." Another long silence. Jesse fought the urge to flee as strong as the urge to take a swing. "What makes you so angry, Jesse?"

Jesse's skin rippled in response to hearing Magnusson say his name. "Nothing that's your business," he said. "Sir," he added awkwardly.

"I make a point to know all my staff personally."

"And Tom," he said before he could stop himself. "How *personally* do you know him?"

"Ah...so that's it?"

"*What's* it?"

"He is a very good-looking young man,"

Jesse blushed, grateful for the dark. "That's not what I mean."

"You don't think he's attractive?"

"Yes... No... I mean, *yes*, he is. He's...nice, but not my type."

"Interesting. What is your type?"

"You're kidding, right?" Jesse asked after he forced his tongue to obey him.

"Am I?"

Jesse couldn't move or think what else to say. He groped for offense, for anger, indigence or even bemusement, but all he found was a low, steady flame gathering heat.

"If you're asking about Tom's scarring," Magnusson said, breaking the spell and turning back to the path, "that wasn't me."

"It wasn't?" Jesse said, glad to get back into the low light of the garden.

"No." Magnusson's face was blank as stone.

"So, who did it?"

"That's his story to tell. Come," he said, glancing at his watch. "I have a few people I would like you to meet. Then I will have Greenway take you home to pack."

Jesse stepped into the warmth of the house gratefully, rubbing his hands together to restore feeling.

"I'm registered independent, as I'm sure you know." Magnusson spoke in a low, level voice as they moved through the house. "But I often have some of my kind to visit. Some of my friends are here tonight. I would ask you to extend to them the same respect you extend to me."

"Why wouldn't I?"

Magnusson sent him an inscrutable glance. "Let's just say your predecessor wasn't quite as accommodating, not that I entirely blame him. We can be…alarming, especially in a group."

That's one word for it.

"I don't get why you need humans to protect you at all," Jesse said out loud.

"We really are vulnerable in the day," Magnusson replied simply, then opened a door and waved Jesse through. "More now than ever. We need humans as our allies, or we won't survive these changing times."

Jesse stepped into the parlor. Several figures sat on the loungers or stood with their backs to the LED fire that spanned the length of the wall. They fell silent as Magnusson and Jesse entered. They were all tall, with limbs so lithe and long that they appeared elongated. Their range of skin tones from espresso to ivory glowed as if lit from within. The brightness of their varied eye colors reminded Jesse of a collection of gemstones, but there was an alienness about their beauty that sparked fear in Jesse's chest.

This was not helped by the fact that they all held crystal glasses of thick, red liquid that left a strange coppery tang in the air.

"So glad you could all make it."

"Glad to be here, Emory," the woman by the fire said, her voice low and like the purr of a tiger. "Though, I must confess, I never thought you would ask us to be in the same room as this human."

"Come again?" Jesse scowled.

"This is the one who broke in," the woman continued, addressing Magnusson. "I could smell him the second I came through the door."

"Mr. Truelove is now a member of my security team. I brought him here to introduce him to you all."

"He tried to trick you into hurting someone," said another haemophile who stood near the window, his unreadable eyes locked on Jesse. "Just so he could be famous."

"Not him," Magnusson countered smoothly. "His friend."

"We try so hard to make this work, Emory," a red-haired haemophile with a ghost of an Irish accent and venom-green eyes said from where he sat in an armchair near the fire. "And yet they are still intent on destroying us. Maybe Magister Morak had the right idea."

"I will *not* have that name spoken in this house," Magnusson said, his voice low and threatening. "And Jesse is my guest. I ask that you extend him some courtesy."

"You and your human tolerance, Emory," the first woman said, setting her glass aside. "It'll be the end of you. I'm warning you now."

She strode from the room. A couple of the haemophiles watched her go. The rest watched Jesse.

"You must forgive Haji," a white-haired haemophile, dazzlingly beautiful with the suggestion of a Scandinavian accent, said as he stood from the sofa. "She has trust issues, shall we say." The haemophile held his hand out to Jesse. "Terje."

Jesse stared, taking the cool, long-fingered hand in a daze. "*That* Terje?"

The corner of his bloodless mouth tilted, and he exchanged an amused glance with Magnusson. "I suppose I must be."

A potent mix of fear and wonder stole through Jesse as the silver eyes bore into his. Magnusson came to his rescue by laying a hand on his shoulder.

"Jesse has had a long day. I'm sure you won't mind if we send him on his way."

"Of course," Terje said. "No doubt we'll meet again. Emory," he said, turning his penetrating gaze to the baron, his expression suddenly grave, "you won't be long? We have that matter to discuss."

"I'll be back presently," Emory replied, putting his hand on the door handle.

"He really is back, you know." Terje's voice was heavy with warning. Jesse's blood ran cold.

"Of course I know." Emory's face might have been carved from marble. "As I said, I'll return shortly."

The other haemophiles said nothing, but Jesse sensed their eyes on him as the baron took him from the room. He still hadn't unstuck his tongue by the time they'd reached the front door, where they found Greenway waiting.

"What was that about?" Jesse asked.

"Nothing you need to concern yourself with," Magnusson replied.

"Sorry," Jesse fumbled. "I didn't handle that well, did I?"

"You did better than most."

"Does, uh...?" Jesse glanced over his shoulder and lowered his voice. "Does Terje Kristiansen stop by often?"

"Sometimes. Terje does a lot of work for the rights of registered independents—those that choose to live outside a commune, like myself."

"I hadn't heard much about him in the last couple of years."

"He's a very private individual."

"He lives with a human, right?"

"Lord Aviemore. That's correct."

"Still?"

Magnusson studied him for a moment. "Why do you ask?"

Jesse shrugged, warmth spreading through his face. "He's not here."

"Alec is even more private than Terje. I have met him...but infrequently. He is not the social sort. Any more questions?"

Jesse blushed and looked away.

"It's okay," Magnusson said softly. "I want you to ask me questions, Jesse. Knowledge is our greatest weapon against fear. So long as it doesn't endanger anyone, I will always endeavor to answer. Trust works both ways, after all."

Jesse absorbed the expression on his handsome face for a long moment. "Okay then, I will."

"Good. Now Greenway will take you home. Tomorrow we will send people to collect you and your things."

Jesse nodded dumbly, staring around the marble hall and trying to make himself believe what was happening.

* * * *

He still wasn't quite able to believe it, even when a team of movers arrived at his building the next day with a van and enough men to move his pitiful amount of stuff ten times over.

Jesse escaped to the cafe on the corner to get a coffee, unable to decide how he was feeling. Soon he stood on the threshold of the stripped flat, shivering in the chill and wondering why he was sorry to leave it. Then he spotted the pencil marks on the wall where they'd measured Oliver's growth, and his chest tightened.

He drew his phone out to call Anton, like he had a dozen times between that moment and the night before, but he still couldn't think how to explain. He put his phone away, shut and locked the door and left, dropping his key through the landlord's letterbox as he passed.

Tom was waiting for him when the moving van arrived at Oswald House. He shook Jesse's hand with another of those spine-tingling smiles then hustled him away to start work on the firewall while the movers took his stuff upstairs.

"I heard you met the others last night," Tom said.

"Huh?" Jesse said, distracted by his workstation powering up. "Oh, the other haemophiles." He shook his head. "Yeah, that's something I won't forget in a hurry. How often do those charmers call around?"

"Fairly regularly, depending on what the baron's got going on. He does a lot of outreach work and tries to involve other independents as often as possible." Jesse glanced at him, confused by his guarded tone, but he didn't meet his eye. "Say, was Darragh Kelly there?"

"Who?"

Tom focused on his monitor. "Redhead…Irish."

Jesse blinked. "Uh, yeah, I think so. I didn't catch everyone's name. Why?"

"No reason," Tom said quickly, finally looking over and giving him a disarming smile. "He's Emory's lawyer. He's supposed to be helping me with some legal stuff."

"A vampire lawyer?"

"Is that so weird?" Tom said with an amused smile.

"Everything about this is weird," Jesse said, shaking his head as he loaded the system's base program. "What do you need a lawyer for? Been skimming the baron's funds?"

He laughed. "Nothing so interesting. Just some property thing with my family. I guess we need to start with these foundation systems, if you're going to rebuild our firewall?"

Jesse allowed the subject to be changed and buried himself in the task at hand.

It kept him busy enough that he didn't have a moment to ruminate for the rest of the day. Tom fetched food at intervals and talked to Filip when he came in, grunting and sweeping snow off his black coat, but largely left Jesse to it.

He was so engrossed that the only way he knew that night had fallen was Tom yawning and saying it was time to call it a day.

"We'll pick it up tomorrow, yeah?"

"Uh, yeah, sure," Jesse said, swallowing the last bite of the bagel he'd been working at since dinner time and draining his now-cold coffee. He followed Tom up the stairs, suddenly very aware of the heaviness of his limbs.

They hovered in the hall, and Jesse wondered if Tom was hoping he'd ask him in or if it was the other way around, when Tom said goodnight, opened his own door and disappeared inside.

Jesse shook his head and went to his own room.

His few battered sci-fi paperbacks were arranged neatly on the bookshelf. His framed Misfits poster hung on the wall over the desk. All his clothes, newly laundered, were folded away in the drawers or hanging in the wardrobe. He noted with surprise the new pairs of hard-wearing trousers and jeans in his size. There were new trainers in a box on the floor of the wardrobe, a sturdy pair of walking boots next to them — also both in his size.

In another drawer he found a number of the shirts and jumpers, and there was one of the black coats Filip had worn hung on the back of the door.

He wondered if he should be impressed or unnerved — and couldn't quite settle on either.

He moved to the desk and had to admit that the moving team had done a good job setting up his systems. The extra sockets he'd asked for had been installed already. He itched to boot it all up and have a go with their super-speed internet connection, but if he started web-diving now, he knew he wouldn't stop until dawn.

Then he noticed the text from Anton.

Hey. How's it going? Keeping outta trouble?

Once again, he had no idea how to handle the instant and unreasonable annoyance that flared in him, let alone how to reply.

He set his phone aside, stripped and climbed into bed. He lay in its embracing warmth, enjoying the feel of the new sheets against his bare skin. He sighed deep and ran his fingers over the soft quilt. He paused, bit his lip then gave the headboard a tentative pull. It was sturdy. He pulled harder. It didn't creak or rattle. He imagined being tied to it with someone large and strong bent over him while he lay helpless. In the dark he wasn't sure what sort of face this man had, but he had a powerful build and strong, capable hands.

Jesse closed his eyes, reached under the covers and grasped his cock. His skin fizzed at the contact. He tugged at the bar through his right nipple with his other hand. The flash of sensation sparked electricity along his nerves. He began to stroke himself, his imaginary lover's hands in place of his own, teasing pleasure from him, not allowing him to move, to cry out or to come until he commanded it.

He imagined the ghost of sharp teeth grazing over his belly and came. He blinked into the dark. He ran a hand over his abdomen, almost expecting to feel scratches, but the skin was smooth.

He fought the hot flush of shame and went to the en suite to clean himself off before returning to bed and falling into a deep, exhausted sleep.

* * * *

The new equipment started arriving the next day, and Jesse busied himself with its installation. Tom worked at his side, and Jesse was gratified to see the engineer seemed to instinctively know the sort of thing Jesse was doing and was able to work with barely any instruction.

A sense of ease spread over Jesse's habitual prickly discontent. He wondered at it, wondered why this would happen whilst working for a vampire, of all people.

"So, what do you do for fun, anyway?" Tom said, stirring sugar into his latte as they took a break late in the afternoon.

"Fun?" Jesse asked, frowning at the tablet he was using to monitor the new motion detectors.

"Yeah, you know—the stuff you do because you enjoy it rather than get paid for it."

"That's the same stuff," Jesse said, nodding at the iPad. "Though I've never been paid for it before…at least not this much."

"That's surprising," Tom said mildly.

Jesse sipped his coffee and didn't meet his eyes. "I'm not the most employable person in the world."

"No?"

"No."

"Okay," Tom said easily. "So you like computers. What about humans?"

"What humans?"

"Friends, family…significant other?" Tom asked, a little too casually.

Jesse examined him a long moment before turning his attention back to the iPad. "One married brother and a nephew. That's about it."

"No folks?"

"No."

"Oh. I'm sorry."

"It's okay," Jesse said, tapping commands he didn't need to, just for the sake of doing something. "Mum died when I was young. Dad went last year. He hadn't been well for a while."

"That sucks. I'm sorry."

"It's okay, like I said," Jesse said, a little too firmly. "We weren't close. What about you?"

"Me?"

Jesse looked up. "Same question."

Tom smiled. "Lots of sisters, but they all live down south. My folks live in Spain. Oh, and very much single." His smile widened. "So, who was the girl you broke in here with?"

"A friend. Well...sort of. She's my tattoo artist."

"I thought she was some sort of social media star?"

"That, too—even if all she seems to do these days is get us both in the shit. Though..." He looked around the break room with a half-smile. "I seem to have lucked out this time."

"Perhaps the universe owed you one," Tom said. He dropped his gaze to his mug and fiddled with the empty sugar packet. "We should both get a bit of time off this Saturday. Wanna—I dunno—do something?"

Jesse examined the nervous set of Tom's face before swallowing. "I can't, I'm sorry. I'm spending the day with Oliver, my nephew," he added when a questioning frown crinkled Tom's brow. "I promised to take him to the Christmas markets."

"Oh well, you can't break a promise like that," Tom smiled. "Next weekend then?"

"Perhaps you could try dating a nice guy. You know, just for the sake of variety."

He made himself study Tom's handsome face, sloping shoulders and the tightness of his grip on his coffee cup.

"Sure," Jesse made himself say. "I'd like that... That is, if we're allowed?"

"Allowed?"

"You know, working together and all that..."

Tom chuckled. "Emory's not a conventional boss. You'll find that out pretty quickly."

Jesse had a hundred questions in response to that but couldn't find a way to ask any of them.

That evening he was still running tests on the sensors in Magnusson's study when the fire bursting to life made him jump. He turned. The baron stood in the door with his hand on the room controls and a quiet smile on his face.

For a frozen moment they just stood, staring at each other. Finally, he spoke.

"Tom said I'd find you here."

"Sorry," Jesse fumbled, embarrassed at how he'd let time slip away from him. "I was just checking the new stuff was working."

"Why are you sorry?" Magnusson said smoothly, taking a step forward. Jesse fought the urge to back away.

"Tom said these were private rooms. I guessed —"

"You're welcome in any part of Oswald House you care to be in," Magnusson said, halting a foot away. "I'm relying on you to make it safe, after all. Tom says it's going well?"

"Got a way to go yet," Jesse said, "but getting there."

"Glad to hear it. Actually," Magnusson added as he drifted past Jesse, heading for a drinks counter in the corner, "I have something I'd like to discuss with you. Discreetly. Whiskey or brandy?" he asked as he poured amber liquid from one of the heavy decanters into a tumbler.

Jesse blinked, struggling to process. "Uh…brandy, I guess."

Magnusson picked up a different decanter, poured a measure and held out the glass. It smelled warm and strong, but Jesse's stomach was bunching, and he didn't drink.

"What's this about?"

"I have a task for you," Magnusson said after a pause. "A very specialized job."

Jesse narrowed his eyes. "That sounds ominous."

"Please." Magnusson gestured to the sofa. Jesse hesitated, suddenly aware he was alone with the Undying Baron in a room without cameras. The frisson of excitement that chased his fear through his body made his cheeks color as he blinked stupidly at the sofa.

"Mr. Truelove, if you please."

The command in Magnusson's tone was unquestionable. Jesse downed a mouthful of the brandy, willing the burning alcohol to help him think straight, and took a seat. When he could focus again, Magnusson had sat at the other end, his long legs crossed, whiskey untouched in his hand.

"I do hope you're not afraid of me," the haemophile said after a long silence. "I will not hurt you."

Jesse gripped his glass so hard his knuckles ached. "I know that," he said, hoping he sounded more sure than he felt.

Magnusson was no longer smiling but something like dark amusement lit the back of his eyes. "Could I tell you more about this task?"

"Uh...sure."

Magnusson sipped his drink, set it aside then drew an envelope out of his jacket. He handed it over. Jesse downed the rest of his brandy. Suppressing a cough, he set the empty glass on the floor and opened the envelope. Inside was a slip of paper with a printed address.

Ivor, Harrison & Associates
7 Stonehead
York

Underneath was a hand-written series of letters and numbers — M-E76-890-DH.

Jesse frowned at it. "This is a law firm...and a case number."

"I'm impressed."

"I've had a few case numbers of my own over the years," he muttered. "What does this one mean?"

Magnusson paused then spoke without breaking eye contact. "This firm is representing the other side in an ongoing legal dispute I am having. The case number is mine. I have every faith in my legal team, but an idea of the sort of case the opposition is mounting would go a long way to helping them plan their own."

It took Jesse a long time to find his voice. "You want me to hack a law firm?"

"Yes, I do." Magnusson said, interlacing his fingers. "Though there's a catch, as you've probably guessed."

"Besides it being horrifically illegal?"

Magnusson lifted an eyebrow slightly. "I did not have the impression that that would be a problem for you, Mr. Truelove."

Jesse clenched his jaw.

"You would be suitably compensated."

"Money's not much good if you're rotting in prison."

"I assure you it will not come to that."

"How do you know?"

"Because I know how skilled you are," he said smoothly, "and I will give you the added assurance that you will have my legal team on your side should any consequences arise. And they are very, very good at their jobs."

"The redheaded guy, right?"

Magnusson nodded. "Darragh Kelly heads up the team. Though he's been practicing the law for at least a hundred years longer than any of my human representatives. Do what you do best, do it well and, trust me, I can shield you from all potential recrimination."

Jesse stared hard at the paper. "Even if I said yes, their files will be on a closed system. No access from outside." Jesse lifted his head. "You want me to break in, don't you?"

"I want you to do what you do best."

"Is this why you really hired me?" Jesse said, unaccountably hurt.

To his surprise, Magnusson smiled. The hint of a sharp canine glinted against the redness of his mouth.

"I believe in utilizing all my staff's full potential," he said.

"What sort of case is it?" Jesse demanded. "If you're wanting me to help you get off from assault or murder or any shit like that…"

"Jesse, I'm hurt. It is nothing of the kind. Besides, don't you think you and the whole world would know if I was facing those kinds of charges?"

"Not if you are good enough at hiding them."

Magnusson's face was serious. He shifted down the sofa until his thigh was almost touching Jesse's. Jesse resisted backing away as Magnusson gazed into his eyes. "I haven't hurt anyone, Jesse. Quite the opposite."

"What do you mean?"

"You'll find out, in time," he said and glanced at the paper in Jesse's hand. "So, what do you say?"

"Surely one of your guys is far better at sneaking into locked offices with no one hearing or seeing anything?"

"This is a human problem with human consequences. My kind aren't interested."

"What about your undead lawyer friend?"

Magnusson's face hardened, and Jesse stiffened.

"I think you're trying to provoke me. It won't work."

"Why would I wanna provoke you?"

"You're like your friend," Magnusson said, his voice soft. "You're worried I'm going to hurt you, so you're trying to make me do it on your terms. At least then you're in control."

Jesse stared hard into the fire. His skin was hot. His heart thumped against his ribs. The touch of a finger under his chin sent a jolt through his body. Magnusson turned Jesse's head so he was looking into his eyes.

"So much fear, Jesse," he whispered. "And anger. And pain. You want me to add to it. I'm not going to."

It was like an iron band was clamped around Jesse's chest. He was caught between a desperate urge to crush himself against the haemophile's body and an equally desperate one to run for the door.

Magnusson dropped his hand, and the spell broke.

"I think you are the best person for this job," he said. "It means a lot to me. And I know I can trust you. You can turn me down. I just hope you won't."

Jesse stared at the address on the paper. "It'll take a few days to plan," he finally said, his voice hoarse.

"Anything you need. Though there is one more thing I have to ask of you."

"*Another* thing?"

Magnusson's eyes flickered. "I must ask you not to read the case file yourself."

Unease tightened Jesse's chest further. "You say that there's nothing dodgy in these files, but you're telling me *not* to read them?"

"I'm not telling you. I'm asking you." Jesse bit the inside of his cheek and made himself hold the measured gaze. "You will have your explanations,

Jesse, I promise. When the time is right. I'm asking you to trust me until that time comes. Can you do that?"

Jesse's throat was aching. It was like he was teetering on a tightrope, trying to decide which way to fall.

Chapter Six

"Hey, are you okay?"

Jesse looked over at Tom. He sat at the next workstation with a concerned frown on his face.

"Huh?"

"You've been quiet all morning."

"I'm fine," Jesse said, gulping coffee. "Just didn't sleep well, that's all."

"Everything all right?"

Jesse stared hard at the code scrolling on his screen. "Course."

"It's okay if it's starting to freak you out," Tom said after a pause. "My first few weeks working for the baron were hard. It took me a while to get my head around it all."

"I said I'm fine." Tom blinked, and Jesse rubbed his face. "Sorry," he muttered, dropping his hands. "I'm just shattered."

Tom gave him an uncertain smile. "You need a break. Have you got your day with your nephew tomorrow?"

"Yeah."

"Well, don't hurry back."

"But the fingerprint scanners arrive tomorrow night."

"They can wait until Monday. Take your Saturday, Jesse. Emory won't mind."

Emory.

Jesse's blood stirred, and he looked away.

* * * *

Jesse was on his third beer and fourth hour of analyzing the blueprints of Ivor, Harrison & Associates' office building when his phone buzzed on his bed. His brother's name flashed on the screen, and Jesse's heart sank.

"Jess, there you are." There was only a touch of annoyance in Anton's tone, for which Jesse was grateful. He was so wound up that he didn't know what he'd say if his brother rubbed him up the wrong way, and it wouldn't take much right now to get him to ban him from the house and Oliver…again.

"Sorry, Ant," Jesse said, getting another beer from the mini-fridge under his desk. "I've been busy."

"Busy?" Anton sounded dubious. "Doing what?"

Planning to break into a lawyer's office for a vampire who's as hot as he is terrifying.

"Uh, a job," he said after unsticking his throat with beer. "I got a job."

"A job? A real one?"

"*Yes*, a real one.'

"I'm sorry. No, you're right. It's just been…" Anton made a frustrated noise. "Sorry. What's the job?"

"Digital security engineer."

"That's great." Anton was so enthused guilt lapped up Jesse's throat. "And do they, well....know?"

"Know what?"

"Don't hate me," Anton said after a pause.

"Do they know *what*, Ant?"

"They know about your record and everything, right, Jess? You didn't falsify references or anything?"

Despite his best efforts, Jesse bridled. "You really think I'm a complete screw-up, don't you?"

"I just know it's been tough, little bro," Anton said, his regret so audible that Jesse again tasted sour guilt "I want to know you're okay."

"I am," Jesse said, more calmly. "This is a real job, I promise. And yes, they know about my past. They gave me a chance, anyway."

"That's great...really great. Where is it?"

Jesse froze with the beer bottle to his lips. "Where's what?"

"The job?"

Jesse fidgeted. "It's sort of confidential."

Another pause, more weighted this time. "Confidential?"

"It's legit, I promise." *Mostly.* He winced. "I'll tell you, I promise...when I can."

"Okay," Anton replied after another heavy pause. "I'll take your word on that. So you can pay your gas bill and shit now?"

"I, uh...I moved out of that place. This is sort of a live-in position."

Another pause. "What the hell is this, Jess?"

"Look... I said I'd tell you, and I will. Just not yet."

"Why not?"

"I just wanna get settled in. See if it's what I really want."

"If you've moved in, I'd say you're pretty committed, little bro."

Jesse bit back a curse. "Can you just trust me for once? Please?"

"I'm trying, Jess. But this is your last shot, understand? If you're up to something dodge and you're not telling me…"

"Can I still take Olly tomorrow or what?"

A moody silence fell. Jesse could hear Sareena in the background. Anton answered in a mutter then came back on. "Yes, you can take Oliver, but just to the Christmas markets, you hear? No jaunts to the seaside or taking him to your new mystery job or anything."

"I promised him the markets," Jesse insisted. "We're going to the markets."

"Good. 'Cause he's really looking forward to it."

Despite everything, Jesse's heart warmed. "I'll pick him up at ten."

"Great." Anton took a moment, and when he spoke, Jesse could hear him making the effort to sound friendly. "We'll see you tomorrow, Jess. Take care, hear?"

Jesse stared at his phone for a long time after Anton hung up. Fatigue was dragging at him, but he took a breath and booted up his deep search application. The only new hit was another article on a national news website about Magnusson's Christmas lights. There was one paragraph about the installation and three more about Oswald House's proximity to the city. The language was careful, but it cited a much-quoted interview with the head of Askham Moor Primary School, in which she discussed the number of parents who had withdrawn their children since Magnusson had taken up residence nearby.

Parents are scared. And you can understand why. Questions have been raised with our Representative to the Assembly for Haemophile Affairs, but local feeling is very much that basic safety concerns are being overlooked in favor of politically motivated international issues.

Jesse shut the article down. He rubbed his mouth, drained the beer then added another subroutine to the search.

Adding term *'Ivor, Harrison & Associates'*...

He hesitated with his finger hovering over the Enter key. He clicked it and shut the monitor down.

* * * *

"Uncle Jesse!" Oliver barreled into Jesse's legs and wrapped his arms around his waist.

"*Oof...* Easy, mate," Jesse said, rubbing his gloved hand over Oliver's tousled hair. "Ready to go?"

"Yeah." Oliver grinned, accepting his backpack and bobble-hat from Sareena. Anton stood with his hand around her waist and studied Jesse.

"Looking good, Jess. New coat?"

"Yeah," Jesse said, sticking his hands in the pockets of the black wool overcoat from Oswald House. "Nice, huh?"

"Yeah, it is. New shoes, too?"

"New everything," Jesse said, helping Oliver into his backpack. "Got a job, don't I?"

"That's wonderful, Jesse," Sareena beamed. "I'm so pleased for you."

"I'll be more pleased when you can tell me who you're working for," Anton said, ignoring Sareena's disapproving frown.

"And I told you," Jesse said with measured patience, "I will."

"Come on, Uncle Jesse," Oliver said, tugging on his hand. "What if they run out of hot waffles?"

"That's highly unlikely mate," Jesse said, but allowed himself to be dragged toward the road.

"He's allowed *one* sweet treat," Sareena called after them. "There's fruit in his backpack."

"Be good."

Jesse heard his brother's weighted words as Oliver, already chattering about hot chocolate, gingerbread and toy stalls, hurried him along.

"Dad's right, you know, Uncle Jesse," Oliver said a little while later, grinning through a smear of chocolate sauce. The crowds weaved around them, and the mouth-watering smells of deep-fried food and spices were thick in the cold air. "You do look good. The clothes are nice."

"Thanks, mate," Jesse replied as they made for yet another craft stall.

"I think the leather coat was way cooler, though," Oliver said as he examined the counter of carved Christmas tree decorations.

"I still have it," Jesse said, reaching for the wooden train Oliver was eyeing. "But it was never much good in the winter. You like this?"

"It's great. But is it for the tree?"

"Yeah, but you can run it on the ground, too. See?" He ran the train along the edge of the counter while the stall owner smiled maternally. "Want me to have a word with Father Christmas, see if he'll let you have an early present?"

Oliver beamed and Jesse handed over the money. They moved toward the Shambles, and Oliver ran the train along walls and fences. But his sound effects quieted then stopped. His face turned thoughtful.

"You all right, mate?"

Oliver sniffed. "Will you be coming over for Christmas, Uncle Jesse?"

Jesse took a breath. "I dunno, mate. I have to be asked, don't I?"

"Dad hasn't asked you?"

"Not yet. But either way, you'll have your mum and dad. That's what counts, right?"

Oliver wiped his face with the back of his mitten. "Dad's still acting weird."

Jesse's heart clenched. "He's just missing Grandad, mate. That's all."

Oliver looked up, eyes round. "Do you miss Grandad, too?"

"Course I do. Why do you ask?"

Oliver was silent for a moment, expression grave. "What about Grandma?"

Jesse paused, trying to control his face. "What about Grandma?"

"Do you miss her, too?"

Jesse sighed, a familiar weight suddenly leaden in his chest. He drew Oliver onto a nearby bench and sat. "You never even met Grandma, Olly. Why are you asking?"

"Dad talks about her a lot, even more at the moment," Oliver said, listlessly spinning the wheels on his wooden train. "I think he thinks you don't care about her—and I think that's why you fight all the time."

A needle went through Jesse's chest.

"Olly, you have to understand..." He fumbled for the explanation that had never satisfied anyone other than himself. "I was very small when our mum died, smaller than you are now. Of course, I miss her, but I never really knew her." He kept his expression mild as he met his nephew's penetrating gaze. "Your dad and I...? We're just different, that's all. And, you know, sometimes brothers and sisters fight. You'll learn that one day."

"No, I won't."

Jesse blinked. "What's that?"

"Mum and Dad told me last week that I won't ever have a brother...or a sister." Oliver sniffed louder. "Mum seemed sad, but Dad said I'm all they need."

"They're right," Jesse said, patting his nephew's knee, even as his chest tightened. "You're the best kid anyone could ask for."

"But I wanted a sister."

"Oh, mate." Jesse put his arm around Oliver's shoulders and drew him close. The boy buried his face into Jesse's chest and clung tight but didn't make a noise. "I'm sorry, lad. I really am. But your folks are right. And you got lots of friends at school, haven't you? That's almost as good."

Oliver rubbed his face into Jesse's coat. Jesse grimaced and searched in Oliver's backpack for tissues. He made Oliver sit up so he could wipe his face. When Jesse had finished cleaning off the chocolate and mucus, he looked brighter.

"What about a cousin, Uncle Jesse?" he ventured. "I could have a cousin one day, couldn't I? If you have kids?"

Jesse blanched. "Uh, that's a little harder for me than most guys, mate."

"I know you have boyfriends and not girlfriends," Oliver said with a frank look. "Mum explained everything. That guy Glen... He was your boyfriend, wasn't he?"

Jesse flinched. "A while ago...yeah."

"He talked about you guys having kids once. I remember. He said that you might adopt or whatever."

The chocolate and banana waffle Jesse had consumed threatened to return up his throat. "That's...complicated."

"But you could get a boyfriend easy," Oliver prompted. "And they can't stop you adopting just because you're both boys. Mum said so."

"That's not the only thing they look at, mate," Jesse said helplessly. "They look at your history, your job..."

"But you have a job now," Oliver said excitedly. "And you told Dad you're gonna be good from now on. I heard you."

"You really gotta stop eavesdropping," Jesse said, rubbing his hand over his face. "This... Ah, I can't even explain."

"But it's *possible*, right, Uncle Jesse? One day you *might* have a kid?"

Jesse heaved a big sigh and made himself meet his nephew's hopeful eyes. "You never know, mate," he said. "You never know."

Oliver beamed. "That's all I want for Christmas, Uncle Jesse. The *only* thing I want."

"Jesus, way to put a deadline on me, lad."

Jesse forced a smile and allowed himself to be dragged toward a carol service tent. He tried very hard to listen to the singing and smell the mulled wine and mince pies and not think about the fact that he could see the sign for Ivor, Harrison & Associates through the door.

* * * *

"We'll be waiting here," Greenway said in a low voice as Jesse got out of the car. "You have one hour."

"Yeah, yeah, I know," Jesse muttered, putting on his gloves and trying to push the conversation with Olly from his mind.

"Sure you're up to this?"

Jesse gave Greenway a look. "Just be ready, lady."

Greenway lifted an eyebrow. Jesse yanked up his hood and slunk down the alley. It was dark and smelled like piss and rubbish. He swore to himself as he stepped over spilled trash and hauled himself onto one of the overstuffed bins. It wobbled alarmingly under his weight. He grabbed the window ledge over his head to steady himself. His heart was clamoring. His palms were sweating.

He pulled out his phone, cursing Trixy, Magnusson, Ivor, Harrison and everyone else he could think of as he waved it until it flashed red where a sensor wire ran on the inside of the window frame. He loaded his custom scrambling app and activated it. The glowing red wire flickered then went dark. He sent up a prayer, stuck a knife into the gap where the wooden frame had warped and jimmied the window until it lifted with a grind of protesting wood.

He held his breath. *No alarms. No flashing lights.* He let out a breath, grabbed the windowsill and heaved himself through.

He fell onto a thin carpet with a curse and a bloom of pain in his hip. He swore and fumbled blindly for his head torch. The beam fell on desks, computers and filing cabinets. He grabbed a chair and hauled himself upright with more muttered curses.

"Getting too old for this shit," he growled to himself as he sat at the nearest desk.

He booted up the computer, stuck a thumb drive into a spare port and began trying passwords. He was into the terminal in seconds—the legal secretary had used his girlfriend's name and birthday as a password, both of which Jesse had found on social media—and quickly found his way into the company's case files. He entered the case number but got no hits. He frowned, tried a system-wide search instead, but still, nothing.

He tried searching for Magnusson's name next. Zero results. He sat back in the chair with a heavy frown. Then he looked past the computer to the filing cabinets. He chewed on his lip for a moment then made for the one labeled H – M.

He made short work of the lock and yanked it open. Inside were a number of paper files, the fattest of which was labeled M-E76-890-DH.

He lifted the heavy file from the drawer then cast about until he spotted a desktop scanner. He hacked into the machine it was attached to and began feeding papers through its tray. The machine whirred, and the size of the digital file grew as the page count ticked up.

Jesse watched the papers feeding while fighting the urge to bring them into the beam of his torchlight. His hand hovered over the summary page at the top.

He'd never know...

Magnusson's cobalt eyes rose in his mind. He swallowed, shivered and dropped his hand.

"Come on. Come on," he urged, checking his watch. Finally, the last page was scanned. He saved the files to the thumb drive, ran a quick wipe program to remove all superficial traces of his activity, then returned the paper file to the cabinet. He returned to the window just as his scrambler app began to pulse a warning.

He clambered through the window, swearing when he caught his shin on the sill. He slammed the window shut and deactivated the scrambler seconds before the system's internal disruption alarm was triggered.

* * * *

Jesse spent over an hour staring at the shadows on his bedroom ceiling before he admitted that there was no way he was going to sleep that night. He thrust the covers back with a growl and paced the room, running his hands through his hair and trying to banish his brother's disapproving voice from his ears — his dad's disappointed one, his nephew's hopeful one.

He shoved his chair against the desk so it clattered — and swore, loudly. There was a knock at the door. He looked at the time, cursed again, pulled on some underwear and went to the door.

Tom stood in the doorway wearing nothing but a pair of striped pajama bottoms and a concerned look. Jesse lifted his gaze from the sculpted, hair-dusted pectorals with an effort and attempted a smile.

"Sorry. I woke you?"

"Everything all right?"

"Yeah." Jesse rubbed his face. "I just can't sleep."

Tom's eyes searched his for a moment. "I find swimming can help, you know, if you're struggling to relax."

Jesse spent a charged moment trying to analyze his tone. "I thought we were only allowed to use the pool during the day?"

"He's away."

"He is?"

Tom nodded. "London…until Monday."

Jesse rubbed his sore neck. "You know, that's really not a bad idea."

"I could come, too…if you want."

Jesse held Tom's sleepy and slightly hungry gaze. A tickle stirred in his abdomen, but he made himself give Tom a regretful smile. "I don't think I'd be great company tonight, mate."

"No problem," Tom said, after the slightest hesitation. "You need alone time. I get it. But we're still on for next weekend?"

"Yeah," Jesse forced out. "Course."

"Okay then. Enjoy."

Tom padded away, throwing a smile over his shoulder as he disappeared into his room. Jesse remained where he was for several moments more, trying to decide what he was feeling.

He sighed, changed into swim shorts and an old Iron Maiden T-shirt, grabbed a towel from the bathroom and padded down the corridor toward the staff stairs.

It was eerie moving through Oswald House in the dark. Nighttime was usually when it was at its most brightly lit. Jesse felt like an intruder.

He snuck through the library and study with the skin of his back prickling. But all his anxiety fell away when he activated the underwater lights in the pool room. They filled the space with a soft, blue glow that was so inviting he thought nothing more of stripping off his T-shirt and diving right in.

The water was just the right temperature—not too warm, not too cool. He did three lengths sidestroke before pausing to catch his breath. He pushed his wet hair from his eyes and hooked his elbow on side, letting the water sway him. His pulse calmed, his breathing slowed and he found his mind was quieter. Sleepiness settled heavy behind his eyes, and for a fleeting moment, he wished he'd asked Tom to join him. He shook the thought away and was just turning to swim back to the steps when he floundered. He spluttered and grabbed the side again to keep his head above the surface.

The baron sat in a chair at the side of the pool, watching him.

"Christ," Jesse cursed. "You scared the shit outta me."

Magnusson didn't move. His long legs were crossed. His alabaster hands were curled around the arms of the chair. His face was masked in shadow, but even from the other end of the pool, Jesse could see the glint of his unblinking eyes.

Jesse's stomach plunged. "Shit. Tom said you were away. I'll bugger off. Sorry." Jesse hauled himself out of the pool and hurried toward his clothes.

"Stay."

Jesse paused in the process of bending for his towel. The tone had thrummed his nerves like plucked wire.

"It's a bit late, boss…"

"I want to ask you a question."

"Can I get dressed first?" Jesse said, aware of his wet shorts sticking to his skin.

"No."

A thrill went up Jesse's back. He crushed his eyes shut until he had control. When he opened them, Magnusson still hadn't moved.

"A question?"

"You didn't read the files."

Jesse swallowed. The water dripping from his body onto the tiled floor was loud in the warm silence. "That's not a question."

He didn't speak.

"How do you know I didn't read them?" Jesse prompted, clenching his hands at his sides to stop himself reaching for the towel. The heat of the eyes burning into him from the shadows was scorching his exposed skin, even from meters away.

"You would have a lot more curse words for me if you had."

Jesse blinked water from his eyes. His blood was burning, and he was becoming accurately aware of the way it had started to pool in his groin.

"Sorry, boss. Do you have a question or not?"

The only sound was the lapping of the water in the pool and the pounding of Jesse's heart. Then, eventually,

"It was a paper file, wasn't it?"

Jesse nodded.

"Which made it harder to get a copy, yes?"

"Impossible, from the outside," Jesse said, resisting the urge to shift from one foot to the other.

"Could anyone else get a copy?"

"Not unless they did what I did, and I don't think anyone else would be that daft."

"Good. That's good."

"Okay then," Jesses said, bending for the towel. "Can I go?"

"Leave it."

Jesse blinked. The command made his skin ripple from his toes to his scalp. "Huh?"

"I said…leave it."

Jesse clenched his jaw. His groin throbbed. Heat warmed his face, and his nerves buzzed. The shadowed eyes pinned him to the spot. He felt exposed, helpless, and the excitement coursing through him threatened to make him tremble.

Finally, Magnusson stood and stepped into the light. He wore no tie. His shirt was crisp, snowfall white and open at the collar. Jesse gazed at his neck muscles sliding into his clavicle and watched in dazed fasciation as he swallowed. The haemophile's blue-black eyes were like twin wells into nothingness, but the way they roamed over Jesse's body caused a very human reaction to stir in his chest. He cursed inwardly and willed his body to calm.

"Has anyone ever told you you're an extraordinarily striking young man?" Magnusson murmured as he approached.

"Sure," Jesse said, astonished he didn't choke on his rising desire.

Magnusson circled Jesse like a shark. Jesse couldn't move. Magnusson stopped behind him and was still for so long that Jesse almost gave in to the urge to run. But then the haemophile leaned close enough that his warm breath brushed Jesse's neck.

"But has anyone ever made you *feel* it?"

Jesse swallowed painfully. His fingernails were digging into his palms. His skin was on fire. The thin cushion of air between them was maddening.

"Look, mate," he started, but Magnusson inhaled deeply, like he was smelling his skin, and the words dried in his mouth.

"I suggest you call me 'sir'."

Jesse shut his eyes tight, clenching his jaw to stop the helpless sound attempting to escape his throat. "Are we...are we really doing this?"

"You like this, yes?" Magnusson whispered, like Jesse hadn't spoken. "To be commanded?"

"I..."

"Don't move."

Magnusson's clothing brushed against his back. Jesse went rigid. He longed to lean into the large body, to feel the muscles against his skin, to dig his fingers into it. But the low noise of warning Magnusson made had him gasping and clenching his fists harder.

"That's good. Well done."

Magnusson ran his fingers up Jesse's arms — a touch as light as feathers, hardly enough to push the water drops over his skin. Jesse swallowed a moan.

"Do as you're told, and you'll be rewarded," Magnusson rumbled in his ear. "Disobey and I will be forced to punish you."

Jesse nodded stiffly. "Yes..."

"Yes, what?"

"Yes, *Sir*."

"That's better."

Jesse's blood heaved through his body as Magnusson glided his fingers up his arms and across his shoulder blades.

"Your tattoos are very interesting," he said as he traced a finger over the words *Burn Out* inked across his shoulders in Tudor lettering. "We can't have them, you know. The Blood washes them away from the inside." The finger swept down the ivy twirled over Jesse's spine, making him quiver. "What do they mean?"

Jesse forced his eyes open but then he realized he could see himself in the window, pale and mostly naked, shaking, his erection painfully obvious through his damp shorts. Magnusson stood behind him, his eyes on Jesse's in the window. He inhaled as Magnusson slid his finger farther, to the death's head moth inked across his lower back.

"I asked you a question, Jesse."

Jesse bit his lip and lifted his gaze to the ceiling. "I'm sorry, what? Sir?"

"What do the tattoos mean?" he repeated, sliding a hand around Jesse's ribs.

Jesse made a strangled noise. "Nothing. I just thought they looked cool...*ah.*" He clamped his mouth shut as Magnusson tweaked his nipple bar. Fire blazed along his nerves and hot gold pooled under his belly.

"Not yet," Magnusson rumbled, digging the sharp fingernails of his other hand into Jesse's side. The sensation sent shocks of pain needling through his peaking arousal.

Jesse took a deep breath, then another, and fought himself back from the edge.

"Good," Magnusson purred in his ear. "Very good. Now, this little addition," he said, tugging the nipple piercing again. Jesse swallowed a groan with a monumental effort. "Is this just to 'look cool'? Or is it for quite a different purpose, I wonder?"

Jesse couldn't have answered if he'd tried. Magnusson flattened his hand over the nipple and massaged it, scraping his sharp nails up his side with his other hand. Jesse twitched, clenched his eyes shut.

"Not yet." Magnusson was right by his ear. "Hold on."

"I...I can't," he gasped as the fire surged in his abdomen.

"Yes, you can," the haemophile said, "I'm ordering you to."

His left hand tightened around Jesse's biceps as his other hand left his nipple to slide, maddeningly slow, down his stomach.

"Jesus..."

"No sounds, Jesse — or I'll punish you."

"But...ah, *fuck.*" Magnusson ran his tongue up his neck. His grip on Jesse's arm was like iron. His other hand pressed against Jesse's belly, just above the waistline of his shorts. "Sir, fuck, *please.*"

"Now you've disobeyed," he whispered, "so you will have to wait."

Jesse whimpered and reached for his cock, which was now so hard it was almost painful. But a vise-like grip clamped around his wrist.

"You're testing me. Stay still, Jesse. Stay silent. *Obey.*"

Jesse heaved breaths into his choked chest and nodded. Magnusson released his wrist. Jesse kept his hand at his side, though his arm shook with the effort.

"There," Magnusson muttered into his neck. "I knew you had it in you."

The haemophile ran a hand up Jesse's arm again, over his shoulder and down his back, the touch softer than silk, even as his hold on the other arm was hard as steel. He traced circles at the small of Jesse's back. Jesse fought another whimper, feeling the fire burn, blisteringly hot, behind his balls. Too hot to bear.

"Almost time," Magnusson whispered, tracing his lips up the back of Jesse's neck. He made a low rumbling noise as he slid his fingers over the waistband of Jesse's shorts to grasp his hip through the damp fabric. Jesse quivered like a bowstring. "With me you will learn the reward is always sweeter if you wait just a bit longer than you think you can."

Jesse wanted to swear, curse, grab the teasing hand that was now sliding down his thigh, thrust his cock into it and come harder than he had in months...years. But Magnusson pricked a warning against his arm. Jesse quivered, still and silent, though wondered if his heart might burst under the pressure.

Slowly, seemingly slower than tectonic plates moving, Magnusson reached toward Jesse's groin. Jesse inhaled deeply, watching the reflection. Magnusson met his eyes in the dark glass then, finally, grasped him through his shorts.

Jesse cried out and the world dissolved into a glittering fountain of shattered crystal. It seemed to last for hours, but then he was sagging with his hands on his knees, blinking at the wet tiles.

He straightened, dizzy and sated. Magnusson was gone.

Jesse fumbled for his towel and hurried to the door. Both study and library were empty. He stood in the dark, shivering and blinking, trying to figure out exactly what had happened.

Chapter Seven

"Sorry," Jesse said, flustered as hurried into the security room late the next morning. "I overslept."

Tom smiled as he held out a mug of coffee. "Swimming helped?"

"Yeah," Jesse said, taking the coffee and not meeting Tom's eyes. "You could say that."

"I wouldn't worry," Tom said, turning back to his computer. "I think you're on the way to being the boss's new favorite."

Jesse froze with his coffee mug to his lips. "Huh?"

Tom gestured at the screen. "Seems he came back from London early. He's requested a meeting with you...tonight."

Jesse loaded his emails and blinked until the message came into focus. "Seven p.m.," he said, fighting his voice to be steady. "We were gonna do that dead-run of the new firewall."

"I can do that," Tom said. "You're his first meeting of the day...night." He chuckled. "Must be important."

Filip came in carrying a mug, bringing with him the smells of fresh snow and beef tea, and the conversation turned to the installation of the new lock on the moor gate.

Jesse stood, shifting from one foot to the other, outside the doors to Magnusson's study at six fifty-eight that evening. He was trying so hard not to remember the scrape of those sharp nails, the power in the hands that had teased and taunted him, the sternness in the voice that had commanded him. But it filled his mind and swelled through his flesh like billowing steam, and he wondered again what he was going to say when they came face-to-face again.

He was chasing his thoughts around in the same circle yet again when the door opened. The baron stood there, his eyes dark and deep as the night sky, with a soft smile playing on his lips.

"Jesse. So glad you could join us."

"Us?"

Magnusson gestured into the room. Jesse moved inside. The fire was glowing, making the room warm and fragrant. Its golden light was augmented by lamps, but the low illumination made the red-haired haemophile on the sofa look as though he had been painted into the scene. His emerald eyes fixed on Jesse, assessing. A glass of red liquid sat on a table at his elbow.

"Jesse. Darragh Kelly. You met the other night?"

Jesse nodded, willing himself not to look away from the unblinking gaze. "The lawyer, right?"

"That's not what I was called in my day," Kelly said, his rolling accent soft but words level as stone. "But I suppose that's what you'd call me now. I hear we've you to thank for our insight into the case against Emory?"

Jesse's face heated. He looked to Magnusson for guidance, but it was like trying to read a cliff face. "Uh...yeah, I guess?"

"Jesse performed exceptionally," Magnusson said, pouring a brandy. "And you told me yourself, there have been no consequences, as promised."

"So the human can break the law without getting caught," Kelly went on. "That doesn't mean this plan of yours is a good one, Emory."

"I have as much faith in your abilities," Magnusson said, holding out the brandy to Jesse, "as I do in Jesse's."

Jesse took the glass with numb hands but didn't drink. He looked between the two men—haemophiles—with his mind reeling. The silence stretched on as they stared at each other.

"Uh, sorry to interrupt the meeting or whatever," he said. "But why am I here?"

"You're not making my job any easier, Emory," Kelly said, standing with the fluid grace of a dancer and draining his glass of blood. "That's all I'll say."

"At this point, I can't see that they've left me any choice," Magnusson intoned.

Kelly sighed and set his glass aside. "I'll do what I can, old friend. Thank you at least for informing me in advance...this time." He straightened his immaculate pinstripe suit and turned to Jesse. "As for you, young man. I trust the luck that has kept you alive this long extends at least until this thing is done. Emory, is your security engineer on site? We have a meeting scheduled."

"Tom? Yes. You'll find him in his room."

"Thank you. Goodnight." He strode for the door and left. Jesse blinked after him.

"Do I get to know what that was about?" Magnusson looked at him. Jesse swallowed. "Sir."

"In time," the haemophile said, pouring a drink for himself.

"So breaking into that office wasn't enough to prove you can trust me?"

"I trust you, Jesse," he said, raising a glass to his lips and sipping. "It's everyone else I'm having trouble with right now. But you will know all you need to—and soon." He put the glass down and stepped close. Jesse's hand tightened around his glass. "I would like you to accompany me to a function this weekend."

"A 'function'?"

"Yes. A Christmas party...at the mayor's house. I have some business to conduct there."

"At a party?"

"She wants it discreet, so thought it was best to meet while the household is distracted."

Jesse sipped the brandy. It burned pleasantly in his throat but didn't still his nerves. "I'm not exactly date material."

"You mistake me," he said. "This would be in a professional capacity." Jesse dropped his gaze to hide any potential hint of disappointment. "I want you to look around the mayor's house while I'm in the meeting, ensure we are not in danger of being spied upon or recorded."

"That sounds like a job for Greenway."

"Greenway will be there as my personal security," Emory continued smoothly. "But I also want your unique perspective. Just look around to make sure I'm safe—that the house is safe."

"I can do that."

There was a pause. "You're not looking at me."

Jesse fought a shiver and lifted his eyes. Magnusson's face was close to his. His lips were set, and his eyes searched Jesse's face. "I'm looking at you. Happy?"

"This is about last night."

"Yeah," Jesse rasped. "It is..." Magnusson didn't move or speak, but Jesse thought he saw warmth gathering in his eyes. "So we don't talk about it. Is that it?"

"I'm more than happy to talk about it."

"It was...something."

"It was. Something you enjoyed, I think."

Jesse's skin rippled. "Where did it come from, huh? You don't even know me."

"I know you're not regretting it, Jesse. Why are you pretending you are?"

Jesse frowned. "You think you know what I'm feeling?"

A small smile turned up the corners of the full lips. "Humans don't realize how little of what they feel is secret. It broadcasts, like a beacon. It's one of the things that makes you so fascinating."

"Whereas you feel nothing?" he said, putting the glass on the table with more force than was necessary.

"That isn't true."

Jesse made a noise of frustration. "So, what? What *was* last night?"

"Has no one ever cared about just what you need before?"

"You jerk off all your employees if they have a bad day?"

"No," he said, smile warming, "just you." Jesse went very still. His heart was slugging in his chest. Magnusson bent close and inhaled. The air brushed over Jesse's temple. He shivered. "I've upset you."

"You haven't *upset* me. I'm not a kid."

Magnusson gazed down at him. "I'm sorry. I thought I knew what you wanted."

You did. More than any other guy I've ever known...but you're not human. Just my luck.

Jesse kept his mouth firmly closed over the words, not wanting to admit them, even to himself. Instead, he said, "I just don't get...why?"

"You won't believe the answer to that question until you're able to answer it yourself," he said. "But I can see what I did has made this difficult."

"You're my boss..."

He blinked once, slowly.

So he does blink.

"I currently employ you. That is correct. But after last night...and considering the way you looked at me when we first met..." He paused. Jesse held his breath. "Forgive me. You are a fascinating human. And my instincts told me there was more to your interest than professional curiosity."

Jesse looked away.

"I'm sorry," Magnusson continued after a moment. "It has been a very long time since I understood the nuances of human emotion. I sometimes forget that."

"No kidding...Sir," he added after an awkward moment.

"I think you really had best start calling me Emory."

Jesse's skin heated. "Okay...Emory."

Emory surveyed him for another long moment. "You have a date this weekend, yes? With Tom?"

Jesse blinked. "I guess I do."

Emory nodded. "Tom's a fine man."

"Look... I don't need you to —"

"Go on the date, Jesse," the baron said, lifting Jesse's unfinished drink and downing it. "Experience a bit of normality. It's important you know what you want before anything goes any further. But either way, we head to the mayor's at six."

He left. Jesse was alone with the flickering fire, the taste of brandy in his mouth and the lingering scent of mint and ice water that was the smell of Emory himself. Jesse scrubbed his hand over his face and retreated to his room.

He sat heavily in his chair and fired up his systems. His searches had found a list of Ivor, Harrison & Associates' public cases — mostly family law, to Jesse's surprise. There were several employment and property cases, too, but nothing Jesse thought could relate to Magnusson. He remembered the baron's promise to fill him in when the time was right, hesitated, then shut down the searches.

He went to shower, willing all the weirdness to make sense in the morning.

It didn't. But he and Tom had enough work that he found it got easier to ignore as the days slipped by.

Jesse caught himself smiling more and more. He had a job — a real job, a decent roof over his head. And, he thought as Tom snuck another look his way, the possibility of something more than a hurried fuck over a kitchen counter on the horizon.

Then why the hell couldn't he stop thinking about the goddamn Undying Baron? The new systems in the study and library had already been successfully tested, but he found excuses to go into those rooms more than he should. But he and Magnusson did not cross paths again. He was not summoned or even emailed by the haemophile. Greenway was the one who confirmed the schedule for the following Saturday.

"Hey, you okay?"

Jesse shook his head and blinked. "Huh?"

"You were a million miles away."

Jesse blinked until Tom came into focus. He was clad in motorcycle leathers and was holding out a helmet.

"Sorry," Jesse said, taking the helmet. "Yeah, I'm fine."

"Because we don't have to do this if you've changed your mind." Caution flickered in Tom's eyes.

"No, I swear. All good. Fuck, we really heading out on this?" Jesse said, running his hand over the cherry-red chassis of Tom's motorbike.

Tom's face brightened. "If that's okay with you. I love riding these roads. But I can always borrow a car from the estate, if you'd prefer?"

"Are you kidding?" Jesse said, zipping up the leathers Tom had lent him. "I always wanted a go on one of these."

"Okay then," Tom said, nervousness tightening his smile as he loaded a bag into the panniers. "Climb aboard."

Jesse watched with a tickle of anticipation as Tom straddled the bike. He climbed on behind, and the tickle fizzed brighter as he spooned Tom's body.

"Hold tight, okay?"

Jesse nodded, then they were off.

They wound along the country lanes with slush spraying from their wheels. The roar of the engine was distant beyond the sound canceling in Jesse's helmet. The afternoon sky arched cool and gray overhead. Jesse wished he could take the helmet off to feel the cold wind in his face. Instead, he settled for enjoying the sensation of Tom's strong body between his legs and resolved to put Emory Von Magnusson firmly from his mind.

Almost too soon, Tom was slowing the bike and turning into the carpark for Fountains Abbey.

"Christ, it's freezing," Jesse said after he shrugged off his leathers, his teeth chattering and breath fogging in the air.

"At least it's not raining," Tom smiled as he retrieved their coats and the bag from the panniers. "Last couple of times I've tried to bring a guy on a romantic picnic here, it pissed it down."

"Bring many guys on romantic picnics?" Jesse asked casually as they strode along. The sky had brightened to ice-white. Snow lay in an even, unbroken blanket over the grass, glinting here and there like it was scattered with diamonds.

Tom's smile made his eyes crinkle. "Not that many, in fairness. These last few years, well, I guess romance hasn't exactly been the first thing on my mind."

"What has?" Jesse asked, keeping his hands in his pockets and his eyes ahead.

"Work, I guess," Tom said neutrally. "Getting over an ex, too. You know…the usual."

"Yeah," Jesse said, a little strained. "Yeah, I know."

"A conversation for another date maybe," Tom said with a slow smile. "Let's get there before the pie gets cold."

"Pie?" Jesse beamed.

Tom laughed. "Yes, there's pie."

"Whoa…" Jesse's eyes widened as the ruins of the abbey appeared ahead. The butter-colored stone made up sweeping arches and looming walls, so intricately carved that it was like looking at a painting. A church tower, its missing roof and empty window frames was the only indication of its ruinous state, towered overhead, so tall Jesse had to crane his neck to see the top.

It was so quiet that Jesse's breathing was loud in his ears.

Tom stopped to gaze at it. "It's quite something, isn't it?"

Jesse just nodded.

"I've never seen it in the snow before," Tom said, his eyes distant. "Somehow it makes it even…emptier. Even more beautiful."

Tom's pleasant face was set in thoughtful lines, his brown eyes shining. Then Jesse caught sight of the scarring above his scarf and looked away.

"You said there was pie?"

"Let's sit." Tom drew out a blanket, a thermal food box, a flask and some plastic plates and cutlery. Their fogged breaths mingled in the air as Tom unpacked a slab of steak pie, uncapped a sealed cup from which wafted the mouth-watering scene of tomato soup and set out plastic-wrapped slices of buttered bread.

"You sure know how to treat a guy," Jesse said as he accepted a piece of the pie and a cup of soup.

Tom poured his own soup with a smile. "Well, they say the way to a man's heart is through his stomach."

"That's where I'm going wrong, then," Jesse mouthed around his food. "I go for at least three other body parts first."

Tom snorted as he dunked his bread in the soup. "Perhaps I should try your way."

He lifted his eyes, and Jesse grinned. He reached for the flask, deliberately brushing his gloved hand against Tom's leg and watching his face. His eyes glinted and a spark lit in Jesse's gut, but it was small—a candle flame…real, warm, but not quite reaching the dark corners inside him.

He lowered his gaze and poured coffee.

"Did you have a nice time with your nephew last weekend? I forgot to ask."

"Yeah. It was good."

"You close?"

"With Olly? Yeah. He's a little diamond. So curious, you know?" Jesse allowed a different, more private smile to show on his face. "So much hope, too." He looked away over the snowy landscape. "I hope he never loses that."

"And your brother?"

Jesse winced. "Not so close with him."

"Sorry. That must be hard."

"*Meh*, not really," Jesse said, lifting his eyes to the slate-colored clouds. "It's always been that way. What about your folks? Sisters?" Jesse said, shoving the last of his pie into his mouth. "Do you see much of them?"

"Not for a few years now."

"No?"

"No," Tom said, setting down his coffee. "There was a bit of a falling out."

Jesse cursed himself. "Sorry, man. My big mouth."

"No, it's fine," Tom said. "I haven't talked about it to anyone except my shrink. I'm glad you asked."

Jesse held his troubled gaze and asked quietly, "What happened?"

Tom tore more bread apart but didn't eat. "Your family ever get funny with you? You know, for being like we are?"

Jesse raised his eyebrows. "For being gay? No. That was the one thing they got right. Did yours?"

"Not for being gay," Tom said, laying the bread down. "But for my choice of partners? Yeah…that happened." He brushed crumbs off his gloves. "You ever get that?"

Jesse forced himself not to stare at Tom's scar. "Only when I was sleeping with dickheads. Though, to be fair, I did that a lot."

"Past tense." Tom's smile warmed. "Broke that habit, then?"

"Sort of," Jesse said, nibbling bread. "Glen, my last ex, he was...nice. My family couldn't get enough of him."

"But you could?"

Jesse dunked the crust of bread into his soup. "I thought this was going to be a conversation for another date?"

"Sorry," Tom said, draining his coffee and screwing the cap back on the flask. "I'm an idiot, getting all heavy on you in the first bloody hour."

"Hey," Jesse said, putting his hand on Tom's, "I asked, didn't I?"

"You did." Tom's lips twitched then he looked away. "I was with some...unusual partners. They didn't like it, which I get, now. But they didn't exactly handle it well. Neither did I."

"That's rough."

"Yeah, it was," he said. "But it's better now. Or...I'm better. Even if things are still hard with my family, at least I know I've got my shit together now, you know?"

"I don't know, actually," Jesse said with a nervous laugh. "But I get the idea. That's good, mate. Really good." Tom smiled. Jesse drank the last of his soup and looked up again at the ruins. "So how old is this place, do you reckon?"

"It was first built in 1132," Tom said, following Jesse's gaze to the soaring tower. "So almost a thousand years, if you can imagine that."

Jesse shook his head. "I can't. Time like that? It doesn't make sense."

"It can't, really," Tom replied, pouring more coffee. "We're not meant to know time that way."

"But haemophiles do," Jesse mused. "Do you think *he* saw this place when it was still running?"

Tom chuckled softly. "It was dissolved in 1539, well before the baron's time."

"Do you know how old he actually is?"

"No, not exactly. But I've never heard of a haemophile older than four hundred years. Well" — his face changed — "maybe one, but that's a whole other story."

"I thought they all lived forever?"

"Nothing lives forever," Tom said with a smile, packing the empty plates away.

"But the Blood… Doesn't that heal everything? Keep away disease and stuff?"

"Yeah, but they can still have accidents — or be killed or…deliberately harm themselves."

Jesse blinked. "That happen a lot?"

"Not compared to us. But yeah, I've heard of a few that couldn't hack it anymore. The endless years… Losing connection with the world… That's why they normally live in communes — for protection, yes, but also to try to maintain a society, of a kind."

"So how do the independents keep going?"

Tom shrugged. "I guess they all find their own ways. Terje Kristiansen has a human partner. Darragh Kelly practices law. Christ knows how many times he's taken the bar exam to stay current." Tom's smile seemed to change, becoming softer. But he shook his head, and it was gone as quickly as it had come. "I've heard of a few that curate art, study anthropology — or just wander aimlessly, detached from everything. Anything that makes them able to stand time passing by without them."

"And Emory?" Jesse said after a pause. "What does he do?"

"You know, I'm not sure," Tom said after a thoughtful pause. "Before Austria, he lived alone in Bavaria, in the mountains, for years and years. I don't think anyone even knew he existed. Then he appeared in Vienna out of the blue about eight years ago, just when all the international haemophile stuff was kicking off. I started working there a couple of years later." Tom shrugged. "And now he's back in Yorkshire, reclaiming his ancestral lands, running businesses, engaging with the community. Maybe that's how he's reconnecting?"

"Why now? Some sort of fourth-lifetime crisis?"

Tom chuckled. "Maybe."

"He's been…good to you, right?"

Tom's eyes were intent. "You can ask me about it, you know."

Jesse inhaled. He lifted a hand, hesitated, then ran his fingers over the scarring at Tom's neck. Tom watched his face with interest.

"Was this him? He said not."

"It wasn't Emory."

"But it was a haemophile?"

Tom nodded.

"Who?"

"An ex," Tom said, voice low. "Several exes."

"Jesus, man."

"Yeah…not good," Tom said, in a voice barely above a whisper. "But as I say, I've moved on…or I'm trying to."

Jesse lowered his hand. Tom's face was close. Their noses were almost touching. He smelled like coffee and caramel. The heat in his eyes was warming the cold air between them.

Jesse opened his mouth to say something, then Tom kissed him. Slow heat poured through Jesse. He closed his eyes, clutched at Tom's coat, tilted his head and opened his mouth. Tom swept his tongue in. Jesse tasted him, swallowing the richness of caffeine and sweetener. The way he breathed Jesse's scent in and sighed it out, shifting his head the other way to kiss him deeper was warm and comforting. Pleasing.

So why wasn't Jesse's blood burning the way it had before Magnusson had even touched him?

Tom broke away. His face had changed.

"There's nothing here, is there?"

Jesse rubbed his eyes. "Shit."

"It's okay," Tom said with a tired-looking smile. "Really."

Jesse drank in the look on his face — disappointment, but also resignation and acceptance.

"I'm not what you really want either, am I?"

"I wouldn't say that," Tom said, putting his hand on Jesse's leg. "You're fun—hot, different. All the good stuff."

"You can't order your heart to stand to attention," he said, trying for a smile. "Or your dick, for that matter."

Tom snorted. "No, I guess not."

Jesse tucked Tom's hair behind his ear and rubbed his thumb over the scar again. "What was it like?" he whispered.

Tom took his hand, drew it away and held it in his lap. "You don't want to know."

"Why?"

Tom frowned, staring hard at their hands. "Biting went wrong. More than once. After the third hospital admission, my family intervened." Tom raised his eyes. "The falling out I mentioned."

"Shit."

"Yeah." Tom looked out over the snowy grounds. The wind tugged at his curls. All traces of the smile had gone from his face. "I'm still seeing a therapist about it. I know I can't let myself do it again, but I've never stopped wanting to."

Jesse's throat was tight. The set of Tom's face made fear uncurl under his belly, but he couldn't deny the crackle of electricity that went up his spine. Tom suddenly looked at him like he guessed his thoughts.

"Don't ever do it, Jesse."

"Huh?"

"Promise me." He tightened his grip on Jesse's hand. "They're not supposed to do it. It's illegal for them to even ask, but some of them still do. It's how they...get off."

"Look, Tom..."

"I know I'm the last person to lecture people on lifestyle choices..." He paused to swallow, gripping Jesse's hand still harder. "But I know what I'm talking about. Don't do it, Jesse. Don't even think about it."

Jesse clamped his mouth shut, trying to not let the fact that Tom had just made the idea more exciting than ever show on his face.

"You need something more, though," he said, his voice catching. "More than me. More than human. Is that so bad?"

"Yes," Tom said, "it's bad."

Jesse's stomach filled with ice water. "But Darragh Kelly, the lawyer? He seems interested."

"I *can't*, Jesse," he whispered, his voice harsh. "I can't let myself get close to one of them again. I'd never survive it."

Jesse took in the fear tightening Tom's face. The fear and the desperation. "You can control pain, you know, with the right partner. It doesn't need to control you."

Tom smiled a shaky smile. "I'll have to take your word on that."

Chapter Eight

Jesse helped Tom pack up the picnic things in silence. He shouldered the bag then held out his hand for Jesse's. Jesse held it as they walked through the ruins. Tom pointed out the old dormitory and refectory before guiding him through the arching cloisters in and around the echoing bell tower. There was sadness between them, but the feel of Tom's hand was comforting.

"Hey, Jesse." Tom paused as they made their way back to the path. "We're friends, right?"

Jesse blinked, surprised. "Yeah. Course."

"I think we both need friendship right now. Maybe more than we need...all that other stuff."

"I dunno," Jesse said with a crooked grin. "All that 'other stuff' is usually high on the list of things I need." He chuckled at the look on Tom's face then kissed his cheek. "But yeah, I think the friend thing could be good."

Tom smiled. "I'm glad. So, remember you can talk to me, right? About anything."

"Sure. You, too."

Tom put his arm around Jesse's shoulders, and they made for the car park.

"Perhaps we could try this again sometime," he said, too easily, as he handed Jesse his helmet. "When the weather's a bit warmer, maybe. Sometimes things look different in the sunshine."

"Sure...maybe."

Snow started falling on the journey home. Tom drove slower, taking the bends with caution. The sun was setting by the time they got back.

Greenway was waiting at the bottom of the staff staircase with a suit in a hanger bag. She held it out as they approached.

"You have twenty minutes."

She strode away, and Jesse stared at the suit in his arms.

"I heard Cinderella was going to the ball tonight," Tom said as he shrugged himself out of his coat. "Just remember what I said, yeah?"

He disappeared up the stairs before Jesse could reply.

The last time Jesse had worn a suit was at his mother's funeral at age three. He'd worn jeans and a T-shirt to his father's, much to Anton's disapproval. He shook away the memories as he finished tying the sage-colored tie. That and the evergreen shirt enhanced his eyes, and as he blinked at himself in the mirror, he had to admit he barely recognized himself. He looked older and younger all at once and wasn't sure what to make of it.

He contemplated his reflection for another long moment then took out his lip, nose and earrings then spent a fruitless five minutes attempting to tame his hair with wax.

Greenway was waiting in the hall. She had arranged her hair in a neat bun and put in a pair of diamond earrings but otherwise looked the same as she always did. The wind picked up as they left the house, blowing flakes of snow into Jesse's face and undoing what little he'd been able to do to control his hair. Greenway led them around to the stables where a limousine was waiting. To Jesse's consternation, she held open the back door for him.

He swore under his breath and climbed in.

Emory wore a fine navy wool coat and gray cashmere scarf. He was sipping from a glass of red liquid as Jesse took the seat next to him. The haemophile smiled.

"You look very nice, Jesse."

"How long do you think this thing's going to take?" he said, tugging his coat tight and folding his arms.

"I couldn't say—a few hours, maybe more. I would like you to use the time to survey the house. Find out what systems they use, if you can."

Jesse narrowed his eyes. "I thought I was coming to stop people from spying on your meeting?"

"That," Emory said smoothly, drinking from his glass, "and assessing the security of the house. It's all part and parcel, surely?"

Jesse tried to read his face, but the haemophile's expression was guarded.

"I trust you had a pleasant day?" Magnusson said after a few minutes of traveling in silence.

"Yeah. It was nice."

"Nice?" Emory said. "That's all?"

"It was *nice*," Jesse insisted. "What do you want?"

Emory looked at Jesse until his skin started to ripple, then opened a cabinet at his side. "You like beer, I seem to remember?" He pulled out a chilled bottle of lager and opened it with the bottle opener in the cabinet top then held it out to Jesse.

"Aren't I working?" Jesse said as he took the bottle.

"Of course. But we are going to a party. Cheers." He held out his glass. Jesse hesitated before he clinked his bottle then swallowed a large mouthful…then another. He was grateful when the alcohol took the edge off his thrumming nerves, but when he came to the end of the beer his head was already starting to swim, and he didn't dare ask for another.

Soon they were stopping outside a floodlit Victorian manor house. Christmas lights were wound around the columns at the entrance. A valet opened the car doors, and Jesse stepped out into the icy wind. He could hear an orchestra playing Christmas music and smell spices and champagne in the air.

"My lord," a smartly dressed man in a red tie was saying, smiling at Emory as the car pulled away. "The mayor is expecting you. If you would like to follow me?"

They were shown through a side door with a coded lock and a motion sensor set in the frame. Jesse memorized the code out of habit then the red-tied man was leading them down a richly furnished corridor with oil paintings on the walls and Persian rugs under their feet.

"The mayor will be with you shortly, my lord," he said, opening a door.

"Thank you," Magnusson said, pulling off his gloves. "I trust she won't mind if my security manager takes a look around?"

"Not at all, sir," the red-tied man said with a narrow look at Jesse.

Emory drifted into the room. Greenway followed, throwing Jesse a loaded look before she closed the door.

"Can I help you with anything in particular? Sir?" The man deliberately added the last as an afterthought. The suggestion of a sneer curled his lip.

"I'm good, mate. You run along and get that mayor now. The baron's waiting and all."

The man's face pinched then he turned on his heel and marched away. Jesse muttered under his breath then brought out his phone. He took a moment to scan the door frame but found no electrical currents that would indicate any hidden recording equipment. He moved farther down the corridor.

There were motion sensors set in the wall at regular intervals and a camera at the junction of the hallway that led to the main entrance and what Jesse guessed was a ballroom. The music and voices got louder, the smells of food and drink stronger. Servants hurried by with trays. A well-dressed security guard stood to one side, nodding to the guests as they arrived.

Jesse scanned the entrance hall, seeing nothing out of the ordinary, then moved outside to check the front of the house. He spotted some large security floodlights, currently deactivated, and more cameras. He shivered and made his way to the window of the room where Emory and the mayor were having their meeting. Again, he scanned but again...nothing.

He shook his head, wondering if his boss was careful or paranoid, but completed a circuit of the whole building, just to be sure. He found nothing beyond a standard CCTV set-up and more security lights. He went back in at the key-coded entrance, stamping his feet in the cold and found the corridor beyond deserted. He could hear the sound of soft voices behind the closed door of the meeting room but otherwise, all was quiet.

He wandered to the ballroom, scanning the faces of the servants and guests for anyone who might be a journalist or an intruder looking to snag the next viral video of a haemophile. But everyone in sight was obviously rich, elegant, laughing and totally absorbed in themselves.

Jesse hunched his shoulders as he skirted the edge of the ballroom. The orchestra was so loud and the laughter so raucous that it set his nerves jangling. He made straight for the bar and buffet table, searched fruitlessly for beer and grabbed a flute of champagne instead.

It was then he spotted a small figure slumped on the floor at the foot of the towering Christmas tree. She was in a crystal-pink party dress. Her light hair was teased into ringlets and tied with a matching ribbon. Her bottom lip stuck out as she pushed a wooden car, a decoration from the tree, back and forth on the carpet with her chin propped on her fist. A flustered-looking woman Jesse vaguely recognized came over to the child and yanked her to her feet, smoothed her dress and scolded her in an undertone. She snatched the car off her, hung it back on the tree then drifted back into the crowd. The girl stuck her tongue out at the retreating figure and slouched once again to the floor with a scowl.

Jesse moved over, making sure the woman was out of sight, then crouched down next to the girl.

"Hey there. Dimity, right?"

She looked up, her eyes round. She blinked. "You're the man who bought me that ice cream."

"Sure am," Jesse said, going for a reassuring smile. "How's it going?"

She narrowed her eyes. "You look different."

"Do I?"

"You did something to your hair. Your old clothes were better, too."

Jesse chuckled and loosened the tie. "I have to agree with you on that one. But hey, why are you down here all by yourself?"

She screwed up her face. "There are no other boys or girls here, but they made me come down anyway. I wanted to draw in my room. Hey..." Her face brightened. "Is that boy here? Olly? Did you bring him?"

"No, sorry, honey. I'm here working." Her face fell. "Why are you here if there are no other kids here, huh?"

Her lips pressed together. "Aunt Helena says we have to stay here for Christmas."

"Well, that's not bad, is it? Pretty fancy place for Christmas — big tree and all."

"Yeah," she said, her lower lip trembling. "The tree is nice, though I'm not allowed to touch it. But..." She cut off as inhaled sharply, fighting tears.

"But what, sweetie?"

She sniffed. "We've moved so many times this year — to different countries, even. I don't think Santa will know where I am."

"Hey," Jesse said, dropping down to sit cross-legged next to her, ignoring the curious and disapproving looks from the nearest guests. "You don't need to worry about that. Santa knows where every kid is, every year...all of them."

"Really?" She looked at him with uncertainty.

"Even if they moved to the moon." He smiled. "And here..." He reached past her, plucked the car decoration off the tree and handed it to her. "These are toys. They are meant to be played with."

She smiled, the tears in her eyes glinting in the lights from the tree. She clutched the car tight. But then her face fell. "All I really want for Christmas is to see Daddy again."

Jesse's chest clenched. "I know. I'm sorry, honey. Your aunt said that can't happen."

She stared at the car, spinning a wheel with one finger. Then she looked up, her face bright again. "Hey, do you want to see my drawings?"

Jesse looked around to see more curious gazes starting to be directed their way.

"Yeah, sure. Let's go now."

Dimity sprang to her feet, grabbed his hand and dragged him to the door. She tugged him across the hall then up a grand staircase and along a colonnaded gallery. Jesse stared around him at the richness and splendor with a sort of dull wonder. Dimity took him down one hallway then another, up some more stairs, watched by another camera, Jesse noted, then stopped outside a wide door. He frowned as he noticed another of those oversized security lights over the door frame.

Indoors?

But then Dimity hustled him inside.

He stared around at the child-sized four poster bed, the miniature dressing table and wardrobe, the crystal ponies in a line on the mantelpiece. Dimity made straight for the writing desk in the corner, tugged open a drawer and wrestled out an armful of papers. She drew Jesse down onto the powder-pink rug and spread them out on the floor. There were pictures of horses, unicorns, rainbows and she had a story for them all.

"Hey, who's this?" he asked, selecting a drawing of a tall man in a dark suit. His hair was done in a black crayon and his mouth a curving line of scarlet.

"That's Daddy." She smiled, patting the picture fondly. "That was the night he took me sailing. He was in his blue suit that night."

"Looks like a nice bloke," Jesse said, his heart clenching as he scanned the other pictures. "Any of your mummy?" he hedged.

She shook her head. "I don't really see my mummy. She had me when she was very young, you see. I've met her a couple of times. She's nice. But Daddy looks after me, really — or he did." Her face fell again.

Jesse grimaced. "What happened to your dad, huh?"

She shrugged listlessly. "One day he just wasn't there anymore."

"Hey, it's okay," Jesse said, squeezing her shoulder. "My dad's not around anymore, either. But it gets easier, I promise."

"He was supposed to be at the lights," Dimity sniffed. "If only I hadn't got lost."

"Hey, it's okay, love…really. Your aunt will always make sure you're okay," he said, praying that was true. "That's what families do."

"I guess…" she said, dragging the picture of her father closer.

"She wouldn't have come to get you in such a hurry if she didn't care, right?"

"I guess," she repeated, tugging at a ringlet that had fallen in her face.

"Hey," he said, bringing out his phone and loading a design app. "You ever tried drawing on a computer?"

"I had a go on an iPad at school once," she said, looking uneasily at the phone. "But I wasn't very good at drawing with my finger."

"You can use a stylus. Here," he said, grabbing a pencil from her box on the floor and turning it eraser-side down. "Have a go. How about a Christmas tree, huh?"

She gave him a wary smile then took the phone and the pencil and carefully, tongue between her lips, outlined a Christmas tree on the screen.

"There," he said, "just like the one downstairs. And here..." He took the phone, tapped a couple of commands and the tree filled green and sprang to life with sparkling lights. Her eyes widened.

"Wow. How did you do that?"

"That was an easy trick," he said, showing her the options menu. "You use layers, see? Things the computer has ready to go. But the stuff you draw yourself is always the best."

"Will you teach me?"

"I would, kiddo, but I don't think we're likely to cross paths again. In fact" — he checked his watch and grimaced — "I better get back downstairs. But hey," he said, standing and dusting off his knees. "Ask at school for a graphic design course. I'm sure they'll have something for you."

"I will. Thanks!"

He smiled then froze as he heard footsteps outside.

"Oh no," Dimity said with her brow furrowing. "It's Maria. She'll be taking me back to the party."

"Chin up," Jesse said with a smile, padding to the door. "Maybe she's come to send you to bed. Then you can do more drawing under the covers." He winked at her, cracked the door, saw the coast was clear, even though the footsteps were getting louder. "I gotta dash, honey. You take care, okay?"

"Will I see you again?" she said, getting to her feet and clutching the toy car to her chest.

"Maybe," he said, trying again for a real smile. "But until then, you look after yourself, all right?"

She nodded, smiling bravely, and Jesse ducked back out into the corridor. He hurried in the opposite direction to the footsteps, turning a corner just as he heard the voice of Dimity's minder scolding her for leaving the party without permission. He shook his head and continued down the hall, searching for another stairway down.

His phone buzzed in his pocket. It was Greenway.

"We're out at the car," she said, then hung up.

Jesse hurried outside, shivering in the cold wind and made for the limo waiting near an iced-over fountain.

"Well, that was different," he said as he climbed in, sighing noisily as the warmth of the car wrapped around him.

"Did you find anything?" Emory was scanning a document on a tablet. The light from the device washed his skin bone-white.

"No one is trying to spy on you or anything like that," he said, tugging off his tie and unbuttoning his collar with relief. "Wasn't the sort of party the internet trolls could sneak into, either, even if they wanted to. Don't know what you were so worried about."

"So the house has pretty standard security is your assessment?" Emory was still focused on the iPad.

"Yeah, apart from the fact that they seemed rather big on floodlights." He sent Emory a penetrating look. "So, are you gonna tell me what I was really looking for?"

"When we get home," he said, putting the iPad away.

He didn't speak again for the whole journey back. His face appeared harder than usual. Jesse kept his mouth shut with an effort, aware of Greenway watching him in the rear-view mirror.

"Thank you, Greenway," the baron said as they entered Oswald House. "That will be all for tonight. Jesse, if you wouldn't mind joining me in my study?"

Jesse's pulse quickened. He tried to make sense of the haemophile's tone, but it was flatter than sea ice.

The fire was already burning in the study. The lights were low. Emory moved to his desk and put the iPad away, checked a couple of papers then put those away, too.

"Help yourself to a drink," he said as he opened a letter from the rack next to an open laptop.

"I don't want one," Jesse said. "I wanna know what's going on here."

Emory read the letter in silence, then slipped it into one of the drawers. Jesse heard a key turn then, finally, Emory looked at Jesse.

"Perhaps we should sit."

"I don't want to sit, either. You want me to steal something from that house, don't you?" Emory drifted toward the sofa without meeting his eyes. "*Don't* you?"

The haemophile poured himself a drink then unbuttoned his suit jacket and sat on the sofa, draping one arm along the back. He met Jesse's eyes over the rim of his glass. When he lowered his drink, he was smiling.

"I knew I couldn't fool you."

Jesse swore. "You really think I'm just some dirty low-life thief, huh?"

"That is very far from the truth."

"Then what *is* all this?"

"Jesse, please." Emory gestured at the sofa. "Sit. I'll explain everything."

Jesse eyed him another long moment then dropped himself onto the sofa, crossed his arms and glared at him. "Okay, I'm sitting. Start talking."

Emory was regarding him levelly. His eyes were impossibly deep, like a night sky in midsummer. But for the first time Jesse thought he detected something else, something fragile. He wanted to look away but sensed it was important that he didn't.

"Firstly, I genuinely did have a meeting with the mayor," he said. "I want to sponsor a financial support scheme for local families struggling with the cost-of-living crisis. She didn't want the meeting known about. Well…" His face darkened. "Didn't want the meeting, full-stop. But in the end, she agreed to meet me if I came over when everyone's attention was elsewhere. But you're right…" He paused. "I took *you* there for another reason."

"*What* reason?"

"You looked around the house, yes?"

"Yeah."

"Did you meet anyone? Talk to anyone?"

"Like who?"

"I already know, Jesse. But I'd like you to tell me yourself."

Jesse blinked. "You know about the little girl?"

"Dimity Hawthorn. Yes."

"Wait. How??"

"She's my daughter."

It took Jesse several moments to find his voice. "Come again?"

"Just as I said."

"That's not possible."

"Why not?"

"Why not?" Jesse blinked stupidly. "There's a million 'why nots'. For one, you can't, you know…breed, right? Biologically I mean."

"You and your ex-partner couldn't, either," Emory said smoothly. "But you still discussed having children."

"How do you *know* that?"

"I needed to be able to trust you, Jesse. I know about your family, your relationships, your criminal record…everything."

Jesse bristled. "But how —?"

"It's true, though, isn't it? You and your partner Glen Winters discussed having children? How was that to be achieved?"

Jesse's heart clenched in his chest. When he spoke, his voice was raw. "He wanted to adopt."

"Well then."

Jesse stared again. Emory stared right back. "You adopted Dimity?"

"The day she was born — legally and completely. I have the certificates in my desk. Dimity is my daughter."

Jesse remembered Dimity's drawing of her father. The dark hair, the blue eyes. "You're her…*you're* 'Daddy'?"

"I am."

Jesse pinched the bridge of his nose. "This doesn't make any sense."

"Perhaps I can explain," Emory said, getting to his feet and drifting to the drinks counter. "Are you sure you won't have one?"

"Make it a double."

Emory brought him a large brandy and resumed his seat. Jesse swallowed a burning mouthful then gestured impatiently. "Go on then. Explain...if you bloody can."

"I'll do my best," Emory replied, a slow smile warming his mouth but not his eyes. "Dimity's biological father was a young man called Cooper Hawthorn," he said, settling back into the cushions. "He had a one-night stand with an Austrian exchange student shortly before he was killed in a boating accident. He didn't even know she was pregnant." He was looking into his glass. The amber liquid glowed in the firelight. "Cooper was the last descendant of my family."

Jesse frowned. "But he had a different name."

"I was never married." He gave Jesse a direct look. "But my sister married a man named John Hawthorn, a Yorkshire businessman."

"You...you had a sister?"

"Yes...and parents, once." His smile was back. "We all start off human, though it's hard to remember, now." He looked into the fire. "My sister's marriage was quite the scandal. I've found reports on it. Marrying below her station, everyone said. But Hawthorn was a good man. She was happy. They had children—and their children had children." He sipped his drink. "I've kept my distance, out of necessity. But I've always watched over them. We've dwindled, though. Ever since Oswald Hall burned down, we've been blighted by misfortune."

"How's that?" Jesse asked in a low voice.

Emory's face was set. "The official explanation was that it was an accident. A servant knocked over a candle. But I watched over the hall in those days. I saw the villagers setting the fire, blocking the doors. I tried to help, but it was too late." He drew a breath. "Only three of the family escaped."

"Jesus," Jesse breathed. "Why?"

Emory smiled a grim smile. "There were rumors the hall was the lair of a vampire."

Jesse stared at him, unable to find any words.

"It was all nonsense," he continued, looking away. "I hadn't lived there for over a hundred years by that point. The hall was home to my sister's grandchildren and their families. But rumors are like venom. They spread before anyone has stopped to consider the source of the problem, which was another local landowner getting angry that my great-great-niece refused his proposal of marriage." He sighed. "He set his servants gossiping in the inns and at church. Since stories around my disappearance still circulated, it quickly gained traction. The next thing I knew, the whole county was turned against us."

"Shit, Emory. That's awful."

"It was," he said quietly. "My family's home was destroyed. Their land was taken from them. They tried everything to survive over the years — some bad things, some desperate things. We limped on into this century. But Cooper was the last." His eyes were far away. "His parents died young. It was a real tragedy. He never really got over it. Headed down a bad road — drink, drugs, women." A line appeared between his dark eyebrows. "I wanted to intervene but couldn't. We were still too mistrusted, hiding our numbers and commune locations, breaking into blood banks to survive." His eyes hardened. "I watched his life fall apart from afar, like I had so many other members of my family, unable to do anything. Then he died, and I thought it was all over…" He raised his eyes. "But then I heard about Dimity. I heard how her young mother wanted to give her up for adoption. I moved to Vienna. I arranged it all."

"But how?" Jesse stammered. "How is it allowed? You're not… I mean…"

"I have a very, very good lawyer." Emory smiled. "And I am related to Dimity — I have proof — and I care for her…greatly."

Jesse wrestled through his thoughts then finally asked, "So what happened?"

"Helena Hawthorn was Cooper's aunt by marriage," he said, draining his drink. "About a year ago, somehow, she found out about Dimity's existence. She hired a private security team to break into my home during the day, while I was helpless. They took her away and brought her to England. I've been fighting to get her back ever since."

"But" — Jesse rubbed his temples — "how can she even do that?"

"The British police are on her side."

"Well, if there really is disputed custody, shouldn't she be in care or something until it's settled?"

"Dimity's had so much disruption to her life already," he said quietly. "I would never do that to her."

Jesse snorted and drank more brandy. "Might be better than what she has now."

"What do you mean?"

"The poor lass is miserable. Those toffs have no idea how to treat a kid. They dress her up, and they tell her off all the time. She's not allowed ice cream, for God's sake."

"So you agree. She would be better with her father."

Jesse stared at the fire. "This is unbelievable."

"Why?"

"So many reasons," Jesse said. "You drink blood, for one thing."

"Donated blood only," Emory murmured in a low voice. "To the very letter of the law."

"And you really think that's not gonna mess her up? Donated or not, her 'daddy' drinks human blood."

"We have no more choice about feeding to survive than you do."

"Then what about the immortality shit, huh?" Jesse said. "You're gonna live forever. She won't."

He smiled. "I'm not going to live forever."

"You know what I mean," Jesse said with an impatient gesture. "How can you have a relationship with a kid, with anyone, when they grow, and you never change?"

Emory examined him closely. His face was serious. "I will *always* be there for Dimity. *Always*. Both her mother and her father, everything she needs, for her whole life. She will never be left alone in this world. Wouldn't you have liked that, Jesse?" he asked quietly. "Wouldn't you have liked to still have both parents in your life?"

Jesse's chest ached. "I think I've gotten on okay, considering."

Emory was quiet. Jesse's mind was not. He stared at the fire until he was able to loosen his hands around the glass. He sipped carefully. It tasted like smoke and apricots. It warmed him down to his belly, made his blood tingle in his veins. The quiet in the room was starting to permeate his flesh and still his nerves. But the questions still circled in his head.

"Haven't you thought about what it will be like when she...you know, dies?"

Emory was quiet so long that Jesse looked up. The baron was gazing at him with grave intensity in his dark eyes. "The memories will sustain me."

"That's it?"

"Memories are all my kind ever really have, in the end."

"What's that like?" Jesse asked quietly.

"That depends on the memory."

Chapter Nine

Something had changed in Emory's eyes. Jesse's skin tightened. The hairs rose on his arms and the back of his neck.

Emory's lips parted. They were shining from his drink. His pupils had dilated.

"Would you like me to touch you again?"

Jesse clutched the glass. "I..."

"You can tell me, Jesse," he breathed, setting his glass aside and sliding up the sofa toward him. "You can ask me for anything."

"I...I don't get this," he said. His voice was hoarse. "Do you want...want to eat me, is that it?"

Emory looked shocked then laughed a low, rumbling laugh. "Not in the way you think." Before Jesse could respond, Emory had put his hand on Jesse's leg, bent his head and run his tongue up Jesse's neck. Jesse gasped, dropping the glass. Emory's hand was cool but strong. His breath was hot. He nipped Jesse's earlobe, making a noise low in his throat. Jesse whimpered, reason fleeing as swiftly as smoke blown in the wind.

He arched against Emory's body, straining for friction against his hardening cock. Emory let out another low sound and grasped Jesse's hip to hold him still as he mouthed at his jaw.

"Christ," Jesse growled as he tried to move and couldn't. "If we're gonna fuck, let's just fuck already."

"I thought you were enjoying our little game," Emory murmured against his skin, grasping Jesse's wrist. Jesse swallowed a groan as Emory drew his arm over his head and pinned it to the sofa arm. He loomed over him, unfastened his tie and ran his tongue down Jesse's throat to his collarbone. "You taste so good," he whispered against Jesse's skin.

"Like lunch, you mean?" Jesse said between clenched teeth, fighting the rising tide of arousal and losing.

"Humans smell and taste like life itself," Emory breathed. "But you in particular, Jesse Truelove…"

"What?" Jesse grated, straining against the strong hold, excitement fizzing over his skin like a shower of champagne. "Big Mac and fries? What?"

"Mmm," Emory purred, pushing back his jacket and shirt and mouthing the joint between his neck and shoulder. "You taste like Paris in the summertime, warm stone, spilled wine in the sun."

"Fuck," Jesse swore again as Emory dragged his teeth across his skin. "Why are you doing this?" he rasped. "Do you even get off this way?"

"Of course we do," the baron said, running his hand from Jesse's hip to his abdomen. "We're red-blooded, breathing creatures, just like you. And you are a very hard man to resist."

Jesse threw his head back as Emory grazed his nipple bar through his shirt. "Guessing the age gap doesn't bother you…"

"Not if it doesn't bother you," Emory said, lifting his head and looking into his face, suddenly serious. His lips were parted and wet, but his cheeks were cool, pale. Jesse swallowed.

"I don't know," Jesse whispered, awkwardness clenching his chest. "Are you even turned on right now?"

A slow half-smile. "It takes us longer to get there, but it's more intense when we do."

"Jesus…"

"Shall I show you?"

Jesse nodded frantically. "Yes, fuck. Whatever you want. Just please, God…" He grabbed Emory's hand and thrust it toward his crotch. But Emory chuckled, reversed the hold and pinned Jesse's wrist above his head with the other.

"Not yet," he whispered in his ear, taking both Jesse's wrists on one hand and trailing a finger down his jaw. "You have to earn that, remember?"

Jesse made a noise, closing his eyes and lifting his spine. But Emory tightened his hold. Jesse gasped at the power in his grip. Emory brushed his hot mouth down Jesse's face and neck as he pulled off Jesse's tie then unbuttoned his shirt.

"And so, we return to this interesting adornment," he breathed against Jesse's neck as he slipped his hand into Jesse's clothing and tweaked the nipple bar. Jesse jerked and groaned. "Interesting," Emory said, raking his fingernails down Jesse's chest, not hard enough to break skin but enough to stripe fire into his flesh.

"Sweet Mary and Joseph."

"Not people I'm intimately acquainted with," Emory went on, brushing Jesse's shirt aside to reveal his tattooed chest and quivering abdomen. "Though I'm happy to make you call their names a few more times before this is done." He lowered his head and took Jesse's pierced nipple into his mouth.

"Christ," Jesse cursed and blinked blindly at the ceiling.

"Him, too," Emory murmured against his skin. "Maybe his father by the end?"

Emory ran his free hand up Jesse's leg, skirting around his throbbing cock, and undid his belt buckle. "I'm going to take these off," he whispered, looking up at Jesse through his thick eyelashes. "But you are not to touch yourself, not until I say. Understand?"

Jesse nodded, the sight of Emory hovering over his groin almost too much to bear.

"You have to say it, Jesse."

"Christ, yes, fuck, whatever. Just please—"

"And you must be quiet," Emory said, holding himself very still. "Remember, young Tom is just a few rooms away. We wouldn't want to upset him."

"Tom isn't arsed about me."

"Oh, he is," Emory whispered. "I can smell his interest in him. He wants to like you—and he's almost there. So, you must be quiet."

Jesse clenched his jaw. Emory locked gazes with him and slowly released his wrists. Jesse didn't move.

"Good," he murmured. "Very good." He slid Jesse's trousers and pants down together. His erection sprang free. He bit his lip until the tidal wave building in his belly subsided. Emory examined him hungrily.

"Undress," he commanded as he began to undo his own belt. "I want to see all of you."

The tone in his voice made Jesse quiver all over. His legs shook as he stood and shrugged himself out of his shirt and jacket, kicked off his shoes and bent over to rid himself of his trousers and socks. He straightened, naked, breathing hard. Emory's gaze roamed his body, a dark hunger burning in his eyes. Some color had crept into his cheeks, and he was no longer smiling.

"The anticipation is quite potent, isn't it?" Emory said in a low voice as he unbuckled unfastened his own fly. Jesse watched the movements with his mouth filling with saliva. But then he paused. "Are you sure you want this, Jesse? We can stop."

"Fuck that," Jesse forced out of his tight throat. "I've not stopped thinking about... Fuck, yes, I want to."

Emory smiled then reached inside his trousers and drew out a thick semi-erect member. "Come here."

Jesse obeyed as soon as he had regained control of his limbs. His eyes were level with Emory's throat. The haemophile ran his hands down Jesse's arms, grasped his wrists and guided Jesse's hands toward his cock.

"I want your touch, Jesse," he breathed into Jesse's hairline. "I want you to feel me. Know me."

Jesse shut his eyes and closed his hands around the warm, firm flesh. It took both his hands to grasp the entire length. Emory made a noise deep in his chest that made Jesse's skin tighten across his body.

"You're..." he croaked, cleared his throat and tried again. "You're not hard."

Emory inhaled, gliding his hands up Jesse's arms and taking a gentle hold of his jaw. He tilted his face up and brought their lips together. His eyes were hooded, his breathing low and slow. "Make me hard," he breathed against his lips.

Jesse shuddered with pleasure. He began to stroke Emory's cock. Emory sighed against his mouth. His flesh stiffened. Jesse's own cock quivered and throbbed, the head just brushing Emory's trouser leg. Jesse longed to rub against him, but the baron's commands still rang, deep and insistent, in his bones.

Emory groaned. He held Jesse's head in place with both hands as Jesse, panting, pumped his hardening cock. Soon the flesh was like iron in Jesse's grip, and Emory swept his long tongue over Jesse's lips.

Jesse opened his mouth with a low moan, and Emory slid his tongue inside. Jesse shivered to taste him — whiskey and smoke and a rich, autumnal taste like the darkest of red wines. He stepped closer, tilting his head to kiss him back. The taste was intoxicating. When his tongue snagged on a sharp tooth, Jesse froze, pain lancing through him. He tasted blood and Emory tensed, shuddering, sucking on Jesse's tongue and swallowing.

Jesse's blood pounded in his temples, his groin, his chest. But Emory broke the kiss. "No, I can't taste you that way, Jesse. No blood. Understand?"

Jesse was too dizzy with desire to answer. He kissed Emory's neck, tasting the cool, fresh skin. He continued to pump Emory's cock while pressing his own against his thigh. "What now?" he rasped, his voice harsh and distant, even to himself.

"On your knees."

The command in Emory's tone undid something inside Jesse. He dropped to his knees. The heat from the fire warmed his bare skin. The low light cast shadows all around them. He grasped Emory's hips, staring at the huge, trembling cock before him with his mouth open. He looked up. Emory was gazing at him. His mouth was open. His large chest swelled as he breathed.

"Make me feel it, Jesse."

Jesse leaned in, closed his eyes and took the swollen head of Emory's cock into his mouth. Emory didn't make a sound, but his muscles bunched under Jesse's hands. He tasted so weird and wonderful, like bonfires and autumn wind, dizzying as the brandy but richer. Jesse drew his tongue along the underside and swirled it over the head before taking it into his throat as far as he could. This time Emory groaned, a low, seismic sound like a storm out at sea.

Jesse listened to and felt him, tasted him and breathed him in. He ached to jerk himself off, to crash into the swollen tempest of orgasm that had been building under his chest ever since Emory had first moved along the sofa. But he kept his hands on Emory's hips, digging his fingers in, feeling his strength, drinking in his taste, savoring every last second of the anticipation.

His knees began to ache, as did his jaw. He started to use his hands, rubbing and pumping his cock as he lathered attention on the head with his mouth.

Emory watched with burning eyes. His breathing had deepened. He clutched at the mantlepiece. Then, when Jesse moaned and took him in as deep as he physically could, Emory shuddered and let out a long, low groan.

"Now, Jesse," he rasped. "Touch yourself *now*."

Jesse fumbled for his cock. The world splintered and exploded. Heat coursed through him. His helpless cry was muffled by the solid weight of flesh in his mouth. He heard Emory moan as if from a great distance and hot, silky fluid poured down his throat. He swallowed it all, beating the last blossoms of his own orgasm through his body with a few more tugs. He sat back on his heels, panting with his eyes closed and head spinning.

Emory helped him to his feet and kissed him. It was languid and slow, lazy and intense all at once.

"How was that?" he whispered against his lips.

"Good," Jesse said, his voice hoarse, blinking to try to regain his focus. "Different. But good."

"I'm glad," Emory murmured as he tucked himself back in his trousers and straightened his clothing. "Now you should go to bed. It's been a long day."

"Yeah…yeah," Jesse muttered and started to collect his clothes. Emory helped him into his trousers and shirt then passed him his shoes. "Look," Jesse said, frowning heavily even as a pleasant sleepiness weighted his body and his mind. "I…I don't know what this is between us…don't know if I need to know…but…"

"Yes?" Emory's face was pale again. Every hair was in place. There was no visual indication that anything had happened. But Jesse could still taste him…feel him.

He stared at the floor. "If you wanna do it again… I dunno. I might be up for that."

"I would like that," Emory said after a pause so long that Jesse's throat closed over.

"So…you like me?"

Emory blinked. "Of course I do."

"Out of all your fit haemophile friends and all your adoring human staff, you like *me*?"

"Yes," Emory said, "I do."

"Okay then," Jesse said, slow pleasure seeping through him like treacle. "Great."

"Before this goes any further," Emory said, his face suddenly unreadable, "I feel I need to say this." He paused. His gaze was intense. "You need to know...I'm never going to hurt you, Jesse, not in the way you think you want."

A red prickle of anger stole through the pleasant glow in Jesse's chest. "And what do I *think* I want, huh?"

Emory raised an eyebrow. "Pain."

Jesse frowned. "Isn't that up to me?"

Emory pressed a kiss to his forehead. Jesse's annoyance drained away as quickly as it had come.

"I'll find ways to please you," he whispered against his skin, "for as long as you want me to. But you can't ask me to hurt you. I won't do that."

Cold chased heat through Jesse's limbs. "What if that's what I want?"

"I'll show you other ways," Emory said. "Other ways I can give you what you need."

"You really think you can?" Jesse asked, very quietly.

"I'd like to try."

Jesse lifted his head to meet Emory's eyes. They were serious but sincere. He was so beautiful that Jesse didn't know what to think.

"Guess it's worth a try."

Emory smiled. "And try I will."

Jesse nodded and turned for the door but paused. Realization chilled his skin. "The thing you want me to steal from the mayor's house..."

Emory looked at him, then nodded. "Dimity."

Jesse went very still. It took him a long moment to marshal his words. "That's not stealing, Emory. That's kidnapping."

"Until anyone proves otherwise, I am her legal guardian," he said. "She has been removed from my custody without permission. I am merely redressing the balance."

"I'm *not* kidnapping any kid for you, Emory, no matter how good a shag you are."

"I understand this is a lot—"

"Understatement of the millennia."

Emory regarded him a long, silent moment. "Why don't you ask her?"

"What?"

"When you go, ask her what she wants. If she doesn't want to come to me, I'll leave her with Helena, and that'll be the end of it."

"Why don't you just go get her yourself, huh?"

"I can't."

"Bullshit."

Emory stared at him, hard. "You saw the floodlights around the mayor's house?"

"Yeah?"

"Daylight floods," he said. "Helena has them installed wherever she and Dimity are staying. They are usually turned on as soon as the sun goes down. They made an exception for the Christmas party. The mayor doesn't know. She was just told they are part of Helena's standard security set-up. I would never have been allowed in the house otherwise, and obviously, I couldn't do anything with so many people around. But under normal circumstances, I can never get anywhere near her."

"That's harsh."

"Yes. Yes, it is. So, will you help me?"

Jesse stared at the fire without seeing it.

"Christmas Eve," Emory said, brushing his hand up Jesse's arm. "The mayor's household is going to the Minster for midnight mass. Dimity will be at home with just her minder."

"The bastards aren't taking her? I used to love midnight mass."

A small smile played on his full lips. "They don't often take Dimity outdoors after dark—in case her evil vampire father tries to steal her back." His face turned serious. "You can get past that house's security easily, Jesse. The daylight floods won't hurt you...or Dimity. You can be in and out in minutes. Then she'll be home for Christmas...her real home. Please, will you help?"

* * * *

Jesse lay staring into the shadows on his bedroom ceiling. Emory's touch was still hot on his skin. The taste of his seed was in his mouth and throat. It had been everything Jesse had anticipated and more—and it felt like they'd only just begun.

But Tom's warnings drifted back. He was a killer. Even if he wasn't now, at some point he must have been. Jesse wondered if Emory would tell him if he asked—or if he really wanted to know.

He had already asked Jesse to break into a lawyer's office and had now asked him to kidnap a kid.

"She's my daughter."

Jesse made an impatient noise and turned onto his side, staring at his computer stations blinking and flashing in the dark. There was nothing to find online. He'd looked. If even one internet journalist knew that a haemophile had adopted a human child, he was sure there would be no end to the articles. But all he'd found had been dry, political discussions about haemophile rights.

He gnawed on his thumbnail.

"I care about Dimity...a great deal."

Jesse screwed his eyes shut, willing himself to sleep and escape it all, however briefly.

It must have worked, because the next thing he knew he was opening his eyes to dawn sunshine and a bone-deep contentment he didn't remember feeling for years. Then his thoughts caught up with his feelings, and his belly dipped. He covered his face with his hands and groaned.

He made himself get up and dressed. He stood debating himself for several minutes, then went to the door. The hall was deserted. The night shift would still be monitoring the CCTV, but if anyone asked, he could just say he was checking the systems.

He went downstairs, making an effort to walk naturally, crossed the hall, went through the silent, dark library and into the study. He tapped in the code to deactivate the motion sensors and turned the lights on. He found the locked drawer in Emory's desk and made quick work of it with his pick tools. It contained a number of files, one of which was labeled by hand.

Dimity.

His mouth dried. He set the file on the desk and stared at it. It was thick, stuffed with papers. Even now he hesitated but made himself open it, but none of the contents made any sense to him. Then, at the back, he found an adoption certificate. He drew it out carefully. It was in German, but Jesse could see it was signed, sealed and countersigned.

He took a deep breath, photographed it with his phone then locked everything away again. It took him the best part of an hour to walk to the nearest bus stop then the bus took almost the same again to get to the city. Jesse spent every minute telling himself he was doing the right thing.

But it still took him a long time of hovering on Anton and Sareena's doorstep before he pressed the bell. There was a pause then the door opened. Sareena, wearing a tracksuit and a flour-dappled apron, blinked at him, startled.

"Jesse, hi. Uh, Ant's at work..."

"I wanted to see you, actually," Jesse said, brushing snow from his hair. "You got a sec?"

"Of course," she said, stepping back. "I'm just getting lunch ready, but come on in. You hungry?"

"God, yes," he said, his stomach instantly rumbling as he stepped into the rich smells of spice and frying chapatis.

"Go on in and take a seat. Oliver's just out with a friend, but they'll be back soon."

Jesse moved through to the kitchen where the air was thick with steam and a myriad of tantalizing smells. Jesse snagged one of the fresh chapatis from a pile on the griddle and ate it in two wolfish bites, suddenly realizing he hadn't eaten since the picnic with Tom the day before. Sareena chuckled, passed him another and a jar of pickles.

"So, how's it all going?" she said, stirring one of the many bubbling pots on the stove. "With the new job and everything?"

Jesse swallowed his mouthful and sucked his fingers clean. "Good. At least. I think so."

Her brow crinkled. "You 'think' so?"

"Could you take a look at something for me?" he said, producing his phone and loading the photo of the adoption certificate. He checked it for the tenth time to make sure he'd blanked out all the printed names then handed it over.

Sareena pushed her glasses up into her hair and peered at the phone. "It's an adoption certificate. Austrian?"

Jesse nodded. "Is there anything weird about it?"

"What do you mean, weird?"

"I dunno. Anything that don't look right?"

She examined it again, pinching the screen to zoom in. "It's been a long time since I did family law."

"You know more about it than I do."

"It all looks sound." She raised her eyebrows. "There's only one adopting party. A little unusual but not unheard of."

"So, this is legit? There's nothing dodgy going on?"

"Like what, Jesse?"

"I don't know. Anything."

She held the phone out. "Without knowing who the parties are, I can't say one hundred percent. It's the human element that's always the fishy bit where the law is concerned."

"*Human* element. Right," said Jesse, somehow reluctant to take the phone back.

She looked at him closely, then again at the phone. "I don't know what you want me to tell you. But legally, yes, this is a perfectly legitimate document. Wait…" She brought it closer to her face.

"What?"

"The solicitor's signature. I know it…"

"Shit," Jesse swore and tried to take the phone, but Sareena held it out of reach.

"Darragh Kelly?" she said, her eyes sharp. "What are you doing with a document signed by a haemophile lawyer, Jess?"

"It's a bit of a long story," he said, holding out his hand with a pleading look on his face.

Sareena pursed her lips and handed the phone over. "What exactly are you mixed up in?"

"Nothing. You said yourself, there's nothing dodgy here, right?"

"Haemophile legislation is a painfully new field. Precedent changes every day." She looked right into his eyes. "You have to be so, so careful with anything like that. Please, tell me what this is. I can help."

"You've already helped." Jesse stood, pocketing his phone. "Thanks, Sareena. And, don't mention this to Ant, yeah?"

"I'm not going to lie. He's already stressed about this job you won't tell him about. I can't *not* tell him that you've turned up here with—"

"Please," Jesse said. "I swear I'll explain everything. I just need to figure some shit out first."

"Jesse," Sareena said, sounding tired, "this doesn't sound good."

"It is," Jesse insisted, meaning it. "This is good... good for me."

Sareena's brow furrowed again in concern, but then the front door opened and in raced Oliver and another boy.

"Uncle Jesse," Oliver cried and flung his arms around his waist.

"Hey there, mate," Jesse said, patting his nephew's head. "How's it going?"

"Great," he said, grinning. "We just had this great big snowball fight in Lee's backyard. Even his dad jointed in."

"That sounds great."

"Hope you're hungry, boys," Sareena said, her eyes still on Jesse. "Lunch is ready."

"I'm *starving*," the other little boy declared and scrambled onto a stool at the counter while Oliver took the one next to him.

"Are you having lunch with us, Uncle Jesse?"

"I can't, mate. Sorry," he said, catching Sareena's eye.

"Oh *why*?" Oliver cried, face falling. "He can stay, can't he, Mum?"

"Of course," Sareena said firmly, indicating the table. "Stay, Jesse. Eat with us."

"I really can't," he said, making for the door. "I gotta get back. Another time, though, yeah?"

"Like Christmas Day?" Oliver said hopefully, looking between Jesse and his mother. "He can come for Christmas, right, Mum?"

"I said we'll see about that, mate," Jesse said before Sareena could speak. "Enjoy your lunch, guys. See you soon."

He heard his sister-in-law trying to call him back but hurried out into the snow before guilt made him say anything more that he might regret.

Chapter Ten

"Jesse?"

Jesse jumped and turned. He hadn't heard Tom come into the security room. He was holding two steaming cups of coffee in his hands. Jesse's veins sang out at the smell.

"Hey," he said, eagerly reaching for a cup. "Thanks for this. I need it."

"You've been pulling a lot of hours the last few days," Tom said with a concerned look, taking his seat. "It's less than a week until Christmas. You can slow down, you know."

Jesse sipped his coffee. "The new firewall," he said. "I'm still not happy."

"It's solid," Tom said with an uncertain smile. "Nothing will get through that any time soon."

"Still," Jesse muttered, running his hole-hunting subroutine for the tenth time.

"You worried about anything in particular?" he asked carefully.

"Like what?" Jesse asked, not looking at him.

"I dunno. But I know you were up late with the boss the other night." Tom's tone didn't waver, but he was suddenly strangely fixated on the contents of his coffee cup. "Perhaps he's told you something? Something he doesn't want the public to know?"

"I just wanna do a good job."

"Pretty sure the only one that could get through this security system is you."

Jesse gave him a wan smile. "Let's hope."

"You really look like you need a break," Tom said gently.

Jesse hesitated. "If you're serious, I do have some other stuff to get on with."

"That doesn't sound like taking a break, Jesse."

"It's a break from this," Jesse said, waving at the scrolling numbers on his monitor.

Tom shook his head with a smile. "I guess you're right. Go on. Get outta here. But if you're up past midnight again, I'm putting you to bed myself."

Jesse managed a smile, trying not to examine the unasked question in Tom's eyes. He thanked him and returned to his room.

The blueprints and security maps for the mayor's house were saved in several encrypted files on his hard drive. He already had them memorized, but he hadn't been able to stop checking and-rechecking them, as well as going over his photoshopped overlay marking the locations of daylight floods and security cameras.

He was reviewing the mayor's staff schedules that he'd hacked from their network when he registered that night had fallen. His eyes were aching, but his heart was unsettled in his chest. He ran the computer simulation of his infiltration again so he wouldn't have to think about whether any of this was okay.

He jumped when someone knocked on the door. He checked the time. Eleven fifty-five. Tom was coming to make good on his promise. Jesse hurriedly shut down the programs and went to the door.

Emory stood on the threshold. He almost filled the doorway.

"Emory," Jesse breathed, his body suddenly on fire. "I... What are you doing here?"

"You are working too hard," he said softly.

"Can you blame me?" Jesse said in a furious whisper. "You've asked me to break the law...again."

"Technically, I haven't."

"There's no lawyer in the world good enough to make that 'stealing-back-what-was-stolen-from-me' shit stick, Emory."

"I told you you would face no consequences."

"I'd still like to try to make sure consequences won't be a thing from the get-go."

Emory was silent. Jesse could hear him breathing, low and deep like a slumbering monster in a deep, dark cave. Jesse's skin fizzed with an excitement he couldn't control, but he held the door tight and didn't move.

"If you really don't want to do this, Jesse, I won't make you."

"If I refuse, then I'm the arsehole who left the little girl with the evil stepmother."

"Aunt."

"Whatever."

"You're scared."

"I'm not."

"I can smell it, Jesse. You're scared. I understand. If you want me to, I'll withdraw the request. Kelly will find another way, eventually—just not in time for Dimity to have Christmas with her father."

"For fuck's sake, man," Jesse said, covering his face in his hands. "Right in the Christmas. Cheers…"

"I'm not trying to manipulate you."

"Well, you're managing it pretty well without trying."

Jesse jumped when Emory pulled his hands away from his face. He threaded his fingers through Jesse's hair. He lifted one hand and brushed it back from Jesse's face.

"Forget it all for now…all of it. I'm sorry I've troubled you."

"Troubled…right," Jesse said, his voice catching as he resisted reaching out and crushing the large, powerful body to his own.

"I forget how much you feel things, how fast and strong your emotions are."

"Well, I got news for you, pal. I feel them faster and stronger than most, so unless you really wanna call this whole thing off—which I know you won't 'cause you love the damn kid—I suggest you leave so I can get on with—"

Emory cut him off with a kiss. Jesse shivered, closed his eyes and stepped into Emory's embrace. He mouthed Emory's lips hungrily, and he opened them, allowing Jesse to delve his tongue in. He met Jesse's tongue with his own, and the sharp canines made Jesse shiver. Emory straightened. He was smiling.

"Swimming helps you relax, yes?"

"I…uh…"

"Come," he said, stepping back into the hall.

"I haven't got my shorts."

Emory's teeth glinted in the starlight. "Neither have I."

Jesse's chest tightened. He shut his door and hurried to keep up with Emory's long, loping strides as he led the way downstairs.

"What if someone sees us?" Jesse whispered, glancing up at the cameras in the hall.

"I'm not keeping our relationship a secret," he said as he entered the library. He glanced over his shoulder. "Unless you'd rather it was?"

"Since when did it become a relationship?"

Emory paused and turned to face him. "Isn't it?"

"Shit, what? I dunno… I thought we were just… *Christ*. Way to put a guy on the spot."

Emory's face was still. He was quiet for a while then smiled. "You don't enjoy this part, do you?"

"What part?"

Emory brought up Jesse's hand and brushed his fingers against his lips. "Intimacy."

Jesse fought to keep his voice steady. "Nowadays we just call it 'fucking', mate."

"But we haven't even done that yet," Emory murmured against his fingers, his eyes lighting with a dark fire.

Jesse shivered. "You were right. Tom can't know. Like you said…I don't think he'd like it."

"Indeed," Emory said, dropping his hand. "Tom is a good man and a valued member of my household. But he's had some…unfortunate experiences with my kind in the past. They would probably color his views on the subject." Emory swept through the study and into the pitch-black pool room with Jesse hurrying behind. "I'm sure it's within your skills to ensure he doesn't find out."

Emory turned on the underwater lights, bathing the room in the flickering turquoise. He held out his hand.

Something inside Jesse snapped, and all thoughts of Tom, Dimity and the mayor's house fled. He shoved Emory's hand aside and claimed his mouth with a demanding groan as he began wrestling with shirt buttons.

"Such impatience, *liebling*," Emory said as he undid the button on Jesse's jeans. "Did I not explain we go slow?"

"You've seen me naked," Jesse said between kisses, tugging Emory's shirt open and pushing it off his shoulders. "It's only fair."

"I concede," Emory rumbled, grinning against Jesse's lips and letting his shirt drop to the floor. Jesse, despite his shaking hands, then made quick work of the rest of Emory's clothing. He stepped back and stared.

The haemophile's skin was a uniform, unbroken almond-color. His muscles moved beneath it like waves on a windswept sea. His arms were the bunched knots of tree branches, and his chest was broad and hairless, bulging above an abdomen ridged like a mountain range. His obliques were solid shelves, sliding tantalizingly to his groin, where thick hair framed his large cock, which was just starting to swell. His thighs were thick, dusted with hair and the muscles shifted delightfully as he stepped closer. He smiled so his canines glinted against his lips.

"So glad you approve."

"You work out, right?" Jesse cursed himself and his ridiculous mouth. But his stupefied brain was struggling to make sense of a body he'd seen in Greek statutes but never on anyone real.

Emory chuckled low in his throat and lifted Jesse's T-shirt over his head. "One benefit of the Blood," he said huskily, as he stripped Jesse, slowly, grazing

Jesse's flesh with touches as light as snowflakes, "is a very efficient metabolism."

"It's definitely working for me," Jesse said, grabbing him by the hips and yanking Emory against him, grinding their cocks together and thrusting his tongue hungrily into his mouth. Emory smiled against his lips and brushed his fingers down Jesse's arms, slowing and deepening the kiss with long sweeps of his tongue. When Jesse began to struggle to breathe, Emory pushed him back and cold air rushed between them.

"Swim first."

"Really?" Jesse whined.

"Really," Emory said, steering him toward the pool. "The cortisol is streaming through your system. You need to relax."

"Coming hard and fast would help with that," Jesse grumbled, standing on the edge and stroking his aching cock.

Emory pushed his hand away from his groin with just a hint of his strength. "It's always better if you wait," he whispered against the back of Jesse's neck. "You'll see. Swim."

"Fine," he cursed, then jumped in. The water was cool and pleasant and doused some of the urgent fire under his skin. He came to the surface with a splutter, wiping water from his eyes and taking a deep breath, feeling his heart start to calm.

"Better?" Emory swam toward him. His large body barely rippled the surface.

"I guess."

"Come. Swim with me."

Jesse splashed to catch up as Emory sailed past him. They did a length of the pool, then another. Their breathing fell in time. Jesse's body cooled. His pulse slowed.

"So you can really smell how I'm feeling, huh?" Jesse said as they turned to swim another length.

"Smell, taste, hear, feel." Emory shrugged a shoulder as he swam. "It's a combination of all those things, really."

"You can *hear* how humans are feeling?"

"You can, too," Emory said, sliding him a glance. "From their tone of voice. And see it in the way they move or look at you." He slowed as they reached the deep end and took hold of the edge. "We have all the same senses as you. They're just stronger."

Jesse trod water, swallowing saliva. The water had darkened Emory's hair to black. Droplets like gems sparkled on his skin. He was so gorgeous that he took Jesse's breath away.

"So, what are you sensing right now?"

"That you're ready for another kiss," Emory said, taking Jesse's hand under the water and drawing him close. Jesse swallowed. He pinned Jesse against the poolside before claiming his mouth. Jesse moaned. Emory plundered his mouth, clutching the pool's edge at either side of Jesse's head and using his powerful legs to hold him against the side.

Jesse ran his hands up the hard, muscled back, feeling every last cell in his body light with a slow flame. He wrapped his legs around the powerful hips and gasped into the kiss as Emory tilted his hips forward and Jesse felt the large, swelling cock press against his arse.

"So, tell me, Jesse," Emory whispered as he broke the kiss to mouth along Jesse's jaw. "You like to be... There's a word for it..." He paused to take Jesse's earlobe between his teeth and crush Jesse harder into the wall. Jesse gasped. The water suddenly felt very warm. "Dominated, is that it?"

"Fuck, yes, that's it," Jesse managed.

"Well," Emory breathed, thrusting against Jesse again, making him gasp. "That is something I can undoubtedly do. But I wonder…"

"Christ, wonder *what*?" Jesse said, tilting his head back as Emory nipped at his collarbone.

"Have you ever thought about doing the dominating?"

"Uh, yeah, I mean…" Jesse cut off, crushing his eyes shut as Emory thrust lazily against him again. "I've tried a few things, over the years, but I know what I like."

"To be commanded?" Emory said, sliding one hand under the water to grasp Jesse's arse and squeeze. "To be possessed? Made to beg?"

"Fuck." Jesse wrapped his legs tighter. His cock throbbed against Emory's hard belly. The water lapping at his skin was like velvet. "Yes," he said, despite barely having enough breath to make a sound. "You've done this before, right? I can tell you have," he said, leaning in to talk against Emory's mouth. "You know what I want."

"I've done most things in my time," Emory whispered, trailing a hand up Jesse's ribs. He spread his fingers on either side of Jesse's pierced nipple but didn't touch it, making Jesse whine in protest. "That's why I think I can show you things you don't even realize you want."

"Like what?" Jesse inhaled sharply when Emory tweaked his nipple.

"There are ways I can be restrained," Emory said after a pause, rubbing his hardening cock into the crack of Jesse's arse, making him catch fire. "Rendered powerless."

"You?" Jesse panted, sliding his hands down to the powerful, hard buttocks and grinding himself into the iron-hard belly. "Whatever."

"Oh yes," Emory said, sliding his lips along Jesse's jaw to kiss his neck. Jesse was gratified to finally hear arousal weighting his voice. "I can be made to submit. I could show you how."

Emory slid his hand down Jesse's belly and grasped his cock, hard. Jesse moaned, closed his eyes and thrust into the hold.

"I'll take that as a yes," Emory whispered into his ear. He began to stroke him — lazy, slow, but hard.

"Fuck," Jesse swore again, digging his hands into the hard flesh of Emory's arse. "Jesus. God."

"I was wondering when God would make an appearance." Emory smiled and thrust against Jesse's skin.

"God," he cried again. "You're so fucking big."

"And you," Emory rumbled, stroking Jesse faster and starting to grind against him under the water. "You're so warm, so full of passion." He ground harder, lifting Jesse higher out of the water as he beat his cock with fast, precise strokes, sending molten silver flowing through Jesse's body. "When I finally have you, Jesse Truelove," he panted against his jaw. "When I finally take you, you'll never forget it. *I'll* never forget it."

"Do it now," Jesse cried, clutching at Emory's shoulders, feeling like he could drown, even with his head above water. "Fuck me. Put it in me."

"Not when you're this close. I want you to really feel it, to savor it...for as long as you can stand it...then a bit more."

Jesse came, crying out and shuddering hot stickiness into the water.

* * * *

Jesse's phone woke him. Daylight bled between the heavy curtains. He squinted at the clock on the wall. It had gone nine. He swore again then finally found his phone in the pocket of his discarded jeans.

Ant calling...

He almost hung up. Emory's touch was still warm on his skin. Then he remembered Oliver's expectant face when he'd asked about Christmas.

"Yo."

"Hey, Jesse, it's Ant."

Jesse frowned. "What's up? You sound different. Is Olly okay?"

"Oliver's fine. Look, Jess, I don't suppose we could meet this afternoon?"

Jesse rubbed his sleep-bleared eyes. "Aren't you working?"

"I've got an afternoon off. What do you say to a cheeky afternoon pint with your big bro?"

Jesse frowned harder. "Are you sure you're okay? You sound weird."

"Weird?"

"You know...cheerful."

"I'm making an effort here, Jess. Can you meet me or not?"

"Uh, yeah, sure," Jesse said, pushing back the covers. "I'm sure I can sort something.'

"Great. Valhalla on Patrick Pool?"

"The Viking place? Won't it be rammed?"

"Let's live a little. See you at three?"

"Three? Sure."

"Great. See you then."

Anton hung up, and Jesse stared at the wall. His hair smelled like chlorine. His skin smelled like Emory. He rubbed his eyes.

"What the fuck are you doing, man?" he asked aloud.

But he couldn't make himself feel guilty. It had just been so damn good.

"When I finally take you, you'll never forget it. I'll never forget it."

His cock was already twitching. He shook himself and hurried to the en suite to splash cold water on his face. The next day was Christmas Eve, and there really should be other things on his mind than Emory's huge, hard...

"Stop it already," he said out loud, slapping his reflection in the mirror. "Stop thinking with your dick."

But it wasn't just his dick—and that's what really scared him.

Thankfully it was Tom's day off, though Filip gave Jesse his usual disapproving scowl as he hurried into the security room just before ten. Jesse gave him his best smile, and the older man scowled and turned back to his screens.

Jesse made sure Filip was still focused elsewhere, then set about downloading the security footage from the night before. He watched Emory and himself crossing the hall together, Jesse's hungry expression so plain it was painful. Then Emory kissed his hand, and Jesse's face flooded with color.

He quickly deleted the footage and patched in some film of the empty hall from earlier in the night, tweaking the time stamp with a bit of image editing.

When Jesse made it into York that afternoon, the city center was heaving. Jesse swore inventively and at length as he struggled through solid crowds that packed the pavements all the way from the bus station to the bar.

Valhalla was also packed, as he expected. The sweet, malty smells of mead and spilled beer thickened the close atmosphere that was already filled with the chatter and laughter. Anton sat at a table in the corner and waved eagerly as he squeezed in the door. Jesse wove his way over, shedding his coat and scarf, already sweating.

"Christ, it's smaller than I thought," Jesse said as he inched past an older couple to reach his seat.

"You not been before?"

Jesse sat with a wry smile. "I try to avoid the tourist spots."

"Apart from the Evil Eye," Anton said with a lifted eyebrow.

"That's different," Jesse said.

"Because it's easier to pull there?" Anton said, but his smile was amused.

Jesse gave his brother a look. "You wanted to talk?"

"Truelove is a Viking name, you know," Anton said, pushing a glass of amber liquid across the table to him. "Our families probably lived around these parts for hundreds of years."

"Perhaps we should have learned to branch out by now," Jesse muttered, taking the glass. "What's this?"

"Mead," Ant said, smiling a little uncertainly. "It's Christmassy, right?"

"Sure," Jesse said, downing the fiery drink in one go. He coughed and lowered the glass. "Well, better get to the bar."

"I queued for half an hour for that," Anton said with an exasperated look.

"Well, I'd better get back in that queue."

"Jesse, please," he said, putting a hand on his arm to stop him from rising. "Here." He pushed his untouched glass across the table. "We can share this one."

Jesse muttered under his breath, sipped from the glass, feeling the sweet drink unknot some of the tension in his back. He slid it back across the table to his brother. "So what did you want to talk about?"

Anton spun the glass in his fingers but didn't drink. He stared hard at the table. "I wanted to apologize."

Jesse blinked. "You did?"

"Yeah. I'm sorry." His brother finally looked at him. There were shadows under his dark green eyes and stubble on his jaw. Jesse noticed he'd lost some weight. Concern bloomed in his gut, but he held his brother's gaze without speaking. "I know I've been a bit of a dick, Jess. And Dad dying isn't really an excuse."

"Well," Jesse said awkwardly, "it is…really."

"No, it's not. I just worry about you…every day."

"You don't need to worry about me, Ant. I'm not a kid."

"I know you're not." He sipped his drink. "It's just taken me a while to realize that. And Dad? Well" —he shrugged—"perhaps you were right about him not being the greatest role model where handling emotion was concerned."

"You think?"

Anton clenched his jaw a moment but then smiled. "Yeah, maybe not."

"Okay," Jesse said, reaching for the drink. "Was that it?"

"No," Anton said, sitting straighter. "I wanted to say I'm sorry, yes, but I also wanted to say I'm not going to push you anymore."

"Push me?"

"About your choices. About your decisions to keep things private." He drummed his fingers on the table, staring hard at the surface and not at Jesse. "If you don't want to share everything about your life, that's up to you. But you should just know I can't help you with anything I don't know about."

"I don't *need* help, Anton."

"Sareena told me…about the adoption certificate." He met Jesse's eyes. Jesse felt the blood drain from his face. "Don't be mad at her. We don't keep things from each other."

"I'm not mad."

"Well, don't be scared, then," he said. "I told you. I'm gonna trust you to make your own decisions — and that they are the right ones."

Jesse regarded him levelly. "You on drugs or something?"

"No," Anton said easily. "I've just realized this is better for you, better for me, better for Oliver."

"Okay. Thanks." Guilt soured the mead in his gut.

"But—"

Jesse sighed. "I knew there'd be a 'but'."

"*But…*" Anton continued, firmly, "you know this goes both ways, right? I trust you to do the right thing. That means you gotta do it."

"Yeah, I get it, Ant," he said, a little testily. "Wanna get it tattooed on my arse?"

"I didn't think there was any space left down there," he said with a strained grin. "And swiftly changing that subject, we'd like to have you for Christmas."

Jesse blinked. Warmth blossomed in his chest. "For real?"

"For real. Oliver wants you there. *I* want you there."

Jesse fought a smile. "Now I know you're either high or bullshitting."

"Neither." His brother did smile, wide and warm, though the dark sadness that had become part of him since their father passed still shaded his eyes. "So, what do you say? You'll come?"

Jesse hesitated then lowered his gaze. "So, I'm sort of…working…late…on Christmas Eve."

Anton blinked at him. "You're working Christmas Eve night?"

"Yeah."

A dozen questions flickered over Anton's face, but he drew a breath and just asked. "How late?"

Jesse chewed on the inside of his cheek, watching the emotion harden his brother's eyes. "Fuck it. I'll be there."

A smile washed away the pensiveness in Anton's face. "That's great. Early, yeah? Want to surprise Oliver."

Jesse nodded. "I'll try."

"Great," Anton said, standing. "More mead, I think."

"Hell yes," Jess muttered. "Line them up."

Anton brought more mead, pork pie and halloumi fries, and they ate and drank and talked about Oliver. It was easier than it had been since their dad had died, and Jesse gradually started to relax. Though when it came time for Jesse to leave, their hug was still awkward, that ever-present barrier between them stiffening their movements.

"See you Saturday, yeah?" Anton said as they stepped out into the darkening evening.

"Yeah," Jesse replied, turning to hurry away without meeting his brother's eye. "See ya Saturday."

Jesse dug his hands in his pockets and hunched against the icy wind blowing down Church Street. The alcohol had dulled his thoughts but had also weighted the unease that lay in his gut like concrete.

A message from an unknown number flashed on his phone screen as he sat on the bus making its way out of town.

Please meet me in the library at your earliest convenience. Please also note, this is my personal number, not to be shared with anyone.
Emory

Jesse blinked at the message for several minutes, fired off a quick reply, saved the number in a hidden sub-folder on his phone and fought an idiotic smile.

* * * *

"I trust you had a pleasant trip to town?" Emory said as he took a seat in one of the deep armchairs of the library and gestured to the one opposite.

"I did," Jesse said as he sat. "Met my brother. It was nice."

"Good. I'm glad to hear it. Are you hungry?"

"We ate." Jesse fidgeted. "This is about tomorrow night?"

Emory regarded him levelly. "I wanted to see how you were feeling about it all."

Jesse grimaced. "The answer to that question changes every ten minutes."

"I can understand that. Let's start off with the objective matters. Are you confident you can get Dimity out safely?"

"I am," Jesse said, staring at the carpet. "But only if she wants to come." He raised his eyes. Emory wasn't blinking. "I'm not forcing her."

"I'm certain she will want to come," he said. "But please ask her first. That is a given."

Jesse nodded. "You got your fastest driver on this?"

"Greenway will wait in the lane as agreed." He reached down the side of the armchair and produced a small backpack. "I'm sure she already has warm clothing, but there's a coat and snow boots in here, just in case." He handed over the bag. Jesse took it with numb hands.

"And what happens when they find out she's missing?"

"Darragh has everything arranged."

Jesse examined him for a long moment. "I get you want your kid back, Emory. I just hope you've thought about the blowback."

"I've thought of everything."

"Really? Like what people will say if a haemophile kidnaps a human kid and holds her hostage?"

"I know you don't think that's what I'm doing."

"*I* don't," Jesse said. "But the news? Social media? The internet?" He snorted, shaking his head. "You thought rumors were destructive in your day."

"Like I said, I have considered everything."

Jesse gave a helpless shrug. "Okay. I'm just surprised your fancy-ass advisors haven't tried to talk you out of this to save you the sheer PR shitstorm it's going to be, if nothing else."

"Who's to say they haven't?"

Jesse examined him. His face was blank, his dark eyes unreadable. Jesse fought the sensation that Emory was a hundred miles or a hundred years away from him. "We'll need to hire extra security at the very least."

"What aren't you asking me, Jesse?"

Jesse gnawed a thumbnail and stared at the wall. Emory came over and perched on the arm of Jesse's chair.

"I understand this is a demanding task," Emory said softly. "And maybe you're wondering what my intentions toward you are in all this?"

"Can you blame me? A job. A home. Mind-blowing sex." Jesse took a shaking breath. "Was it all just so I'd do this for you, no questions asked?"

Emory was quiet a long moment. "I admit when I found out about your break-in here, getting Dimity back was the first thing that came to my mind," Emory said softly. "At the time, maybe I thought money and security would be enough to secure your loyalty." His eyes were hard but earnest. "But it means the world that I can now trust you with this on a personal level, too."

"So now it's…different?"

"Don't you think so?"

Jesse shrugged. "I'm having trouble telling up from down right now, to be honest."

"Jesse," he said softly. "You can still say no."

Jesse stared hard at the wall for several long moments. Then he dared to meet the haemophile's eyes. "I've met Dimity before, you know. The night of the Christmas light switch-on. She knew you would be in the square. She tried to get to you but got lost. She was crying. All she wanted was her daddy."

"All I want is what's best for my daughter," Emory said, his voice barely above a whisper.

"I think so, too," Jesse said after a brief pause. "But doing it this way has consequences, Emory — to you, to her. Wouldn't it be best to wait for the legal shit to work itself out?"

"The legal wrangling could take years. I resent every day Dimity has to spend away from her family." He looked into Jesse's eyes. "I promise you, I really have thought of all this, including the impact on you, Jesse. And you have my promise I will protect Dimity…and I will protect you."

"And yourself?"

He smiled so his sharp teeth glinted. "Have no concerns on that front."

Chapter Eleven

Jesse had wanted to stay with Emory, lose himself in his intoxicating embrace and forget everything for as long as possible, but Emory insisted he get some rest.

"Tomorrow, *liebling*," he murmured, pressing a chaste kiss to Jesse's cheek in the doorway of the library. "Tomorrow night, we'll have everything we want."

Jesse went to bed tingling with a combination of trepidation and excitement. He woke, not feeling rested, to the sound of Christmas music drifting up from somewhere on the lower floors.

When he went downstairs, he found a stream of people flowing between the entrance and the library, all carrying Christmas decorations. The music was coming from the in-house speaker system, and many of the staff were wearing tinsel in their hair, festive earrings or Christmas jumpers.

"Happy Christmas Eve," Tom said as he joined Jesse in the hall. "Guessing the boss had a last-minute attack of the festive spirit."

"Yeah," Jesse said hoarsely, "I guess."

"You okay?"

Jesse tried for a smile and made for the break room. "Yeah, all good. Hey, I was just thinking... We should get some more security staff in, just for the next few weeks." Jesse went to the coffee machine. "You know how holidays send people nuts."

"We can do that," Tom said, leaning against the counter and folding his arms, "if you think that's necessary."

"I do — booze, family bust-ups, disappointing presents." He shrugged. "That shit gets people all riled up. They're bound to lash out at the local pariah more than usual."

"I'll get on it this morning." Tom fetched mugs from the cupboard. "So, big day tomorrow. What are your plans?"

"I'm supposed to go over to my brother's, to see my nephew."

"That sounds lovely." Tom paused as Jesse fetched the milk without making eye contact. "Not looking forward to it?"

Won't be going if I'm in fucking jail — for good this time. Jesse swallowed the words and poured the milk. "Just a lot to get done first, is all."

"Like what?" Tom said, taking his mug and following Jesse from the room. "Systems are all online. Holiday cover is arriving at noon. I'd say we're free and easy."

Jesse made sure the security room was empty then went in and shut the door behind them. "You were with Emory in Austria, right?"

"Yes..." Tom said carefully. "Why?"

Jesse gripped his coffee mug, hard.

"It means the world that I can now trust you with this on a personal level." Emory's words echoed in his head. He let out a noisy sigh and sat at his workstation. "Nothing. Forget it."

"Jesse, you seem unusually tense this morning, even for you."

"It's just this bloody holiday," Jesse snapped, then shook his head. "Sorry. I'm a dickhead."

Tom chuckled and sat next to him. "You're not a dickhead. Sometimes Christmas is hard. I get that. And I guess a lot has changed for you, coming here. How about I get us some breakfast, huh? The holiday pastry should be arriving any minute."

Jesse smiled. "That sounds good."

"One thing Christmas is good for," Tom said, moving to the door, "is comfort eating. I'll be right back."

"Hey," Jesse said. Tom paused in the doorway. "What are you doing tomorrow? I never asked."

Tom put his hands in his pockets, looking a little sheepish. "They put a pretty good staff meal on in the break room. Plenty of booze, too. With any luck, I'll be passed out under a table by three p.m."

"You're not going to see your family?"

"Nah," Tom said with a shrug. "Easier to stick around here."

Something tightened in Jesse's chest as he watched old pain cool the warmth in Tom's eyes. "Okay, man. Well, I hope they push the boat out."

"They usually do." Tom returned his smile and left. Soon he returned with a plate stacked high with Danishes, croissants, cinnamon whirls and pecan plaits, plus a tub of jam, one of cream and another of butter.

He and Jesse allowed the excellent food to move the conversation on as they did their routine morning system checks and joked about what their dads had looked like in Father Christmas suits when they had been kids. Jesse was surprised to find the memories less painful than usual.

At noon, the temp staff came in to relieve them for the holiday weekend, but it was close to one before Jesse was satisfied that they knew what they were doing. Tom finally dragged him from the room, then they were standing, slightly awkwardly, in the hall outside their bedrooms.

"Hey, wanna go for a walk or something?" Tom said hesitantly. "There are some nice routes over the moor. And there's an amazing pub in the next village over."

Jesse was sorely tempted. He thought about walking out over the snowy horizon with handsome, kind Tom, about booking a room at the pub and not coming back, leaving all the complexity and uncertainty behind. But then he remembered Emory's face…and Dimity's.

He shook his head. "Sorry, man. I've got some stuff of my own to get on with. But hey, if I don't see you, have a good one, yeah?"

"You, too," Tom said. He squeezed Jesse's arm. "You deserve a nice Christmas, Jesse. I hope you get one."

"You, too, mate," Jesse said sincerely, moving toward his door. "Really."

Jesse slumped against the inside of his door as the reality of the coming hours dropped on him like bricks.

All too soon darkness had fallen. The weather forecast had promised more snow, but it hadn't started falling by the time he was getting ready. He cursed. They needed snow to cover tracks. Snow, tonight, was his friend. But as he shouldered his bag and went downstairs, the sky out of the window was still blank and dark.

Greenway was waiting for him at the side door. She was silent and rigid as they left the house and made for the garages.

A shadow detached itself from the rest along the wall as they approached.

"Sir," Greenway greeted the shadow then went to open the garage.

"Shit, *you're* coming?"

"Of course I am."

Jesse shifted from one foot to another. He could feel Emory's eyes on him but neither of them spoke as Greenway brought a car round.

They drove down the winding country lanes in silence. Jesse's jaw ached from clenching. His palms were sweating inside his gloves. Greenway took a round-about way down back roads to the mayor's house, but it was all too soon that Jesse spotted lights between the trees on a rise to their left.

Greenway pulled in and shut off the engine. Jesse sat for a long, tense moment in the warmth of the silent car, the presence of Emory solid at his side, then climbed out into the frigid air.

The only sound was the ringing of church bells drifting through the air from somewhere far away. He climbed over a gate into a field. The snow was a dull gray in the moonless dark. As he trudged through the shin-deep snow, fresh flakes began to fall. His chest loosened slightly. But then he took in blinding light on the horizon, and his stomach knotted all over again.

The daylight floods around the mayor's house bathed the snow in brightness for twenty yards in every direction. Jesse hung on the edge of the pool of light, glaring at the mansion and clenching and unclenching his fists. He checked his watch. The fake security footage he'd looped into the CCTV feed had been rolling for almost a minute. He had a maximum of thirty before the next patrol when the security guard watching the feed would realize something was up. But it was still hard to make himself step into the light.

He glanced up at the window of Dimity's bedroom. The curtains were open, and the low light of a nightlight bathed the pink ceiling.

He dashed across the lawn to the side door that he and Emory had entered by the night of the party. He shook his head when he entered the same code from that night and the door clicked open.

"Amateurs," he muttered, then ducked inside. He donned night-vision goggles and hurried along the corridor as quietly as he could manage. He took a circuitous route to avoid passing the security room door then crept up to the third floor.

The corridor was flooded with brightness from the floodlight over Dimity's door. He squinted against the glare. His heart was thumping wildly in his chest. The room was just three doors away. There was still time to turn back…

Two doors. One.

He checked his watch. Ten to midnight. Twenty minutes left. Was he really going to do this?

A footstep on the stairs had his heart lurching into his throat. He tried the handle of the nearest door and almost buckled with relief when it turned, and he ducked into the dark room beyond. A quick sweep with his goggles showed an empty bedroom. He stood there in the silence, holding his breath and listening. He heard a door closing somewhere below…then silence.

He was about to leave when he noticed the coat hanging on the back of the door. Something about it was familiar. It was pale green in the night-vision, but when he lifted his goggles, he could make out it was pale orange. *No...peach.*

He looked around at what must be Aunt Helena's room. It was meticulously neat. Silk pajamas were folded on the bed. Her makeup stood in a neat line on the dressing table. A laptop sat in the precise center of the desk. Jesse made himself put a hand on the door handle. Then he cursed and turned back. He was into the laptop in seconds and had accessed her encrypted hard drive a few seconds later. He typed in Emory's case number from memory and there it was—the lawyer's file.

Jesse glanced at the wall, thinking of the little girl sleeping on the other side, then opened the file.

It was similar to the one in Emory's desk. Most of it didn't make any sense to him. Applications. Affidavits. Precedent statements. Then he caught sight of the evidence list. An entry at the bottom made his heart jerk behind his ribs.

Kill List.

He swallowed. His hands throbbed. He clicked the link. A scanned document displayed. Jesse's mouth dried out as he read.

His watch buzzed on his wrist. A ten-minute warning. He slammed the laptop lid and backed away from the desk with his heart hammering. He stood against the foot of the bed, shaking. A cold sweat stood out on his back.

Then light flooded the room. Jesse spun around. The door was open. A small figure stood outlined against the light.

"Who's there?"

Jesse froze in the shadow of the bed curtain, his heart racing.

"Who is it? I'm calling Maria."

"Hey, hey, hey," Jesse said hurriedly, "hold your horses, Dimity. It's just me."

"Who are you?" Her voice tightened with fear. "Why are you in my aunt's room?"

Jesse pulled off his hood and knelt in front of her. "It's Jesse. Remember me?"

She opened the door a little wider but didn't move closer. "I think so. The Christmas party?"

"That's right. You showed me your drawings."

Silence. Seconds ticking by. Jesse didn't dare move. "What are you doing in here?" she said.

"I, uh..." He looked back at the laptop then back at the little girl in her pink nightdress, clutching a stuffed rabbit to her chest.

"I'll get Maria," she said and moved to step away, but Jesse held his hand out.

"No, wait, Dim." She stopped, eyeing him warily. He took a breath. "You're right. I'm not supposed to be here. If you get Maria, I'll be in trouble."

Dimity took an uncertain step into the room. "Why will you be in trouble?"

"I..." Jesse fought himself. He could just make out her face in the darkness, crumpled with a mixture of sadness and fear—not the face a child should have on Christmas Eve. "Your dad sent me."

Her face transformed, lighting from inside. "Daddy?"

"Shh," he hushed her, shuffling forward on his knees. "This has gotta be a secret, right?"

"Daddy's here?" Her words came out in the strangled squeak of someone trying to keep their excitement quiet.

"He's not far," Jesse said, checking his watch and wincing. "He sent me to get you. Thought you might want Christmas with him."

"Hurray," she called, jumping up and down, swinging her rabbit about.

"Hey, hey," Jesse said urgently. "Quiet down, eh? I'm not supposed to be here, remember?"

"But why not?" Dimity said plaintively. "I want to see my daddy. You're here to take me to him. What's wrong with that?"

Jesse swallowed. "Dim, this is very, very important, okay?"

"*What* is?" she said, her voice lowering, brow wrinkling.

"You said you want to see your daddy, right?"

"Yeah…?"

"Is that the truth? One hundred percent, cross your heart, swear on your bunny's life the truth?"

She giggled, covering her hand with her mouth. "Of course."

Jesse's uncertainty prickled over his skin. "You want to live with him again?"

"That's all I want from Santa this year—all year, every year." Her face crumpled. "I miss him so much."

Jesse's heart clenched. "You know…you know what he is, right?"

"Of course I do," Dimity insisted. "He's a haem-er-phile." She pronounced it carefully then beamed. "Like a vampire, but real…and not bad. He was related to me, like, a million years ago. But now he's adopted me so I'm his real daughter."

Jesse fought his tight throat to open. "So you know what he does, right? What he drinks?"

She shrugged. "I drink Ribena, so not that much different."

"It's a bit different, love…"

"Not to me."

"And you're okay with never seeing him in the day? And knowing that perhaps, sometime, a long time ago…" Jesse took a breath. "Know he might have hurt people? Badly?"

Dimity's face was serious. "I know he used to do bad things. But it was so, so, so long ago, and he doesn't do it anymore. Please, Jesse. Can I see him now?"

Jesse took a deep breath then let it out in a long, slow, sigh. He checked his watch. "We've got less than ten minutes. Hurry. You need to get dressed."

Dimity sprinted back to her room and was dressed and ready in her new coat and snow boots in less than a minute, chattering away the whole time in an excited whisper.

"You must promise to be as quiet as a mouse. Quieter," Jesse whispered as he fastened her coat. "And do as I say, right?"

"I swear one hundred percent, cross my heart, on Bunny Bella's life." She giggled, waving the rabbit in Jesse's face.

"Okay then," he said, struggling to fight a smile. "You got everything you want?"

She stuffed the bunny into the top of the backpack, nodding.

"You don't want your drawing things? Any other toys?"

"Daddy already has all my favorites," she said, pushing the bag toward him. "Come on. Let's *go*."

Jesse shouldered the bag, took Dimity's hand and crept from the room.

Dimity was good as her word. She didn't make a sound as they moved through the dark, silent hallways. Even when they were out in the freezing night air and

Jesse scooped her up and ran across the illuminated stretch of lawn, all she did was cling on and hold her breath. Only when they were back in the shadows did Jesse slow. His heart pounded and sweat ran down his back. He set Dimity on her feet, took her hand and hurried across the dark field toward the road. She ran at his side, stumbling occasionally, but never once made a noise. In the low light, he could see her face was tight with excitement.

Jesse listened intently for an alarm that never came. He checked his watch. The security footage he'd planted would have stopped looping by now, but there was no noise, no lights, no barking dogs. He picked up their pace.

A dark figure became visible by the gate. Dimity let out a squeal, let go of Jesse's hand and raced forward.

Emory bent over the gate and scooped her up into his arms. She was chattering, high and loud, her voice choked with tears. Emory replied in whispers before returning to the back of the car with her. The engine was already running. Jesse scrambled into the front. Greenway gunned the accelerator without turning the lights on.

Jesse swore and clung to the door, but Greenway steered them expertly down the dark, winding roads. Only when the brightness of the floodlit mansion had disappeared from their mirrors did she turn the headlights on and slow the car.

Dimity had not stopped to draw breath. She sat in Emory's lap, chattering about Jesse, her bunny, their escape from the house, how much she'd missed him, how much she hated Aunt Helena and Maria, her minder. Emory gazed at her. His face glowed with a low, fierce warmth. His smile was like nothing Jesse had ever seen him wear before.

Warmth bloomed in Jesse's cheeks, and he felt a telltale prickle in his eyes.

Then the vision of Aunt Helena's laptop screen rose before his eyes, and cold swamped him.

"Thank you, Greenway," Emory said as they entered Oswald House. "I owe you much."

"All in a day's work, sir," Greenway said, then, stepping forward and lowering her voice, "Don't fuck it up, yeah?"

Jesse blinked, startled. Emory's face was serious. "I don't intend to."

Greenway nodded then looked between them. "Merry Christmas, gentlemen. Miss." She nodded to Dimity then made for the staff stairs.

"Daddy, Daddy," Dimity said, tugging on Emory's hand. "This house is amazing! Is this where we're going to live?"

"That's right, darling. Do you like it?"

"I really do! Look at the tree!" she said, gesturing at the fiber-optic tree that was rotating colors in the corner of the hall.

"That's not even the main tree," Emory said with a slow smile. "Come on. It's Christmas morning. Father Christmas may have already visited."

Her eyes widened. "Already?"

"You were top of the list this year," Emory said, brushing her curls back from her face. "Take your coat and boots off first, though. They go in there." He nodded to the door under the staircase. Dimity raced to the cupboard, flung it open and disappeared inside, still talking.

Emory turned to Jesse. His face had grown serious again.

"Thank you, Jesse," he said. "Thank you from the bottom of my heart."

Jesse took off his gloves without meeting the haemophile's eye. "Already had thieving and hacking on the rap sheet. Why not kidnapping, too?"

When he looked back, Emory's expression had darkened. "Something's wrong. What is it?"

Jesse's throat closed again. He tried to speak, but then Dimity was racing out of the closet and tugging on Emory's hand. "All done, Daddy," she said. "Where's the tree? The *real* tree?"

"This way," Emory said, steering her toward the library. "Jesse? Are you joining us?"

"Me?"

"Oh, please, Jesse," Dimity begged. "Let's go see what Santa has brought us."

Jesse looked from the haemophile to the child and back, seeing very different but similarly expectant looks in their faces. Despite everything, it warmed him through.

"Well, if he puts you at the top of the list, it's only right to see what he's brought."

Dimity danced about, shaking excited fists. Emory smiled. He took his daughter's hand and led her to the library.

Dimity shrieked and ran inside. Jesse stood on the threshold and stared. The bookshelves were wreathed in holly and ivy. Their fresh, woody fragrance filled the air. The sound of a choir singing carols drifted from a hidden sound system. A huge fir tree, reaching almost to the ceiling, stood in the corner, decorated in red, green and gold stained-glass hangings. Tea lights flickered in colored glass globes from almost every branch, pooling the tidal wave of presents below in golden light.

The sight, the warmth, the color, the smell flooded Jesse with something unfamiliar, something like a glow.

"He's been here. He's been here," Dimity cried, diving straight into the presents. "And he knew where I'd be, just like Jesse said he would."

"Uncle Jesse is usually right about these things," Emory said in a low voice, catching Jesse's eye. He held out his hand. Jesse hesitated then took it. He drew Jesse toward the love seat that had been placed next to the tree.

"Go on, then," Emory said as he sat and crossed his legs. "Open them."

Dimity started tearing paper from a jigsaw puzzle.

"St. Stephen's Cathedral," she said, delighted, holding up the box. "I love it, Daddy. Can we go see it again sometime?"

"Of course. We can spend the whole of next Christmas in Vienna, if you like. How about the next one?"

They watched Dimity make her way through the presents, listening to her delighted commentary as she went. At one point, Emory fetched them drinks — beer for Jesse, hot chocolate for Dimity. Jesse sipped and allowed himself to relax. That curious warmth stole through him again as he watched Emory take delight in Dimity's joy as she opened sketch pads, an easel, paints and canvas.

"She's very good at art," Jesse said as she attempted to set up the easel. "She showed me some of her drawings."

"We've had many acclaimed artists in the family over the years," Emory replied as he helped her tighten the screws in the wooden frame. "I'm very confident Dimity will be included in that list."

"You should get her an artist's tablet," Jesse said around a yawn, rubbing his eyes. "She had a go on my phone. I think she'd be a whizz at digital art."

"Would you like that, darling?" Emory said as he opened a box of pencils for her. "Would you like to try making art on a computer as well?"

"If Uncle Jesse will teach me," she said with a wide grin.

Emory looked at him expectantly. Jesse smiled, propping his head on his hand. "Sure. I can do that."

He yawned again and Dimity followed suit.

"Yes indeed," Emory said, standing and gently moving the easel into the corner. "I think it is time for bed."

"But you'll be up for ages yet, Daddy," Dimity complained, just the edge of a whine in her voice.

"We've discussed this before, haven't we, Dimity?" he said, his voice firm. "Tonight was a special night. But just because I'm awake all night doesn't mean you can be. Little girls need their sleep."

"Uncle Jesse," she pleaded, even though her eyes were drooping, "you tell him."

"Dad's rules, Dim," he said, standing. "It's been a long night for all of us."

"Okay," she said, rubbing her eyes. "If you're going to bed too?" She peeped at Jesse from under her curls.

He glanced at Emory. He was smiling. A low heat was starting to smolder in his eyes. "Sure," he said, though his blood had started to race. "My bedtime, too."

"Okay then," Dimity said, fetching Bunny Bella from where she had been set in an armchair to watch the proceedings. Dimity held her hand out to Emory. "Bedtime."

Emory took his daughter's hand and led her to the door. Jesse stood, stretching and moved to follow. Emory paused at the doorway.

"Have another drink," he said in a low voice, that dark fire sparking in his eyes. "I haven't given you your Christmas present yet."

Jesse was instantly awake. He swallowed, nodded. "Sure."

Emory leaned in and brushed his lips along his jaw. "I won't be long," he whispered in his ear, then turned and took his daughter toward the stairs.

Jesse went to the drinks counter and poured a brandy. He downed it, enjoying the burn in his throat and poured another. He sipped, surveying the room. The carols still wafted in the air. The scent of the fire, the candles and the greenery wove among the sounds like golden threads. He searched for the fear from earlier, for the anger, the confusion. But that now lay beyond a curtain of contentment that Jesse wasn't sure he understood—just like he wasn't sure he could handle the sparking electric storm building in his abdomen at the memory of Emory's expression before he left the room.

By the time he returned, Jesse was on a third brandy and the alcohol was starting to burn in his veins. Emory had removed his tie and jacket and unbuttoned his collar. His eyes were glowing with dark fire. He gazed at Jesse and slowly put his hands in his pockets.

"I would like to show you just how truly grateful I am."

All Jesse could manage in reply was a noise in the affirmative. Emory drifted forward. Jesse clutched his glass tight. Emory took the glass from his hand and set it aside. His face was close. Jesse could smell his whiskey-scented breath.

"Shall we retreat to the study?"

Jesse remembered the large sofa before the fire and nodded dumbly. Emory preceded him through. The roaring fire was the only light source in the room. It sent shadows dancing over the walls, the furniture and Emory himself. Jesse's blood rushed as Emory held out his hand with a suggestive smile.

Jesse ignored the hand and threw his arms around Emory, pressing himself against his muscled torso and kissing him. Emory opened his mouth to Jesse's searching tongue. Jesse drank in the taste, wine and moorland heather, running his hands up his back and growing painfully hard.

"You must slow down," Emory said, taking a firm hold of Jesse's arms and pushing him back. "Or you'll be spent long before I'm done with you."

Jesse fought air into his lungs. "Tell me what you're gonna do."

Emory's blue-black eyes glinted in the firelight.

"Two rules," he murmured as Jesse stood there, aching and hard, his mouth dry and longing to kiss again. "No talking. No using your hands. Break either rule," Emory said, leaning close and speaking against the hollow in Jesse's throat, "and you will be punished. Understand? You may answer."

"Yes," Jesse rasped, grappling at Emory's shirt. But Emory took him by the wrists and guided his arms back down by his sides.

"No hands, Jesse...not until I say." He straightened and looked him in the eye. "You want this, don't you? Want me?"

Jesse nodded frantically, desperate to rip the clothes from Emory's body. But he held still, not blinking, not looking away.

"Then you shall have me," Emory whispered. "It will be different to what you're used to—and it will take time. But I think it will be worth it."

Jesse nodded again, swallowing curses, then inhaled sharply as Emory unzipped his hoodie. He pushed it off Jesse's arms then leaned in to mouth his neck as he slid his hands inside Jesse's T-shirt. Jesse closed his eyes, his shoulders aching as he forced himself not to move. They were so close, and yet the only contact between them was Emory's mouth on his throat and hands running up his back.

"So warm," Emory breathed against his skin. "So fragrant. So...colorful."

He fought for control as Emory drew his T-shirt over his head and threw it aside. He trailed his fingers over Jesse's tattoos, his gaze following the path his fingers made with hunger in his eyes.

"So many stories here," he whispered. "I hope soon you'll trust me with them."

Jesse swallowed. Emory bit his earlobe. Jesse's earring clicked against his teeth. He ran his hands up Jesse's arms and down his chest. Jesse's skin rippled in the wake of the touch. His throat was painfully tight, as were his jeans. Thankfully, Emory's next move was to strip him entirely.

Jesse gasped with relief when his erection sprang free but then moaned in frustration when Emory didn't touch it. He kissed him on the mouth, sweeping his tongue against Jesse's. He inhaled as his hands skimmed Jesse's chest, belly and the front of his thighs. Jesse keened in frustration, but Emory pricked his sharp fingernails against Jesse's legs in warning.

"Patience, *liebling*," he whispered, then stepped back to unbutton his shirt.

Jesse ached to touch him. But when he finally stood before him, naked and glowing in the firelight, all Emory did was hold his hand out. Jesse took it in and allowed himself to be led around the back of the sofa. Emory backed him against it, leaned into him and kissed him. Jesse sobbed to finally have some friction against his throbbing cock but then Emory was breaking the kiss and whispering in his ear.

"Turn around." Jesse shivered with excitement and obeyed. "Hands on the back of the sofa." Jesse gripped it tight. He stared into the fire, feeling Emory's body draw close. "Don't let go. Understand?"

Jesse nodded, crushing his eyes shut. Emory kissed the back of his neck and ran his hands down his back, over his arse, around his hips. Jesse fought a groan. Emory continued his hands' slow, meandering exploration. He stepped close and Jesse felt the swelling flesh of his cock against his arse cheek. Jesse shivered. Sparking starlight began to gather under his balls.

Emory lifted Jesse's right hand from the sofa. Emory bent it back then cool, slick liquid was squeezed into his hand. Emory pressed his mouth into Jesse's hair.

"You'll have to prepare yourself," he whispered, the building heat in his voice sending sparks along Jesse's nerves. "My nails mean I can't. Make sure you do a thorough job. I'm watching."

Jesse drew in a deep breath then reached back and plunged two fingers into himself, a cry strangling in his throat.

"Slower," Emory ordered, squeezing Jesse's other wrist as he fluttered kisses over his shoulders.

Jesse nodded stiffly and eased his fingers out and into himself, swallowing groans, the pleasure already almost overwhelming.

"Here," Emory whispered, gripping the wrist of the hand half-buried inside Jesse. "I'll help." Emory guided a third of Jesse's fingers inside him. Jesse couldn't stop the choked sound that escaped him. The delicious stretch and the strength in Emory's hold was too much. Emory moved Jesse's fingers for him, in and out, so slow that Jesse wanted to scream. Emory's breathing was deep and loud in his ear. The haemophile crushed Jesse's legs against the sofa and the huge, hard cock was like steel against his arse.

Jesse swore under his breath, reaching deeper, trembling, but before he could reach release, Emory moved his hand back to the sofa. Jesse made a noise — half pleasure, half agony — then Emory was chuckling against his neck.

"Almost, my dear," he whispered. "Almost."

He then heard the click of a bottle lid and the sounds of Emory lubricating himself. He longed to watch, but the haemophile was kissing his neck, shoulders and down his spine and he was almost dizzy with it all. The fire blurred before his eyes. He felt the thick carpet under his feet, the sofa under his hands and the heat of the flames against his face. But none of it compared to the feel of Emory so close and the anticipation prickling beneath his skin.

"Permission to speak…" Jesse's voice was tight.

"Go ahead," Emory said as the sound of him lubricating himself continued.

"What about a johnny?"

Emory kissed his shoulders. "The Blood prevents us from carrying infection — or contracting it. I will fetch one, if you prefer…"

"No," Jesse said hurriedly, his legs and arms aching as he held himself rigidly. "I want to feel you…all of you."

Emory made a low noise of satisfaction and gripped Jesse's hip. There was a blunt, hot pressure against Jesse's entrance. He almost came right there but he sucked in air and fought himself back from the edge. His muscles were strung through with hot wire, but Emory didn't move.

"Now, dearest," he breathed into Jesse's ear, "I'm about to fuck you within an inch of your life. But remember the lovely Tom is only a couple of floors away, so you are not to make a sound. Understand?"

Jesse nodded frantically, pushing back against the hard cock, but Emory tightened his grip, stilling him.

"There will be one exception to the no-noise rule," Emory said. "If you want me to stop, you say so. Is that clear?"

Jesse made a pained noise in his throat, nodding again.

"I mean it, Jesse," Emory said against his temple. "You must tell me if you need me to stop, or we can't do this."

Jesse turned to look at him. Emory's cheeks were flushed. His pupils were dilated. He was so beautiful that Jesse could hardly breathe. But he made sure to hold the penetrating gaze and nodded a third time.

"I promise."

Emory's mouth turned up at the corners. He pressed his lips to Jesse's, then dusted kisses over his cheek and down to his throat. He clenched Jesse's hip hard and pushed forward.

Jesse's entire world spun away into a glittering veil of sensation. Emory was huge. He moved slowly, stretching Jesse inch by agonizing inch, expanding him to the point of pain. Needles of quicksilver flashed up Jesse's spine and down his legs. The burn was so delicious that he wanted to pant and yell. But he gripped the sofa and choked the noises down.

It felt like it took an eternity, but finally, Emory was fully sheathed. His chest swelled against Jesse's back with each breath. The exhalations poured over Jesse's skin like heated spring water.

Emory held himself there, so big and so deep inside Jesse that he wasn't sure he'd ever walk again but didn't care. The powerful muscles in Emory's legs were bunched, and the hard abdomen quivered against the small of Jesse's back. They were so close and complete it was like they were one and the same. Ripples of flame, hotter than those in the hearth, licked through Jesse's body. For a moment, he forgot to breathe.

Then Emory was sliding back, a couple of slick, teasing inches, then slamming home again.

Jesse couldn't swallow the cry that billowed out of his throat. Emory, panting against his shoulder, squeezed his hip in warning then repeated the motion.

Jesse's groan drowned somewhere in his chest. He crushed his eyes shut, fought breath into his lungs but then Emory was thrusting again...and again. He shifted, widening his stance, bending Jesse lower. He thrust in faster, deeper. Jesse hung his head, fighting to stay quiet, fighting the flesh-searing pleasure that boiled over him.

"God, Jesse," Emory panted in his ear. "Tell me to stop..."

Jesse kept his mouth clenched shut. Emory tilted his hips higher. Jesse was lifted onto his toes. He gripped the sofa tighter. His knuckles ached. Emory grasped Jesse's other hip, adjusted his stance, then banged into him, so hard and so deep that pleasure exploded through Jesse like a bomb. It blinded him, deafening him, filled him so completely that he couldn't tell if he'd really come or if this was still just the best build up he'd ever had.

Time became unreal. He could feel the points of pain where Emory's fingernails dug into his flesh. All this registered beyond the flickering shell of ecstasy that swelled to the point of unmanning him. Then, when he began to feel like he couldn't possibly take any more, Emory groaned deep in his barrel-like chest, changed his angle and grasped Jesse's cock.

Jesse came so hard he could no longer see, hear or think. All there was was the feeling — drowning, cartwheeling through a blinding inferno laced with sparks of pain that consumed him.

Chapter Twelve

Jesse was jerked awake from a very deep and dreamless sleep, unsure what had woken him. He didn't remember coming to bed. His arse burned. Every muscle was aching. But he felt amazing. Even thinking about the night before was making him hard again. He turned over, cursing the empty bed next to him. But then the sound of his phone buzzing made him sit up.

That was when he caught sight of the clock on the wall. It was almost eleven.

He scrambled out of bed, reaching for whatever clothes first came to hand. His phone was still buzzing as he laced his trainers. There were four missed calls and increasingly furious messages from his brother.

He swore again, grabbed his coat and phone and raced from the room.

It was only as he was stumbling down the staircase that the noises that must have woken him penetrated. He moved into the hall and frowned to see the front door wide open. The house security staff raced in and out, yammering on walkie-talkies.

"Hey, what's going on?" he called.

One of the men hurried over. "Where's Greenway?"

"I dunno. What's the drama?"

But the man shoved past him and made for the stairs. Jesse went to the front door with a sinking feeling.

Blue lights flashed at the gates. Jesse could make out at least two police cars blocking the road. The sound of raised voices reached him as another security man pushed past him to join the throng around the gate.

Every wonderful feeling that had filled Jesse upon waking swept away like fog on the wind.

"Jesse?"

Jesse turned. Tom was standing in the hall, a mug in his hand and a confused frown on his face. "What's going on?"

Jesse couldn't find words so just gestured outside. Tom came forward. His frown deepened as he took in the scene at the gate. "Shit. What's happened?"

Jesse opened his mouth, still not sure what he was going to say, then a small, high voice from behind said, "Uncle Jesse?"

They both turned. Dimity stood at the top of the stairs in a pair of unicorn pajamas with Bella Bunny clutched in her arms. Her ringlets were sleep-rumpled, and her face was tight with fear.

"Uncle Jesse? Is something happening?"

"*Dimity*?" Tom's eyes widened.

The girl's gaze moved from Jesse to Tom and her face brightened. "Mr. Tom," she chirped, hurrying down the stairs. "It's really you!"

"It's really me, Miss Dimity," he said with a shaky smile, shooting a confused look at Jesse. "I didn't know you were here."

"Uncle Jesse brought me home last night," she said with a grin. "We had Christmas in the library."

"*Uncle* Jesse?" Tom said, staring at Jesse again.

The commotion at the gate increased in volume. Dimity stood on tiptoes, trying to see. Jesse moved her away from the door.

"Look, sweetie," he said, trying to keep his voice steady. "You had a real late night. Why don't you go back to bed, huh?"

"I'm not tired," Dimity said, tugging against Jesse's hold. "What's happening?"

Greenway strode out of the staff door in jeans and a Christmas jumper, her grim expression a stark contrast to her clothing. She was followed by several harried-looking security staff.

"Good morning, gentlemen. Miss Dimity. Merry Christmas."

"Merry Christmas, Kate," Dimity said with the beginnings of a smile.

"Might I suggest Miss Dimity retire to her room?" Greenway said. "I have a small situation to deal with."

"*What* situation?" Dimity demanded.

"Nothing that concerns you, miss," Greenway said, ushering to the security guards ahead of her. "Back to your room now, like I say."

She shut the door behind her. Tom stood staring at the door then down at Dimity.

"What did Santa bring you, Mr. Tom?" Dimity said brightly.

"I haven't opened my presents yet, miss. Why don't we get you back to your room like Greenway said?"

"Fine," Dimity said sulkily, then grinned at Jesse. "You'll take me, right, Uncle Jesse?"

"Uh," Jesse met Tom's blank look and rubbed his neck. "I don't know where it is, honey."

Dimity giggled. "Silly you. I'll show you."

Dimity took them upstairs. Tom was close on Jesse's heels. She led them along the corridor of the first floor.

"You said these were guest rooms," Jesse muttered.

"Some of them are," Tom replied in a low voice. "But along here are the family rooms."

"*Family* rooms?" Jesse frowned but then Dimity opened a door and dragged Jesse inside.

The room was decorated in all shades of blue. The bed was piled high with quilts in indigo and azure. There were matching drapes over the window. Soft toys were arranged on a dressing table in the corner. A child's painting of a unicorn was framed on the wall over the chest of drawers. Against the opposite wall was a bookcase stuffed with books. Her easel and art supplies were set up next to the bed, and she went straight to them, explaining them eagerly to Tom.

"And no pink in sight," Jesse observed.

Dimity folded her arms. "I don't like pink. Aunt Helena liked pink."

"Fair enough," Jesse said as Tom hovered in the doorway. "Look, love. I have a few things to sort. Will you promise to stay here? Maybe do some painting?"

"Sure, I guess," Dimity said, scraping her slipper over the carpet. "Are those policemen here to take me back?" she then asked, very quietly.

"Course not," Jesse said, dredging up a smile.

"But what if they do?"

"I've made this place very, very safe," Jesse said, patting her arm. "Tell you what... Why don't I take you around the gardens later? Show you just how safe it is?" A small smile brightened her face, and she nodded. Jesse patted her cheek. "I'll see you later then, yeah?"

"Yeah," she said with a brighter smile. "And we'll *both* see Daddy later, right? Once it's dark."

Jesse swallowed. "I'm sure we will."

"Jesse," Tom said. Jesse managed a reassuring smile for Dimity then followed him out into the hall.

"What the hell?" Tom said as soon as the door was shut. "Dimity's *here*?"

"You *knew* about her?"

"Of course I knew," Tom said in a harsh whisper. "How does *she* know *you*?" Jesse stared at him, wondering where to start. Tom took in his expression and waved his hand impatiently. "Forget that for now. Just tell me, what is she *doing* here? The custody battle can't be over. We'd've known."

"Why was she a secret, huh?" Jesse asked. "Why did no one tell me about her?"

"Because it's a delicate situation."

"Not as delicate as me breaking into the fucking mayor's house to bust her out."

Tom's eyes widened. "You did *what*?"

"He wanted me to," Jess said, running his hands through his hair. "Said legally that Helena woman had no right to have her."

"Emory *asked* you to steal Dimity back?"

Jesse dropped his hands with a sigh. "Yes."

"Jesus." Tom put a hand to his head.

"This is bad, isn't it?"

"I don't know," Tom said carefully. "It wasn't clever, that's for sure. And he's usually clever."

"Was he right?" Jesse asked quietly. "When he said Helena wasn't supposed to have Dimity in the first place?"

"Technically," Tom said, gesturing wearily. "But now he's essentially kidnapped her—"

"But he's her legal guardian," Jesse said, not unaware they were having the same argument he and Emory had already had. "So it's not kidnapping. Right?"

"Well, I just hope Darragh can prove that," Tom said, looking worried. "Otherwise, Emory just hammered a nail into the coffin of his custody case."

"You mean I have."

Tom examined for a moment then sighed. "You were just doing what he asked you to do. Hey…" His expression hardened. "Was this why he hired you?"

Jesse winced and looked at the floor. "To begin with, yeah. But it's more than that now."

"More?" Tom paled. He stared at Jesse for a long moment and the silence grew loaded around them. When he spoke again it was in a hoarse whisper. "Jesse, are you two…?"

Jesse felt like the floor had disappeared from under him. "I don't know what you want me to say."

Tom blinked. Several questions flickered through his eyes then back out again.

"He can hurt you, you know—and I mean *really* hurt you."

"I'm tougher than I look."

"That's not what I mean," Tom said softly. "He's lived for hundreds of years, been with who knows how many people—men and women, human and, well…not."

Jesse's skin prickled. "What's your point?"

"The point is..." Tom raised his hands, checked himself and lowered them again. "Look... I know you're special, Jesse. If we were able to make it work, I'd spend every day showing you that."

Jesse's throat ached. "There's a 'but', coming, right?"

Tom sighed. "Do you really think any human can ever be special enough for one of *them*?"

"What about Alec MacCarthy and Terje Kristiansen, huh?"

Tom's face tightened. "I still haven't figured that one out. But..." Tom went on gently. "It's a lot of pressure. Don't you think?"

Jesse stared at him. "Is this what you tell yourself? Why you won't go near another haemophile? Even though you're clearly nuts about that lawyer?"

Tom blinked. "Darragh?"

"Come on, mate. It's clear as day."

Tom was silent for a moment. His face was grave. "I won't date a haemophile because I'm addicted to getting bitten. That's the beginning and end of that story."

Guilt was sharp in Jesse's gut. "I'm sorry."

Tom's expression softened. "Don't be sorry, Jesse. Just trust me on this. It's simply too easy to get hurt."

"Emory understands me," Jesse insisted. "He knows what I need."

"Do you even know what that is yourself?"

"I gotta go," he said, pushing past Tom. "I'm late."

"Late for what?"

"Christmas with my nephew," he said, hurrying down the stairs. He reached the bottom just as Greenway came back in. Her face was flushed, and her mouth set in hard lines.

"Greenway?" Jesse said, joining her. "What's going on?"

"The situation is under control," she said. "The police had no warrant, as I suspected. They can't enter the grounds."

"But they're still here," Jesse said, peering out at blue lights flashing at the gate.

"They're camping out in hope someone leaves who they can then question," Greenway said, glancing between Jesse and Tom. "I suggest you gentlemen get comfortable."

Greenway swept away, and Jesse cursed.

"The delivery entrance then...?"

"Police will have that blocked, too," Tom said.

Jesse swore again. "If I miss today, I'm screwed. Ant'll not let me see Olly ever again."

Tom sighed. He stared at the wall, his mouth twisting.

"Do you know a way?" Jesse asked. "Tom, please."

"I guess we could wheel my bike over the moor? Get it onto the back road?"

Jesse's heart lifted. "You'd do that?"

Tom's smile was tentative. "Life or death, is it?"

"Life or death...definitely."

"You need to be back to take Dimity around the grounds later. You promised."

"I will, I swear."

His eyes warmed. "Fine."

"Thanks, man. Thanks so much. I owe you."

"I'd say you do," he said. "Come on."

They went out to the garages, keeping out of sight of the gates. They wheeled Tom's bike awkwardly down the lawns and through the moor gate. There were some fraught moments getting it over the bumpy moorland to the road, but finally, Jesse climbed on behind him and they were zooming toward the city.

Jesse fought guilt as he climbed off outside his brother's house, thanking Tom again.

"I'll come back at about four, shall I?"

Jesse hesitated. "Do you want to come in?" He found he'd asked the question before he'd fully decided to.

Tom lifted his eyebrows. "I haven't been invited."

"You've done so much. The least I can do is make sure you get fed."

"Are you sure your brother won't mind?"

"Let me handle Ant," Jesse said. "Come and have some bloody Christmas dinner."

The door opened before they reached it and out sped Oliver. He cried Jesse's name and grabbed his hand, bouncing.

"Hey, buddy," he said. "Sorry I'm late. Merry Christmas."

"I knew you'd come," Oliver beamed at him. "Dad said you wouldn't, but I knew you would."

"So you made it."

Jesse looked up. Anton stood in the door holding a beer and wearing an expression somewhere between fondness and annoyance.

"Better late than never, right?"

"I'll put that on your gravestone, little brother," Anton said. His gaze slid to Tom, and he raised his eyebrows.

"This is Tom," Jesse said. Oliver's smile widened and his brother's turned knowing. "Is he okay to join us?"

"You've got a boyfriend, Uncle Jesse?" Oliver grinned.

Tom colored rather fetchingly, and Jesse fought a blush of his own. "Tom's a friend, mate. Tom, this is my nephew...Olly."

"Pleased to meet you, Olly."

"You guys are gonna have kids, right? So I can have a cousin?"

"Jesus, Olly," Jesse said.

"How about you let them come in for a bit before planning their lives out, lad?" Anton's eyes were amused.

"This way," Oliver said, running for the door. "I gotta show you my new train set, Jesse. It's amazing."

"Thanks, Ant," Jesse said as he reached the door. "I appreciate it."

"The more the merrier," Anton said, assessing Tom.

"How do you do?" Tom said with a warm smile, shaking Anton's hand.

"Wow. Posh," Anton grinned. "Not too posh for beer before lunch, I hope?"

"I should hope not," Tom said and sent a small smile Jesse's way. Anton took their coats and directed them to the sofa by the electric fire. Oliver commenced showing Jesse all his presents. Anton pressed beer into their hands, and Sareena darted to and from the kitchen, vocally ecstatic to have another guest to help with all the food.

Tom laughed easily with Anton, discussed cooking and books with Sareena and trains and motorbikes with Oliver. When they sat down to lunch, Jesse had the uncanny feeling that Tom was already more a part of the family than he was.

* * * *

The meal was cleared, champagne was poured and the sun, visible through the patio doors, began creeping toward the horizon.

"Do you really have to go?" Oliver said as Jesse and Tom put on their coats.

"Now, Oliver," Anton said. His face was slightly ruddy with drink as he beamed at Jesse. "I'm sure these guys have their own plans for the evening."

"Ant," Sareena scolded but she was smiling with her hands on Oliver's shoulders. "It was lovely to meet you, Tom."

"And you, Mrs. Truelove."

"Sareena, please. Come again, won't you?"

"That would be nice, but rather up to Jesse." Jesse opened his mouth without knowing what would come out of it, but then Tom took his hand. "Come on. We should get back."

"Right," Jesse said, nodding a little too quickly. "Right."

They didn't speak as they climbed back onto the bike. Sunset blushed the sky with gold as they wheeled the bike back into the garage at Oswald House.

"Come on," Tom said quietly, not meeting his eye. "Dimity will be waiting for you to take her on that walk."

"Thanks for today," Jesse said as they made their way back to the house. "I mean it. It meant a lot. Kept my brother from quizzing me about everything at the very least."

"Hey, what are friends for?"

Guilt lanced in Jesse's chest.

Dimity sat on the stairs. She had her chin in her hand and a sulky look on her face. Jesse frowned as he took in her riding coat, aquamarine jodhpurs and the tiny whip in her hand. The sulky look vanished when she spotted him. She sprang to her feet.

"There you are," she said, putting her hands on her hips. "You're very late."

"Sorry, love," Jesse said, ignoring the amused look on Tom's face. "I was with Olly. Remember Olly?"

Her face brightened. "Is he here?"

"Sorry, sweetie…no."

"Oh." Her face fell but then she squared her shoulders and gestured at the door. "Never mind. It's time for our walk, like you promised."

"Why are you dressed like that?" he asked warily.

"I'm riding Ruby. Hector's saddling a horse the right size for you, too. You have a helmet, right?"

"Uh…what?"

"Don't worry, I'm sure Hector has one for you."

"Who the hell is Hector?"

"The groom, silly. Now come on."

Tom was grinning openly now. He raised a hand. "Happy Christmas, Jesse. See you tomorrow."

"Wait…"

"Come on, Uncle Jesse," Dimity said, grabbing his hand. "I want to be back when Daddy gets up."

Jesse fought nervousness as Dimity led him to the stables.

"I don't really do horses," he said.

"Don't worry. Thor's gentle. And Ruby'll lead the way."

"It's called *Thor*?"

"Good evening, Miss Dimity." A round man in a flat cap and worn overcoat stepped out of a door at the end of the stable block. He was leading a caramel-colored pony. "Ruby is ready and waiting for you. Just go slow with her. You're both new to these grounds."

"I will, Hector. Is Thor ready, too?"

"He is, miss. Here…" He made a stirrup with his gloved hands and boosted Dimity up onto the pony then disappeared back inside the stable. Jesse stood, stiff and awkward, as Dimity's pony nuzzled his coat. The groom reappeared leading a beast that, to Jesse, looked the size of an elephant.

"You know what, mate," Jesse said, raising his hands. "I think I'll pass."

"Oh, Thor's a softy," the groom said, stroking the horse's glossy neck. "All you gotta do is sit on him."

Jesse winced, the burn in his arse from the night before still pulsing when he moved. "Yeah, I don't think so."

"Oh, *please*, Uncle Jesse," Dimity pleaded. "I haven't seen Ruby in so, so long. And if you're not riding, you won't keep up."

Jesse let out a sigh. "Fine. Got a helmet, mate?"

Soon Jesse was helmeted and flushing furiously as the groom assisted him, flailing, onto the back of the animal.

"Jesus, fuck," he muttered, looking down at the ground seeming all too far away.

Dimity giggled, and the groom gave him an exasperated look.

"Sorry," Jesse muttered, grabbing the reins tight. "Come on. Let's get this over with."

Dimity kicked her pony on and, thankfully, Jesse's beast seemed happy to plod along in her wake. He clung on grimly but then as they left the stable yard and stepped out onto the lawns, he began to get a feel for the rhythm and relaxed a little.

"So no one can get in, right, Uncle Jesse?" Dimity said as they turned toward the boundary wall.

"That's right," Jesse said, nodding toward the motion sensors, the cameras and the security man doing a patrol. "We've got it all set up here. You're safe, see?"

"And Daddy's safe, too?" Her face was grave. "In Vienna, people tried to break in a few times. Daddy said they wanted pictures." She shook her head. "Why are people so weird?"

"No one's getting in, love," he said, because he couldn't for the life of him think of how to answer that question. "I've made sure of that."

They crested a rise, and the delivery entrance came in sight. A police car was visible through the iron bars. Jesse jerked the bridle of his horse.

"Let's head back toward the gardens," he said but Dimity stopped to look. Jesse heard the distant sounds of car doors opening then uniformed figures appeared at the gate. "Dimity. The other way."

Dimity obeyed, steering her pony around and kicking it into a trot. Jesse swore, clinging to Thor's mane and cursing with every jerk until Dimity slowed to a walk again.

"They want to take me back to Aunt Helena, don't they?" she asked quietly.

"Yes," Jesse said, easing his grip. "But they won't get to."

"Promise?"

"They'd have to go through your dad first," he said grimly. He managed a crooked smile for her. "That's not gonna happen, right?"

She smiled and some of the care fell from her face. Shadows lengthened between the trees, and the fairy lights started to wink to life.

"It's so pretty," Dimity said, pulling on her reins so Ruby ambled to a stop. "This is where Daddy was born, you know."

"Yeah. I'd heard that."

"His family are from Saxony." She sent Jesse a proud smile. "That's in Germany. But he lived here, on this very spot, hundreds of years ago." She looked around her with a dreamy look in her eyes. "I'd like to grow up here, I think."

"Yeah?"

She nodded then grimaced. "I just wish there didn't have to be guards and stuff."

"Me, too, love," Jesse said. "Even though I'd be out of a job."

Dimity sent him a curious look. "Do you and Daddy love each other?"

Jesse opened and closed his mouth a few times.

"Uncle Jesse? I saw him kiss you."

"He's my boss. So, it's not... I mean —"

"I've also seen the way you look at him — and the way he looks at you, too. He doesn't look at the other people who work here like that."

Jesse again groped for words. "We've, uh... Well, we've not known each other that long, love."

"Why does that matter?"

"Well, we're not... I mean." He shook his head. "I'm human. He's not."

"I'm human, too, and I love him. So why not you?"

"It's a bit of a complicated question."

"No, it's not. I love my daddy, and I love you, too. It just makes sense that you should love each other as well. Then that's all of us."

Jesse blinked. "You love me?"

"Of course I do. You rescued me — twice."

Jesse's pulse was fluttering in his wrists. He blamed the icy wind for the burn in his cheeks.

"Hey, it's nearly dark," he said. "Let's get back. Your dad'll want to see you."

Dimity *hmphed* and turned her pony's head back toward the stables. "Fine…if you're really not going to answer my question. But I won't forget."

Chapter Thirteen

By the time they were back in the warmth of the house, Jesse had sore legs and the chafe in his arse was worse than ever. But the only thing that mattered was a strange flutter in his chest.

Emory was in one of the sitting rooms. There was a laptop open on the coffee table and papers and files strewn around him. Darragh Kelly was in the chair next to him. They were conversing in low tones but stopped as Jesse and Dimity entered. Kelly said something in a low voice, nodded to Emory and withdrew. Dimity raced across the room. Emory got to his feet, swept her into his arms and kissed her curls, answering all her questions about the house, how he slept and listening intently as she told him about their ride.

Emory looked at Jesse and raised an eyebrow. "A ride?"

Jesse winced. "On some bloody animal named Thor."

Emory gave him a knowing smile then looked back at his daughter. "So you had a good Christmas, then?"

"Best Christmas *ever*, Daddy," she said, flinging her arms in the air. "Can we have another tomorrow?"

"Well, I'm not sure if Father Christmas is free to visit every day," he said, tapping her nose. "But I promise I will make every day here so special it will feel like Christmas."

She grinned. "And once Christmas is over, it's almost time for my birthday."

"That's right. Just seventeen sleeps until January tenth."

"Can I stay off school this time?"

"Yes, darling. You're off school until Aunt Helena and I have decided which school you're going to. That'll take a little while yet."

Her face clouded. "Do I have to go back to Switzerland?"

"No," Emory said firmly. "Whatever happens, you won't be going back to boarding school. I promise."

She flung her arms around his neck. Emory met Jesse's eyes over her shoulder then set her on the floor. "Okay, darling, it's your supper time. They're preparing it in the kitchen. You run along and eat, then after dinner you can bring that puzzle down, okay?"

"Yay," she cried. "Can we do it here, together?"

"We can," Emory said. "Ah, Joanna…"

"Evening, sir. Miss Dimity." A woman Jesse recognized from around the house had appeared in the doorway, holding out her hand. "Your supper's ready, miss."

Dimity continued chattering as she was led away.

"Helena sent her to boarding school?" Jesse shook his head. "Poor kid."

"The *Collége Monta Rhina* is one of the finest schools in the whole world," Emory said levelly. "Helena had high hopes for Dimity's future. I can't help but approve of that. But I agree with you. I think she would be happier coming home each night, even if that home isn't here." His eyes had darkened, but he blinked and the look was gone. "Are you hungry, too? I could ask them to bring some food through."

"No, I had a big lunch, thanks…" He glanced around the room, Dimity's question still buzzing in his brain, making it hard to look Emory in the face. "You know cops are at the gates, right?"

"Yes, I know."

"And you're not worried?"

"Darragh is handling it."

Jesse nodded, sliding his hands into his pockets and staring at the floor, trying and failing not to think of Emory's hands on his body the night before.

"I hope you had a good Christmas, too."

Jesse raised his eyes. Emory was watching him with an unreadable expression. "Yeah…" Jesse fumbled, bit his thumbnail and tried again. "It was great…really great. Last night, I mean."

A corner of a smile turned up Emory's mouth. "I thought so, too."

"I, uh…" Jesse ran a hand over his hair. "I went to see my brother's family today, for lunch."

"That sounds nice."

"I took Tom." Emory didn't answer. It seemed he was even more motionless than usual. "It wasn't, you know…" Emory still didn't speak. "He got me out past the police" — Jesse gestured awkwardly — "and gave me a lift. I couldn't just leave him out in the street."

"Of course not," Emory said, sitting and starting to gather papers.

Jesse hesitated. "Are you mad?"

"Should I be?"

"I dunno." Jesse shrugged. "It wasn't a date or anything. But I think he still likes me."

"Of course he does." Emory smiled. "He's only human."

Jesse made an impatient noise. "You're gonna have to help me out here, Emory. What are we doing? Just fucking? 'Cause if so…" He trailed off, unable to shape his own thoughts let alone find words for them.

"That's not all it is to me, Jesse," Emory replied. "But you need to remember being with me is not like what being with a human would be."

"I know that, don't I? That's why it's so fucking good." He clamped his mouth shut.

Emory's expression didn't change but his eyes glinted. "I know you're conflicted."

"I'm not."

"Jesse," Emory interrupted softly, holding his gaze. "I'm not mad. But let's not hurt Tom. He's been through enough."

Jesse scuffed his foot on the rug. "So this…between us?" He swallowed. "Not just sex, huh?"

"Not to me," Emory said quietly after a pause. He stood and drifted close. His eyes locked on Jesse and stayed there. "You make me feel things I haven't for a long time. I like feeling connected to someone. I think I can have that with you. I think our needs are similar." His face softened when he took in Jesse's expression. "But I'm happy for this to be whatever you need it to be."

"I need sex," Jesse stated. "Good sex. Sex that makes me feel things. I need that in my life, Emory, and I think you can give me that. But..." He held the penetrating gaze, taking a breath, letting it out slowly. "But I still work for you. That's not awkward?"

"Is it awkward for you?"

Jesse hesitated then shook his head. "I want to keep you safe...and Dimity, too."

Emory kissed his mouth. Jesse sighed, slid his arms around him and held on tight, taking the kiss deep into himself and feeling himself strengthen.

Emory broke away, pressed a kiss to Jesse's forehead and stepped to the door. "Later, *liebling*. I have some business to attend to"—he opened the door—"but perhaps you could join Dimity and me for the puzzle?"

Jesse searched his face then dropped his gaze. "You should have her to yourself for a bit. I need to check the CCTV to make sure the coppers aren't trying anything dodgy."

"I appreciate that," Emory said. "I'll message you when it's her bedtime. Perhaps you could help me put her to bed?"

Jesse smiled. "Sure. I could do that."

"Lovely." His lips curved. "Happy Christmas, Jesse."

Jesse relieved the cover security engineer and sank himself into a full system review to avoid overthinking the rollercoaster that had been that day. All the systems were secure and all cameras online. There were still two police cars at the front gate and one at the delivery entrance. He tried to ignore the discomfort oiling over his skin and made himself focus on the work.

Some time later, a message pinged into his phone.

Putting Dimity to bed.

The nanny, Joanna, was standing outside Dimity's bedroom, gazing through the door fondly. She smiled at Jesse as he approached and withdrew to the room next door.

Emory was in the small chair by the bed. His large body dwarfed both pieces of furniture. He was reading a story in a low, rhythmic voice. Dimity was curled in the quilts with her eyes half-closed. The sight sent something soft and delicate coiling through Jesse's chest. Emory beckoned, not missing a beat in the story. Jesse stepped inside. Dimity rolled her head to look at him, smiling just as Emory finished and closed the book.

"Night-night, darling," he whispered, kissing Dimity's forehead.

"Night, Daddy," she mumbled, then reached for Jesse. Emory nodded encouragingly. Jesse moved to the bed a little stiffly then bent and let her put her arms around his neck. He hugged her back. She smelled like chocolate milk and strawberry shampoo.

"Night-night, love."

"G'night, Uncle Jesse."

She was asleep by the time they'd turned the light out.

"She's a good kid," Jesse said.

"Yes, she is." Emory gestured down the hall. "I'd like to show you something."

Emory took them to a door at the very end of the corridor and opened it. "The master bedroom," he said.

Jesse stared. The carpet was cream. Floor-to-ceiling windows looked out over the starlit grounds and the snowbound moor beyond, sparkling under the moonlight. A wood-framed bed stood against the opposite wall. Emerald drapes framed the carved headboard. Lamps stood on wooden bed stands, bathing the room in a low light. Prints of forested mountains decorated the walls.

"Whose is it?"

"It would be my room," Emory said, looking around a little wistfully, "if I were a human."

"You built yourself a master bedroom you're never gonna use?" Jesse asked, moving farther into the room to gawp at the white-marble en suite.

Emory's smile turned suggestive. "I'm never going to *sleep* in it. That's not the same as not using it."

Jesse's mouth dried. Emory held out his hand. Jesse took it, and Emory pulled him close. They kissed. Jesse's blood was instantly on fire. His breathing caught in his throat. His pulse pounded in his temples and groin. But he made himself go slow, sliding his tongue against Emory's, allowing his taste and scent to anchor him. Emory slid his hands to Jesse's lower back, drawing him close. Jesse ran his hands up Emory's arms and shoved his jacket off his shoulders.

Emory allowed Jesse to undress him. Jesse made himself take his time, very aware of his own building need but also of the lack of answering hardness in the front of Emory's trousers. He sank himself into the low noises his lover made as he unbuttoned his shirt and kissed the skin as it was revealed.

"Jesse," Emory breathed as Jesse stripped off his shirt and kissed his chest, licking his nipple. Emory inhaled.

"Tell me what you want," Jesse murmured, moving across to the other nipple as he ran his hand down

Emory's hard abdomen. "You did what I wanted last night. Tell me what you want me to do tonight."

Emory chuckled softly, rid Jesse of his shirt then captured his mouth.

"I want you to experience dizzying pleasure," Emory said into the kiss as they unfastened their belts. "So hot and strong you forget everything else, so powerful you almost know what it's like for me when we're together."

Jesse moaned against Emory's lips. Emory drew him toward the bed. He lay down and pulled Jesse on top. Their kiss grew hungrier, wetter, their teeth and tongues clashing. Jesse thrust his rigid cock against Emory's thigh while reaching between them to grasp Emory's with both hands.

Emory rumbled low in his chest as Jesse began to stroke him.

"How do I do that to you, Jesse?" he whispered as he ran his hands through Jesse's hair, tilting his head to push his tongue deeper. "Tell me how best to make you feel that way."

"You already know," Jesse breathed. Emory hardened in his hands. Jesse trembled to remember the sensation of the huge cock inside him.

"Not good enough," Emory growled and rolled over, pinning Jesse to the bed. Jesse arched his neck, whimpering as Emory nipped and licked at the tender skin. "You need more. What?" He ran his hands down Jesse's sides to grasp his ass. "More discipline?" He squeezed and Jesse moaned.

"Fuck, yeah," Jesse said, still beating Emory's cock lazily, every inch of his skin alight. "Make me beg for it."

Emory smiled against his sternum. "I believe that can be arranged."

Emory left the bed. Jesse made a noise of protest. But then went very still as he watched his lover produce a bottle of lubricant, a tapered plug and a length of velvet rope from the nightstand. He held up the rope. His lips were parted and his breathing heavy. His sharp teeth glinted in the low light. His blue-black eyes burned like molten metal. Jesse clung to the covers.

"How about this?" Jesse could only nod dumbly. Emory still didn't move. "You're certain?"

"Hell yes, I'm certain."

Emory studied his face a moment then smiled. "Your wish is my command, *liebling*."

He kissed Jesse hard, the kiss both possessive and commanding, as he ran his hands down Jesse's arms, took hold of his wrists and drew them over his head. Jesse whimpered as the soft rope twined around his wrists then pulled tight. Emory moved up the bed to fasten the rope to the headboard.

Jesse's blood sang. The stretch in his shoulders was divine. The sight of Emory kneeling above him with arousal darkening his eyes as he looked Jesse up and down was like fire under his skin.

"Just when I thought you couldn't get more appetizing." Emory grinned, again showing teeth. A delectable frisson of fear flickered through the heat in Jesse's chest. Then Emory's face turned serious. "We need a word."

"What?"

"A safeword."

"Seriously, I can take anything."

Emory's face was set. "I won't be part of your self-punishment, Jesse. *Ever*."

Jesse scowled, desire dampening. "You think that's what this is?" he snapped. "That I want to punish myself? For fucking *what*?"

"I don't know you well enough yet to answer that question."

"Can't I just like it this way?" Jesse exclaimed, yanking at the rope. "Can't it just be about fun?"

"I'm never going to ask you to explain what you like or why," Emory said softly, leaning down so his face was above Jesse's. "But I do insist on a safeword."

"Fine," Jesse grated, skin burning with frustration. "'Shambles'. Let's use 'Shambles'."

Emory smiled softly. "Like the street?"

Jesse nodded. "It's where I first saw the poster for your Christmas light switch-on. Now, can you please —?"

Emory thrust his tongue deep into his mouth. Jesse whimpered but Emory kept the contact exclusively to mouths. He trailed his tongue up Jesse's jaw, then down his neck. Jesse swore under his breath. Emory rasped his fingernails up Jesse's ribs as he kissed his way down Jesse's chest. Jesse swore again, louder.

"You'll be pleased to hear," Emory said, dragging his fingernails over Jesse's hip as he fluttered kisses around Jesse's nipple, "that this room is soundproofed."

"Thank *fuck*," Jesse cried when Emory took his nipple bar between his teeth. His spine curled. His cock twitched. Emory traced the text *Fade Away* etched across Jesse's chest with his finger, his mouth following in its wake. Jesse cursed and panted, and Emory moved on to the roses that wound over his ribs, following every line with his fingers and mouth, lighting fires as he went.

"Jesus, Emory," he panted. "Touch me already."

"When I'm ready," Emory murmured against his belly, licking the swallows inked around his navel. "I'm enjoying the taste of these tattoos too much."

Jesse's breathing hitched. His skin tightened, and his cock cried out for attention. "You can taste them?"

"Yes," Emory murmured, grasping Jesse's hips and shifting to lie between Jesse's legs. "I can." He ran his tongue down Jesse's belly and grasped his thighs.

"Fuck, Emory... *Please*."

Emory hovered over Jesse's trembling cock. He met Jesse's eyes and grinned. "I'm not sure I believed your desperation there, dearest."

"Fuck. *Please*."

Emory grinned and squeezed his thighs again. Jesse was just opening his mouth to beg again when Emory took him all the way into his throat.

Jesse came, straining against the rope and crying out, long and loud. Liquid fire poured out of him and stars pinwheeled behind his eyelids.

His vision hadn't unblurred before Emory climbed up the bed to kiss him, slow and deep. Jesse tasted himself on the haemophile's tongue and shivered with a slow fire pulsing in his veins. He jerked when the slick tip of a lubricated plug pressed against his entrance.

"I hope you're not done," Emory whispered, "because I'm only just starting."

"God, Emory..."

"God is making an early appearance tonight, I see." He nipped Jesse's bottom lip and rocked the plug against his entrance, teasing. "I'm going to prepare you slowly. I hope you're ready to be patient."

"Fuck, Emory," he panted, nodding. "Yes."

"A convincing performance," he said, biting Jesse's ear, "but I think we can do better."

Emory slid the end of the plug in. Jesse's breath hitched. Emory stilled.

"All right, dearest? Not too sore?"

Jesse shook his head. "No, all good. All, ah..." Words escaped Jesse as Emory pushed the plug deeper. "My Christ," Jesse breathed, trying to push back. "More."

Emory drew the plug out. Jesse swore and Emory smiled against his neck then pushed it all the way in. Jesse cried out and flung his head back. His sated cock began to throb.

"There?" Emory said, rolling the plug inside him. Jesse yelled out some nonsense he didn't even hear as sparks flickering across his vision. "Good to know," Emory said, rolling it again and pushing deeper, stretching and probing. Jesse swore and cursed as his body trembled and gave way to the toy. The invasion burned, delicious and fulfilling. Jesse panted, blood again pooling in his groin, then Emory withdrew the toy. Jesse whined in protest.

"Oh, it's not over," Emory said huskily in his ear, lying between Jesse's legs. "Are we ready?"

"Yes," Jesse begged. "Emory, please."

"All in good time," Emory whispered against his mouth. "I was quite rough with you last night," he said, rubbing the tip of his swollen cock against Jesse's entrance, making him jerk against the ropes. "So we can stop here...or we can go slow."

"I want it hard," he said through clenched teeth.

Emory shook his head, running his hand down Jesse's thigh and tucking his fingers under his knee. "Not on the list of options, Jesse."

"Fuck," he swore as Emory crooked his knee and moved his leg outward, thrusting lazily against him.

Jesse's desire spiked. His oversensitive cock pulsed. "Go slow then."

"Mmm." Emory nuzzled the hollow under his jaw. Then, so slow Jesse almost screamed, Emory pushed the head of his cock inside. Blooms of pain radiated up Jesse's body. He sucked air between his teeth. Emory held still, but Jesse could feel the tension in his body, the hot breaths against his neck.

"Shambles?" Emory's voice was husky.

Jesse shook his head, let out a long breath, drew another and made himself relax. "I'm good."

Emory pushed farther in, and Jesse groaned, loud. The stretch was both amazing and frightening in its intensity. He'd never been so full in his life, not even the night before. Face-to-face it was like Emory was reaching parts of Jesse he didn't even know he had.

It must have taken several minutes for him to slide fully in. He held himself there, panting against Jesse's skin. Then he raised his head and looked into Jesse's face. His pale skin was ruddy. His red lips were parted and wet. His eyes burned like boiling water.

"Jesse," he breathed, and his voice sounded different—raw, dangerous. "My God…"

"Move, please," Jesse panted.

Emory plundered Jesse's mouth with his tongue and pulled out halfway. Jesse cried into his mouth then Emory slid back in again, slow as ocean ice. Jesse made more noises, begging without words. Emory withdrew, farther this time, then pressed back in again—and again, and again. He never gained speed, but with each slow thrust, he lit a deeper, darker fire in Jesse's body.

Jesse's cock was hard again. His skin was burning. He drew in desperate breaths between Emory's deep, searching kisses and wondered if his body really could take this without imploding.

Emory broke the kiss with a growl and pressed his forehead to Jesse's as he rocked slowly in again. "I'm close," he said, his voice low and fierce. "I'm close, Jesse."

Jesse couldn't speak. He closed his eyes, opened his mouth and cried silently as the sensations swelled in him. Emory lifted Jesse's knee higher and thrust deeper. Emory's body tensed. His powerful thighs hardened, and he groaned, long and low, as liquid heat flooded Jesse's body. Finally, he grasped Jesse's aching, swollen cock.

Jesse didn't think there was anything left to allow him to orgasm again, but he did — and it was seismic. He heard himself make a noise as if from a great distance. His body melted into a rush of electricity, without beginning or end.

Jesse's focus returned as Emory untied the rope. The burn in his shoulders and arms was beautiful, complimenting the other sensations like cream in coffee. Emory kissed his shoulder, his elbow, his palm.

"Not hurting?"

Jesse shook his head, too breathless to speak. Emory moved off him and his cock slid out, leaving Jesse stretched and bereft. Jesse blinked, surprised to feel Emory trembling as he moved. He sank into the pillows and drew Jesse next to him. Jesse wrapped his arms around Emory's torso. They rested together, their faces close, sweat and stickiness cooling on their bodies as their breathing slowed.

"Thank you, Jesse."

Jesse blinked, not realizing he'd been drifting. "I think I should probably be thanking you."

Emory shook his head. His face was serious. "You have to understand…" He was quiet for so long Jesse didn't think he'd continue. When he spoke, his voice was quiet and his expression careful. "Dimity's made me feel like a parent, but you've made me feel like a man. I thought that had been lost to me forever."

Jesse shifted his head on the pillow to meet his lover's eyes. "You're not kidding, are you?" Emory shook his head. "Well, what can I say?" he continued, a little awkwardly, unsure of how to handle the emotion filling him. "Glad to be of service."

Emory chuckled, planted a kiss on his nose and let out a deep, long sigh. They lay in sleepy, contented silence for a while then Emory traced the *Fade Away* on Jesse's chest again.

"Is this a statement?" Emory murmured. "Or an instruction?"

"Whatever you want it to be."

"And the same for the *Burn Out* on your back?"

"Sure," Jesse said with a yawn. "Why not?"

Emory kissed the corner of Jesse's mouth and sat up with a sigh. "I'm very sorry, but my working day is only just starting." He stood and moved to the bathroom. He paused in the doorway. "You're welcome to sleep here."

An odd hopefulness humanized his expression. Jesse looked around the room, feeling both sorely tempted and extremely out of place.

"I've got some stuff to check in my own room."

"Okay," Emory said with a quiet smile. "Whatever's best for you." He frowned as Jesse ran his hands over the covers. "What's wrong?"

"We won't ever actually sleep together, will we?" Jesse raised his eyes. "I mean sleep. Really sleep."

Emory's face shifted. "No, dearest, we won't."

Jesse nodded.

"Is that okay?"

"It'll have to be, won't it?"

Emory didn't reply straight away. "I'm going to clean up. Would you like to join me?"

"I don't think I have a third go in me," he said, wincing slightly as he moved off the bed.

Emory held his hand out with a smile. "That can wait until tomorrow night."

They showered, rubbing lemon-scented shower gel on each other, not talking, just exploring each other in intimate silence. By the time they were dressing and leaving the room, it was all Jesse could do to stay awake long enough to return to his own. There were reports to read and searches to check on his computer, but his bed was calling. He collapsed without undressing.

Chapter Fourteen

Jesse wasn't sure where he was. The room he was in was pitch dark, but he knew there was a peach coat hung on the back of the door. He knew makeup was lined up on the dressing table in an orderly line. The blinding light of a laptop screen shone from the desk. There was a document on the screen. He didn't want to read it but he was moving forward, unable to stop. He sat. He was reading a list...a list that made his blood run cold.

He choked and sat up, gasping for air. He was in his own room at Oswald House. He was sweating. The stretch of Emory was still hot in his arse but the rest of him was cold. He rubbed his face.

His phone was buzzing somewhere in the bed. He squinted at the clock in the low light. It wasn't even seven. He grumbled and scrabbled for his phone, blinking tired eyes. By the time he found it, it had stopped ringing. There were seven missed calls from Anton.

His blood chilled all over again. It was then he noticed the warning symbols blinking on his computer monitors.

His legs were shaking as he scrambled to his desk and opened the notifications. His deep searches of Emory's name had trawled thousands of hits in the last two hours. His stomach dipped like he was on a rollercoaster. He desperately searched through tweets, posts and reaction vlogs until he found the article that had sparked it all.

It was an online article on a small local news site.

The Undying Baron Kidnaps Human Child.

It took several moments for Jesse to bring the text into focus. Dimity wasn't named and neither was Helena. But one sentence had Jesse's heart climbing into his throat.

Sources now confirm that Baron Emory Von Magnusson engineered the kidnapping of a human girl from the mayor's residence on Christmas Eve and is holding her hostage at Oswald House.

The hit counter was ticking up as he watched. The Twitter chatter had reached around the world. The membership of online haemophile hate groups had shot up and was still rising. Jesse jumped when the sounds of shouting came from outside.

He hurried to the window and jerked back the curtains. The police cars were just visible in the pre-dawn gloom. Beyond them was a crowd so dense it filled the road for several meters. Shouts and curses rose and fell. The ground inside the gate was littered with bottles, cans, bricks and broken glass. Jesse watched, horrified, as someone tried to scale the wall, only to be pushed back by the joint efforts of the police and Oswald House's own security.

A frantic knock on his door then Tom came in without waiting for an answer. His hair was rumpled, and he was hurriedly fastening his jeans.

"We have a situation."

"No shit," Jesse said and gestured for Tom to lead the way, hurrying along in his wake and trying not to limp. "How did they find out about Dimity?" he said as they reached the ground floor.

"One of Helena's scumbag lawyers leaked it, that's how," Tom muttered, anger hot in his voice.

"Why?"

"They must have tried the police first," Tom said with a shrug. "But they have no legal grounds to take her back. Still don't. So now they're trying this."

"Mud-slinging? They really think this'll make Emory hand her over?"

"No. But it'll make it all a hell of a lot harder for him when this goes to court." Tom shook his head. "This is why all this was a stupid idea."

"Hey," Jesse protested as they passed the staff canteen, empty but for abandoned half-full cups, "Emory wanted his daughter back. That's all I thought about."

"I didn't say it was *your* stupid idea," Tom said with a look over his shoulder.

Greenway was in the hall, directing operations. More security staff than Jesse had ever seen before at Oswald House were rushing around, reporting to Greenway and taking her orders.

"We need more security guys," Jesse said as he ran after Tom.

"Many more," Tom said as they took their seats. "But I don't know how many external agencies will hire to us now."

"Shit," Jesse cursed, typing commands and scrolling through the security reports. "People have tried to get over both gates and the rear wall."

"We need to pull men away from the front," Tom muttered, tapping keys, his brow furrowed. "The police are holding them off down there."

"So the police are now on our side," Jesse muttered.

"No one wants a riot," said Tom grimly.

"How long do you think they can hold them back?" Jesse said, swiveling a camera to try to establish how large the angry crowd at the front gates actually was. More cars were already arriving.

"More police are on their way," Tom said, tapping at his phone then putting it to his ear. "I heard Greenway say so. I'll see if I can get any more security."

"Talk fast," Jesse said as the new cars disgorged more angry-faced protestors with signs and spray paint.

Tom was talking into his mobile when Filip hurried in. His round face was grave. "Someone's throwing stones at the moor gate cameras," he reported.

Jesse flicked to the rear feeds just as one fuzzed and went dead. "Shit. Where can I get a ladder?"

"Jesse, you can't go out there," Tom protested.

"If any of these fuckers manage to get in," he said, grabbing a coat, "we need photographic proof of them breaking the law."

He ignored Tom's warnings and followed Filip outside. They retrieved a step ladder then rushed across the lawns. Jesse's breath misted in the air as he ran. The snow was crisp under his feet. If it wasn't for the ugly shouting coming from beyond the wall, it would have been idyllically peaceful.

Jesse blanched as they passed under the trees and he heard the true extent of the violence being meted out on the gate.

"Pervert! Sick fuck! Murderer!"

Another bang as something large clanged against the steel.

"How many are there?" Jesse whispered as Filip conversed with the two guards positioned inside the gate.

"Three or four," Filip said. They dodged to the side as a stone flew over the wall, catching the camera and landing with a thud at their feet. Filip shook his head. "Maybe more."

"Go tell Greenway we need the police around here," he said, setting the ladder against the wall. "This is criminal damage."

"The police don't care," Filip growled. "They want the little girl back."

"The little girl is with her legal guardian," Jesse snapped. "And these people will be scaring her shitless."

"I know that," Filip said, scowling at the gate. "But bloody English police don't believe it."

"They'll believe they can't let this get any worse," Jesse said, pushing Filip back toward the house. "Go. Tell Greenway. And check Dimity's safe in her room, will you?"

He expected the older man to argue but his face shifted. Something like approval smoothed its hard lines. "I will do that, sir," he said, then rushed away.

"Sir," one guard said as Jesse set his foot on the bottom rung. "You really shouldn't go up there."

"We need that camera working," Jesse insisted.

The guards exchanged doubtful glances, but Jesse was already climbing. He reached the camera and was gratified to see it was only the casing that was damaged. He detached it from its mounting, being careful to stay out of sight, opened the casing and realigned the damaged wiring. The red transmission light flickered back on. He glanced up at the mounting, braced himself, climbed another rung and peered over the wall.

There were three of them. They were big men bundled in thick coats, smoking, cursing and throwing rocks and frozen sheep dung. One had a square jaw and close-cut corn-blond hair. Jesse started, recognizing Tyler from the Evil Eye.

His heart pounded as he attempted to refasten the camera, but Tyler spotted him.

"Hey, fucker," he shouted and launched a stone.

Jesse swore and ducked. The stone sailed over his head.

"Show your face, you twat," he cried again, and there was a crash as a stone struck the wall. "Protecting a child rapist. Stringing up's too good for you." Another crash and the camera wobbled.

"Jesus, Tyler," Jesse shouted. "I see you're as good a shot as you are a fuck."

Silence fell for a breathless moment, then the projectiles started again, and the curses grew fouler.

Jesse scrambled down. He was on the bottom rung when a stone struck his head.

He was aware of pain, flashing lights and hitting the ground, hard. The shouts of the guards muddied in his ears, and it felt like his guts were trying to crawl out of his mouth. The next thing he knew he was on his feet with a strong arm around him and Filip was at his side, urging him on. Jesse wrenched himself free, bent and vomited into a rose bush.

"We need to get you to a hospital," Filip said. Through his blurred vision, Jesse could just make out that his grave face was lined with concern.

Jesse shook his head then swore as pain swirled through his skull. "They'll..." He swallowed rising sickness and drew a deep breath. "The coppers'll have me the second I step outside the gate."

"Greenway'll drive you," he said, taking Jesse's elbow and drawing him back toward the house. "They couldn't stop her if they tried."

Jesse blinked through the pounding red waves as someone pressed a bag of ice against his head. Tom's face was there, pale with concern. Then there was a car. Shouts. Bangs on the doors, windows and windshield. Jesse vomited into a bag someone had thoughtfully provided. The engine roared then, thank God, blessed silence.

By the time Greenway was braking outside A & E at York Hospital, the pounding had lessened to a point where he could at least see straight.

"You okay on your own?" Greenway said as she helped him to a seat in the waiting area.

"Get back," Jesse said, waving her away. "They need you."

"Call if you need anything," she replied, and Jesse was surprised to see her face tight with anxiety for the first time since he'd met her. Then she was gone.

He squinted at his phone screen as he scrolled news sites for any more updates. The story was headline news on every UK and some international sites, though there were still no names, interviews or statements from the police. But the lack of hard facts wasn't stopping the story's momentum.

Anger tangled with fear fisted around his heart.

His phone buzzed in his hand. Still dizzy, he answered it before his brain had caught up with his hand. He recognized his brother's irate voice and closed his eyes, unable to make sense of the words. Finally, Anton wound himself to a stop.

"Jesse? Are you there? Answer me."

"I've got a headache, bro," he croaked.

"You've got a *headache*?" he snapped. "That'll be the least of your problems when I'm through with you."

"What's going on?"

"What do you mean? I just told you."

"I didn't catch…" Nausea rolled through Jesse. He wanted to hang up, even though moving his thumb was too much effort. His head pulsed. Bitterness washed over his tongue. His brother was talking again. "Hey, mate…slow down, will you?"

"What the hell is wrong with you? Are you pissed?"

Jesse blinked his eyes open, groaned and shut them again. "No, I'm not fucking pissed. I've got a head injury."

"You… You what?"

"I'm in A & E. Can tearing me a new one wait?"

Anton said something else Jesse didn't catch and hung up. Jesse slumped back in his chair, shifting the melting ice pack and groaning when the bright lights on the ceiling shone red through his eyelids.

"The triage nurse will see you now."

Jesse shambled after a young woman to a curtained bed where he lay down, and the world started spinning all over again. He answered her questions and followed her finger with his eyes then she was gone, telling him that the doctor would be with him shortly.

He gratefully closed his eyes again. He tried to chase his thoughts into order, then tried to make himself look at his watch to figure out how long until it got dark and Emory would find out about all this, but both actions seemed far too much effort.

He was jerked from his stupor when someone yanked back the curtain. Anton stood there with a face like thunder.

"Ant..." he mumbled, attempting to sit up. "This isn't really the best time."

"What the hell happened to you?"

"Some fucker threw a rock at my head, that's what."

"So it's true."

"What's true?"

Just then the doctor pulled back the curtain and blinked at Anton in surprise. He stepped to the side and glowered like a gargoyle during the examination, apparently immune to Jesse's bleary glares. By the time the doctor had diagnosed Jesse with a mild concussion, had glued and dressed the wound on his head and urged him to go home and rest, Anton's expression had shifted from stormy to stony.

He tried to help Jesse off the bed, but Jesse yanked his arm out of his grasp. "What are you doing here, huh?"

"What do you think I'm doing here?" he said as they moved outside. Jesse lifted an arm that felt like lead to shade his eyes from the sunlight then stumbled to a stop when Anton stepped into his path. "Jesse, we are going to talk about this."

"Talk about *what*?"

"You're working for that fucking vampire, aren't you?"

"Ant—"

"I'm so stupid. All that money out of nowhere? The live-in job that didn't care about your record? And now some kid gets snatched out of one of the highest security houses in town?"

"It wasn't that high security..." Jesse cut himself off and swore under his breath.

"It really was you."

"Ant—"

"I can't believe this." His brother clutched his forehead. "Just when I thought you were finally getting yourself sorted, and all along you were being paid to kidnap little kids?"

"That is *not* what happened."

"What else do you call it, Jesse?" Anton's face was stricken. "I can't believe I've let you be part of my son's life."

Jesse blinked, nausea rising again. "What are you saying, Ant?"

"You helped one of *them* gain access to a child," Anton said in a low, dangerous voice. "What do you think I'm saying?"

Words wouldn't come. Dread flooded Jesse's body. He stared at his brother, who was going blurry beyond a wall of bitter tears. "That's not what this is."

"Then explain it to me, Jesse." Anton's voice was hoarse. "Explain what the hell is going on."

"She's *his* kid, all right?" Jesse cried. "She's his *daughter*. *They* kidnapped her from *him*."

"What the hell are you talking about?"

"She's the baron's great-great-great niece or whatever," Jesse said, wrapping his coat around him as the cold wind picked up. "He adopted her. I was just helping return a miserable kid to her dad who she loves." He met his brother's eyes, and a tear spilled down his face. "I just thought about how Olly would feel if someone took him from you and Sareena. That's all that was in my head. I had to do it."

Anton examined him for a long, silent moment, disbelief and rage chasing each other through his eyes. Jesse clenched his jaw to stop his teeth from chattering. Anton looked him over, made an impatient noise and drew Jesse over to his parked car. They both climbed in, and Anton started the engine and turned up the heat. Jesse's shivering eased, and the pounding in his head receded but he couldn't meet his brother's gaze.

"The adoption certificate," Anton said, "the one you showed to Sareena?"

Jesse made himself look over. His brother was staring out of the windshield with his hands tight on the wheel. "It's legit, Ant. Sareena said so."

"And this," Anton said, gesturing at his head. "How the hell did this happen, huh?"

"The story got leaked now dickheads are attacking his house," Jesse muttered, touching the cut and wincing. "Throwing stones. Threatening to lynch him."

"And you still think that's a suitable environment for a child, do you?"

Jesse frowned. "I'm their security engineer. I'm the one who makes sure it's safe. So yes."

"Why didn't you *tell* me?"

"Because you wouldn't understand."

"You don't know that."

"Ant. You didn't come out here to check I was okay, did you? You came here to yell at me...again."

Anton stared at him, his face strained. Silence billowed between them like poison gas. Then he shook his head in disbelief. "How did this happen, Jess?"

"How did *what* happen?" he demanded impatiently.

"When did we stop understanding each other? Stop trusting each other?"

"You're kidding, right?"

Anton blinked. "What do you mean?"

Hurt bloomed in Jesse's chest but the anger was stronger. "We've always been apart, Ant. Always."

"That's not true."

"Of course it's true. I was always on the outside."

"Outside of *what*?"

Jesse stared at him. "Are you really pretending you don't know what I'm talking about?"

Emotion colored his brother's cheeks. "Jesse, tell me what you're getting at."

Sour heat boiled up from the deepest, darkest parts of Jesse's body. "I'm getting at me spending my entire life on my own, because I wouldn't join you and Dad's fucked up little 'I-miss-mum' club." Anton stared at him like he'd hit him. Jesse hunched his shoulders and looked away. His mouth tasted bitter. The anger slumped out of him, leaving a dark, throbbing hollow behind. "Look... I loved Mum. She was our mum. But I don't *remember* her." Jesse dared to meet his brother's eyes. They were brimming with silent tears. His jaw was tight. Jesse tried to clench his own shut, but the words poured out of him like blood from an open wound. "Her dying was all that mattered to you...and to Dad. It defined you both, man."

"That's not true, Jess."

Jesse's breathing hurt. "All anyone ever said when I was a kid was 'Mum woulda loved this' or 'Ellie would have been so proud.' And I get it. I do. Of course I do...*now*. But I was a *kid*." He paused to draw a shaking breath and let it out slowly. "I felt like I'd come along too late to be part of the family."

Silence like seawater filled the car. Jesse gnawed his thumbnail and stared at his lap. He was shaky and dizzy, but he was pretty sure this wasn't all from the head wound.

"So, it's our fault then," Anton eventually spoke, his voice painfully even. "Me and Dad forced you into all this — dropping out of college, never holding down a job or a relationship. *We* made you break into that museum and hack those business tax records."

"That business was stealing from their staff's pension fund," Jesse argued. "Trixy was gonna expose them."

"You're basically sitting there and telling me," Anton continued like he hadn't spoken, "that the reason you're a total screw-up is all because *we* missed Mum?"

No. It's because you couldn't live without her. But I had to.

Jesse swallowed the words and the emotion that threatened to choke him. Instead he said, "I am who I am, Ant," he said hoarsely. "That's nothing to do with Mum. She wasn't there, remember?"

"Yes, I remember." His words were laced with venom.

Jesse rubbed his aching head gingerly. "Look. Working for the baron... It's really not what you think."

"And yet at no point during *any* of this did you feel like you could *tell* me about it. Wasn't that a warning sign, Jess? Wasn't that a voice telling you how fucked up this all is?"

"It's *not* fucked up," Jesse pleaded. "That's my point. I just knew what you'd say. Please, Ant. He's not a monster."

"You are joking, right?"

"If you ever met him, you'd see..." He trailed off. Anton's gaze was locked on his wrist. Jesse blinked at the rope burn with a slow, dull terror.

"What's that, Jesse?"

"None of your business," Jesse said, tugging his sleeves down.

"Jesse."

"I need to get back," Jesse said, "Are you giving me a lift or what?"

"Get out."

Jesse stared at his brother. Ice-hard hatred masked his face. "Ant—"

"Out of my car, Jesse. I don't want to see you. I don't want any calls from you. And you are to *never* go near my son again. Understand?"

"Ant, please!"

Anton reached across him and opened the passenger door. The cold air rushed in. Jesse swore then staggered out. His head spun, but he bent to lean back into the car. "Ant, if you would just listen."

"I always knew you were different, Jess," Anton said, eyes wet and his jaw trembling. "But I never thought you were dangerous, not once."

"I'm not *dangerous*, Ant. I swear. You know me."

"Shut the door."

Ice water pumped in Jesse's veins. His brother wouldn't look at him. He shut the door, and Anton drove off. Jesse staggered aside before his foot got run over. He was alone in the hospital car park with his head hurting, his limbs shaking and his heart breaking in his chest.

"You look like you're having a day."

Jesse swore, clutching his pounding head. Trixy stood at his shoulder in a violet furry coat. Her black-painted lips were smiling, but her eyes were icy.

"Trixy. What the fuck?"

"Come on," she said, jerking her head toward her hot-pink Mini parked three rows back. "I'll get you a drink."

"It's not even eleven a.m.," Jesse said, squinting at his watch.

"Never stopped you before."

"I have a concussion," Jesse protested. "I'm not drinking."

"Coffee, then," Trixy said, clicking her key so her Mini beeped and flashed. "Tea. Fucking wheatgrass juice, for all I care. All I'm saying is, we need to talk."

"I've got a kind of a situation. I don't really have time."

"That 'situation' is likely to get a whole lot worse if you don't come with me now." She held up her phone. He took it with shaking hands. Bile threatened to rise again. On the screen was a photograph of him, spreadeagled on the master bed in Oswald House. His wrists were tied to the headboard and Emory was on top of him, his face buried in Jesse's neck and his arse tensed between Jesse's spread knees. Jesse's mouth was open, his eyes shut, his face a mask of blind ecstasy.

"Where...?" Jesse choked. He coughed, and tried again. "Where did you get this?"

"You're not the only one good with surveillance," she said, taking the phone back.

"Trixy..."

"How do you think this'll help his kidnapping case, huh? Photographic evidence of him abusing one of his employees."

"That was *consensual*."

"He's still your boss. That's abuse."

"It's not." Jesse made an impatient noise. "He's my... We're..." He growled in frustration. "He wasn't abusing me."

"He tied you up." Trixy shrugged one shoulder. "Could be argued—"

"Now you're gonna slut-shame me in the same breath?"

Color flooded her face under her pale foundation. "Don't blame the player, Jesse, especially when you *got* something out of all this." She waved the picture under his nose. "And what did I get?" Her face twisted. "Nothing. Worse than nothing. Another hyped-up lead that never went anywhere. Do you have any idea what the trolls did after my tweet about getting arrested?"

"So the internet's a cesspool. That's not news."

"They photoshopped me into prison rape porn, Jesse." Her voice shook. "They sent it to my mum." She suddenly looked painfully young. Jesse's throat ached. Trixy took a breath and squared her shoulders. "So, I'm taking control back."

"The world is full of dickheads," Jesse said, his voice raw. "Ruining Emory's life won't change that."

"It'll change the news cycle."

"Trix," he pleaded, but she turned her back.

"I'm just saying come for a drink," she said, sweeping to her car. "Take it or leave it."

By the time they had found a quiet corner in the emptiest coffee shop they could find, Jesse felt ready to throw up again. Trixy smiled as she sat, tapping at her phone as her skinny oat milk latte steamed on the table between them.

"Sure you don't want something?"

"Say what you gotta say, Trixy."

Trixy placed her phone on the table and met his eyes. "I want an exclusive."

"An exclusive what?"

"Interview. To get the truth out there."

"To go viral, you mean."

She shrugged. "The truth should be viral, don't you think?"

"Fine," Jesse said, his patience snapping. "The truth is that, yes, I'm fucking Emory Von Magnusson. And it's the best fucking sex I've ever had. And that's all there is to that story."

"I believe there's more to it." Jesse kept silent. Trixy regarded him with narrowed eyes. "You know he's killed people, right? That's a fact."

Jesse shifted in his chair. "Of course I know."

"And you're okay with doing the dirty with a killer?"

"He's not—" Jesse cut off, making an impatient noise. "That was literally hundreds of years ago."

"And what if you found out he'd killed kids, huh? Even back then? Would you still feel the same?"

Jesse stared at her. "You…you don't know that."

"It's as possible as anything else, isn't it?"

"No," Jesse said firmly. "It isn't."

"So you won't mind if I release these pictures, then?" She said, picking up the phone and swiping. "There's a video, too, you know. Quite good quality. The camera you recommended has a great zoom. And you know if you stand out on the moor at night, with Oswald House all lit up, you really can see everything. Of course, I wasn't expecting to see you—"

"What do you *want*?"

"Like I said…an interview," she said, pocketing her phone. "Tell me what's going on at Oswald House. Is the kid dead?"

"Of course she's not bloody dead."

"Tied up like you, then?"

"Trixy, that's sick."

"Come on, then. Who is she? Why'd he take her?"

"She's his—"

"His *what*?" Her eyes danced. "Jess?"

"It's no one else's bloody business."

She raised her painted eyebrows. "You owe it to the world to let everyone know what's really going on up there."

"I owe the world shit. That's all it's ever given me."

"Just give me the kid's name, Jess. I can dig up the rest."

"You're not digging anything up," Jesse said, standing so quickly his chair hit the wall. "Not outta me, anyway. Release the damn video. See if I care."

"I think your brother will care."

"My brother already hates me," he said, turning away. "You can't make him hate me more."

"Tell me what he's like then," Trixy said, hurrying after him as he made for the door. "What's the Undying Baron like in bed, Jess? It certainly looks like he knows what he's doing."

"Fuck off, Trixy."

"Is he rough? Does he bite you? Is he going to make you a vampire, too?"

Jesse stormed out into the icy cold street with his emotions rioting in his chest.

Chapter Fifteen

Jesse was no closer to calming down by the time he got back. He had to wait at the end of the lane for security, sent by Tom, to elbow their way through the crowd and escort him back inside. Cameras flashed and phones were thrust in his face. He blinked until finally he was in the warm stillness of the house where he sank to the floor and buried his head in his arms.

"Jesse? Jess?"

Tom's voice came from an echoing distance, somewhere on the other side of the wall of storm water that swirled all around him. When Tom touched his arm, he jumped and scrambled away.

"Jesse—"

"I've got to see him," was all he could say, glancing out of the window to see, thank God, it was starting to get dark.

"Jesse, wait."

He didn't. He rushed to the basement door, set his eye to the scanner then shambled down the stairs before the door had fully opened. It was so quiet he could hear his heart hammering. He hovered at the bars, staring in at the secured sleeping chamber beyond. He checked his watch, over and over. The seconds slugged by like hours.

"Jesse, come away." Tom had come down behind him and took his elbow. "This isn't safe."

"I need to see him."

"Jesse, we shouldn't—" Tom started, then cut off when an alarm started blaring upstairs. He swore and pulled his phone out of his pocket. Jesse's own was buzzing, but he ignored it.

"Something's happening," Tom said. "We gotta get out of here."

"No."

"You don't get it," Tom insisted, his grip tightening. "We don't know how he'll be."

"Tom, let *go*."

They both froze when there was a click and a hiss. The sleeping chamber was opening.

Emory appeared as if out of nowhere. Jesse's blood froze in his veins. His lover towered over them, clad in nothing but sweatpants and a T-shirt, the thin cotton pulled tight across his heaving chest. His eyes blazed with submarine fire. His lips were drawn back from his lips, revealing his canines, gleaming against his red mouth. His fists were clenched, and his huge arms bulged.

"Move aside." His voice was thunderous. Jesse trembled. Tom stood frozen next to him.

"Emory," Jesse said, his voice sounding small in his ears. "*Please.*"

"Out of the way," Emory growled. "*Now.*"

"Emory, *wait.*"

But the haemophile shoved Jesse aside like he was nothing more than a doll. Then he was gone, just gone — like he'd evaporated.

It took several moments before Jesse could gather his senses enough to race back up the stairs.

"Emory, fucking *wait*."

He burst into the corridor, but it was empty. The garden door swung in the cold breeze. Jesse raced outside, running as fast as his legs would take him. His head pounded with every step. He kept calling Emory's name, terror and confusion pumping in his veins. There were no footprints, but he had no problem following the shouting.

By the time he reached the moor gate, the shouts had risen to screams. Jesse staggered out onto the open moor and froze.

Emory stood barefoot in the snow, still as stone. His breath billowed in the air. Several men were scrambling in the direction of the road. One remained. He was yelling nonsensical threats, kicking the snow, waving his arms, almost hysterical.

"Emory, don't hurt him," Jesse cried. "Please."

"Go back inside," Emory ordered.

It was only then Jesse realized the hysterical man wasn't yelling at Emory. Tyler was there, stood some distance away, just visible in the darkness. He was stiff as a board, and his head was tilted at an awkward angle. Jesse could make out the whites of his eyes and the violent shaking in his limbs.

It was then Jesse realized there was someone behind him. Long, pale fingers gripped Tyler's arm and his neck. Eyes like red coals burned in the shadows of the bone-pale face. A red mouth was open, close to Tyler's shoulder, the white teeth glinting.

"Lucien," Emory said, voice low as an earth tremor, "let him go."

The unknown haemophile's hands tightened. Tyler went rigid. Jesse watched in horror as the front of his jeans darkened with urine.

The other man was screeching now. He stooped, grabbed a stone and lifted it. Jesse yelled a warning and flung himself at the stranger, colliding with him at full force and tumbling him into the snow. The man writhed and raved, striking out wildly.

"Fucking *stop*," Jesse cried, straddling him and grabbing his arms. "You're gonna get us all fucking killed."

The man stilled, panting, his spittle hitting Jesse's face. He clutched Jesse's coat like he was about to throw him off but didn't move. He was staring wide-eyed at Tyler and the horror clutching him.

"This is not how things should be." The voice out of the darkness was like the low, slow flow of lava. The accent was beyond anything Jesse's adrenaline-flooded mind could identify. But the utter and explicit threat made his flesh turn to ice.

"Let him go," Emory commanded.

"This. Is. Not. How. It. Should. Be."

"Lucien…" Emory took a step closer. Tyler sobbed as the long fingers tightened on his arms. "Go. Now. Before it is too late."

The silence that descended was colder and harder than hoar frost.

"It is already too late, my friend."

Tyler crumpled bonelessly into the snow. The haemophile had vanished. His friend threw Jesse off and ran to him.

"Get up, man," he cried, shaking his arm. "Get the fuck up."

Tyler got shakily to his feet, then the man was dragging him toward the road. He continued to scream obscenities until the distance rendered him inaudible.

Jesse stood, breathing heavily. The icy air burned his lungs. Emory hadn't moved. His face was hard. He still looked like a stranger.

"Emory?"

Jesse blinked but Emory was gone. He stared around but he was completely alone. The silence was dark and cold as the winter night around him.

He drifted back to the house in a daze. Tom was on the terrace, scanning the dark anxiously. He slumped with visible relief when he spotted Jesse.

"Jesse, thank God," he said, hurrying to meet him. "What the hell happened?"

"I...I don't even know."

Tom took him by the arms. "You look awful. Come on. Get inside."

Jesse stepped gratefully into the warmth but couldn't go any farther than the inside of the door. He slumped against the wall and closed his eyes.

"You were right, Tom. You were right." His voice shook.

"Right about what?"

"His face," Jesse said. "He was..."

"It wasn't him," Tom said quietly after a pause. "He sensed a threat. That's when the Blood takes over."

"But he can't control that, right?"

Tom shook his head. "No. No, he can't." He put his hand on Jesse's arm. "Jesse, you don't look well."

"My fucking head," Jesse groaned, rubbing his temples.

"You should lie down."

"If I lie down, I'll throw up." Tom's walkie-talkie crackled. Jesse waved him away. "You go, mate. I'm not much use to anyone right now."

"Tell me what happened first. What did Emory do?"

"I can't even say."

"Try." Jesse blinked at his tone and finally met his eyes. They were hard. "Did he hurt anyone?"

"No," Jesse said softly. "He saved someone."

Tom blinked. "From *what*?"

"It looked like another haemophile."

Tom blanched. "Who?"

"I don't know," Jesse breathed. "I've never seen him before—never seen anyone like him before."

Tom bit his lip. When he spoke, his voice was hoarse. "And where's Emory now?"

"Gone after him, I think..."

Tom hesitated. "Did this haemophile have red eyes?"

Jesse opened and closed his mouth. The memory made him shiver. "I thought it was a trick of the light."

"Shit," Tom swore, running his hands through his hair. "Lucien."

"That's what Emory called him," Jesse whispered. "Who's Lucien?"

Tom took Jesse's elbow and tried to urge him along the corridor. "You really should go rest, Jesse."

"Who is Lucien, Tom?"

"That's not for me to tell you."

"I just watched him almost rip some guy to pieces," Jesse said, halting. "Who the fuck is he?"

Tom shook his head regretfully. "I'm sorry Jesse. I really can't tell you. Emory will...if he wants you to know."

Jesse's head started to spin again. Tom escorted him as far as the stairs, but his phone started ringing. He answered with an apologetic look and raced back to the security room.

Jesse sank onto the bottom step and pressed his forehead to the cool wall. His own phone started vibrating. He groaned and took it from his pocket.

Ant calling…

Jesse's blood surged. "Ant?"

"It's me, Uncle Jesse."

Jesse's chest clenched. "Olly…mate. Are you okay?"

"I think so."

Jesse closed his eyes, head aching more than ever. "Does your dad know you're using his phone?"

"No…" Olly said in a small voice. "But I needed to speak to you, and he wouldn't let me."

"What's the matter?"

"I saw her…on the news. Dimity."

Jesse sat up, heart pounding. "You saw her? A picture?"

"Yeah," Oliver said, his voice small. "They're saying that vampire kidnapped her—and Dad says you're working for him."

"Hold on a second, mate," Jesse said, trying for a cheery tone. "No one's kidnapped anyone, okay?"

"Do you work for him, Uncle Jesse? Have you seen her?"

"Yes, mate. She's here with me. She's fine."

"Really?"

"Would I lie?" Jesse said, making sure his smile was audible in his voice. "I can't explain all this right now, but I swear Dimity is fine." Something moved in the corner of his eye, and he turned his head. Dimity stood in the doorway with her rabbit clutched tightly to her chest. Her eyes were wide and round.

"Hey, Dim, love," he said shakily, holding out his hand. "You all right?" She nodded stiffly after a moment's consideration. "I've got Olly on the phone here. Wanna come say hi?"

Her face brightened a little, and she came forward.

"Is she there?" Oliver said, his voice cheering.

"Yeah, buddy, she's right here. Say hello, love." Jesse handed the phone to Dimity. She held it to her ear, smiling shyly.

"Is that you, Olly? Yes, it's me. I'm okay." She was quiet a moment as she listened, then she giggled. "That sounds *so cool*. I got paints for Christmas…and painting stuff. And Daddy says I can have ice cream for breakfast for a week."

"I don't think he did," Jesse said with tired amusement, holding out his hand. "Say goodnight now."

"Goodnight, Olly. See you soon." She handed the phone back.

"We gotta go," Jesse said, smiling at Dimity. "And you better get to bed before your dad realizes you've been on the phone."

"Have you had another fight?" Oliver's voice had sunk again.

"Yeah, we did. But things'll be right as rain again soon."

"Promise?"

"Promise." He hung up, swallowing guilt at the lie, and smiled at Dimity. "Hey, love. Why are you out of bed?"

"What's happening?" Her eyes shone with fear. "There were alarms…and shouting."

"It's nothing you need to worry about," he said, holding out his hand. She allowed him to draw her onto the stair next to him.

"Where's Daddy?"

Jesse flinched. "You know what, love? I'm not sure. But he'll be back soon."

Dimity frowned as she examined his face and lifted her fingers to touch the bandage on his forehead. "Did you hurt yourself?"

"Just a bump," he said, trying for another smile, even though it made his head pound. "Don't you think we should get you back to bed?"

She shook her head defiantly. "Not before I see Daddy."

"Okay," Jesse said, getting stiffly to his feet and holding his hand out for hers. "Tell you what... We'll go to your room, and we'll both wait for Daddy."

She weighed him up for a long moment, then nodded and took his hand. Joanna met them in the corridor, visibly relieved to see Dimity.

"You promised me you'd stay in your room, miss," she said, kneeling to brush her hair back from the girl's face.

"I'll stay with her," Jesse said tiredly, "until her dad comes back."

"Thank you," Joanna said with a heartfelt smile. "I need to check in with Tom."

Jesse took Dimity into her room. Soon they were both crouched on the floor with paper and pencils, drawing Father Christmas and his reindeer.

"Your reindeer are very wobbly," Dimity said with a critical frown.

"My artistic talents are limited, even without a headache," he said, handing the pencil back to her. "Here... You take over. I'll watch."

"See? They need two antlers each," she said, correcting Jesse's drawing, the concentration intent on her face.

"Dimity?"

They both looked up. Emory was in the doorway. He had changed into trousers and a navy jumper. His hair was combed back with not a strand out of place. He was smiling. Jesse found it hard to summon the image of his bared teeth and twisted scowl.

Dimity sprang to her feet and ran to him. He lifted her from the floor, murmuring non-answers to her questions, kissing her hair.

He caught Jesse's eyes over her head, and his expression fell. He set her back on her feet.

"It's late, darling," he said when she tried to draw him into the room. "Can you let Joanna read you a story? Uncle Jesse and I need to talk."

She narrowed her eyes, looking between them narrowly. "You'd better not be fighting."

"We're not fighting, dearest," he said, patting her cheek. "Be a good girl now." Emory stepped back and Joanna reappeared, smiling warmly and bearing a mug of warm milk. Dimity kissed her father goodnight, hugged Jesse and allowed herself to be guided to bed.

"Night, love," he said as he closed the door. Then he followed Emory down the hall, his head spinning.

Emory held the door to the master bedroom open. The neatly made bed and soft fragrance of the sheets and carpets brought memories rushing back. Jesse ignored them, went straight to the windows and closed the drapes.

"Jesse."

"What the hell happened back there?"

"Can you look at me, please?"

Jesse turned. Emory stood with his hands in his pockets. His face was blank, but emotion simmered in his eyes.

"You're hurt," he said, reaching out to touch Jesse's head, but he stepped back out of reach.

"Answer my question."

Emory drew a deep breath and sighed it out. "Lucien is a very, very old friend."

"He almost ripped Tyler's head off," Jesse said, his voice rising, despite his desperate clutching for control.

Emory frowned delicately. "You knew that human?"

"We're not talking about me," Jesse retorted. "We're talking about *you*—and this *Lucien*. He almost dismembered that guy—and just a few feet from your fucking house, Emory. The house where your kid..." He trailed off, blood rushing to his face. His head ached worse than ever. He clenched his jaw and swallowed the fear-fueled words, watching Emory's face ice over.

"You have something you wish to say to me, Jesse," he said. "I would like you to say it plainly."

Jesse looked at the bed, his skin tingling, then dropped his gaze to the floor. "I saw the list, Emory."

"List?"

Jesse made himself meet his lover's eyes and not flinch. "Your 'Kill List'."

Emory was silent for a long moment. His face did not change, but the emotion that had been in his eyes drained away, leaving cold cobalt in its place. "You promised me you wouldn't read that file."

"Helena Hawthorn... She had it on her computer."

Emory still didn't move. Jesse's skin felt too tight for his body, but he refused to look away.

"Why did you look?"

Jesse shrugged. "I dunno. It was an impulse."

"An impulse?"

"I wanted to know, Emory," he snapped. "Wanted to know what the hell I was in the middle of."

"So you hacked into Helena's computer. You saw the list of people the authorities have proved that I have killed."

Jesse nodded stiffly.

Emory did not immediately speak. When he did, his voice was softer. "And yet you still brought Dimity back to me."

"There was no one on that list since eighteen-hundred-and-whatever," Jesse said. "So I told myself Aunt Helena was probably the worse monster. But now…"

"Please be careful using that word, Jesse," Emory said. "It has done my kind a lot of damage over the centuries."

"Words don't kill people, Emory," Jesse said. "But when this Lucien psycho turns up on your doorstop, assaulting protestors, and you wake up all Blood-fueled and not yourself…" Jesse's breath was heaving. He couldn't blink, couldn't see straight. Emory didn't move. Angry, fearful tears threatened to spill, but Jesse swallowed them back. "Do you really think you're safe to raise a kid?" he finally said, the emotion in the words rubbing them raw.

"Yes," Emory said without hesitation, "I do. And until tonight, you thought I was, too."

"That Lucien would have killed Tyler if you hadn't talked him down."

"But I did," Emory said quietly. "And Lucien wouldn't have involved himself in the first place if those men hadn't been threatening my home."

"You can't *hurt* people," Jesse said desperately, stepping close, "even if they are dickheads. Don't you see? They're all waiting for an excuse to lock you up, wipe you out, who fucking knows what?"

"I didn't hurt anyone, Jesse."

"Your *friend* did," Jesse retorted. "Or would have."

"Lucien is very old. Very...troubled," Emory said softly. "He does not often come anywhere near human settlements."

"So why this time?"

"Because my family was being threatened."

Jesse made an impatient noise. "Don't blame the victims."

Emory touched the dressing on Jesse's head. "They attacked you, Jesse," Emory said softly. "That makes them enemies, not victims."

"A friend of yours attacks someone in your back garden. Your house is surrounded by an angry mob. You only get up when your daughter is about to go to bed. You can't control your actions if the Blood thinks shit is going down." Jesse drew a deep breath. "How is this okay for her, Emory?"

Emory held himself very still but didn't speak until Jesse met his eyes. "She is my daughter, Jesse. I love her. I would kill, and I would die for her."

"Kids don't want you to do either of those things," Jesse said despairingly. "They want you to give them breakfast, take them to school, throw them birthday parties. They just want you to be..." He closed his mouth.

Emory raised an eyebrow. "Human?"

Jesse looked away.

"If I thought that being with her aunt's family would be better for her, I would give her up in a heartbeat," Emory said after a long pause. "But I am her father. I am not conventional, but I love her."

"And if this Lucien psycho shows up again?"

"Lucien is my maker. We share a bond. He would never hurt someone I cared for."

Jesse stared at him, unsure how to handle his reaction. "Your...your 'maker'?"

Emory nodded.

"What does that mean?"

Emory tilted his head. "He's the one that brought me into this existence. Transformed me."

"From being human to...this?" Jesse lifted his hand to touch Emory's face, froze and dropped it again.

"That's right."

Jesse fidgeted. "How?"

"I can't tell you that," Emory said softly. "It's forbidden."

"What were you like?" he asked softly. "When you were human?"

"I can't remember." Jesse made a disbelieving noise. "It's true, Jesse. That life fades after a while."

"How do you not remember a whole lifetime?"

Emory shrugged gently. "It would be like you trying to recall memories from your infancy, from before your capacity for memory had fully formed."

"Mum died when I was three," Jesse said. "I only know what she looked like from pictures. But I still remember *feeling* something, once. You don't even have that?"

Emory was silent for a long time. Then he looked away. "I know I had a sister. I know I lived in a house on this land." He gazed around the room a little sadly. "But I have very little recollection of what it was like — or what I was like."

"So your oldest memory is...Lucien?"

"That's right. And even now, we can sense each other."

"You can *sense* each other?"

Emory nodded. Extreme emotions. Pain. Fear. The closer we are, the stronger it is. Though if we were on different continents, we would still get something."

"That's impossible."

"I can assure you it's true."

"He was the one Terje meant, wasn't he?" Jesse said after a moment. "When Terje Kristiansen said 'he really is back'?"

Emory sighed. "Lucien can be a concern. He lives by his own rules."

"So he's dangerous."

"That depends on your definition of dangerous."

"I'm pretty sure making a guy piss his pants in terror counts as dangerous."

"He didn't hurt anyone," Emory repeated. "We try to make sure he never does."

"'Try'?" Jesse swallowed. "That's not exactly reassuring, Emory."

Emory didn't flinch. "Nothing could ever induce him to harm someone I cared about."

The floor dipped under Jesse's feet. "Do you, like, love each other?"

Emory frowned in thought. "I imagine at one time it was something like what you call love, yes. But it is different — like family but…deeper. And unbreakable."

"So what the fuck do you need me for?"

Emory examined his face. Finally, he smiled and ran a finger down Jesse's cheek.

"My darling Jesse," he said, his voice barely above a whisper. "I cannot help what is between me and Lucien. We are linked by the Blood, whether we want it or not. But you…" He lowered his voice. "You I *choose* to love."

Jesse's breath left his body. "You…you what?"

Emory kissed him. "I love you, Jesse," he whispered.

"That's crazy," Jesse said, shaking his head. "You've only known me a few days."

Emory brushed his hair from his face. "I knew you were special the second I saw you at the Christmas lights." Emory smiled softly. "Yes, I saw you, with your nephew on your shoulders. I heard the things you said…and saw the way you looked at me."

"I'm not saying it back," Jesse returned after a breathless silence. "This is all too…I don't know."

Emory brushed his knuckles over Jesse's cheek. "You don't have to. Not until you're ready."

Jesse cleared his throat. His face was hot. "So if I admit that Dimity is safe with you…" He looked intently into Emory's face. "What about everything else? School, birthday parties, university graduations? A wedding? Sometimes loving a kid is just not enough."

Emory tucked Jesse's hair behind his ears. "I plan to enroll Dimity in the best school in the district. Joanna and my security staff will get her to and from the facility safely. The first thing I do upon waking every night is see her and hear about her day. As for birthday parties, graduations"—his eyes glittered—"weddings…? I will join for whatever part of those celebrations happen after sunset. All of Dimity's birthday parties so far have been after dark. She has a January birthday, thankfully, when the days are short. She doesn't seem to mind."

"What about the other kids? Their parents? Do they mind their children going to a birthday party after dark at a vampire's house?"

A line appeared between Emory's eyebrows. "I know you're tired and in pain, so I'm going to allow you some latitude in this, Jesse, but the answer to your question is no. In Austria, Dimity's friends' parents were all very understanding. They are a little more progressive in that part of Europe. Haemophiles have lived in the open there for some time." He sighed deeply. "I would do my very best to give Dimity a happy life. But, ultimately, none of it is up to me." He took Jesse's hand. "The court will know all about what has happened tonight. They will know about my 'Kill List'. They will know everything. And they will decide if I can be Dimity's parent. And I will accept their judgment."

"You will?"

Emory nodded. "I believe Dimity belongs with me, but if the world decides she can't be, I'm not going to fight. Fighting would make everything worse for her. I won't do that to her."

Jesse had run out of words, run out of questions, run out of energy. He sank onto the edge of the bed and put his head in his hands, willing the aching to ease, inside and out. The bed shifted as Emory sat next to him.

"I'm so sorry," he whispered, putting his fingers under Jesse's chin and lifting his face to examine the dressing on his forehead. "I really didn't want you to get caught in the middle like this."

"I'm the silly bugger that climbed the ladder."

"Yes. Filip told me," Emory said, running his thumb over the dressing. "You really are very impulsive."

"We needed the video proof of those guys being arseholes. If the courts are going to decide if you can be Dimity's dad, it's only fair they have all the facts."

"Thank you," he said gently. He ran his hands down Jesse's neck, lighting a low fire in his flesh, before resting it on his chest. "But there's something else. Something that's making your heart beat too fast. Is it something to do with why you drew the curtains?"

"Trixy," Jesse said, his voice catching in his throat. "She's got pictures of us from last night. Videos. She's probably going to release them."

Emory looked thoughtful. "She told you this?"

Jesse nodded. "She said she'd keep it under wraps if I told her all about Dimity. I told her to get lost."

Emory smiled. "Thank you."

"But it's gonna come out." Jesse clenched his fists. "Our fucking sex video. All over the internet."

Emory took his hand. "We'll weather it, Jesse. Together."

"It's not just that…" Jesse rubbed the fading marks on his wrist. "Anton…my brother. He's figured it all out."

Emory was quiet for a long moment. "He disapproves?"

Jesse snorted. "Understatement." He picked at his fingernails. "He's banned me from seeing Olly. He thinks I'm dangerous."

"You, *liebling*? Dangerous?"

"He thinks I'm a pervert," Jesse said, the words raw. "Maybe he always has." Jesse closed his eyes. "It's all gone so wrong so fast. And I don't know what I should have done differently."

"Nothing," Emory murmured. "No one should make you feel ashamed for who you are, Jesse—least of all the people you love."

Jesse swallowed his emotion with an effort. "He's just looking out for Olly."

"Having a loving uncle in his life can only be to the child's benefit," Emory insisted, putting a hand on his leg. "Your brother will realize that, eventually."

"I'm not so sure."

"He's angry and probably scared." Emory gazed at the curtained windows. "There's a lot of fear going around. But give him time, Jesse. Give them all time. It will all come right."

"You think so?"

Emory smiled. "I have lived several hundred years. If there's one thing I've become confident of, it's the healing power of time." He squeezed his leg. "Trust me on this."

The tension in Jesse's chest eased. He let out a breath and nodded.

"Now," Emory said, pushing the hair back from Jesse's forehead and studying the bandage, "I would very much like to fix this, if you'll allow me."

"Fix it?"

"I don't approve of haemophile Blood being abused for recreational purposes," he said, his voice hard. "Darragh and I are campaigning on a number of fronts to strengthen the laws around that. But, if I have your permission..." He peeled the dressing away from Jesse's wound. "The tiniest drop applied here should heal this instantly, with a minimum of side effects."

"These side effects...they, uh..."

"Yes?" Emory promoted gently with the start of a smile on his face.

"I heard it makes you horny as hell."

"That is accurate," Emory replied. "But I believe I am more than capable of mitigating that particular side effect." Jesse's heart began to beat in a very different way. Emory held his gaze. "I would like to take your pain away, but only with your permission."

Jesse nodded dumbly. Emory smiled, ran his fingers into Jesse's hair, drew his face forward and kissed his forehead gently.

"Just relax," he whispered, then pressed the pad of his thumb against his canine. A bead of dark red Blood welled up like a jewel. The air was filled with a heady smell, red wine and bonfires. Jesse's own blood began to pound. Emory smeared the Blood over the cut on Jesse's head.

Jesse's head filled with fire. He gasped and grabbed onto the bed. The sensation was almost worse than the pain. For the longest second of his life, he thought he might expire with the strength of it. But then it dimmed and washed down though his flesh like a strong whiskey, leaving a glowing simmer behind.

He was aware of every centimeter of his body. Everything tingled. He could smell the paint on the walls and the cleaner in the carpet. He blinked. The pain was gone. He touched his fingers to his head. The skin was smooth. He blinked at his fingers and his eyelids drew a shimmering veil across his vision, like there was phosphorescence in the air. Even the oxygen he breathed tasted different, like it was heavy with strong but sweet alcohol.

"How are you feeling?"

Emory's voice swam in his ears, rich as melted chocolate. Jesse gazed at him. The hue of his eyes was now composed of a hundred blues. The smoothness of his pale skin was delectable and perfect as fresh cream. Jesse could see, feel and smell the power in him, as well as the seething mass of ebbing, swollen emotion just below the surface.

He grabbed Emory's jumper and yanked him in for a fierce kiss. He inhaled his smell, plunged his tongue deep into the hot, copper-tasting mouth. The sharp teeth grazed his lips, sending tendrils of fire through his body. Emory made a low growl and ran his hands inside Jesse's shirt, setting his skin ablaze. Jesse climbed into his lap, feeling like he couldn't breathe fast enough to keep the oxygen in his body. His cock was rock-hard. He thrust against Emory's belly with a moan, never breaking the kiss, running his hands feverishly over the haemophile's iron-hard shoulders and chest.

"Fuck me, Emory," he panted against his lips. "Tie me up again. Fuck me. Make me scream." Emory moaned and rolled Jesse under him, tugging his shirt over his head and layering kisses over his neck and chest.

"Being restrained," Emory whispered against the skin under Jesse's ear as he slowly unfastened Jesse's jeans, "it's all about power...control. You like to give your control up to someone else. Have them set the pace. Make the decisions. Drive your pleasure."

"Yes," Jesse gasped, tugging impatiently at Emory's clothing. "Yeah. Do that. Quick."

Emory took his wrists and pinned them above his head. He smiled enigmatically.

"Remember we talked about doing it the other way?"

"Emory, seriously, I'm about to fucking explode. Can you please just—?"

Emory captured his mouth again, keeping his hands over his head, ravaging him with a kiss so deep and intense that Jesse wondered if they might both suffocate.

But then Emory left the bed, and Jesse shivered at the sudden loss of contact. Emory held his gaze as he tugged his jumper off, revealing the endless, rolling planes of his hard, muscled torso. His eyes burned into Jesse's as he unfastened his belt and pushed his trousers down. He stepped out of them, then drifted to the nightstand. His muscles slid under his alabaster skin like waves on the ocean. His arse was the picture of perfection as he bent and drew something that clinked out of the drawer.

Emory held out two heavy sets of metal cuffs. Jesse stared at them with his heart pounding against his ribs.

"I think the rope was enough," he said, his voice hoarse.

"These aren't for you."

Jesse opened and closed his mouth a few times, his skin fizzing with the possibilities. "For you?"

Emory nodded slowly, his eyes burning dark and low.

"But..." Jess sat up, looked at the wooden headboard doubtfully. "Will they be strong enough? Will the bed?"

Emory moved to the foot of the bed and pulled the whole thing out from the wall as easily as if it were a toy, revealing metal rings set in the plaster.

"You had those *built into the wall*?"

Emory nodded again. "They are set in reinforced concrete." He threw the handcuffs on the bed where they landed with a thump. "They will hold me."

Jesse picked up the cuffs warily. They were cold and weighty, cruel looking. "I don't know..."

"I understand the thrill around the giving and taking of control," Emory said, crawling toward him. "We won't do this if you don't want to. But" —he paused with his face a breath away from Jesse's— "I think you'd be very, very good at it."

Jesse fought breath into his lungs to speak. "And this," he said, lifting the cuffs. "This is what you want? What you'd like?"

"I like to feel things," he breathed, brushing his lips over Jesse's. "Deep. Hard. Strong. You are all these things." He kissed him and cupped the flagging bulge in the front of Jesse's jeans. Jesse's blood surged again, a thousand small fires burning along his veins like sparklers. He grabbed Emory's shoulders and pushed him onto his back. He climbed on top and ran his hands over his powerful body, the idea of what it might be like to have it entirely at his mercy shooting excitement through him like lightning.

Emory guided him through the locking mechanisms in a voice husky with arousal. The sight of him prone on the bed, his arms over his head and wrists shackled to the wall, took Jesse's breath away.

"Jesus, Emory," Jesse said, stripping off the last of his clothing then straddling his lover. He ran his tongue over his jaw, neck and pecs as he danced his hands over the hard belly and muscled hips.

"Do whatever you want," Emory said, his own breathing deepening and his cock swelling. "I am yours."

Jesse almost wept with anticipation, burying his face in Emory's neck and thrusting against his powerful thighs. "*Ah*. I...I think..."

"What?" Emory whispered into his hair as he parted his legs, and Jesse shifted to lie between them.

Jesse ran his hands up Emory's thighs. He thrust into the tight, hot space between Emory's sculpted arse cheeks and moaned. He lifted his head. They were both breathing hard. Emory's eyes were hooded and blistering with a thousand hot blues.

"I want you," Jesse whispered.

"You have me."

Jesse kissed him hard and fumbled blindly in the bedside drawer until his hands closed around the bottle of lube. He could smell the cool, clinical fragrance stronger than he ever had before as he smeared his fingers.

Jesse's hand shook as he found Emory's entrance. Emory moaned, the sound raw and throbbing. Jesse almost came right there. He trembled as he slid a finger inside. He kissed Emory's jaw, his neck, his chest, anything to avoid his eyes. The tight heat made him shiver, but the sensation was so unfamiliar that he felt awkward, fumbling.

"That's good, Jesse," Emory whispered against his hair. "Keep going... Yes."

Emory tensed. Jesse reached in again, making Emory groan. His muscles clamped around Jesse's fingers. Jesse's mouth dried out.

"Shit, Emory," he panted as he worked him, in and out, sliding in a second and third finger with care as Emory's breathing sped up. "Are you sure?"

"Jesse," he said, his name sounding more like a growl than a word, straining his arms so the handcuffs groaned, "hurry."

Jesse withdrew his fingers, lubricated his twitching cock with shaking hands and moved up the bed so they were nose to nose. Emory stared into his eyes. Jesse hung there a moment, enjoying the feel of Emory's body, taut and ready, under him.

"I'm yours, Jesse."

Jesse pushed forward. The tight heat swallowing him combined with the Blood firing in his veins was like nothing he had ever felt or knew he could feel. He made a noise, but it was on some far, distant plane that he was momentarily incapable of processing. Emory lifted his hips, taking Jesse deep inside and tightening around him like a fist.

Jesse clung to Emory's body like a drowning man. He pressed his forehead against Emory's chest, breathing the smell of his skin deep and holding himself still until the sensation of being about to fall off a cliff ebbed. Then he drew out of Emory's body, held himself still, then slid in again. Emory panted his name, but Jesse was numb to everything but the waves of liquid sunlight rolling over his body. He thrusted in and out, deeper, faster, clutching hard to the rigid muscles of Emory's back. He needed more, needed to know this body, inside and out—this body that was strong enough to rip Jesse to pieces, but which Emory had chosen to share with him, to let him hold, taste, fuck and be fucked by, experience every inch of it even more thoroughly than his own.

Jesse lifted himself onto his hands so he could see Emory's face as he sped up. Emory's eyes were burning. He was breathing fast through his open mouth, his teeth and lips wet and glistening. His hair was stuck to his forehead by sweat.

"Harder, Jesse," he breathed, and Jesse let out a strangled noise and obeyed. The rattle of the cuffs grew louder. The bed creaked. Jess swore and cursed and made nonsense sounds, feeling his control slip away.

"God... God," Jesse said, throwing his head back as Emory tilted his hips, deepening the penetration. He strained against the cuffs and groaned, open-mouthed. His muscles tightened around Jesse.

Jesse came in a blinding, ruby-glittered curtain of heart-stopping ecstasy. He hurriedly fumbled for Emory's cock and Jesse heard him cry out from beyond the echoing in his ears. Hot, fragrant liquid spattered over his belly.

Jesse lay on Emory's heaving chest for a long time. His skin was oversensitive, rippling at Emory's every breath brushing his shoulder. He was still buried inside and was afraid to move, wondering just which bits of ugly reality were waiting for them once Jesse pulled out and the moment had passed.

"*Liebling*," Emory finally whispered, "are you well?"

Jesse nodded, lifted himself to slide out of Emory and rolled off him. He fumbled shakily with the restraints until he found the releases. Emory lowered his arms with a low groan then drew Jesse to him. Jesse tucked his head under Emory's jaw and let himself lie still.

"How are you feeling?"

"Empty," Jesse whispered against Emory's chest, "but better."

"I'm glad," Emory said, as he traced his fingers over the tribal designs on Jesse's arm.

"You wanted to know," Jesse mumbled. "About the ink?" Emory propped his head on his hand and looked into his face but didn't speak. Jesse lowered his gaze. "I meant what I said. The designs themselves don't mean much." He ran his fingers over the roses on his ribs. "But each time I got one, I felt like I was becoming less the boy with no mum, less the boy who didn't understand how to be sad enough to please his family. Less him and more me."

"That's very sad. But very beautiful."

Jesse rolled his head on the pillow and gave Emory a tired smile. "You're just saying that 'cause you want to go to bed with me again."

"I would very much like to go to bed with you again," Emory said. His face turned wistful. "I'd also like to take you on holiday, teach you to ride, take Dimity to a theme park with you—things human families do. Whatever else I said, I am acutely aware I can't be a normal family to anyone."

"I'm sure we can do some of those things," Jesse said thoughtfully after a pause. "When all this shit's settled down, anyway."

Emory watched him. "So you believe I can be a dad again?"

Jesse gave him a long look. "I think I always did. I was just... scared."

"Inducing fear is something I'm unfortunately used to," Emory said, and the gravity in his tone made Jesse's belly dip. But when he looked back, Emory was smiling. "But I'm just glad you changed your mind." He kissed the corner of Jesse's mouth and sat up with a sigh. "I have matters to attend to, I'm afraid," he said, moving into the bathroom.

"What are you going to do?"

"Meet with Greenway," Emory said, running the tap. "And Darragh. Decide what to do next."

Jesse heard the sound of brushing teeth. He leaned over and saw Emory stood at the mirror, a towel around his waist, brushing at his long canines.

"As if you brush your teeth."

Emory spat then glanced over his shoulder with a raised eyebrow. "Why wouldn't I?"

"I can't imagine there's much sugar in blood," Jesse said.

"There's sugar in alcohol. Fizzy drinks. I like those."

Jesse shook his head in disbelief as Emory went back to brushing. "So, if haemophiles get cavities and shit, how do any of you have any teeth left?"

"What do you mean?" Emory said, wiping his mouth on a towel and baring his teeth in the mirror to inspect them. The sight of his needle-sharp canines and incisors sent an odd shiver over Jesse's skin.

"Human teeth fall out in less than a lifetime," he continued. "You guys live for loads of lifetimes."

Emory came out of the bathroom with a small smile on his face. "If we lose a tooth, we grow a new one."

Jesse blinked. "No way."

Emory stooped for his underwear. "Way."

"So why brush?"

"To smell nice," Emory said, pulling on his trousers and jumper. "To taste nice. And, well...growing new teeth is not pleasant."

"It hurts?"

"Yes."

Jesse hesitated. "Can I see them?"

Emory went still. "Why?"

"I'm just curious."

"You've seen them," Emory said softly, sitting on the bed to put on his socks.

Jesse slid across the bed and ran his hands up Emory's back. "I think..." Jesse said softly, gathering his courage. "I think I'd like to feel them."

Emory went still.

"Em?" Jesse said softly, going cold at the look on his face.

"Never ask that, Jesse."

Jesse frowned. "You're the one who went on about controlling my pleasure, about not being ashamed."

Emory faced him. His eyes were hard. "I'm *never* biting you. You should not ask."

"But why?"

"Did you not see Tom? Hear his story?"

Jesses made an impatient noise. "That wouldn't have happened if he hadn't got something out of it."

"It nearly killed him, Jesse," Emory said in a low voice. "Could still, one day, if he ever slides back. There are bad people among my kind, just as there are in yours—ones that would take advantage of someone's vulnerability. I will *never* do that. And you do not want me to, either."

"You can't tell me what I want and don't want," Jesse said, crossing his arms. "That's up to me."

"Of course it is," Emory said, looking momentarily surprised. "Your sexuality is your own, Jesse. But your need for pain is something else. And I've already told you I won't be part of that,"

Jesse growled and flung the covers back. But Emory took his wrist to stop him storming away. His face was still hard, but when he spoke, his voice was softer.

"This is great, what's between us," he said. "I've not had a physical connection with someone like this in a long time. But you forget I can sense and smell more about you than you can about me. I'm not going to tell you you're wrong for any of the things you want. But I am *never* going to hurt you, even if you ask. You will have to accept that if this is to continue."

Jesse glared at him for a long time with his heart doing somersaults in his chest. Emory kissed the corner of his mouth.

"Sleep, my love," he whispered. "It's been a long day."

"I'm not tired."

"You are. Sleep, Jesse," he whispered. "Heal. Let me take care of things tonight."

Chapter Sixteen

When Jesse awoke the next day in the master bedroom, the clock on the bedside table revealed it was close to noon. He pushed the covers back blearily. The heavy drapes had kept the room dark as night, and he had to turn on the bedside light to find all his clothes. When he drew the curtains back, the day was surprisingly bright. Patches of grass were starting to show through in the snow on the moor.

There was still a police car in the lane and a crowd of people waving placards. But looking at them now, Jesse felt an odd sense of calm.

He touched his head. The skin was smooth. He went to the mirror but there wasn't even a fading mark on his skin. He felt fresh, alert.

When he checked his phone, there were no missed calls, no messages, nothing—not from Ant, not from Trixy, anyone. Even the memory of Lucien's red eyes blazing in the darkness seemed less horrifying in the cool, midday sunshine.

Dimity's bedroom door was open, but her room was empty. He was heading back to his own room to change when he ran into Tom. His face was drawn and pale. There were shadows under his eyes. He was tapping on his phone and almost walked straight into Jesse.

"Did you get any sleep, mate?"

"Jesse," Tom said, blinking. "There you are."

Jesse frowned at the look on his face. "What's happened now?"

Tom bit his lip. "You've not been online?"

Jesse's stomach lurched. "What is it?"

"It's…you."

Jesse swore and hurried past Tom to his room. His displays were blinking with notifications. He sat at the desk, numb, and loaded the content, bracing himself. But it wasn't a sex tape that was doing the rounds. It was a sound clip.

The truth is that, yes, I'm fucking Emory Von Magnusson. And it's the best fucking sex I've ever had. And that's all there is to that story.

Trixy's smiling face then appeared, but her video discussing haemophile sexual arousal and BDSM was a blur. She'd got a hundred thousand hits already, and it was still rising. There were memes. There were spin-off articles, reaction videos. Her proposed human-haemophile sex guide was already getting crowdfunded.

Jesse slumped in his chair. Tom was hovering in the doorway.

"Was that really you?"

"My Christ, Tom," he said, despairing, "is there anything I *can't* do to fuck this up more?"

"It wasn't you who decided to share that with the world," Tom said, coming into the room.

Jesse shook his head. "I should have known she was recording me. I should have known."

"You met with her and said that?"

"I thought she was a friend. Stupid me. She was just using me, like always."

Tom sighed. "Darragh wants a meeting at sunset."

"Shit," Jess said, going cold. "Really?"

Tom nodded. "Hawthorn's lawyer wants you for a deposition next week."

"A...what?"

"They need to ask you some questions, under oath — about Dimity. And Emory."

"Like with a judge and shit?"

"No," Tom said. "Not in court and not with a judge — your lawyer, their lawyer, a recorder. Some questions, that's all."

"Well, I won't do it."

"You have to. It's illegal to refuse. Don't worry," he said, though the set of his face didn't make his words reassuring. "Darragh will prep you. He knows what he's doing."

Jesse tried to unpack the tone of his voice but couldn't.

"This is what they've been waiting for," Jesse said, stabbing his finger at the paused video on his screen. "They want to prove Emory's unfit to be a parent. Get Dimity taken away."

"This way you get the chance to tell them that he is fit." He managed a weak smile. "This may end up being a good thing."

Jesse looked away, blushing. "Is Dim okay?"

"She's fine," Tom said, tapping at his phone. "Joanna took her off for the ride on the moor this morning. Filip went with them," he added, seeing the look on Jesse's face, "and there's no one hanging around the gate anymore."

"I wonder why," Jesse drawled.

"Yes," Tom said, frowning again at his phone. "The stuff about Lucien has come out as well. An eyewitness account from someone called Tyler Lomax, claiming he was assaulted."

"He was," Jesse said. "Fucking psycho nearly ripped the guy in two. He might be an arsehole, but he didn't deserve that."

"Lucien's not psychotic," Tom said gently. "He's just...remote from societal norms."

Jesse snorted. "That's a posh way of saying 'psycho'."

"Did Emory tell you about him?"

"Yeah. He did." Jesse hesitated. "You've met him?"

Tom nodded. "He came by once when we lived in Vienna. He's...complicated. But Emory means a lot to him. He wouldn't intentionally endanger him or his case."

"What do you call this then?" Jesse said gesturing at Tyler's interview on Tom's phone.

"There will be loads of this and more before this is over," Tom said, putting his phone away. "Perhaps it's time for everything to be out in the open — good or bad. Then people can see where the lines are."

Jesse hesitated. "Do you think they'll let him keep her?"

Tom's face was grave. "I don't know. If it were up to me, there'd be no question. I've seen what a great dad he is. But the world might not be ready for it..." Tom trailed off. He was frowning at his forehead. "Your head. It's better." Jesse clenched his jaw. Tom's eyes widened. "Jesus, Jesse. Did Emory give you Blood?"

"Just a drop," Jesse said defensively. "To fix it." Then he swallowed. "Was that wrong?"

Tom let out a long, slow breath. "It's a gray area. Let's just say that. How do you feel?"

"Fine. Better than I have in days, really."

"Muscles not aching, don't feel sick?" Jesse shook his head. "Don't feel like you want…more?"

Jesse thought for a moment. "It was good, that's for sure," he admitted. "But…it's always good with him, even without that."

"That's okay then," Tom said, standing. "He didn't use too much."

Jesse's face heated but Tom initially just appeared to be relieved. But then his face turned thoughtful, and his gaze went to the floor.

"He really is good to me, Tom," Jesse said in a low voice. "Good *for* me. I feel so much when I'm with him, but I'm never scared."

Tom finally looked at him. Regret and uncertainty weighed equally in his eyes. "I'll take your word on that."

"I swear," Jesse said, his voice thickening when he thought of Emory's firm refusal the night before. "There's no risk. Trust me. I know what that feels like."

Tom gave a nervous laugh and ruffled his curls "That makes two of us, then. But thanks, Jesse. I needed to hear that, I think."

"So, what's next?" Jesse said, glad to move the conversation on and turning back to his workstation. "What can we do to counter all this crap?"

"Have your meeting with Darragh at sundown," Tom said, moving to the door. "And do exactly what he says. That's all you need to do. And, Jesse?" Jesse looked up. Tom smiled. "Thanks."

Jesse blinked. "For what?"

"For understanding everything. Understanding *him*. Probably better than I do"

Jesse nodded, unsure what to say. Tom smiled again, a mix of emotions in his eyes, and left.

* * * *

Jesse searched through his clothes for an hour before sundown, trying to decide what you should wear to a meeting with your vampire lover and his undead lawyer. With a frustrated noise, he dressed in plain black jeans and a white T-shirt, zipping a new hoodie over the top. He found Emory and Darragh Kelly in the study, conversing quietly over half-drank glasses of blood.

"Jesse," Emory said, standing as Jesse entered. "Thanks for coming."

"No problem," Jesse said, taking the seat opposite the red-haired haemophile.

Kelly hadn't moved. His emerald eyes were fixed on Jesse. "I thought I recognized the voice on that clip," he drawled in his low, rolling voice.

Jesse winced and caught Emory's eye. "I'm sorry, Em," he breathed. "I really am."

"Why are you apologizing?" Emory said with a slight curve of the lips. "The statement was very complimentary."

"That's not how the opposition will spin it," Kelly said. "But if we prepare for this deposition carefully, we could make it work in our favor."

"I don't know much about all this legal stuff," Jesse said, wiping his damp palms on his jeans.

"Of course, you don't. That's my arena," Kelly said. He turned to Emory. "This relationship you two have. It's grounded in mutual respect, I assume?"

"I believe so," Emory said, looking again at Jesse.

"Yes," Jesse said firmly. "Of course it is."

"Good," Kelly said, picking up a file from the table and leafing through it. "If this human genuinely cares for you, Emory, there's a chance we can make other humans do likewise."

"Look, mate," Jesse said, nettled. "I want to help Emory. I do. But what's between us is our business. I'm not spouting a load of personal shit to some stranger."

Kelly drew out his phone and pressed play. The audio clip played again, and Jesse winced.

"Yeah, yeah, okay," he said, gesturing impatiently. "We don't need to hear it again."

"My point, Mr. Truelove," Kelly said, "is you've already shared your 'personal shit' with the whole world. My job is to turn it into an advantage rather than a catastrophic blow to Emory's custody case."

Jesse winced again.

"I do have some good news," Kelly said, turning to Emory. "The court has now ruled that Dimity can stay with you until the custody hearing."

"That's excellent news," Emory said.

"No shit?" Jesse said, moving to the edge of his seat. "So they admit it was illegal for that woman to take her away?"

Kelly lifted an eyebrow. "More like they've admitted there are no legal grounds at this stage to take her back. But you need to keep quiet about Christmas Eve at the mayor's house," he said, his expression darkening. "They don't need any more ammunition."

"Aren't they going to ask me about that?" Jesse said, keeping his voice steady.

"I don't know what they are going to ask," Kelly said. "But if anything about that night comes up, your response is 'no comment'. Understand?"

"Isn't that gonna sound suspicious?"

"The focus of this case is on our plans for Miss Hawthorn's future," Kelly said decisively. "That is what the judge will be making her decision on. We don't comment on anything that is unhelpful to that end." Jesse glanced at Emory, but he was looking at the wall, his eyes distant. Kelly glanced at him without reaction then back at Jesse. "All the depositions are after sundown, so we will all be together. I've won the motion to ensure Helena Hawthorn is not present."

"Thank Christ," Jesse said.

"No, you thank *me*, human," Kelly said with a hard look. "Christ will be of no use to you in this situation."

"It's just an expression," Jesse muttered.

"You'll have to excuse me on that front," the lawyer said, his jewel-hard gaze again on his files. "I never got used to this modern habit of taking the Lord's name in vain."

"Darragh," Emory scolded softly.

"I would like to meet with you a couple of more times before the deposition," Kelly said, gathering his files and standing. "I will help you prepare. But the most vital part of all this is you focusing on what's important. That's the baron and his daughter. Understand?"

"You don't have to tell me Emory and Dim are important," he said levelly.

"Work on the swearing," Kelly said, then moved to the door. "Baron," he said, inclining his head, then left.

Jesse bit his lip. "Is it really a good idea for me to do this?"

"You have to do it, my love," Emory said, moving to join Jesse. "I'm sorry you do. But that doesn't change things." Emory smiled and ran a hand up Jesse's arm. "But don't worry. I'm certain you're more than capable of handling a few human lawyers. Tell me, how are you feeling today?"

"Fine," Jesse said, touching his forehead. "No pain left."

"I didn't mean your head."

Jesse looked up, their words from the previous evening rushing back and closing his throat. "Fine. I think."

Emory lifted his hand and kissed the knuckles. "Have you forgiven me?"

Jesse pulled his hand away. "You don't need forgiving. I was being an idiot."

"Is that so?"

Jesse waved a hand and turned his back. "I heard Tom when he told me about the biting. About how bad it is. I know I shouldn't have asked. Maybe it was the Blood, I dunno. But I do this, Emory," he added, quietly. "I...push things. I always have. I don't like thinking there's...edges to things. Boundaries."

Emory ran his hands up his arms from behind. He pressed a soft kiss to his neck. Jesse shivered.

"There are no bounds to what I'm starting to feel for you," he whispered against his skin. "It makes me ache that you can never truly know what or how I feel. Seeing you with Dimity, apart from anything else..." He smiled against Jesse's skin, and Jesse's heart fluttered. "It's like a dream. But I've hurt people in the past...inflicted pain." His grip tightened on Jesse's arms. "It's a part of myself that's cost me a lot to change. I can't go back."

Jesse turned in his arms, grabbed his face and kissed him.

"I get it," he whispered, kissing his lips and nose. "I get it, even when I pretend I don't. I'm sorry."

"Don't be sorry, love," he said, kissing Jesse's cheek. "Just be you."

"I'll try," Jesse said with a crooked smile. "And I'll do anything I can to make sure you keep Dim. Whatever it takes."

"Thank you," Emory said sincerely, rubbing his arms then moving to the door. "I have a meeting with Greenway. Then Dimity's new school has agreed to a midnight video call. Are you going to bed? You should rest."

Jesse shook his head. "I'm gonna try to adjust to being up later," he said, shoving his hands in his pockets. "Try to be around more when you are."

Emory was still for a moment. "You don't have to do that."

"I want to. Just like working nights, right?"

"I can't let Dimity do that," he said after a moment. "If you were hoping she would stay up, too..."

"No, no," Jesse said, waving his hand. "That would be too much for a kid. I'm thinking twilight shifts for me though, maybe? One until one or something? Then I'll see her in the afternoons, you in the evening? When you're not working, that is."

Emory smiled softly. "I'd like that. Let's see how that works, shall we?"

"Yeah," Jesse said, fighting a yawn. He checked his watch. "A few hours left. Gonna get a coffee and take a shift in the security room."

"Stay safe, *liebling*."

He left. Jesse gazed into the fire, trying to decide if he had meant to commit that much to Emory before he'd entered the room, then admitted he'd been at Emory's command the minute he met his eyes at the Christmas lights ceremony.

The memory of Oliver made Jesse's heart clench. He brought out his phone. Nothing from Anton. He stopped himself ringing, telling himself it was too late…in more ways than one…then went to the staff kitchen to pour the strongest coffee they had.

* * * *

Jesse spent the next week swinging between a place of joyful contentment and gut-wrenching fear that he'd made the biggest mistake of his life. He woke around noon each day, and the first thing that happened was Ant's words and the image of his face twisted with hatred would race back to him. He would hurriedly get out of bed and bury himself in work until it was time for lunch with Dimity. They usually ate with Joanna in one of the airy sitting rooms that overlooked the grounds. She liked to go for a ride after lunch, usually with Joanna, though Jesse was occasionally cajoled into accompanying her instead. He began to get a better feel for Thor and was reassured that Filip always followed at a discreet distance. They always steered away from the moor gate, though no one had come near it since the night with Lucien.

The crowd at the front gates thinned as the days went by and Emory wasn't arrested. But there was always someone there. Fresh graffiti had to be whitewashed off the gates every other day. But as he rode or walked through the chilly grounds with more grass showing through the melting snow, wind in his face and the sound of birds in the air, it was easy for Jesse to pretend that protestors and hate-fueled headlines didn't exist.

Until he logged into his computer, anyway. The internet continued to churn with supposition and speculation, but it had changed direction since Kelly had finally issued a statement. The legal language he'd used was so dry and remote that it seemed to have taken the wind out of the protestors' sails. But the revelation that a haemophile was fighting for custody of a human child was rippling around the world.

Trixy's crowdfunder exceeded its target in days. She had tried every possible way to get in touch again, he suspected for more insight into his sex life. In the end he blocked all her numbers and distributed her picture to the security team with his cheeks burning.

He was grateful for his time with Dimity, when he could remember what it was all for.

"I met the teacher last night," she said one afternoon when she was chatting her new school as she reined Ruby in from another trot. "And Daddy says I can take biscuits for the class on my first day. Miss Henderson so much nicer than the teacher at my old school," she added with an expressive frown. "He was always angry. And he smelled funny."

Jesse made polite, noncommittal replies and tried not to think about what might happen if this all fell apart.

Joanna would usually meet them at the stables and take Dimity inside while Jesse joined Tom in the security room for the afternoon and evening shift. That day, though, Joanna wasn't alone. A woman Jesse didn't recognize but who looked vaguely familiar stood with her, wearing a small smile on her pleasant face as she watched Dimity dismount. Dimity handed Ruby to the groom and walked over, beaming at the woman as she removed her helmet. Jesse got down off Thor with considerably less dignity and hurried to join them, but the strange woman had already returned to a car parked in the stable entrance.

"Who was that?" Jesse asked Joanna as the woman drove away. "Did she have security clearance?"

Joanna gave him a funny look. "Yes, she has clearance."

"Who was she?"

"That was just Sofia," Dimity explained before Joanna could reply, striding back toward the house. "My mummy."

Jesse blinked, but Joanna was already directing Dimity upstairs to get changed. Jesse stood in the hall, staring after them. But he was already late for his shift, so he turned and made for the security room.

Tom nodded at Jesse's question. "Sofia calls by sometimes, just to see how Dimity's doing. It's all agreed and pre-arranged."

"Doesn't that confuse the hell out of the kid?"

"Did she look confused?"

Jesse sighed and sat at his workstation. "No. She never does."

"Well then," Tom said and turned the conversation to work.

The minute the sun went down, Jesse joined Dimity to wait for Emory. They would spend a few pleasant hours together, watching a film or playing with her art supplies or computer games. It was all so comfortable and domestic that Jesse had a hard time remembering there was anything unusual about the situation. Apart from the fact that he couldn't get enough of 'comfortable and domestic' for the first time in his life, that was.

Then it would be time to put Dimity to bed, and Emory would take him to the master bedroom for more of the most mind-blowing sex of his life. Emory produced ropes, chains, cuffs, toys... There were build ups that felt like they lasted for hours, orgasms so intense they left Jesse breathless and reeling. Whatever had happened that day, Emory seemed to instinctively know what Jesse needed and gave it to him, over and over.

It was so easy to convince himself that this was what he wanted forever. So easy. And yet...

"Are you all right?" Tom asked the night before the deposition.

Jesse started, realizing he'd been staring at a screen of code without seeing it for several minutes. "Yeah...fine."

"You look knackered."

"Just getting used to the new sleeping pattern," Jesse replied, sipping his coffee.

"You sure that's all it is?" Jesse looked over. Tom was tilting his head. "You can still talk to me. You know that right?"

Jesse let out a long sigh, closing his eyes. "I'm just feeling like I'm living in two worlds at once," he said softly. "And I don't know which is real."

"Maybe they both are — or neither."

Jesse looked at him. "Thanks. That really helps."

Tom smiled and patted his shoulder. "Everything's very new right now. And with the custody case and everything" — he shook his head — "it's got us all off balance."

"You don't seem off balance," Jesse said, eyeing Tom, who looked bright-eyed, well rested and even more chirpy than usual.

"Don't I?" His smile widened. "That's good to know."

Jesse examined him for a long moment then looked away, smiling. But then he sighed again. "The whole world is watching this case," Jesse said quietly, shaking his head. "It's so scary big." He swallowed. "I can't get my head around it."

"You should probably decide how you feel...and soon."

"It's nothing to do with me."

"It's everything to do with you," Tom said quietly. "She could end up being your daughter, too."

Jesse didn't let himself meet Tom's eyes, however, worried his colleague might see the mingled excitement and terror he suddenly felt.

Chapter Seventeen

"You need to answer their questions honestly," Emory said to a nervous-looking Dimity as she sat between him and Jesse in the limo on their way to the deposition. "There are no wrong answers. And you can't get in trouble, no matter what you say." He added this last as he met Jesse's eyes.

"But I don't want to talk to them," Dimity said. "They want to take me away."

"They want to do what's best for you," Emory said, holding her hand tight. "For them to decide that, they need to know how you feel — really feel...about everything."

A knot of people were outside Ivor, Harrison & Associate's building when they arrived. Emory's security urged them back before they allowed the car door to be opened. When Emory emerged with Dimity and Jesse in tow, shouts broke out and phones were held over the heads of the security guards to film them.

Dimity didn't look around but held Emory's hand tight and went with him up the steps to where Darragh Kelly, blank-faced and intent, stood in the open doorway.

He took them through the empty offices at a brisk pace, tapping on a large-screened phone as he went.

"Miss Hawthorn is scheduled first," he said to Emory. "Then Mr. Truelove. Then you."

"Good," Emory replied, slowing his pace as they approached a glass-walled meeting room with a number of grim-faced people sitting around a large table. "Joanna is coming in an hour, then she can take Dimity straight home."

"Don't I get to stay with you, Daddy?" Dimity said, looking perturbed.

"It's late already, darling," Emory said, kneeling in front of her so they were on eye level. "But I promise we won't be far behind you."

A young woman in a smart suit opened the door.

"Good evening," she said. "I'm the representative from Child Services. I understand the necessity of having these depositions so late in the day, but perhaps we could get Miss Hawthorn's interview done as quickly as possible?"

"I don't want to." Dimity flung her arms around Emory's neck. He held her close, stroking her back. His face was tight with emotion. Jesse's heart clenched.

Emory whispered something to Dimity that Jesse couldn't hear. She straightened, wiped her eyes and nodded. She took the woman's hand and allowed herself to be taken into the meeting room. Kelly followed Dimity in. Emory took a seat on one of the deep sofas set against the wall. Jesse sat on the edge, his elbows on his knees, one leg jigging.

Dimity sat with her back to the glass. The Child Services rep was on one side and Kelly on the other. One of the suited men pressed a button on a recording device in the middle of the table, and the court reporter began typing as the large, square-faced man in the middle of the row began to talk.

"What are they going to ask her?" Jesse said quietly.

"They'll ask her about her daily routine," Emory replied in a monotone. "How much time she spends with me. And what she's seen and heard about the house."

"Then there's nothing to worry about, right?" Jesse said carefully. "She loves living with you."

Emory didn't answer. He was still as stone with his hands folded in his lap. His blue-black eyes were locked on the small figure beyond the glass. Jesse dropped his gaze to the floor.

On one hand it seemed like the poor girl was trapped in that room for hours. On the other, it was all too soon that someone was saying Jesse's name. He blinked and sat up.

Dimity put on a brave smile as Emory talked to her off to one side. The Child Services rep stood a polite distance behind them. Joanna was waiting in the doorway in her coat, her expression guarded.

"Go on home now, darling," Emory said, standing and urging Dimity toward Joanna. "We'll see you soon."

"Mr. Truelove," the man in the doorway repeated, and Jesse's heart began to race. Then Emory was at his side, taking his hand.

"Remember what I said. There are no wrong answers," he murmured softly. "Just tell them the truth."

"I don't know what that is," Jesse said, his voice hoarse. "That's the problem."

Emory pressed his hand to Jesse's chest. "In here you do."

Jesse gazed into his eyes. His mind raced and his blood surged. Emory held his gaze for a long moment, gave him a minute nod then pushed him toward the door.

Jesse sat facing the line of lawyers, finding it hard to focus. Kelly was on his right, rigid as a carving with his long fingers interlaced on the table in front of him.

"Mr. Truelove," the square-faced man in the middle spoke while scrolling through something on his tablet. "Have you had the deposition procedure explained to you?"

The courter reporter clicked away in the corner. Jesse swallowed. "Yes."

"And you understand that everything you say will be provided as evidence in the custody case of Baron Emory Von Magnusson and Dimity Hawthorn?'

"Yes," Jesse said, a little steadier.

"Good." The man raised his head. "I'm Brandon Harrison. This is my associate Francis Ivor," he indicated the balding man on his right. "And these other people are senior partners in my firm. We are representing Helena Hawthorn in this matter, but I suspect you already know that,"

"Mr. Truelove has had the procedure and your role in it explained to him," Darragh Kelly cut in. "That is now on record. Please, can we proceed?"

Jesse resisted looking over his shoulder to where Emory sat, alone, beyond the glass behind him as Harrison spent a moment looking Jesse over. He was suddenly glad he'd caved to Kelly's nagging and put on a suit and tie and tidied his hair.

"Very well," Harrison began, swiping the tablet's screen and picking up a stylus. "Firstly, what is the nature of your relationship with the baron?"

Jesse tilted his chin. "We're fucking."

Harrison raised his eyebrows. The other people went very still. Kelly's face was unreadable.

"So, it's a sexual relationship?"

"That's what I said, wasn't it?" Jesse kept his voice level, despite his heart doing cartwheels in his chest.

Harrison carefully scribbled a note on his tablet. "I thank you for your candor, Mr. Truelove. Now perhaps you could expand how you think your relationship impacts Dimity Hawthorn."

"Impacts?"

"Yes," Harrison said. "It's a challenging enough situation to have someone of another species as the parental figure. To be aware of that parental figure being involved with a male member of his staff—"

"That sounds like gay-bashing to me, mate," Jesse said. "You might wanna be careful there."

His balding associate gave Harrison a pointed look. Harrison's jaw tightened.

"Is your relationship consensual, Mr. Truelove?"

"Yes."

"We obtained a warrant for the security footage from Oswald House," Harrison went on, looking him in the eye. "There is some footage missing from not long after you took over as security chief."

Jesse swallowed. "Missing...?"

"Part of the footage was looped to cover a gap. Our technical analysts have tried to retrieve it but, alas, they are not as competent as you." Harrison tilted his head. "Why did you wipe that footage, Mr. Truelove?"

He looked imploringly at Kelly, who tapped his long fingernail on the tabletop. "Have you got evidence that it was Mr. Truelove that wiped this footage?"

"None beyond what our analysts have termed a 'digital signature', which they attribute to Mr. Truelove, though it is far from proof."

"Then perhaps you would like to get to the point," Kelly said levelly.

"My point is to raise the question as to whether Mr. Truelove is wary, ashamed even, of his relationship, if he felt the need to erase evidence of it?"

"You don't know that it was what was erased," Kelly said, his face blank.

"The time and date of the missing footage are telling," Harrison returned. "But that is not what we're here to prove. I'm merely trying to ascertain whether this is an abusive situation or not."

"It isn't," Jesse insisted.

"He's your employer," Harrison said levelly. "Controls your pay. Your living circumstances. You can see why we would be wary."

"He's good to me," Jesse said firmly. "Too bloody good."

"How so?"

Jesse swore under his breath. He dropped his gaze to the table. "I haven't had anyone treat me like this before. He makes me feel... I dunno." He shifted in his seat.

"Please be frank," Harrison insisted. "It is important the judge gets a clear picture of the situation."

Jesse clenched his teeth. "He makes me feel special, all right?" he said, his face heating. "Makes me feel like

I actually matter — that what I want matters and that I'm not a freak for wanting it."

Harrison referred to his notes. "So now we come to it." He twiddled his thumbs. "How would *you* describe Baron Von Magnusson's relationship with Dimity Hawthorn?"

"He's crazy about her," Jesse said vehemently. "Loves her to pieces. She is literally everything to him."

"So you would say the baron puts Dimity first?" Harrison continued, still looking at Jesse. "In everything?"

"Yes," Jesse said. "And before you try to trick me into saying that pisses me off, it doesn't. That's as it should be."

"Could you expand, Mr. Truelove?"

"The kid comes first," he said, "before everything else — before anything you want…need. Before you deal with your shit, you deal with theirs. That's the goddamn rules."

Harrison regarded him steadily. "And the baron does this?"

"Every time."

"And how would you say kidnapping her from her aunt's house in the middle of the night was putting Dimity's needs before his own?"

"Mr. Truelove will not be answering any questions about December twenty-fourth," Kelly said.

"Oh?" Ivor said, wrinkling his high forehead as he raised bushy eyebrows. "That's very interesting."

"How Miss Hawthorn came to be restored to her adopted guardian has already been reviewed by the judge and ruled on," Kelly said, his voice never wavering. "It is not the subject of this deposition."

"You're right, of course, Mr. Kelly," Harrison continued, an unpleasant smile on his face. "Mr. Truelove is the subject of this deposition. So perhaps he wouldn't mind answering a few questions about himself?" Jesse went cold. "Before your employment at Oswald House, what did you do as a living Mr. Truelove?"

Jesse looked at the lawyer at his side. Kelly gave him a small nod.

Jesse cleared his throat. "I was an independent IT consultant."

"And who hired you...and for what?"

"Mr. Truelove's client list is protected information," Kelly put in. "If the judge really wants it, she would issue a warrant. Has she done so?"

"Please ensure the report reflects Mr. Truelove is declining to answer," Ivor said with a sneer.

"It's not relevant, that's why," Jesse snapped. "She's not *my* kid, is she?"

"But if you plan to continue a relationship with the baron, you could end up with a role in her upbringing," Harrison said smoothly. "This is why we need to know the sort of people the baron allows into his home...into his family. Fortunately, your arrest record is on file, so we don't need you to tell us about that."

"So I'm a screw-up," Jesse grated. "*Was* a screw-up. It's all in the past."

"You've left it all behind? Just like that?"

Jesse shifted. "Yes."

"And what triggered this change of character?"

"Emory did."

The people across the table's faces tightened with scorn. "A haemophile inspired you to be a better human being?"

"Yes. No," Jesse corrected himself. "He convinced me I was *already* a good human being."

"So, if the baron ever requested you do anything illegal, for example, break into a law office to steal confidential information" — Harrison gave him a hard look — "you would refuse?"

Jesse couldn't breathe.

"Please note that, again, Mr. Truelove has declined—"

"Hypothetically speaking," Jesse said in a low voice. "I would do anything to help level this twisted playing field of yours."

"Perhaps you'd like to expand on that, too?"

Jesse leaned forward in his chair. "If this was all because he was gay, or another race or gender, the world would be up in arms. But no, just because he's a haemophile, it's okay to treat him like some sort of pariah — someone who shouldn't be allowed anywhere near a kid, just because he's *different*."

"Let the record show that I'm now placing before Mr. Truelove evidence exhibit Eight-A — Baron Emory Von Magnusson's registered Kill List."

Jesse stared at Harrison's tablet with his vision blurring. He didn't want to read it again, didn't want to see that they were so many men and women, different ages, different backgrounds, from all over the world.

"This is what makes him different, Mr. Truelove," Harrison said, tapping the screen. "It's not because he looks different — or his skin color, or because of his sexual orientation. It is because he has *murdered* people. Many, many people."

"To survive," Jesse said quietly, still staring at the list. "To live. Before they had a choice."

"These first fifty names," Harrison went on, running his finger down the list. "These deaths all occurred within the first two years of the baron being transformed. Early research suggests a haemophile can subsist on one full human feed for up to a month. This number of deaths far exceeds the amount minimum needed for the baron to feed. And this is only the ones we know about."

Jesse shook his head. When he spoke, his voice creaked. "I don't know what you're saying."

"I'm asking if you really think that every single person on this list was killed by the baron simply to allow him to survive? Not out of malice, enjoyment or sexual thrill?"

Jesse shoved the tablet away. "You can't judge him on stuff he did over two hundred years ago."

"I'm afraid that is what we are here to do," Harrison said.

The list, the table and the room blurred. Jesse looked at Kelly desperately, but the lawyer's eyes were fixed on Harrison.

"Would you like to revise your statement, Mr. Truelove?" Harrison said quietly. "As someone who knows him intimately and as someone who knows *this*." He tapped the screen again. "Do you really think Baron Emory Von Magnusson is a suitable guardian for a human child?"

The silence was like freezing winter fog. Kelly's hard eyes were now on Jesse. The court reporter sat still in the corner. The lawyers waited.

"I love him," Jesse eventually said, so softly someone asked him to repeat himself. "I love him, you hear me?" He shouted, clenching his fists. "And he loves Dimity. That's all that matters."

He hurried for the door. Several people called him back, but he couldn't make out the words. Emory stood. His face was a mask of concern. Jesse wanted to fling himself into his arms, bury his face in his huge chest and will the world to go away, but Harrison's voice was raised behind him. Kelly's clipped responses cut through it, and Jesse suddenly couldn't bear to hear or see anything else.

He rushed past Emory, through the building and out into the icy air. He shouldered his way through the line of security and ignored the crowd of onlookers. He thought he saw a flash of electric-blue hair among the crowd but kept moving.

He stumbled along with his heart in his throat, everything hurting until he realized he was standing outside Anton and Sareena's house. His thumb was on the doorbell, and his forehead was pressed against the glass.

No one answered. It was dark inside. He checked his watch, winced but pressed the bell again, as a sob threatened to choke him.

"Jess?"

Jesse turned. Anton stood at the side gate in a large coat with an open beer in one hand and a log in the other. His face was lost in shadow, but Jesse could tell he was frowning. He stood very still.

"Hey..."

Anton didn't move. "What do you want?"

"Can I come in? Just for a bit?" Jesse asked with his voice quavering and small.

Anton still didn't move for a long moment. "You're not wearing a coat."

"I kinda left somewhere in a hurry..." Jesse said, rubbing his arms as shivering started to set in.

Anton was still for several pained heartbeats. Then he stepped back and held open the gate. Jesse moved down the side of the house and into the back garden. A fire danced in a firepit on the patio. A cooler of beer was set next to a chair drawn up to the flames. Anton moved over, threw his log on the fire and dragged up a second chair.

"Sareena's taken Oliver to her mum's for a few days," Anton said, a little sluggish, as he sat and drained his beer.

"Is everything okay?" Jesse asked, hovering at the edge of the firelight.

Anton's face twisted. "I don't think I'm easy to be around at the moment."

Jesse clenched his fists. "I'm sorry, Ant. I'm *really* sorry."

Anton met his eyes over the flames. A hundred unsaid things flickered through them before he lowered his gaze again. He gestured at the extra chair. Jesse sat, drawing close to the warmth of the fire. Anton held out a beer. Jesse snatched it and swallowed half in one go, but it still felt like there was a shard of glass wedged between his ribs.

"It's all been on the news," Anton muttered, staring at the fire. "Just like you said. A vampire suing for custody." He shook his head. "What's happening, Jesse?"

"You really want to know?"

Anton glanced at him then away. "No," he said flatly. Then he grimaced. "But I should. Tell me, Jess. Help me understand."

Jesse rocked in his chair with his teeth chattering. "Honestly? I don't know what's happening anymore," he whispered softly. "I thought I knew, thought I understood. That everything was simple."

"Simple?" Anton raised his eyebrows.

Jesse shrugged. "That's just it. From the outside looking in, yeah, it must look like the world's most almighty shit parade, the worst thing since Blood Winter." He winced and Anton looked away. "But on the inside..." He turned to face his brother, waiting until he met his eyes. "On the inside, Ant, it really was just about him — and how he loves his kid. And how I... How I love them both."

The lines in Anton's forehead disappeared as his face flattened. "Come again?"

"I love him, Ant," Jesse whispered. "I know what I said. What I sounded like on that clip. But it isn't just about the sex."

"Jess, I don't wanna hear this."

"But you need to," Jesse said, drawing his chair closer. "Don't you see? You're like everyone else, and that's not your fault. Of course you were scared of him...of what he's done. But don't you see...? It's just because you don't *know*."

"Know what?" Anton asked wearily.

"That he's incredible," he said. "He gets me. And, whatever he is, whatever he's done... he's good for me."

"And what about that poor sod you brought here for Christmas, hey? Tom, was it?"

"Tom's a friend. I didn't lie about that."

"He didn't look at you like I look at my mates, Jess," Anton said.

"He's a friend," Jesse insisted. "a really good friend."

"But why is he just a friend?" Anton said despairingly. "He's nice. He's *normal*. He's clearly crazy about you."

Jesse put his head in his hands. "I tried to like him, Ant. I swear I did, for all those reasons. But they're all things *you* want for me—not things I want for myself."

"You don't want a partner that treats you with respect and decency?"

"Who's to say I don't?"

"So why bring him to Christmas, huh? Was the poor bastard just a decoy? Christ, Jesse. That terrible thing about all this is you don't see this as messed up."

"It wasn't like that," Jesse pleaded. "He gave me a lift. He was on his own. He had a great day."

Anton shook his head. "It's like Glen all over again."

The glass in Jesse's ribs twisted. "What?"

"You mow down these nice blokes because what you want is some twisted fantasy that no human can live up to."

Jesse swallowed. "Emory lives up to it. That's what I'm trying to tell you."

Anton clenched his jaw then gestured wearily. "Go on then. I'm listening...for ten seconds. That's all the time I'm giving this."

Jesse cleared his throat with another swallow of beer. "He's the most amazing person I've met, Ant. He's lived so long—seen and done so much, regrets so much. But, under it all, the thing that matters the most to him is family." Jesse watched his brother stare into the fire. "You get that, right?"

"Yeah," Anton said slowly after a long moment. "Yeah, I get that. But he's not human, Jess." He raised his eyes. "Whatever else, nothing changes that."

"Why is being human such a big deal?" he whispered. "It sucks, in my general experience."

Anton's face was pained. "You don't mean that, little brother. Not really."

Jesse looked away.

"Look... I'm sorry about the other day," Anton finally said in a low voice. "I was angry. Really angry. But it's like you said. All that matters is family, right? I have to think of Oliver. I have to put him first, understand?"

"I would never hurt Olly," Jesse said, his voice wobbling with pain. "You know that."

"You would never mean to," Anton said carefully, grasping Jesse's arm. "Of course, I know that. But you've got so much going on in your life, Jesse. You're still trying to figure all that out. And maybe that's my fault."

"Ant..."

"Or maybe it's Dad's. I don't know," he said, waving a hand. "I'm exhausted trying to figure out where it all went wrong. But you break the law. You can't hold down a job. You let strange blokes tie you up then splash it all over the internet. You took a kid out of her home at night—"

"That wasn't her home."

"I know you've justified it all to yourself," Anton said, sitting forward. "And I know you did it all for what you thought were good reasons. I'm starting to get that. But at the end of the day, what the world sees matters. What people say matters. And it impacts Oliver." He let out a deep sigh. "I'm not saying never, mate. But you have to see why it's best you stay away from us until things are better."

"But this is the best life's ever been for me," Jesse said, his voice choking.

Anton grimaced. "That's my point."

Jesse left without another word.

* * * *

Emory hadn't returned by the time Jesse got back to Oswald House. He ignored the cold feeling that stole through him when the taxi driver eyed the graffiti on the walls, and he went straight upstairs. Dimity's bedroom door was closed. He resisted opening it and went to the master bedroom. He closed the curtains, sat on the bed in the dark and waited.

An indeterminable time later, he heard a car outside and the front door opening. There were voices in the hall. A few moments later, the bedroom door opened, spilling dim light into the room. Emory came in and moved toward the bedside lamp, but Jesse went to him and took his wrist before he could turn it on.

They stood there in the dark, Jesse clutching Emory's wrist, his own breathing coming fast. Emory's was slow and heavy in the darkness.

"How did it go?" Jesse asked.

"We won't know that until the hearing," Emory said. Jesse jumped when Emory tucked his hair behind his ears. "Kelly told me what you said, Jesse," he said quietly. "I hope that's okay."

"I fucked up," Jesse said. "Again."

"You told the truth," Emory replied. "That's what you needed to do."

"Even if it's cost you your daughter?"

"If anything costs me my custody of Dimity, it won't be your honesty," Emory said softly. "An important part of all this is that I and my kind be understood. I believe as part of that, I should be allowed to parent Dimity. If that doesn't happen but the world at least starts thinking of us differently, it will be progress. And it might mean that the next parent won't have to go through this."

"You can't really think that," Jesse said, his voice edged. "You can't be that decent, after everything we've put you through."

"We've put you through worse, over the years," Emory replied. "Change is never easy. But it's important it happens, anyway." Emory kissed his hair. "Thank you...for everything."

"I can't do this anymore, Emory," he whispered.

"Do what, *liebling*?"

"Go on like this," Jesse said, swallowing a sob. "All these feelings. All this shit inside me." He clutched the front of Emory's shirt so tight that his fingers ached. "Good ones. Shit ones. Loads of them somewhere in between I can't figure out." He reached out in the dark, found Emory's hair and drew his head in for a feverish, clumsy kiss. The taste and smell of him, smoke and wine and power, sent sparks along Jesse's veins. "Please, Emory," he panted against his mouth. "Please make it stop."

"I can't stop your feelings, my love," he said. "I wouldn't want to. But I'm happy to change them, for a while." He ran his tongue down Jesse's neck and slipped his hands inside Jesse's shirt.

"Not like that," Jesse said, shaking his head, clutching Emory's arms so tight it had to be hurting him. "I mean change *me. Please.*"

Emory stiffened. Jesse sensed him lift his head. It was several moments before he spoke.

"I hope I've misunderstood."

"You haven't," Jesse rasped, pressing his body against Emory's. "I want to be like you. A haemophile. I can't deal with all this human mess anymore. I can't."

Emory withdrew his hands from Jesse's body and stepped back. Jesse whimpered and reached after him, but Emory guided him to the bed and sat. He clicked on the light. His face was guarded.

"You can't ask that of me," he said firmly. "It is illegal."

"But that Lucien turned you, right?" Jesse said desperately. "And someone turned him. And Darragh. And Terje Kristiansen and all the others." He grabbed Emory's hand. "You were all human once, and you aren't anymore. I want that."

"You don't mean that."

"Yes, I fucking *do*," Jess shouted, standing. "And I'm sick of everyone telling me what I mean and don't mean, want or don't want." Emory sat very still as Jesse stood with his fists clenched, watching him until his pulse slowed and the heat left his body. "Please," Jesse begged. "*Please*, Emory."

"No one should make you justify what you want in the bedroom, Jesse," Emory said quietly. "Or what you want from a partner. Or from your future. But it's like biting... You *cannot* want this the way you think you do because you don't understand what you're truly asking."

"You're so in control. Everything's easy for you. I don't want any of this hard stuff anymore."

"My dearest," Emory said, taking his hand. "Becoming a haemophile doesn't leave emotion behind. It doesn't let you escape the fear, the anger." His grip tightened. "Quite the opposite."

Jesse blinked. "What do you mean?"

"You wouldn't escape these feelings. They would get worse."

"But you said you don't remember being human..."

"I don't. Not now. But there was a time when I did. And I carried everything with me so strongly I didn't know how to handle it." He stood, looking hard into Jesse's face. "Why do you think so many people died those first few years, Jesse?" he whispered. "It was nothing to do with hunger."

Jesse stepped back. His skin rushed with chills.

Emory didn't blink. "I've learned to understand who I am and handle how I experience the world. But it took hundreds of years, too many lives — and cost me far more than I would have ever willingly paid, had I known." He ran a thumb down Jesse's cheek. "I wouldn't do it to my worst enemy, let alone someone I care about."

A whirlwind rose inside Jesse's chest, clogging his throat and flooding his head with rage and sorrow. He buried his face in Emory's chest and sobbed. He choked and cried — ugly, loud crying that soaked and slimed Emory's shirt and made his face grow hot. But he didn't stop...couldn't stop.

Emory held him until the crying slowed and eventually eased. Jesse held his face against his chest, breathing heavily, not wanting to move. Finally, Emory brought him back to the bed. He undressed him, slowly, kissing as he went. It wasn't long before Jesse was overwhelmed with a very different mix of sensations. Emory moved slowly, teasing and licking, lighting fires, forbidding Jesse to talk or move as he prepared him, slowly and thoroughly, with a well-lubed plug until he was writhing and crying and beyond conscious thought. That was when he leaned over Jesse's quivering body and whispered an instruction in his ear.

"Turn over, my love."

Jesse scrambled to obey then Emory was filling him, inch by glorious inch, plunging to his depths with his long, rock-hard cock. Jesse lost himself in the burning pleasure, the smell of the sheets, the feeling of Emory's sharp nails digging into his hips.

Emory continued to thrust into him, slowly and languidly, until time lost all meaning.

"I love you, Emory," Jesse whispered as he clutched the sheets. "I fucking love you... *Ah...*"

Jesse came, hot and hard, spasming around Emory's cock. Emory wrapped an arm around his chest and drew him up, so he was sitting in Emory's lap, penetrated so deep Jesse thought they may never be parted again. Emory nuzzled his face in Jesse's neck, thrust several more times then shuddered and came, flooding Jesse with warm, sticky heat.

They lay in each other's arms in silence as their breathing slowed. Jesse was aware of the clock on the wall ticking closer to dawn, but Emory didn't leave.

"So that's a no to being turned, then?" Jesse murmured into Emory's jaw, only half-joking.

"It's a definitive 'no'," Emory said, turning his head so he could look into his eyes. "You don't want it, Jesse. It won't fix anything." He ran his finger over Jesse's lower lip. "Especially as nothing needs to be fixed."

"I dunno. I feel pretty broken right now."

"I'm sorry this has been so hard," Emory said. "But I can't be sorry this has happened between us."

"Even if I can never really understand you or how you feel, see, think? Or even join you for a meal or anything like that?"

Emory grimaced. "You really want to join me for my sort of meal?"

"I would if I was like you," Jesse went on doggedly.

Emory sighed. "Think about what people who care about you would feel if you became a haemophile. Would they be pleased for you?"

"What I want is nothing to do with anyone else but me."

"Most of the time, yes," Emory agreed with a nod. "But with this, no. In this circumstance, you have to think of yourself as if you were a friend…or a parent." Emory looked at him hard. "What would you think if Olly asked this of someone one day?"

Jesse went cold. "That's different."

"But it's not," Emory whispered. "Just imagine what your father would feel, were he still here. Or your mother. That's how you need to start thinking of yourself, as someone you love rather than someone you're trying to escape."

Jesse rolled onto his back and stared at the ceiling. "Right in the orphan thing. Cheers, Emory."

"It's important to think about it, though, isn't it? And talk about it?"

Jesse sighed, a heavy sigh that rattled from somewhere from deep inside him. Into the still silence, he heard himself whispering, "I would have liked to have known her, you know."

"Your mother?" Emory's voice was cautious.

Jesse nodded. "I don't miss her. I can't pretend I do. I don't remember her." He scowled into the dark. "People always ask what it was like, growing up without a '*mum*', never knowing your '*mum*'. People don't ask what it was like never to know *her* — Ellie Truelove, the person." Jesse shook his head, suddenly struggling to speak. "And bloody hell, my family loved her. Still love her. Losing her messed them both up for so long…most of my life. To have inspired so much love…" Jesse swallowed. "Yeah, I think I would have liked to have known that person."

Emory propped himself on his elbow and gazed down into his face. "Perhaps you do know her. Perhaps she lives on in you? Ever consider that?"

Jesse snorted. "I highly doubt that, somehow."

"Perhaps your family didn't show you how much they love you because they assumed it was obvious, just like they assumed it was obvious to you how they felt about her."

"Why do you think I want to escape all this?" Jesse said, covering his face with his arm. "It's just all too damn hard."

"But you're so good at it," Emory said, drawing his arm away from his face. "A lot better than you think you are. And besides…" A guarded smile played on his lips. "Perhaps I want a human parent for Dimity. Didn't you consider that?"

Jesse blinked. "Huh?"

"It's probably time we talk about that, isn't it?"

Jesse's body tensed. "Was this… Was this what you were thinking from the start of all this?"

Emory grinned playfully. "Why? Don't you like her?"

"I'm crazy about her, but —"

"But?"

Jesse opened his mouth, closed it again and looked back at the ceiling. "I just want the pain to stop."

"Pain is part of life, my love," Emory said, ghosting his hand over Jesse's chest, trailing his finger around his nipple bar, making his sated arousal tickle back to life. "But I hope I can continue to balance it for you."

"You are pretty good at that," Jesse conceded, gazing into Emory's face. "That last time... It was...different."

"I believe that was making love rather than just 'fucking'."

Jesse looked away. "Glen, my ex... He liked to take it slow sometimes. But I dunno, I always found it...boring. I know that's bad."

"But not this time?"

"No," Jesse said and kissed him again. Emory returned the kiss, leisurely but intense. Jesse fought a moan and broke away. "You'd better go. It'll be getting light soon."

"I've got some time yet," Emory said, rolling Jesse on top of him and plunging his tongue into his mouth.

"You want to do it again?" Jesse panted into the kiss.

"Being with you keeps reality from becoming too real," Emory whispered as he ran his hands down Jesse's back. "I'd do it forever if I could."

Chapter Eighteen

Jesse again woke up in the master bed. He lay for a long time, feeling Emory's touch still burning on his skin, inhaling the smell of him on the sheets and smiling.

He showered in the en suite and tried to decide what had changed. The hearing was still to come. His sex confession was still doing the rounds. He'd stormed out of the deposition, and Trixy was still in possession of videos of him that could throw fuel on the flames. But none of it seemed to matter as much as it had yesterday. It mattered, but not as much as the fact that Emory loved him — and Dimity loved him, and perhaps, so did Ant.

The date of the hearing came to them via an email from Darragh Kelly a day later. It was scheduled for Saturday evening on the last weekend of Dimity's extended Christmas holiday. Sunday was the tenth of January, Dimity's birthday.

"That's shit," Jesse whispered to Emory. Dimity sat on the other chair sketching dogs as *101 Dalmatians* played on the large screen over the living room fire.

"Really shit. Not only will she not know until the last minute whether she's going to be packed off to Helena's again, but she also has to find out on her birthday?"

Emory squeezed his leg. He was drinking a glass of wine. Jesse marveled at the calm, contented look on his face.

"It is what it is, my love," he said in a low voice. "At least it will be over."

"That can't be all you're feeling," Jesse said, putting his beer aside.

"Of course, it isn't," Emory said with a small smile. "But that's all I'm choosing to acknowledge right now." He kissed Jesse's cheek. "I'm enjoying my evening with my family. I never dared to believe I could even have this. I want to savor it."

Jesse didn't let himself say anything more, though he wanted to…at length. But he bit it back and allowed his new routine at Oswald House to distract him.

People still hung around at the gates, though fewer than before. No new graffiti had appeared in some days. All the security systems were online and registering nothing unusual. Tom was back to being his usual, friendly self, though he seemed to be taking more meetings with Kelly than Jesse thought must be necessary. But he spotted a quiet, private smile on Tom's lips more than once and didn't say anything.

Whenever he wasn't working, Dimity kept him busy. Her skill with her drawing tablet was increasing, and her joy at the effects in some of the art apps seemed unbounded. As soon as it was dark, they shared a few precious hours with Emory. Each day Jesse woke late, and the fragile bubble of ease around his heart wobbled but did not break.

But all too soon he was holding Emory's hand tight as they walked into a courtroom, having negotiated a crowd of reporters and protestors on the courthouse steps. The only other people in the courtroom were Harrison and Ivor at the other table, the Child Services rep in a seat behind them and, finally, sweeping in with her heels clicking on the marble floor, Helena Hawthorn.

She stopped at the end of Jesse's row.

"What is this man doing here?" she demanded. "This is a private hearing."

Jesse bristled, but then a door opened and in walked a gray-haired lady in a gown with a round face and a serious expression.

"Jesse Truelove is here as a court-approved significant other to the baron, Mrs. Hawthorn," the judge said as she took her seat. "Now, if you want to take your own place, we can begin."

Color flushed into Helena's face, but she moved to her lawyer's table.

The judge cleared her throat and opened a file. She sat up straight, and her eyes went over everyone in the room, one at a time.

"This is a private custody hearing to determine the guardianship of Dimity Hawthorn," she intoned. Jesse clutched his hands together in his lap. "As everyone is aware, I have now read and assessed all the statements, depositions and evidence provided by both parties. Today's hearing is simply to inform you of my decision. And, as is my right, to call on any extra witnesses to testify on any areas I still have my doubts on."

"Yes, Your Honor," Harrison said, standing. "And I'm sure Mr. Kelly would agree in saying we hope that this matter can be resolved quickly and fairly for the sake of the child involved."

"I take it as a point of professional pride that I resolve all my cases quickly and fairly, Mr. Harrison," the judge said as she flicked through her notes. "But I appreciate everyone's emotions in this case will be running high. Would Mr. Kelly like to add anything before I proceed?"

Kelly stood. His face was grave, but the deep emotion in his eyes was undeniable. Jesse was flooded with gratitude that Emory's happiness at least lay in the hands of someone that clearly understood the significance of this moment.

"I would first like to thank the court and opposing counsel for their flexibility in allowing this hearing to be held after dark, to accommodate me and my client's admittedly inflexible needs," he said, his voice weighted with just the right amount of sincerity. Harrison and Helena looked unimpressed, but the judge watched him with a measured look. "And I would like to go on to say that, whatever their differences, the baron and Mrs. Hawthorn are in agreement over the need for this matter to be resolved fairly and finally before Miss Hawthorn returns to school on Monday."

"A noble sentiment," the judge said, turning over another paper. "And one I'm also in agreement with. To that end, I only have two extra witnesses I would like to interview before making my decision. First, I would like to call Sofia Graf. Bailiff? Please escort her in."

Jesse stared as the door was opened and in walked the woman from the stable yard. She wasn't smiling this time. Her expression was uneasy as she looked around the room. She caught sight of Helena and stopped in her tracks.

"Please, Miss Graf," the judge said, indicating the seat to the right of her bench. "This won't take long."

A man who had come in at her elbow spoke to her in what sounded like German. The young woman nodded and took the seat.

"Miss Graf is accompanied by Stefan Jurgen, our court translator. Good evening, Miss Graf. Thank you for joining us."

The translator relayed this information to the young woman, who nodded and shot a smile up at the judge. She said something, which the translator then repeated in English.

"Thank you, your honor. Anything I can do to help."

Jesse was looking between the woman, the set look on Helena's face and the unreadable one on Emory's and trying to figure out just what had changed in the room.

"My first question, Miss Graf—"

"I'm sorry, Your Honor," Harrison said, standing, "but we must object. Sofia Graf gave up all parental rights to Dimity when she put her up for adoption at birth."

Jesse watched Sofia, taking in the brightness of her eyes, the soft tilt of her mouth. It was like Dimity was sitting in the witness box, looking wary but not scared. The judge was peering at Harrison over the top of her glasses.

"I am aware of that, Mr. Harrison," she said. "However, Sofia is still the girl's mother. And, I understand, has made an agreement with the baron about being involved in her daughter's life."

"That's correct, your honor," Kelly said smoothly. "Miss Graf was only eighteen years old when Dimity was born. She had — and still has — a whole life to live. She wasn't ready to give Dimity a home. But she is a kind and responsible woman and was keen to see how her daughter's life has turned out. She makes agreed visits to Dimity once or twice a year."

"Is Dimity aware that this woman who visits her is her own mother?" Harrison snapped at Kelly. "Her mother who chose not to keep her? How is that in any way beneficial to her upbringing?"

Jesse's blood heated. Sofia's face clouded as the translator muttered at her side. Emory's face grew grim. Kelly gazed at Harrison with something like contempt. "Yes, Dimity is aware that she is her birth mother. The baron agreed with Sofia that honesty from the start was the best course of action. As she grows older, it will be up to Dimity what sort of relationship she would like to have with her mother. In the meantime, Dimity is growing up aware that her mother does care about her wellbeing."

Sofia burst in with a flurry of German. She held her head high as her eyes bored into Harrison.

"I love Dimity," the translator said, "but I am not in a position to give her the life she deserves. Baron Von Magnusson has given her the sort of home every little girl dreams of. Do you really think I would stand by and do nothing if I thought she was in any way unhappy?" She shook her head. "Shame on you people. Shame on you for bringing this so far and putting Dimity in this position. If her needs really came first, we would not be here."

"Thank you, Miss Graf," the judge said. "I believe you've answered the main question I was going to ask.

But I do have one more, I'm afraid." Sofia looked up at her. "You are aware that the baron is not human. You are aware that, as a race, humankind is still relatively uninformed as to haemophile's day-to-day habits and lifestyle. As the law stands, the baron cannot be held responsible for any of his actions prior to nineteen-hundred, but there is nothing to say that law won't alter as it adapts to changing perceptions. Given all that and knowing the baron's past, do you still really think he could be a suitable adopted father to your child?"

"I do," Sofia said without hesitation, meeting Emory's eyes and smiling. "I was a very young girl when I had my baby. I did not know Cooper, Dimity's father, when I got pregnant. He did not live long enough for me to find anything out about him — or whether he would have made a good father for Dimity." Her eyes moved to Helena, who sat, grim and silent, in her seat. "It was all very hard to take, but the baron came to me. He told me he was Dimity's uncle, from many, many years back. I knew what he was. But *blutfressers* have been accepted more easily in my country than they are here — to their benefit and ours. He told me what he could do for Dimity and that he would be there for her during her whole life, through good times and bad. He could provide her with every material need, yes — but it went beyond that." She took a breath and the translator waited. The whole court waited. "He could give her more love than any human parent can within a lifetime. And I saw in his eyes that he spoke the truth." She smiled warmly. "Dimity and I are friends. She trusts me. She has told me herself how happy she is. I have seen with my own eyes how well she grows." Her focus swung back to Helena. "Her aunt means well. I think so, yes. But she does not have the love that Emory does."

"I *do* love her," Helena snapped, standing. "Judge, of *course* I love her. She's my great-niece, for God's sake. My human, flesh-and-blood relation—"

"Please, Mrs. Hawthorn," the judge said sternly. "I have your statements already. It was Miss Graf's I wanted to hear today."

Helena, ashen-faced, resumed her seat.

"Thank you, Miss Graf," the judge said, nodding to her. "You may step down."

Sofia and her translator left the room. She gave Emory a smile as she left, which he returned. Jesse stared after her, trying to untangle what he was feeling.

The judge had to say his name twice before he realized he was being addressed.

"What? Huh?"

"Can you come to the witness stand, please, Mr. Truelove?"

Jesse looked around, panicked. Kelly was looking at him expectantly. Emory was giving him an encouraging smile. Helena was glaring like she might make him catch fire with thought alone.

"But I already answered all the lawyers' questions," Jesse fumbled.

"I understand that, Mr. Truelove," the judge said, a little impatiently. "I have some of my own…if you please."

Jesse stood. His palms were sweating. His breathing sounded hollow in his ears. He sat at the witness stand. All the eyes focused on him felt like laser sights.

"Mr. Truelove," the judge said as she flicked through her papers. "I have read the transcript and listened to the recording of your deposition many times. I'd like to start off by thanking you for being one of the most honest witnesses in this case."

Jesse blinked. "Well, yeah. You're welcome. I guess."

She looked at him over her glasses. "It is your apparent honesty and forthright nature that has made me want me to ask you this, of all the people involved."

Jesse swallowed. Harrison and Ivor looked wary. Kelly was assessing, but Jesse thought he saw something like a smile shadowing his lips. Emory was gazing at him calmly, his hands on the table, tenderness and tiredness equally weighted in his eyes.

"I'll answer anything you want, ma'am."

"Good man," the judge said, tapping her notes together. "And I'll remind you that your partner may be in court, but it is me you are talking to, and I represent the law. I can guarantee your safety and the lack of repercussions for your answer. Clear?'

"What are you asking?"

"Has the Baron Von Magnusson ever hurt you, Mr. Truelove?"

He frowned. "What? No, of course—"

"Even when you asked him to?"

The room was silent. Jesse clenched his hands into fists, keeping his eyes locked with the judge, despite the pull of all the other eyes on him.

"No," he said, his voice heavy.

"And you have asked him to is my guess?"

"Your Honor," Kelly said smoothly, leaning forward on his elbow. "Forgive me, but nothing in our files or deposition indicated—"

"I read the news, Mr. Kelly," she said sharply. "And, God help me, watch YouTube. Unfortunately, Mr. Truelove's most private desires are no longer private—

which, as much as I regret it, is very much impactful in this case." She looked back at Jesse. Dizziness fogged his head, but he did not blink. "You are a practitioner of BDSM, Mr. Truelove?"

Jesse shifted in the seat. "That's a very fancy way of putting it, but yeah, I guess I am."

"Again, forgive me, but does this mean you enjoy the act of being dominated? Restrained? Even hurt by your partner?"

"Don't knock it 'till you've tried it, love. That's all I'm saying."

"Who's to say I haven't?" The judge's lips twitched. The silence in the room took on a very different quality. Jesse suppressed a smile with only partial success. The judge gave him a tiny nod of encouragement. "So, to return to my point, I'm assuming at some point during your relationship with the baron, you have requested that he hurt you? Inflict pain? Possibly more?"

Jesse glanced at Emory. His gaze was still fixed on Jesse. Jesse looked back at the judge.

"Yes. I have."

"And did he do as you asked?"

Jesse shook his head. "No, Your Honor…not once. And I've asked a lot."

"Thank you, Mr. Truelove," the judge said after a beat, in which she examined his face. "You may stand down."

Jesse was shaking as he returned to his seat. Harrison was saying something, and Kelly was interrupting, but Jesse didn't hear any of it. Emory turned in his seat and smiled, grasping his hand. Then the judge was banging her gavel for silence.

"Don't think I'm not aware of the significance of this case," the judge said, meeting every set of eyes in the room in turn. "The decision made here today will set precedents and therefore affect many families going forward, not to mention the place of haemophiles and their rights within the law of this country. I am more than aware of all this. But, first and foremost, my job is to protect the interests of Dimity." She straightened her back and closed her file. "It is my decision that the parental rights of Dimity Hawthorn should remain with the Baron Emory Von Magnusson."

A stutter went through the room. A buzzing started in Jesse's ears. The judge raised her voice to silence the lawyers. "It is my considered opinion the baron will not only provide Dimity with a secure and prosperous home, but a safe and loving one, too." She looked at Emory. Jesse wished he could see his face as his own blood pounded in his ears. "I trust he is up to the responsibility and will not only do right by Dimity but will do so as a representative of his own kind in this landmark ruling."

"I am, Your Honor," Emory said, standing and bowing. "And I will. Thank you. Thank you from the bottom of my heart."

"Your Honor," Harrison said again, but the judge lifted her hand.

"You have my ruling, Mr. Harrison. Thank you, everyone."

Jesse flung his arms around Emory from behind and buried his face in his fine-smelling suit, choking into the fabric.

"You did it," he cried, not hearing anything beyond the rushing in his ears. "You fucking did it."

"*We* did it," he said as he turned and gathered Jesse to him, wrapping his strong arms around him and crushing him. "Thank you. Thank you so much."

When Emory finally extricated himself from Jesse's arms, Kelly stood by, holding out his hand. Emory shook it, smiling wide enough himself to show teeth, but there was nothing threatening in the expression, the joy in his eyes was too bright.

Helena stepped up to them. Her face was grim.

"Helena," Emory said, stepping past Kelly to meet her, his expression guarded but kind, "I won't say I'm sorry. I love Dimity, and I won't apologize for that. But I know you do, too. And I hope you will still be involved in Dimity's life."

Jesse was startled to see tears standing in Helena's eyes. She opened her mouth to speak, but the only thing that came out was a choked noise and she clamped it shut again, turned on her heel and stalked for the door.

"It's now Dimity's birthday," Emory called after her. She paused at the door. "I have a surprise planned. I'll send the details. I hope you'll consider joining."

Helena glared at her lawyers, who were already checking their watches and packing away their papers, then at Jesse. Jesse tried for a smile. "I think Dim would like that, right?"

Helena exhaled sharply and hurried from the room.

Jesse was so mixed up with relief and joy that he barely registered leaving the court building or the crowds surrounding it. Emory didn't seem to notice them, either. He made for his limo with his hand clasped tight around Jesse's while Kelly hung back to address the crowd.

As soon as they were alone, they were kissing, heatedly, Jesse both laughing and crying and kissing every bit of Emory's face as he kept trying to capture Jesse's mouth. Finally, he did, and their tongues met as the car pulled out, until Emory broke off with a deep sigh that seemed to well up from his soul.

"It's over," he said softly, his eyes burning. "It's finally over."

"Are you kidding?" Jesse said, grinning. "It's just starting." Jesse took his hand. "Can we wake Dim and tell her? Come on, Em," he said, glancing at his watch. "Just this once, let's wake her up."

A slow smile spread over Emory's face. "She's already awake," he said. "Kelly phoned Joanna. She's on her way to meet us."

"Meet us where?"

"For her birthday surprise. I wanted to do something special, especially as this could have been the last birthday I get to share with her. But I should have had more faith," Emory said and took both Jesse's hands in his. "I said it already, but I can never say it enough. Thank you, Jesse...for everything."

"I didn't do anything," Jesse said.

"You made me human," he said softly, "to the world and to myself. You made me remember what it means and confident that I can be what Dimity needs me to be."

"As if you ever doubted that."

"I did," Emory said, his face clouding. "Of course, I did. How could I not when the entire world is telling you that you are not fit to be a parent?" He took a breath, his large chest swelling under his suit and making Jesse's blood burn and his heart lurch. "You helped me believe again, and I will not rest until I've shown you how grateful I am."

"I just want you, Em," he said softly, "as you are...and Dim."

Emory squeezed his hands, and his smile widened. "Then we are both very lucky."

Chapter Nineteen

Jesse was leaning in for another kiss when the car slowed and filled with brightly colored lights. Jesse craned his neck to look at the window.

"No way," he said. "You're freaking kidding me?"

Emory was already out of the car and Jesse followed, not waiting for the driver to open the door. He stared around at the colored stalls, all squalling jangling tunes and piled high with soft toys, computer games and bags of sweets. The smells of cotton candy and popcorn vied with the headier smells of engine oil and fresh donuts. The lights of a Ferris wheel spun slowly over everything like captured stars. Jesse was taking in the carousel and ghost train when a scream of many joyful voices filled the air. He turned just in time to see a crowd of children hurry off a coach and barrel forward, a half-dozen exasperated but smiling adults following them.

Emory stood at the gate. Greenway had appeared from somewhere and was at his shoulder, watching everything as each adult approached Emory in turn, shaking his hand and talking in low voices, their expressions displaying various amounts of uneasiness. Emory smiled as he greeted them, his face warm and sincere.

The children were already piling onto the rides or queuing at the stalls for treats or to have a go at hooking a duck or throwing hoops when another car arrived and out raced Dimity. She completely ignored the theme park. She ran straight for Emory. Jesse's heart lurched in his chest. Emory had already forgotten about the parent he'd been talking to and bent to sweep his daughter up into his arms. He spun her around and clutched her close, beaming. His eyes were only for her as she laughed with her arms around his neck, bright tears running down her face.

In that instant, Jesse could see the uncertain looks on the parents' faces soften. Emory strode through the gates with Dimity in his arms.

Dimity caught sight of Jesse and squealed. "Uncle Jesse!" she cried, and Emory set her down. She ran to him and flung her arms around him.

Jesse sniffed, blinking back tears, and got to his knees. "Come on, lass," he said, his voice shaking. "Gimme a proper hug."

She put arms around his neck and crushed him to her. Jesse gathered her close and kissed her soft hair. Warmth filled him from his toes right to the crown of his head.

"Happy birthday, love," he said, squeezing her tight. "Seems your old dad has really pulled out all the stops, huh?"

"And I can really go on anything, Daddy?" she said, turning back to Emory with wide eyes. "For free? And eat anything I want?"

"It's your birthday," Emory said, stroking her hair. "Of course, you can."

"And is my whole class really here?" she said, gazing round, wide-eyed.

"Most of them, darling, yes. You'll meet the rest tomorrow in school."

It didn't seem possible, but her grin widened. "So I get to go to St Margaret's? I don't have to go back to Switzerland?"

"I made you a promise, didn't I?"

Dimity squeaked with joy, hugged Emory's legs and kissed his hip. "I love you, Daddy."

"I love you too, darling," he said. "Now go. Enjoy your birthday. Meet your new friends."

She ran over the teacups where two girls were ready to help her climb in.

Jesse shook his head. "I don't think I've ever seen a kid so happy."

"I hope she gets to feel like this every day," Emory said, softly, putting his arm around Jesse's waist. "But not every day will be a birthday."

"I don't believe for a second you're regretting anything," Jesse mocked, prodding Emory in the ribs.

"Of course not," he said, smiling as Dimity waved from her teacup. "The battle's over." He raised his eyes to where Darragh Kelly stood off to the side with a knot of security people, murmuring with their heads together before the guards nodded and fanned out to patrol the perimeter. "But there's still a war going on out there. Who knows if the fighting will ever stop."

"The fight's over for us," Jesse said, taking his hand. "You're a real dad. The world will see that, and it will get better for everyone."

"I hope so."

Jesse kissed him on the cheek and sighed, holding his face against his lover's. "Even if it doesn't, who cares. It's working for us."

Emory drew breath to say something else then his gaze fixed over Jesse's shoulder. "Well, maybe you're right."

Jesse turned. Anton stood in the gateway, staring around with a set expression. Oliver was at his side. Anton was clutching his son's hand like a lifeline. Oliver's face was a bright mix of wonder and fear.

"Jesus," Jesse said softly, coming forward. "Ant?"

Anton looked up. Oliver's face transformed in an instant. "Uncle Jesse!" He tore his hand from his father's and raced over.

"Hey, mate," Jesse said, fighting the emotion that threatened to catch in his throat as he knelt to hug his nephew.

"Dad said you'd be here," Oliver said, smiling nervously at Emory. "I don't know if he wanted to come. But he changed his mind."

"We're all allowed to change our minds, mate," Jesse said, ruffling Oliver's hair and meeting his brother's gaze. "Everyone gets a second chance."

"Mr. Truelove," Emory said, holding out his hand. "I can't tell you how pleased I am that you accepted my invitation."

Anton stared at Emory. His face was pale and his jaw tight. "I'm not sure I've accepted anything, yet," he said, taking Oliver's hand and drawing him back by his side. Oliver went mutely, his face falling.

"That is entirely your decision," Emory said. "But if you'll forgive me, I'll still allow myself to be encouraged by the fact that you came at all. It means a lot...to both of us." Emory squeezed Jesse's shoulder but didn't break eye contact with Anton. Anton stiffened but didn't look away. Emory smiled at Oliver then again at Anton. "May I?"

In that moment, Jesse felt like he'd fallen in love with Emory all over again. Anton considered for a long moment, but Jesse could see the surprise and grudging approval in his eyes. Finally, he nodded.

Emory lowered himself to one knee and held his hand out. "It's very nice to meet you, Oliver. Your uncle has told me all about you."

Oliver's face twitched. He took Emory's large hand uncertainly. "I...I liked your lights. The Christmas lights."

"Well, thank you," Emory said. "I especially hoped that children would enjoy them. Did you have a favorite?"

"The moon," Oliver said, smiling shyly. "Definitely the moon. It changed, went from full to a crescent and everything."

Emory's eyes swirled like seawater on a warm summer's night. "The world is a really beautiful place...even at night. Don't you think?"

"Definitely," Oliver said, unaware of his father watching the exchange closely. "Lights always shine brighter at night, don't they?"

"You're a very intelligent young man," Emory said, getting to his feet. "It's a pleasure to have met you."

"You too, sir," Oliver said, grinning and looking over at the other children. "Is it true? Is Dimity here?"

"She certainly is," he said. "This is her birthday party. However..." Emory glanced over to where Kelly was endeavoring to catch his attention. Jesse was startled to see Tom at his side, a tablet in his hand and a warm smile on his face as he raised his other hand in greeting to Jesse.

"I'm sorry. If you'll excuse me," Emory said, bowing his head to Anton. "I need to have a word with my security team, make sure everything is secure. Jesse," he said then kissed him firmly on the mouth and stepped away, "I'll give you a moment. But I believe Dimity requires you on the carousel before too long."

"Carousel, oh, Dad!" Oliver cried. "Dimity's going on the carousel."

"I know, lad," Anton said, staring hard at Jesse.

Dimity's shout was louder than everyone else's as she climbed the stairs onto the red-and-gold ride. She had chosen a horse with a blue saddle. "Daddy, Dad, look! My favorite color!"

Emory instantly excused himself from Kelly and moved over to help her onto the horse's back. Dimity was grinning and giggling, shouting to the other children who were all climbing on the other horses around her, though she still followed her father's instructions to hold on to the straps and put her feet in the footholds properly.

Anton was watching intently.

"Dad," Oliver murmured. "Please?"

Anton drew a sharp breath. "Okay, son," he said. "One ride. Off you go."

Oliver screamed his delight and pelted over to the carousel. When Dimity spotted him, she almost fell off her horse in her attempts to reach out to him. Emory steadied her then bent down to lift Oliver onto the horse next to hers. Even at a distance, Jesse could see the two children chattering, their faces pink with excitement, bouncing up and down on the horse's carved saddles. Oliver turned in his saddle to shout and wave.

"Hey, Uncle Jesse," he shouted, gesturing at Dimity, "you really did get me a cousin for Christmas."

Dimity squealed in delight, and Emory's own smile widened. He ensured both children were sitting securely before stepping down. The music gained volume, and the ride started to spin. The horses moved up and down and the children's delighted cries faded and rose as they moved round and round.

"I can't quite believe you're here, Ant," Jesse said quietly.

"Trust me, neither can I."

"But you are." Jesse hesitated then put his hand on his brother's arm. "Thank you."

Anton looked at him as if seeing him for the first time. "He won custody."

Jesse nodded. "Yeah."

"And you helped?"

"I think I did."

"They really love each other," Anton said quietly as he watched Emory waving at Dimity. She waved back—and so did Oliver. Their laughter could be heard over the music and shrieks of all the other children.

"They do."

"And you love them." Anton's eyes were on him again. Jesse could feel them but couldn't look away from his family.

"I really do." Jesse's breath left his body in a rush when his brother enveloped him in a bone-crushing hug. "Whoa, Ant," he gasped. "What gives?"

"I'm sorry, Jesse," he said. His voice was choked. He sobbed loudly into Jesse's shoulder, clinging to his coat. "I'm *so* sorry."

"Hey," Jesse said, his emotion prickly and pleasing and as strong as sunlight rolling over his skin. "Hey, Ant, it's okay." He patted his brother's back warily then, when the sobbing continued, put his arms around him and rested his chin on his big brother's shoulder.

"All right, so it's not okay—but it will be. And I'm sorry, too. I really am."

"Why are *you* sorry?" Anton said stuffily, not raising his head. "I'm the screw-up. I always have been."

"You're not a screw-up, Ant," he said, pushing him back to look into his face. "Perhaps neither of us are? Okay, maybe we could have both handled shit better. There's no rule book for any of this, right? We're all just doing the best we can."

Anton wiped his eyes. "Yeah. Yeah, I guess so." He swallowed. "There's something I never told you."

"What's that?"

Anton sniffed again and blinked his eyes dry. "Whatever else happened. Whatever else I didn't get or...refused to think about, I've never once doubted how much you love my kid." He took a shaking breath. "And I love you for that, little brother—even more than I already did."

Jesse searched for words, but his mouth was crowded with a hundred things he couldn't express. Instead, he put his hands on his brother's shoulders and kissed him on both cheeks then pressed their foreheads together. "I love you, too, arsehole."

Anton grinned and moved toward the carousel to wave at Oliver. Emory stood ready as the ride slowed then stopped. He climbed aboard to help Dimity and Oliver down from their horses. The only thing that made it look different to any other day at the fair was the wary shadow of Greenway, never far from her master's side, and the black-clothed private security strolling between the rides, their walkie-talkies crackling and eyes vigilant.

"Uncle Jesse," Dimity and Oliver both called in unison as they climbed down. "Ferris wheel! Come *on*."

"You are summoned," Emory said with another smile.

Jesse looked at Anton. His face looked tired, but the haunted look that had become part of his eyes had gone. "Go, little brother," he said. "Enjoy. Just..." He winced. "Watch out for Olly, yeah? And that little girl. And yourself, while you're at it."

"Always, mate," he said, squeezing his brother's shoulder. "Always."

Jesse hurried to where the children were waiting with Emory.

"You're coming on, too, right?" Jesse said as the children scampered off toward the Ferris wheel.

"If you want me to," Emory said, eyeing the ride a little warily.

"I think we all want you to," Jesse said, as Dimity called to both of them to hurry.

Emory smiled and held out his hand. "Then lead the way."

Jesse wondered whether it was possible to actually explode from happiness as he and Emory followed Oliver and Dimity to the Ferris wheel, arm-in-arm. He was aware of the interested looks the adults and some of the children gave them as they passed, but nothing made him look away from Emory's content face.

Apart from when someone with electric-blue hair stepped out of the shadows... Jesse dropped Emory's arm and strode over, ignoring Oliver calling him back. Trixy watched him approach with a blank expression.

"What are you doing here?"

"Well, that's nice," Trixy said, raising an eyebrow. "Don't I get any credit for helping you win your case?"

"*Helping*?"

"Jesus, Jesse," she said, shaking her head. "Don't you read the internet anymore?"

"The last few weeks have sort of put me off it."

Her smile was thin. "My YouTube video about you guys went viral."

"I'm bloody aware of that."

"It's actually influenced how people think of the baron, you idiot," she quipped. "Don't you see? I always knew people wanted to know the truth." She glanced over Jesse's shoulder to where Emory was watching them. Her face paled, but she carried on. "Okay, so maybe I was a tiny bit off the mark about which truth was important, but haemophiles as breathing, sexual beings?" She grinned. "The internet fucking loves it. The whole world is shipping you two—and all the other high-profile vamps, for that matter."

"You really are on another bloody planet, aren't you?"

"I helped you," she said, prodding his coat. "The least you could do is return the favor."

"How?" he asked suspiciously.

"I still want that interview—with both of you, as a couple. Then I'll write a book. It's already funded. And publishers are emailing me figures bigger than my YouTube revenue."

"You're crazy."

"I'm not. I'm realistic. You want people to think of you as a real couple? Let me do this."

"We *are* a real couple," Jesse argued. "I don't need the world's approval for that to be true."

Trixy rolled her eyes. "Then do it for all those other odd couples—people the world don't think belong together. Lord Aviemore and Terje Kristiansen started the ball rolling. You could launch it into space. Promote equal rights, Jesse. Hashtag 'love is love,' right?"

Jesse stared at her, torn between fury and amusement. He shook his head then looked at the floor. "I tracked down the dickholes that made that prison rape video, by the way," he said softly. He looked up. Her jaw had tightened. "I was going to report them to the cops...after I'd talked to you. But I didn't want to speak to you." He let out an impatient sigh. "I was still mad. But I'll do it."

"Thanks, Jesse," she said, her voice catching. "I appreciate that. Tell me who they are."

"Let the police handle it, Trix."

"I can do a far better job eviscerating them than the police ever could. I just need their names."

Jesse sighed. "You don't have to fight everything alone, you know."

"Like you, you mean?"

Jesse shook his head again. "How did you even get in here anyway?"

"I asked her." Emory had appeared at Jesse's elbow. His face was cool as he studied Trixy. All she did was raise an eyebrow, but Jesse could see the cold glint of fear in her eyes. "Whatever the intention, she is right. Everything she has done helped, in the end. And, without her" — Emory smiled at Jesse — "we would never have met. I owe her for that, if nothing else."

"Em..."

"So you'll give me an interview, Baron?" she said, showing her teeth in a wry grin. "An exclusive? Filmed at Oswald House?"

"I invited you here tonight to show you the truth of these narratives you seem so invested in," Emory said in a low voice. He put his hand possessively on Jesse's shoulder. "My people will get back to you about the interview and your book. But if you don't mind, I will be stealing Jesse away now."

Trixy clearly wanted to say something more, but Emory steered Jesse toward the Ferris wheel.

"She won't let it go, you know," Jesse muttered as they approached the car behind Dimity and Oliver's. Jesse was aware of Anton watching from a distance but was pleased to note the smile on his face. Then he stared as Darragh Kelly and Tom approached Trixy. She started when Kelly touched her on her shoulder. They began conversing in low tones. Trixy looked between them with a disbelieving expression. But then Kelly, his face as serious as ever, took Tom's hand. Tom's face lit up, as did Trixy's.

"She'll get her interview," Emory said as he stepped up onto the waiting car, drawing Jesse with him. "But not from us."

"Tom and Kelly?"

"They've been dancing around each other for some time now," Emory said as he sat and fastened the belt over both their laps. "But they were both uncertain about many things." Emory smiled as Kelly and Tom wandered away, hand in hand, with Trixy at their side. "I think we may have influenced more than we think."

"That's great," Jesse said as the car eased forward, and more kids were secured into the car behind them. "I knew Tom needed something...more. More than me."

"The way his family treated him made him very scared of who he was. And for a while he had lost himself in a dangerous place. But he has found himself again, now. And Darragh? Well" —Emory smiled— "you need something more than the law to keep you connected to the world, though he would obviously never admit it."

Jesse clutched the bar as the car swayed and the Ferris wheel began to turn. Dimity and Oliver squealed with delight as they went up and up.

"Holy shit," Jesse said as they climbed higher. "Look who's here."

Helena stood in the gate with her own security at her back, staring around the scene with hard eyes.

"Aunt Helena!" called Dimity from above. The woman blinked and looked up. Dimity waved, her face pink and grinning. Helena's expression warmed ever so slightly and something like relief softened her face. She raised a gloved hand to wave back then her gaze fell on Jesse and Emory. Jesse wove his fingers with Emory's and held him tight. But all Emory did was incline his head. Helena hesitated then nodded in reply, turned to speak to her security and strode through the gate toward where some of the adults were congregating at the free bar next to the ghost train.

As the Ferris wheel turned, she and everyone else fell out of sight. The bright lights of the fun fair shrank until it was like looking down on a starlit sea. The lights of the city glimmered in the distance, and stars shone overhead. The wind picked up, brisk and chill, whipping Jesse's hair about his face. He leaned into Emory's shoulder just as the moon came out from behind the clouds and bathed them in silver.

"I didn't think life could be like this."

"Life can be anything you want it to be," Emory said and kissed him, slow and deep. Jesse sighed, breathing in his scent and swallowing his taste. He broke apart and pressed his forehead to Jesse's. "I'm so glad you came into *my* life, Jesse Truelove."

"Broke into it, you mean?" Jesse said with a smile.

"Crashed into it like a speeding car." Emory smiled wider. "And shook things up in all the right ways."

"I'm glad too," Jesse said, kissing the end of his nose. "It's all still crazy. But it's good crazy."

"I'm glad you think so," Emory said as the Ferris wheel continued to climb higher. "Jesse," he said softly, "I would very much like you to marry me."

Jesse choked. "You *what*?"

Emory's face was so serious in the moonlight that it made Jesse ache. "Marry me, Jesse Truelove. I want you to be my husband."

"You have got to be yanking my chain." Jesse's voice was hoarse. Emory's expression never flickered. "How would it even work? Till death *I* do part?"

Emory took both his hands in his own and held them, looking into his face, unblinking. "I'm yours…entirely, for as long as you'll have me. I want to make that promise to the world."

Jesse's head spun. He remembered Glen getting down on one knee in that restaurant, remembered seeing his heart breaking when Jesse turned him down. He blinked until the vision lifted.

"We can't…" was all he could manage to say.

"We've proved today we can do anything," Emory said, smiling. "Be my husband. Be Dimity's dad. Let's be a legal, registered family."

"Em, I mean…we *can't*. It's not legal. Not even Kelly could swing it."

"Yet," Emory said, reaching into his pocket and drawing out a small velvet box. Jesse's throat closed over. Emory opened it. Two platinum bands lay on the white cushion inside. The Ferris wheel kept turning, but Jesse still didn't speak.

"I'm your family, Jesse," Emory said softly, "whether you say yes or not. Remember that. But whatever the law says, let's wear these." He picked out one of the rings and held his hand out. "I don't care what the world thinks…only you."

Jesse bit his lip, hard, then watched as he held his hand out, like it was being controlled by someone else. Emory's face shifted, and Jesse realized he'd been genuinely scared. But the fear evaporated in a wash of joy, and he slipped the ring onto Jesse's finger. With shaking hands, Jesse pushed the other ring onto Emory's.

He kissed Emory with deliberation, enjoying the simple joy of being able to touch him and not think about anything else. Gradually, he became aware that the ride had stopped, and a small crowd of children and adults were standing around clapping. He blinked.

"Did they know you were going to do this?" Jesse stammered.

"You mean you didn't?" Emory said. He was grinning.

"You'll never stop surprising me, will you?"

"I sincerely hope not."

Blood and Bonds:
Bleed in the Night
S.J. Coles

Excerpt

Summer was at its height. York hadn't felt a breath of wind or a drop of rain in weeks. Even at night, the air was still and heavy, like it was choked by a storm waiting to break.

But the weather wasn't the reason Tyler couldn't sleep.

It had been the same every night for weeks. As soon as he switched the light off, he was back on Askham Moor. Hands stronger than iron crushed his body. Adrenaline coursed through his veins like venom. The smell of his own urine was sharp in his nostrils.

He could hear his own voice bleeding out of him, freezing and dying in the cold night air: "Let me fucking *go*," he cried. "Let me go *now*, or I swear I'll…"

The grip on him tightened. Fingernails sharp as glass shards pricked his flesh.

"Be still." The voice was as smooth as an oil spill. It poured into his ear and down his nerves, stretching them to the point of snapping. The hot, fragrant breath against his skin made his traitorous body shake.

"This is assault. I'll have you arrested, I swear."

"This is what happens when weak men pretend they are strong." The creature tightened his grip in Tyler's hair and pulled his head back, exposing his neck. "Do you still think you are strong?"

Tyler fought air into his lungs, staring at the stars that had started to wheel overhead. "Who...who are you?"

"I am Lucien," murmured the voice. "Whether you live another fifty seconds or another fifty years, you will *never* forget that name."

Tyler threw his pillow across the room. It knocked a hi-fi speaker flying. It crashed to the floor with the sickening sound of splintering wood. He sat on the edge of his bed with his head in his hands, breathing hard, until the red mist swirling before his eyes faded.

He checked his phone. Three-o-one a.m. He threw it at the wall, shoved back the sheets and paced the flat until, finally, the sun began to rise, and he dared open the curtains.

By the time he was nearing Fulford Road Police Station an hour later, he was finishing his fourth coffee, and his body felt like it was strung through with hot wire. There was a bitter, metallic taste in his mouth. His heart skittered in his chest.

He swore and swerved to avoid an ambulance bombing the other way down the narrow street...then another. He pulled over and climbed out of the car, shaking as the sirens faded away. Silence descended. He took a steadying breath and made for the police station on foot.

It wasn't yet six a.m., but when he arrived, the entrance was swarming with activity. Another ambulance was pulled up onto the curb. Paramedics were hoisting up a stretcher on which sprawled an unconscious form. There was blood everywhere — on the man's face, clothes, matting his hair. The ambulance screamed off after the others.

Tyler stood staring for a moment before shaking himself and striding into the police station.

"DI Walker," he barked at the harried-looking desk officer. She held up a finger and continued her conversation on the phone. "*Oi*, lady. I said I want to see Walker. *Now*."

"One sec," she said into the phone then gave Tyler a hard look. "Please, sir. Take a seat."

"I won't take a bloody seat. Get Walker out here. *Now*."

The woman's face tightened. "DI Walker is engaged. If you want to leave your number, I will be sure he contacts you. Yes, I'm still here," she spoke again into the phone. "We need extra techs to go over the CCTV as soon as possible. Yes. Scene photographers, too—"

Tyler reached over and cut the woman's call. "I said I want Walker...*now*."

She held his glare without blinking. "And *I* said he's *busy*, sir."

"Mr. Lomax." Tyler turned. A tall man stood in the doorway. His brown hair was disheveled, like he'd been running his hands through it, but the hard amber of his eyes was as unyielding as stone. "You're up early."

"*Finally*," Tyler said, folding his arms. "I came for an update on my case."

The detective studied him for a moment. "This way, Mr. Lomax," he said, stepping back and holding open the door.

Tyler strode through, muttering under his breath. Walker took them to an interview room and shutting them in.

"You're avoiding me," Tyler said.

"Why would I avoid such pleasant company as yours?" Walker replied, standing with his hands in his pockets. There were shadows under his eyes and spots of blood on his collar.

"I'm *serious*," Tyler said, lifting his gaze from the stain. "You don't think I'm serious? Because I can show you just how serious I am, if that's what you want."

"Is that why you're here so early? To threaten me?" Walker replied, pulling out one of the plastic chairs from around the small table and sitting. "Or have you finally come to confess to that assault outside the *Golden Fleece*?"

Tyler bridled. "I'm talking about *my* assault, arsehole. That psycho haemo that attacked me. You know, the one that no one's trying to find?"

"What about the criminal damage to Baron Von Magnusson's home, then?" Walker said coolly. "Perhaps you'd like to confess to that instead?"

"This is *bullshit*. That thing nearly killed me. *Killed* me."

Walker surveyed him a moment longer then gestured to the other chair. "Have a seat, Tyler."

"I won't have a seat. I want to know what you're doing about this."

Walker's only response was to push the chair out from the table with his foot.

Tyler swore and slumped into it, glaring at the detective.

"Are you going to tell me why you're really here this early?"

Tyler's skin rippled at the look in his eyes. "I told you. I wanted an update."

"So you don't know anything about the four men we found on the stairs this morning?"

Tyler blinked. "What?"

"Four unconscious men were dumped in our doorway at shift change, all severely injured. Know anything about that?"

"Why fucking would I?"

Walker interlaced his fingers on the table and leaned forward. "They are two members of a suspected pedophile ring, a violent drug dealer and an abusive husband. Still not ringing any bells?"

Tyler slammed his fist on the table. "I'm here about *Lucien*, Walker. You know, the murderer you've let get away?"

Walker leaned back in this chair again, watching Tyler closely. "Last year the Chief Inspector came for a visit and found a man chained to the railings in the car park. His name was Jason Parr. He was a suspect in a series of rapes. He had a hair band of one of the victims in his pocket. It led to his conviction."

"I'm not here for a history lesson."

"Parr said *you* put him there."

Tyler clenched his fists under the table and was careful not to blink.

"He said you jumped him in a bar," Walker continued, "and next thing he knew he was chained up in the rain with a hairband he claims never to have seen before."

"I don't know no Jason Parr. And that's nothing to do with this."

"So these degenerates left bleeding on our doorstep before dawn..." Walker narrowed his eyes. "Nothing to do with you?"

Tyler stood so suddenly that his chair crashed to the floor. "You better start taking this seriously, detective," he said, stabbing the table with his finger. "Hear me? You don't want a guy like me as your enemy."

He made for the door.

"You want Lucien found, Tyler?" Tyler halted with his hand on the door handle but didn't turn around. "You ask your sister what she knows about this mess," Walker said smoothly. "Then you give me a call."

Tyler glared over his shoulder. "What's she got to do with it?"

"A well-connected woman, your sister," Walker said, standing and straightening his tie. "What she doesn't know isn't worth knowing, right? See what she knows. Then we'll talk."

Tyler stormed out of the police station.

He searched his pockets for his phone, remembered he'd smashed it against his bedroom wall and swore. He got into his car and drove into town with his jaw clenched so hard it hurt. He parked, made for the nearest phone shop and hovered outside the doors until it opened.

The assistant's enthusiasm soon died when he realized that Tyler's money might have no limits but his patience was quite the opposite. He left the store with a new phone and an even worse mood and dialed a number from memory.

Emerald didn't answer.

Tyler fired off a series of furious messages and made for the *Cafe Rouge* on Low Petergate, somewhere that didn't serve alcohol so somewhere he was unlikely to be spotted by anyone he knew. He ordered a black coffee and took a table in the corner, out of the way of the breakfast crowd.

He tried Emerald again with no luck and gulped the scalding coffee. He scrolled several news sites, searching for any mentions of haemophiles. The local papers were still full of articles about the Undying Baron winning the custody case for his adoptive daughter earlier in the year with the help of his human partner, Jesse Truelove. The kid was going to a local school, and Von Magnusson had just been elected to the school board. Reactions were…mixed.

Tyler shook his head, attempting to dispel the memories of standing outside Oswald House, his blood hot with anger, convinced a little girl was being abused behind the high walls.

Then Lucien had turned up.

He quickly switched to the national sites, trying to find anything about any more cases of haemo-on-human violence and what was being done about it. All he found were posts about the haemophile's parliamentary representative Ivor Novák's latest campaign to allow haemophiles to legally marry. Tyler's stomach clenched. He hurriedly scrolled away.

The next thing he found was a video of a press conference around the de-registration of haemophile communes by one Magister Dragomir Soroka. The very sight of the white-faced, white-haired haemophile made Tyler's blood run cold. The eyes, black and empty, reminded him of a shark's.

Why should our names and addresses be listed for anyone with ill intent to find? Why should we suffer perpetual scrutiny when all we want is a chance to live our lives in peace?

Tyler put the new phone screen-side down on the table. He finished the coffee. If anything, the caffeine increased his tension, but he ordered a second cup.

By the time he was done with his second drink and Emerald still hadn't returned his call, his patience was frayed to the breaking point. He left the cafe without leaving a tip.

Nasir, Emerald's secretary, started when Tyler strode past his desk.

"Uh, Ty," he said, scurrying after him. "This really isn't a good time."

"Go swivel, Naz," Tyler said and shoved open his sister's office door. He shut it in Nasir's face but not before registering his ex's pained frown.

Emerald was on the phone. Her scarlet suit was as sharp as her gaze, which locked on Tyler and stayed there, even though she didn't miss a beat in her conversation.

"Well, that's exactly what I said. I agree. We just have to get ahead of it. Yes. Exactly. Look…" She tilted her head. "Can I call you back? Ten minutes? Thanks."

She replaced the receiver with a deliberate click. "Tyler. What a nice surprise."

"Leave it out, sis," he said, dropping into one of the armchairs that faced her oversized desk. "If you picked up your bloody phone, I wouldn't have to barge in like this, would I?"

"In case you didn't notice," she said with an icy smile, "the appointment of the lord mayoralty is due. Getting appointed two years running would make history — and I *intend* to make history. So I have rather a lot on my plate, to say the least."

"I ain't leaving until you talk to me."

Emerald sat motionless with her fingers twined together for such a long time that Tyler knew a sneak of apprehension up his spine. Then she stood, straightened her jacket and went to the door.

Tyler braced himself to be hustled out by security, but instead she just leaned out and said, "Naz?"

"Yes, Lord Mayor?" Nasir scrambled to his feet, tidying papers.

"Take an early lunch. There's a good chap."

Nasir's eyes flicked to Tyler then back. "Yes, Lord Mayor," he said and left.

Emerald waited until the lift doors had pinged shut before closing the door again. She resumed her seat without meeting Tyler's eyes.

"Okay, little brother," she said, leaning back in her seat. "You have four minutes. What do you want?"

"I saw Walker this morning."

She lifted a sculpted eyebrow. "He hasn't taken out a restraining order yet, then." Tyler glowered. "And did the Detective Inspector have any news?"

"You know he didn't. You'd've known before me."

"What's your point Tyler?" she said in a bored tone, doodling on her notepad.

Tyler watched her closely. "Someone dumped four bodies on the steps of the police station overnight."

Emerald stopped doodling. "Excuse me?"

Tyler shook his head. "Not dead. Beat up...bad. There was a lot of fucking blood..."

The sharp lines of her face tightened. "You were there?"

"No," Tyler said hurriedly. "Like I said, I went this morning. They were just clearing up."

"I see." Her expression was watchful.

"Walker asked me if *I* did it. When I put him straight, he asked me to ask *you*."

Emerald had gone very still. "Me?"

Tyler nodded. "Have you heard anything?" Emerald looked at the wall. Tyler dragged his chair closer and lowered his voice. "Please, Emmy. I gotta find that guy. I can't sleep knowing he's out there..."

"And what's your Lucien thing got to do with four scumbags being dumped at Fulford Road?"

Tyler paused. "Who said they were scumbags?" Emerald's red lips twitched. "You know something, Emmy. What is it?"

"Why do you care?"

He swallowed. "Was it Lucien? Did *he* do this?"

Emerald sighed and leaned on her desk. "This didn't come from me. Got it?" Tyler nodded. "I mean it Ty," she said, her voice deadly serious. "If even a whisper of this comes back to me, you can forget about my intervention the next time you get yourself arrested or worse."

"Yeah, yeah," Tyler said, "I get it. I'll take it to the grave. Come on. What's going on, huh?"

Emerald examined her blood-red manicure for a long, tense silence. "Recently people have been... vanishing. Taken out of their homes at night. No signs of a struggle, nothing. They were just...gone. But I got a call this morning. Sounds like they all turned up at the police station—what was left of them, anyway. I wasn't sure I believed it, but you said you saw it?"

"How many went missing?"

"Four, that I've heard of. But it's only become weird because of this last guy...Terry Fleetwood."

"What's so special about him?"

"The other three were under investigation—two for kiddy pictures, another for drugs. Police hadn't been able to get anything solid, probably never would. When they went missing, suspicion was some cop had gone rogue...until Fleetwood vanished."

"Fleetwood was the wife beater?"

"So Walker figured it out, did he?"

"What's the deal with Fleetwood?"

"He *wasn't* under investigation," she said. "Not even suspected. The wife never reported him."

"But *you* knew?"

"I know people who knew," she hedged. "Guy liked to piss away his money in a few of my places, drink and run his mouth, so word got about. But the police were never involved. That means it can't have been a copper that did this."

"So..." He swallowed, his blood running cold. "Lucien?"

She spread her hands. "No one knows. A pro, that was the guess. No struggle, no mess — at least, no mess at the scene of the abductions. No one left behind to care. Though why a pro was targeting these charmers was anyone's guess. But this morning..." Emerald picked up her phone, tapped at the screen and passed it over.

"What's this?" Tyler said, scrolling through some text full of medical terms.

"The medical reports on your gents from this morning."

Tyler scowled. "I don't know what I'm reading here, sis. I failed biology, remember?"

Emerald sighed and took the phone back. "Blood loss, Tyler. They were all suffering from massive blood loss."

Tyler went very still. "Any of them talking?"

"If they are, my source wasn't able to find out."

"So this was him..." Tyler's blood ran cold. "He's still here...in York. *Biting* people. And that moron Walker's doing *nothing* —"

"It's a haemo attack, sure," Emerald said. "Whether it's this Lucien of yours —"

"He's not *mine*," Tyler's face flushed with heat. "He's a fucking maniac. And he's loose in my town, and no one is taking it seriously."

"The city's packed with haemophiles at the moment, Ty," she said, her voice level and infuriatingly calm.

"There's a whole contingent of them at Oswald House right now. Blew into town over a month ago. Something to do with this marriage bill Novák is trying to push through with help from that haemo lawyer of the Baron's. Why do you think I'm run off my feet trying to play interference?"

"Lucien attacked these men," Tyler said, stabbing his finger on the desk. "I know it."

"Even if he did, who cares?" she said with a wave of her hand. "Let him clear the scumbags out of the city. Saves me a job."

"You won't be saying that when he starts coming after the scumbags who work for you."

Emerald narrowed her eyes. "Careful."

"Why aren't you up in arms, huh?" he snapped. "Why aren't we all out trying to get this lunatic?"

"Leave it to Walker."

"He's doing fuck-all. Even when he knows all this, I bet—"

"This can't go to the police, Tyler."

Tyler chewed his cheek. "He told me—"

"I have to protect my sources," she said firmly. "We had an agreement."

Tyler made a frustrated noise. "So what am I supposed to do? Nothing?"

"Tyler." Emerald used the voice that always reminded Tyler of their father. "You really have to let this Lucien thing go."

"*Why?*"

"Because you can't hurt him, but he could hurt you…*really* hurt you."

Tyler again felt the hot breath on his neck, the hands crushing his body. He heard the voice like liquid mercury flowing through him, lighting fires as it went.

"If no one else will stop this guy," he said, his voice hoarse, "then I'll bloody have to do it myself."

"Tyler," Emerald said, glancing at her phone as it started ringing, "do as I say. Let it go. Take a holiday or something."

"A *holiday*?"

"Get out of town for a while. When was the last time you went anywhere, huh?" She reached for the phone.

Tyler grabbed the phone before she could answer it, lifted the receiver and slammed it back down. Emerald's eyes glinted with dark fire.

"What else do you have?" he said. "Anything you've heard — rumors, anything."

She was silent for a moment then tilted her head. "What about Naz, huh?" she asked, frowning. "What went wrong there?"

"Emerald —"

"You need something, Ty," she went on. "If it's not headspace, then it's to get laid."

"Tell me what you know about Lucien."

Emerald sighed loudly. "This isn't like knocking some creep's head on the bar and tying him to a railing, little brother. Haemophiles are dangerous. You're lucky to be alive as it is."

Tyler ground his teeth. "Well, I guess I'll have to fight fire with fire."

"What?"

"I need one of *them*. A haemo."

"Ty, no —"

"If you won't help me, I'll bloody well help myself," he said and stormed out, just as her phone started ringing again. He passed Nasir on the bridge outside the office. He was carrying a takeaway coffee and a paper bag that smelled of pastry. His face transformed as he saw Tyler approach, but Tyler brushed past him without meeting his eyes.

About the Author

S.J. Coles is a Romance writer originally from Shropshire, UK. She has been writing stories for as long as she has been able to read them. Her biggest passion is exploring narratives through character relationships.

She finds writing LGBT/paranormal romance provides many unique and fulfilling opportunities to explore many (often neglected or under-represented) aspects of human experience, expectation, emotion and sexuality.

Among her biggest influences are LGBT Romance authors K J Charles and Josh Lanyon and Vampire Chronicles author Anne Rice.

S.J. Coles loves to hear from readers. You can find her contact information, website details and author profile page at https://www.firstforromance.com/

PUBLISHING

Sign up for our newsletter and find out about all our romance book releases, eBook sales and promotions, sneak peeks and FREE romance books!